BROTHERS
UNDER THE SKIN...

On the surface Charlie Cumberland and Cal Torrensen could be brothers. Both are intelligent and attractive. Both seem marked for success. Both are at the beginnings of their adult lives.

Both know Elaine—and that's where the brotherhood stops. Cal has had her and cast her off. Charlie's decent instincts are drawn to her. It is Charlie, unknowingly, who will gamble Elaine's future in an effort to find his own way of being a man in the world.

Avon Books by Roderick Thorp

THE DETECTIVE
DIONYSUS

RODERICK THORP

INTO THE FOREST

AVON
PUBLISHERS OF
DISCUS • CAMELOT • BARD

AVON BOOKS
A division of
The Hearst Corporation
959 Eighth Avenue
New York, New York 10019

First Avon Printing, July, 1970

AVON TRADEMARK REG. U.S. PAT. OFF. AND
FOREIGN COUNTRIES, REGISTERED TRADEMARK—
MARCA REGISTRADA, HECHO EN CHICAGO, U.S.A.

Printed in the U.S.A.

For Irwin Stark

INTO THE FOREST

People do not only live in their own lives,
but in the lives of others: in their own they
play leading parts, but in those of others,
sometimes important but sometimes
very small ones.

W. SOMERSET MAUGHAM

INTO THE FOREST

chapter one

I

On a mild Friday evening in September of nineteen fifty-five Alice McCarthy stood within the entrance of the Marboro Book Shop on West Eighth Street in New York City, staring through the half-reflecting glass to the display case walls, to which were taped prints of Van Gogh, Gauguin and Toulouse-Lautrec. The prints were hung beside posters celebrating the *Corrida de Toros* in Seville, Spain, of a Sunday eight years before. The word *Manolete* appeared in large red letters at the bottom of each poster, and it was meaningless to her. In nineteen fifty-five and at her age, twenty, if she had thought about it, Alice might have come to the conclusion that the word had something to do with the fiesta, or the hanging of the posters themselves, on the order of "Post No Bills," in English.

Although she was staring at them Alice was not interested in posters or prints. She had come to buy a book, but she was not interested in books, either. Standing here was a graver admission than the admission it avoided, yet it was an easier one. She had read so many books only to escape that one more had at last become too terrible and desperate, and carrying it back to her room too much of a physical burden. She wondered at the miserable convolutions of her flight. She was slipping into a mood she knew well, one of smallness insignificance and unworthiness. She was hypnotized by her lack of self-knowledge as it moved on her with the safety and terror of a small, locked room.

In the faint mirror of the window she could see people passing, the couples holding hands, their light summer clothes flicking brightly in the blue September shadows. Her self-pity rose more powerfully and she hated herself for it, but it was irresistible. She focused her eyes on the

11

window to use it as a view to the sidewalk; she could not dare turn around.

She was a pretty girl: of medium height, delicate figure, with truly black hair. She had fair skin and blue eyes, but because her lips were thin and her jaw just a little too angular, the effect was that, in a crowd, she was indistinguishable from the next girl. And of late, she was always in crowds.

She had friends, but they were two hundred and fifty miles away in Ithaca, New York. The memory of them now was as remote as they were, as Tompkins County was, faded, gone even from the semi-reality of the immediate past. They were in that deeper and dimmer dimension of faces and times, that decaying wonderland just above dreams. And by Alice's circumstance, they were removed one step further: to yield to calling would be to yield to humiliation; the girls she had never really liked would know how she had failed in this thing she had been so arrogantly confident about. They would have something for their vicious, petty cackling. She would never be able to go home—even if she wanted to.

In the seven weeks she had been in the city she had added only two telephone numbers to her book: that of the office in which she worked, in midtown off Fifth Avenue, and that of the women's hotel on Sixteenth Street where she lived. The job was a good one, but she felt swallowed by it. She was one of thousands of girls, but, she hoped, not like so many of them: the mechanical exotics who were the receptionists, the tough Brooklyn mamas who were the file clerks. They were not all like that though, there were some nice girls. Maybe she was still too shy, but she had made no new friends, not even someone to talk to during her lunch hours.

The women's hotel was something else again, except for a very few young girls, the place was filled with creaking or bloated dowagers, dying by degrees, making their actual physical tribute to death in the bathrooms, which they occupied for hours. Alice hated to think what ghastly services they were performing to stave off what would be a release for most of them. Without television, they had no lives at all.

She turned from the bookstore and looked down the block where over the crowd the movie marquee gleamed seductively. She had not intended to go to the movie, but it was showing a film she had not seen. As if sleepwalking she started toward it.

"Excuse me!" The young man she had stepped into released her arms. "You'd better watch yourself, peaches— I almost knocked you down."

And her hurried into the bookstore.

"—Buddy?" she asked. A whisper, he couldn't have heard it. He pushed on through the glass doors. It *was* him. She chased after him. He paused at the cashier's desk and she stopped still as if playing a game. She could feel her heart pumping.

He was not what she remembered from her first year in high school; he seemed almost short now, although within an inch or two of six feet. He was older now—naturally— but he seemed less mature. His brown hair appeared to have receded a little, but it was still combed in a boyish way, and not carefully. He needed a shave and there were small lines around his eyes, but they were still a bright, light brown, deep and quick. He had a tan left from the summer.

She computed his age. He had been a high school senior over five years ago; he must be twenty-three or -four. He moved toward the back of the store; she followed. He had that same careful walk, not quite leisurely, of the ballplayer who walks to his position while the others trot out like children. It was so controlled. For a moment she remembered the way he had looked as he worked his arm loose before a game, and the slow ritual way he had gone into the windup before pitching. Buddy Cumberland. She remembered it all, the sunshine on the grass, the voices swimming around her, the warm wind coming in across the field into the faces of the crowd in the tiny grandstand.

He could not possibly know her. She had seen him only on the field or in the halls of the school. She had been one of hundreds he had seen—passed, smiled back to, not knowing them. And had he even smiled at her? She could not remember.

But she wasn't going to be stopped. She tried quickly to cover up the faltering she felt in her steps. He was at a counter on which discount-sale books were piled. She touched his shoulder.

"Buddy?"

He turned around.

"Oh, you. Say, you aren't hurt, are you?"

"No."

He studied her. "Wait, do we know each other?"

"I guess not. We went to high school together."

"Well, for Christ's sake—!" He grinned and relaxed against the counter, folding his arms. "Sure, why didn't I know right away? When you called me Buddy just now it didn't register. No one calls me Buddy any more outside my family. I'd never have placed you—"

"Alice." She blushed.

"Alice," he repeated. "So, what are you doing in New York? Are you married?"

"I'm still single. I'm working." Again she blushed—uncontrollably, stupidly. It was going so badly she was not even present now. She was inside herself and being forced to watch.

"I was home this summer," he said. "Every girl I'd meet in town was married. I quit asking. I was going to skip it this time, too, and ask how many kids you had. Seriously, how long have you been in town?"

"Two months."

He nodded. He offered her a cigarette. She took it and could not control the trembling of her fingers. He saw it, but as he held the match for her he went on as if he had not noticed. "I was living in the Bronx when I first came down. For a while, until I started meeting people, it was agony."

"I know," she said. "*How* I know."

"I wouldn't think a woman would have as much trouble as a man. The world comes to her, in a sense."

She was supposed to say something now, but it was

impossible. He had called her a woman, for one thing. And as best as she could tell, he had not looked anywhere but at her face or hands, or at her hair for just a moment; so it was not the sensation that he was stripping her down that embarrassed her, but that he was so confident with her—not as if he knew her well, but exactly the reverse, exactly the truth. He was so far above her in this simple situation that he was trying to show her the way. She was supposed to relax toward him, and it intimidated her.

He glanced at his watch.

"Are you in a hurry?" she asked. "Don't let me keep you, please."

"I have some time yet—wait a minute. Are you doing anything tonight? I have to go out to Roosevelt Raceway. Would you like to come with me? We won't be staying late, if you have something to do tomorrow."

"No, I have nothing to do," she said clumsily. Now she wanted to laugh. She could not even score the points he wanted to give her.

"We could leave now, if you like," he said "We could take our time going out, talk and make a night of it. I'd like you to come."

She hesitated, then smiled.

"Fine." He took her arm and they started toward the door. "Alice," he said.

"Excuse me?"

"I'm just getting your name fixed. I'm sorry."

"People don't call you Buddy now?" she asked.

"You know how that works. Buddy got left at home. My first name is Charlie, by the way."

"I know. I know your last name, too. Cumberland. But may I cal you Buddy? It's the way I know you."

"Call me anything you want, just like everyone else."

She was confused, but let it go. "What are you doing now?"

"Going to City College," he said.

"What are you studying?"

"History—teaching."

"No fooling? You're the last one I'd imagine becoming a teacher."

"Well, you hardly know me," he said.

They were at his car and she had no chance to reply. He kept talking as if she had not offended him.

"I taught last spring, student-teaching, and I'll be doing it again this year. I think it's fine; I wouldn't do anything else."

"I'm so surprised, though."

She shouldn't have said it, for he simply shrugged. Now he really was annoyed with her. Her mind resisted it; they could smooth it over. She looked at the car, an ancient Chevrolet convertible. The top was up, but the windows were all open. She hoped he would say something, anything. She could not apologize, but she did not know why. She was so clearly wrong. She had spent a year at Cortland State Teachers College before she had made her break for New York, and she had hated it. The question was, did she think so much more of him than herself that it was beyond her to imagine him as a teacher? But she *was* thinking that teaching was for people more like her than him, and it made her afraid again.

"You know," she said thickly, "I went to Cortland State Teachers College last year."

"Oh? Why did you quit?"

"I don't know—it wasn't right for me."

"You did the right thing," he said. "It's like anything else you're going to spend your life at. You have to think it's the only thing that matters."

"That's the way I felt it should be. Teaching was my parent's idea. They said I should have something to turn to if I ever needed it. I didn't think that was enough. That's why I'm here."

"You ought to be congratulated," he said. "You did absolutely the best thing you could have done."

She was pleased. But, she knew, if she told the truth as it happened, he would be completely disgusted with her. In arguing her way out of college, she had said to her parents that she wanted to "do something." "Teaching isn't doing," she had said. It was a lie, and he was showing her it was a lie. Teaching was more doing than people like her could handle. She had made the right move in quitting teaching, not because she was better than it, but because she was worse. And this would be his view, if she told the truth.

But there was another part, and she felt it saved her; she had not met anyone at Cortland State or anywhere else who saw learning and teaching as he did, obviously so vigorous and exciting. If she had, perhaps she would have stayed, or transferred to a liberal arts college. At Cortland State the girls had chosen teaching as something easy to do until they found husbands, and the boys—were not really human.

Goons, Alice had called them. The whole thing had been bedlam. She had quit not just because of the pressure of what she knew now was her misconception of teaching, but because of all the pressures. She had had to get out, for what she had felt was her own sake.

They were coming to a darker section of town, past factories and loft buildings. They went on and then out onto a broad bright street that was an approach to a bridge. She was studying it all. On the bridge there was nothing to see because it was old and the car-lanes were surrounded by heavy girders. On the other side, too—on an elevated highway they sped along—there was no spectacular view, which she had hoped for, only rooftops on which drying wash billowed dimly bright, white against the warm far black.

She asked how he had decided to become a teacher.

It had been an accident. He had been in the Army and when he had been discharged, he had come to the city with the intention of just going to college. But a series of confusions, all his, had put him in City College's School of Education. After a year and a half, he decided to stay. The more he learned, the more he loved teaching, or what he thought he could make of it.

It was his decision to make. His parents were dead and what was left of his family was scattered over the state. He had a married sister in Syracuse; another, single, worked in Troy. Only his uncle, his father's brother, remained in Tompkins County. "But," Buddy said, "I went up this summer—as I told you. It was my first year without summer school. All of us get together over the Christmas holidays, usually in Syracuse. We're really close, more than you would think under the circumstances."

She said nothing—she had nothing to say. A moment passed. She could see that she did not know him at all, just one trivial event squeezed into a crowded life. He was still very much the athlete to her, all grace and power, chewing gum and adjusting his cap. She was childish and wrong, but the vision was such a happy, vibrant one after so many weeks of depression and confinement.

It was slipping away. It seemed to be vanishing like a dream.

Now too much time had passed and she could not pick up the conversation. He stayed still, and they drove for a while in silence.

The city would not end. She had been certain that, after so long, they would enter the dark of the country, but it did not happen. They passed mile after mile of stores and homes, all brightly lit. She began to get tense again. Maybe he was lying, and driving her in circles.

He told her why they were going to the track. His uncle was a horse player, and a colt he had been watching upstate was running tonight at Roosevelt for the first time. Since the morning line-up had the horse at better than twenty-to-one the bookies in Ithaca paid, his uncle wanted to get his money down at the track odds. All Alice could really understand of this was that Buddy had received his instructions on the telephone this morning.

"Do you play the horses, too?" she asked.

"Oh, sure. I get out here at least once a month."

She could not think of an answer.

"You look shocked," he said. "Don't be. I'm not getting rich, but it's a better date than a cheap night club. The girls I go with always seem to have more fun."

"Well, you know we don't get much of that up home. It's just strange, that's all. Um, what were you doing in the bookstore tonight?"

"I was seeing if a book I'd ordered had come in. One on the race for Lake Chad."

"I don't follow you."

"I know, nobody does. I'm waiting for the day when somebody will. Lake Chad is in Africa, south of Sahara. The British and French both wanted control of it in the last century. I'll be doing a paper on it for a course in Imperialism I'll be taking."

"Where do you get the time for all this? I mean—"

"Oh, I work Saturdays, too. In a gas station."

"It sounds like a treadmill, now."

"We never say that."

"Oh, okay." She was quiet.

"Well, figure I get a hundred and ten a month from the G. I. Bill. I need the extra fifteen a week I make Saturdays."

"It sounds very hard. I don't know where you get the time for a tenth of the things you've talked about."

"It's not the time, it's the money. I have to budget so I have enough for the important things, like the car, liquor and women. They have to come first."

"Oh."

"That's my joke," he assured her. "Everybody hears it. It *is* the money that's difficult. I have to be careful. I get a job in the summers and save like hell, although this year I worked for my uncle and saved practically nothing. He has a gas station, too; it's where I learned the business. But he helps me out. Every once in a while he sends me something to get me through the rough spots."

"Oh, now."

"No, really, it's not that much. I worked for him this last summer to pay him back. He's single. I kept him company. I could have made a hundred and a quarter a week over at Alcoa in New Jersey. He had some time off for the track this way, you know, June, July and Saratoga. And while he was at the station we kept up a running two-handed game of seven card stud."

She did not understand this, but she did not ask about it. They were nearing the raceway; she could see its huge red sign high against the darkness. Buddy looked at his watch, his face serious. He bore down on the accelerator and wove the car from lane to lane, around the slower-moving traffic. At the parking lot gate he hit the brakes so hard the car skidded a little, but the attendant, instead of getting angry, only grinned. Buddy found a space quickly and pulled up the hand brake. "Can you run?"

"Why?"

"It's almost post time. I can't be late; I couldn't do that to him."

She hurried. Taking her hand, Buddy pulled her across the broad field. From the stands she could hear the rumble of the crowd. Cigarette smoke rose in a vast blue haze; the faces she could see under the lights were very clear and full of color. She could feel her heart pounding hard and her chest aching from the exertion. Buddy would not let up. From the stands a voice boomed over a loud-speaker:

"The Marshal calls the pacers!"

"Do we lose?" she asked.

"Two minutes." He let go of her hand and started to get money out of his wallet for the admission. "After we're inside," he ordered, "go to the program stand, the nearest one, and wait there."

He pushed her through the turnstile first, and then, his arm around her, running again, he said, "that stand, over there."

She went dutifully, not looking back, still running, as though slowing down would penalize him.

"The field is in motion!"

We lose, she thought. She could not lift her eyes to see what was around. Faces flashed by, out of focus. She stood still, clutching her purse to her waist. The thudding of horses' hoofs came to her, growing louder in a steady beat on dirt, but she could not find the courage to look for them down the incline where, she remembered from the movies she had seen, the track was supposed to be. She stood there as the sound faded and a few random shouts shot out of the stands, sweeping magically from this end down to the other.

The lights went out everywhere but over the track and the loud-speaker voice announced, *"They're off,"* and started calling the horses' positions.

Alice hiccoughed.

Buddy was beside her. He took her arm and led her up the incline through the crowd. "Come on, maybe we can see some of it, anyway."

"Is everything all right?"

"We'll have to see. Oh, I got to the window all right. Our horse is number seven. He's running fifth now."

The horses were at the back of the track, coming into the turn. All of them, pulling the sulkies behind them in a smooth rocking pace, looked alike to her. They were in a perfect line, not like any race she could have imagined, and as they came past the stands only those few shouts erupted, the same voices, it seemed, impelling and coarse. The horses continued down and around the turn into the back of the track in the same smooth line, rocking and pulling steadily.

"Boat race!" somebody screamed.

"What does that mean?"

"Hush," Buddy said.

The pack came into the nearer turn again; the crowd, screaming now, rose in a mass. The sulky drivers were pressing forward in their seats, their whips flicking out. Alice could hear the hoofs coming down in the measured clopping sound even through the roar. The horses had bunched into a cluster now, with only three of them behind, still aligned.

"It was going to be a boat race," Buddy yelled, "the sons of bitches, but the seven horse is trying to win, and now the bastards are trying to box him in."

She did not look at him for fear the surprise she felt about his language would be shown to him. And more important, she wanted him to think she understood something about the race. But she could not see number seven. The group of horses was moving swiftly down the center of the track and then under the white wire. The grandstand lights went on again and she could hear the mumbling of numbers around her, one of them seven.

"Who won?"

"Out on the board. It'll be a while; there was a photo, I'm sure of it."

The number seven shined suddenly on the board, and was repeated in a shout by the crowd. Next, in red letters, the word PHOTO gleamed on.

"Do we win?"

"Do we win? You bet we win!" He grasped her shoulders and shook her. Now, looking out to the track, he slapped his right bicep with his left hand. "Right up to here we win! Those lousy bastards, that'll teach 'em." He breathed deeply once and looked at her happily. "Come on, let's get on line while they quibble over place and show."

"Don't you want me to wait here?"

"Aren't you going to cash in your tickets?"

"I don't have any tickets," she said.

"What are those things in your pocket?"

From the pocket of her skirt jutted three yellow stubs.

"Oh, I can't!" she cried.

"If you can't, you'll take the railroad home. Don't try to find out if I'm kidding."

"Please, Buddy, I can't—" But she was giving in. It was a physical thing, through her legs and stomach and head.

"It's the custom," he said. "A man usually buys tickets for the girl he's with. I'm not kidding you."

She looked up at him. He had no idea what she was thinking. She had to kiss him. She was moving as she realized it, closing her eyes before she was really near. He kissed her lightly, holding her at the waist.

"Thank you," he said.

"Thank *you*," she answered without thinking.

"Come on, we'll get on that line." He took her arm and they went down under the stands to the cashiers' windows. People were already waiting.

She asked, "What do we do now?"

"We go home, back to the city."

"It looks so easy."

"Sure. But we're going home."

"I didn't mean we should stay," she said. "I mean it, it does look easy to me." She stopped, worried again. No, there was nothing to worry about. He was interested in her now. She had shown him she wasn't cold. Only to him—would he understand that? Yes. It was going to be all right.

The cashier's window opened and the line moved forward rapidly. Her tickets paid over a hundred and sixty dollars. She busied herself with putting the money away very carefully while Buddy was being paid—an enormous amount, it appeared. She could not ask how much. They started out to the car.

"Listen," he said, "there's a place up near my school where we can get southern fried chicken. It's a colored place. If you don't mind Harlem at night, we'll go there."

"No, no, it's fine." And silence. Why had he asked? Couldn't he assume already that she would be willing to go? What had she done to make him uncertain of her? Maybe he wanted her to talk, she thought, maybe he wanted to hear her opinions.

But there was nothing she could say. She had seen Harlem from the train but that wouldn't be enough. Nothing would be enough. She could not get across the last barrier to him. She has seemed to cross it, then she had slid back. She wondered for a moment if he was toying with her. No ... no. The failure was her fault. She was incapable of saying even that she was having a good time.

In the car she watched him hunch over the dashboard in the intricate process of starting the old motor. Maybe he had written her off already. She wished it was the beginning of summer now, instead of the end. She might see more of him than she was going to. If. She was wishing now, as if the wishing could rise and deepen and overflow and make a good thing happen. This one night had knocked down the last seven weeks like a file of toy soldiers. The rich, happy visions of what would happen if she did more than wish began to take their place ... the jolt of sudden motion snapped her thoughts, and she was moving in the cool night air toward the exit of the parking lot.

Alice was twenty.

But by her reckoning she had been alive only four or five years. Everything prior to a dim and indeterminable moment in her middle adolescence was swept in a glowing semiconscious tide. The sweet maze of childhood, without awareness of time or change, was in retrospect just a blurred study of the seasons, of nights and bright days. Walk down a sandy road and search out the round stones. A hundred times, a thousand, and then know each stone so well it has a secret name, like the smell of a comic book or the feel of a starched pinafore on one's shoulders. With the quiet of a little girl whose brothers were years her seniors, Alice found things to fill the minutes, gather the minutes into pleasant hours. On spring evenings when she had finished helping in the kitchen and her homework was done she would go out, hearing the screen door squeal lightly and slap shut behind her, and walk again, but mostly up a nearby hill whose crest was rocky and blown with a growth of small trees and shrubs. There were places there to sit, trace one's finger through the red dust, run a hand over the weather-smooth boulders. For a time, until the coming of the next winter broke it, she had a habit. She would form a kiss on her lips. She would form a kiss out at the green evening sky and all she could see below in the blue-gray gloom, and whisper, "I love you." On an evening she never thought of any more she had cried. It was dark in the sky and darker still down below, where tiny windows glowed. A car, headlights shining and then red tail-lamps glinting, moved silently on the distant highway. There were fireflies near, floating in random quiet arcs.

"I love you," she whispered. With her fingertips she touched her mouth and tried to imagine what being kissed on the mouth in return would feel like. She kissed the worn fabric of her jeans where they were pulled tight on her knee.

Then, from the house she could not see from where she was sitting, her mother's voice, "Alice! Come on, sweetie, it's getting late! We're going to have ice cream!"

"Yes, Mommie!"

Alice started to cry, she wanted to cry—out of a feeling she had never experienced before and did not know the quality of, whether it was sadness or joy—she wanted to

cry, but there was only an ache in her chest and a choking
in her throat. But she was glad of it, and at last she did
cry in the full joyous relief of crying, and finally she ran
down the hill happily, certain no blotches on her face
would give her away. When the screen door slammed, her
father, who was spooning the ice cream into soup bowls,
looked around and laughed aloud because she was winded
the distant highway. There were fireflies near, floating in
and gasping and laughing and sniffing all at the same
time.

In the nights they listened to "Mister Keen, Tracer of
Lost Persons," and "The F. B. I. in Peace and War." On
Sunday nights there was "Same Spade, Private Eye," and
"The Fred Allen Show." And afterwards, every night,
there was the smell of quilts and pillows.

But then there were events, things that began and ended
and against which one calibrated time and exercised criti-
cal faculties. And changes, the body changed. Lipstick—
she was not allowed to use powder. Hair styles. School:
school took on a happy new depth. It was becoming more
interesting.

But it was time, the coming to the forefront of time,
the ineluctable presence of time stretching and shriveling
always against her wishes, that made her think and become aware of herself against the background of an
unconscious world. The road she walked was transformed
into a thing serpentine and inherently evil, an abductor
ferreting her away to a tedious and fearful existence
wherein time clicked along promisingly and simultaneously
promiseless so that the finer, fragile reaction she once had
had to life began to harden and seethe like an inner
animal. Her anger, with the interminable grinning clicks
of the spinning world, pitched up to such a fury that even
those weekly bland diversions people her age indulged in
became more of the same pacing out, rehearsals in full
fancy dress, for a salvation and ordeal that was never
going to happen.

And just as much it was people, aspects of them childhood never had revealed: their pettiness, the proud way
they prattled news that was no news, pecking along in

time with time. And college, her sole hope for a while, appeared to be the nexus of the superficiality as they, the others, construed it: college was deluxe, crucial to the clucking mothers, for whom it was a place to marry their daughters out of; important to the fathers, whose sons could evermore peck first class; meaningless to children, who went probably most honestly because they were doing what they had been told. Insipid parties, people talking in grave tones difficult even for the dying to mean seriously; idiot rivalry among the student groups, even between dormitories; dates ending in blind attacks at the brassiere, the belly or the bottom, sending a girl up to her room in tears, wondering who or what had stolen her life.

Home was a haven of a kind. She did not have to worry about being uncouth or out of vogue. She could read and sing aloud when she wanted and not feel afraid of sweating when she worked hard. She could say her prayers, *saying* the words, not simply forming them in her mind.

But her feeling followed her. She was not going to let herself be robbed of life, or of any part of it. More and more she thought that she was going to live just once, and she was not going to be an accomplice to the crime being committed against her. With the absurd hope that was the heir to her anguish she argued for her freedom, compromised it that amount necessary to receive her parents' blessing, and enrolled in a six weeks' secretarial course in Syracuse. This past midsummer her doubt and despair became again so great she had to struggle with herself to remake her decision.

But not to affirm it. She went sadly, as if the place she had loved first would be the place she would always love last.

She awakened and felt the soreness instantly. She knew where she was, in his apartment, in his bed. She stared at the unfamiliar wall, adjusting again to the sensation of his heavier body tipping the mattress in his direction. He had to go to work today, she remembered, and she looked at her wrist-watch, which she had forgotten to remove. Six-thirty. Odd. Why had she awakened so early? So rested?

She stayed still. In the car last night, when she had finally been able to tell him how nervous she was, he told her to relax. "Stop making every little thing important. I'm not judging you. I know how strange everything is for you."

"I'm such an idiot, Buddy."

"You're not. Just take it easy."

"I've never been out with a man before. Only boys."

"Thank you, that was nice of you to say."

And outside the restaurant, going back to the car again—things had been going so well—he asked, "Ready for home yet?"

"No."

"Want to go up to my place?"

"Fine."

"I'm not a kid, Alice, and I'm not going to treat you like one."

And with her heart in her mouth, "That's right."

She did not feel good now, but it could have been worse. She was beginning to believe it could not have been better. She had had confidence in him. She had come around to thinking that it would be a splendid idea—she could approach her later marriage with that much more maturity and insight. He had not said anything. About her, about them, about *it*. Later he had done his talking, softly, soothingly, like a father. She had gone to sleep safely.

She eased herself out of bed and gathered up her clothes. He had put an alarm clock on the bookcase and now she pushed the button to keep it from ringing. With her clothes held before her, she looked down at him asleep. His skin was so very white where the sun had not touched it, only his arms and face and neck were brown, like a laborer who wears a tee shirt.

He looked like he was pretending, his eyelids only lightly drawn. He seemed happy, though the smile-lines in his face were relaxed, showing as faint pale rays across the browner skin. Brown hair, straight nose, good chin—

he was handsome. Gentle-looking. She withdrew to the bathroom.

She started breakfast before she awakened him. It seemed like a logical thing to do.

"Come on. Wake up."

"What time is it?"

"Ten to seven. Your breakfast will be ready soon."

"You shouldn't have."

"Well, too late," she said.

"How do you feel?"

"A little sore, but all right." She smiled. "Thank you for being so good to me."

"Don't say that." He sat up now, holding the sheet about him. "Um, step out and let me get something on. Say listen, I'm not very good in the morning. It takes me a while to wake up."

"I'll stay clear," she said.

"Are you really all right?"

"Yes. How many girls have you done this with?"

He looked at her. "You asked that last night."

"No, I didn't!"

"Yes you did. Before you went to sleep."

She was sure he was lying. "I didn't.—What did you tell me, then?"

"I said it wasn't your business."

She paused. "I'm sorry," she said.

"I'm sorry, too. Listen, Alice, I said I wasn't so good when I woke up."

She nodded. "Come on, your breakfast will be ready." She turned and left the room.

Still, she was not sure she could believe it—yet she had gone to sleep in so lovely and secure a way that she could have said anything. Of course he was telling the truth. He had no reason to lie. Why had she asked? She fiddled with the place settings at the table. The original question came back, she did not want to know the answer. Dozens of girls, dozens of times. She knocked a knife to the floor with a clatter.

His apartment was an old building on Twelfth Street east of Seventh Avenue, down from Saint Vincent's Hos-

pital. Three rooms, run together railroad style, the back
room too small for anything but a desk and a bookcase,
the kitchen in the center, the living room, the room in
which he *lived*, to the front, looking down to the street
three flights below. The apartment was neat and clean.
The furniture was the unfinished kind he had painted
himself, but it showed good taste. Now that she thought of
it, it was the self-respecting way in which he lived that had
played a large part in the success he'd had with her.

They sat down to breakfast. He acted very pleased.

"I really did ask that last night, huh?"

He nodded, watching her.

"I'm so surprised at myself," she said.

"Don't be. I'm curious about you, too. *This* never happened to me before."

"Well, you know about me."

"Oh, there are ways to get around that."

"Tell me, please."

"You know. Just so far and no further, baby, and so
forth."

"I never gave it a thought. I really am dumb."

"No, you're not. You're just right the way you are. The
breakfast is delicious."

"You don't want to talk about it," she said.

He grinned. "Actions speak louder than words, and I
have no time."

"Oh, you." For the first time she thought about being
able to do it again.

"And you blush, too. Well."

She looked away. She couldn't stop thinking. She wondered when the soreness would go away. Maybe he was
just trying to cheer her up, but she wanted to take him
seriously. He was going to be pleased when he realized
how much she wanted to take care of that for him. He
had forgotten how much she had liked it.

"Enough," he said. "Will you do me a favor? Send my
uncle's share up to him. That's if you have some free time
today. He would have to wait until next week, otherwise."

"Are you trying to show your confidence in me?"

"Is it so obvious?"

"Yes, but I'll do it. Thank you again."

"Stop saying that. Listen, before I fell off last night I worried about how you'd feel this morning. A little late to start worrying, I know. This is what I wanted to say: you've made it very easy for me this morning. I feel absolved."

"*You* feel guilty?"

"You were a pushover. I should have had more respect."

"I wanted it, too, Buddy. I wanted it very much."

She looked down suddenly. For a moment he did nothing, as if truly he did not understand that she had said far more than she had wanted to, then he reached for her hand, squeezed it, and let go. "Look at me," he said. "I feel the same way, I think. I have no idea why we did what we did. Not really. Certainly we can't go back to the beginning and start over. I don't want to, for that matter." He stopped. "You're very dear to me already, Alice. I have to leave it at that."

"That's fine," she murmured.

They finished and had another cup of coffee and then he kissed her goodbye and left. She had a key with which to lock up and they were to meet his evening in front of the Loew's around the corner. As she closed the door after him she felt a loneliness and depression rolling up, and she looked around for some way to negate it. She went to the window to see if she could see him below. He had the same idea, for he turned around, not to wave, but, as she observed clearly, to smile with genuine pleasure. But the relief she felt was suddenly cut off—for he had stopped just as suddenly and looked up the other way toward Seventh Avenue. Someone was coming, a heavyset, swarthy fellow.

He, too, was looking up. He had seen, Buddy went down the steps to meet him. They stood talking, the swarthy fellow looking up, grinning. For a second it wasn't clear, but then it was: Buddy was telling him about her.

She backed away slowly, taking her arms in her hands. She was cold, just like that. As if he had struck her there, a knot was rising in her chest. She stumbled against the bed, hurting her leg. The tears flooded up and rolled out of her eyes so quickly that she did not have the chance to hold them back. She was collapsing from the inside out. Even as she thought that she did not want to touch his bed he was on it, falling across it. She drew her breath and smelled his odor on the sheets, cried out, and rolled onto her back, digging her nails into her upper arms. Her leg throbbed and felt as though it was bleeding, but she did not move to tend it. She knew that if he were here, she would not be able to get up to hurt him. She herself was hurt too badly. She had never felt anything so bad as this. The sound of her own crying hammered her ears longer and louder than it had ever done.

The telephone rang. It occured to her not to pick it up, but when she realized it might be him she clambered for the instrument, hiccing and sniffing.

"Alice? It's me. I would have come back upstairs but I had to get rid of him—the fellow you saw. You did see him, didn't you?"

"Y-yes." She moved the mouthpiece away again; he wasn't going to hear her cry. She fought to get control.

"I guessed you did. I'm sorry. He saw you, or he saw me look around, which may be the same thing. He asked who I had up there. He pressed it. Of course he doesn't know you, but I did play dumb. I told him I was just glad to be back from the country, and that's why I looked up. Now listen to me hard: this fellow is the type who will call or come up there to check. Don't answer the phone or the bell, either."

"What's his name? What's the matter with him?"

"His name is John Murillo. I'll give you the complete run-down on him when I see you. We won't be able to avoid running into him from time to time—"

"You didn't tell him, then?"

"Of course not. I just told you. I wondered what you'd be thinking. Listen, this makes me mad enough to kill him, but he's just one of those people they haven't caught up with yet. Do you understand me, Alice?"

"Yes, Buddy. Buddy, listen, I thought all wrong things—"

"You don't have to tell me."

"I want to make it up. I'm sorry I judged you." She hoped he would be glad to hear her repeat something he had said to her.

"The only thing I'm sorry about is that I can't be with you now," he said. "Try to take it easy the rest of the day."

"I'm sort of glad it happened," she pressed. "Now I know even more about you, and I still like it."

There was silence. Then, "Okay. Relax. Make yourself pretty tonight. We'll do something nice, I promise."

II

Stiff, aching and hung over, Cal Torrenson shuffled down the hall of the upper floor of the summer bungalow in Groton Long Point, Connecticut. He felt as though he had swallowed the emptyings of a vacuum cleaner, and the fresh, cool salt air of the morning did not hlep him. He continued down the hall to the bathroom where he took three aspirins. With his eyes closed he stood still a moment, then he peered at himself in the medicine cabinet mirror, stroking his soft, day-old beard. No, he was not going to shave. He discerned the red streaks in the whites of his eyes. In disgust Cal Torrenson turned away and went back to his bedroom.

Sunday, early September, nineteen fifty-five, mild and breezy, visibility at sea over five miles. From his window Cal could see at least that far, out over the blue Sound to the white rim of the horizon. More directly below him on the beach were umbrellas with their tines braced into the sand against the billowing gusts. There were only a few umbrellas, and to Cal's right and left was the logical explanation for that: bungalows already closed for the summer. The taste in his mouth, he felt, was the proper finish to the summer, this dreary summer.

Cal had just attained his majority. He was tall and well-built, an inch over six feet and almost two hundred pounds, blonde, blue-eyed, and for the time being, well-tanned. He had spent this miserable summer as a lifeguard down on the beach and his tan wall all, absolutely all, he had to show for it. He dressed quickly and braced himself for what was to come downstairs, a virtuoso performance by the Madame.

She, his mother, was sitting on the couch in the living room, thumbing through the magazine section of the *Times*. Other sections were on the pillow beside her. As she heard Cal on the stairs she raised her eyes, only moving her head slightly.

"A dillar, a dollar, a ten o'clock scholar. How do you feel?"

"No interviews, please." He went on toward the kitchen.

"You weren't home at five o'clock this morning," she called.

"You know how that is," he said.

"Cal, you could be just a little more thoughtful."

"All right."

"All right what?"

"Please, Mother, I just don't want to hear it. Where's Dad?"

"Out in the yard."

He turned to go.

"No breakfast?" she asked.

"I'm not hungry."

"Are you going to tell him about the fishing trip now?" It wasn't a question, it was a command. Cal stood still at the door. Off in the corner of the yard in the shade of a tree his father was sitting in a deck chair, facing away. All Cal could see was the man's legs and the bottom of his shorts. To his mother, Cal said, "Well, I've only got two days. It's either today or tonight."

"You have a lot to learn."

"*Please,* Mother!" He looked at her, thinking, *as if you knew anything about him and me.* He could level with his father, after their own fashion of give-and-take, and she had no idea of that between them. Or between anyone. Her world was a well-ordered fraud. Sunday with the

Times was part of it. Also charge accounts. Also dragging the old man to musicals in Manhattan. Those things, plus the best sellers, were all there was to her.

"Take the sports section out to him, then, please. Do him that one favor."

Cal went back to the couch and took the section of the paper. His mother had another section up to her face and he could not see her, so he glared stonily at the gray mass of print. He turned around and went out of the house, onto the rough, slightly burnt grass of the back yard.

"I brought out the sports section."

His father stirred as if he had been half-asleep. He removed his sunglasses and scratched the white stubble on his cheek.

Here in the sun the man's belly-skin looked sickly and soft. His body was peppered with moles and on his hairless legs tangles of blue veins could be seen. He raised himself to a sitting position and made room for his son on the footrest. Cal sat down.

"What time is it?" his father asked.

"After eleven, I think. I don't know. Why, do you have work to do?"

"Oh, no." He reached down on the grass for his pack of cigarettes, took one, then tossed the pack to his son. "How was your time last night?" He smiled with a good-natured lechery.

"Fine. It turned out pretty good." Like a mouse darting through a maze Cal's mind dodged the truth.

"You're being careful, though, aren't you? Your mother can't helping worrying."

"I know. She makes sure I know."

"That's a woman. When you understand that, you know it all."

"Explain it to me," Cal said, grinning, knowing what he was to get.

"Not me, I don't know any more than you do." The man drew on his cigarette. "But be careful," he said gravely.

"Sure. Hey, I have something to speak to you about."

"Shoot."

"You remember Bix—he came out last year at the end of the season?"

"Sure. The frail boy with the new little Thunderbird."

"That's right. I'll be rooming with him at the frat this year. I got a letter from his last week—he's getting up a fishing trip. There was talk about it this spring, I told you. Well, it's on for this week, at Skaneateles Lake."

"What the hell is that name?"

'Skaneateles. Skan-ee-at-lees. It's one of the Finger Lakes, up near the University. The fishing's great there."

"This week, eh?"

"Wednesday morning. I'd have to leave Tuesday."

"I thought you were going to help us get the stuff back to Darien this year." His father watched him carefully, drawing again on the cigarette and letting the smoke snake up before his eyes.

"I can take a load or two tomorrow, I suppose, if the stuff is ready."

"Out of the question. We'd have to work today."

"Well, then," Cal pushed, alarmed, "I can take two on Tuesday and go straight from Darien afterward. I have to stop at the house anyway. My trout flies are there."

"That's a lot of driving," his father said.

"I'll pace myself. I'll take it easy."

"Your mind is made up already, isn't it?" But he was grinning, Cal was in.

"I *am* asking you," he said respectfully.

"All right, you can go."

"Thanks." Cal stood up.

"Sit down, wise guy. I didn't dismiss you yet."

Still smiling, Cal obeyed. This was the old man's way.

"I wanted to ask you something, how do you stand with the draft?"

"They're not taking fellows in the district until they're twenty-three or -four. I have two years yet."

"Oh. Hm." Now, to waste time, to let Cal sit in attendance, as Cal himself was well aware, his father glanced down at the sports section and examined the headlines. He picked it up and opened it to the second page. "Yes, well—" He looked up. "What I wanted to ask you was, whether you were still interested in psychology—as a career, that is. I was talking with Addison down at the Republican Club and he says there are a lot of jobs in the government, overseas, say, that pay money—why, I was surprised. A kid could work a couple of years out of the country, say in a place like Greenland, and come back with a wad. Of course you'd need a doctorate, but maybe you'll get a deferment. I don't know. But if you want, when you're ready, I can tell him to check into it, ask around, and see how you go about it. He owes me favors from the war, when I was letting him have gasoline and auto parts, so nothing should be too difficult."

"To tell you the truth, Dad, I've just about given that up. It's too long a road and it just isn't worth the trouble. I've been thinking about personnel and advertising and so forth, something I can do with I have. I want to see how the business world is. I've built my course around it this year, so I can really put my teeth into it—"

"You got this personnel stuff from that girl you were seeing last year, didn't you?"

"Well, sure, to an extent—she's going into advertising, really—but I was toying with it before I met her. Long before. This is my own decision. She cleared up a lot of false impressions I had, that's all."

"I'm not saying anything against her. Don't get me wrong. She must be quite a person. All we've ever done was to try to point out what you'd be taking on with a Jewish girl. You're still very much on the defensive—"

Something over the rooftops caught their attention, and together they looked around. High over the slate tiles, a sail, gliding against the sky as though unreal, floated from right to left. Coming to a clear space between the houses, it showed below it a sloop whose deck was angled sharply against the dark water. Cal could see men crawling over the rigging. Again houses blocked it, but for the moment, the image held fast. Cal kept staring, waiting for another glimpse.

"What I was going to say, Cal, was that sooner or later you're going to have to relax about what happened between you and her—Elaine? Was that her name?—And come to terms with things again. I don't know, am I making myself clear?"

"Yes, but I feel pretty good. I'd rather talk jobs than her, if you don't mind. I want to strike out on my own, move to New York, bear down on getting—you know—*doing* something with my life. Does that make sense to you?"

"All the sense in the world. Look at me. I did what I wanted, worked hard, and I have something to show for it. Look what I have. There's not much more a man could want in this world."

"A racing sloop."

"What?"

"A racing sloop," Cal repeated grinning.

Mr. Torrenson snorted. "Oh, shit, kid. You know what I mean." Together they looked out to sea, but the sloop was gone, skimming over the top of the water, cracking the wavecrests, moving on.

Cal took the opportunity to get up and go back into the house. The talk was working toward one of his father's stories—how he had persuaded his drivers to invest in the bus company and thus had saved it from the hands of the bankers, for example—and although Cal was very interested in spite of having heard the stories before, this morning such attention as he would be required to pay was beyond him. He hoped his father would not be offended.

His mother was working through the real estate section now—she liked to look at the room layouts in the ads—and Cal went by silently, waiting for her to say some more on last night. Nothing. He got up the stairs and into his room. Already the choice of sleep or wakefulness was ebbing out of him. Sleep really was the best way to avoid thinking about last night's disaster. Sleep would restore him.

He awoke near four o'clock, sweaty but more alive than he had been before noon, thinking of the vivid dreams he had had, and he went downstairs to get a snack.

The house was dark. His father was on the couch now, asleep, and the television set was on, showing a fuzzy

Eddie Cantor film. Cal's mother would be outside walking
on the beach. After his sandwich, Cal went out and hosed
down his Plymouth two-door; then he hosed down his
father's car, a two-year-old Packard Patrician four-door
sedan which already had a half-dozen scratches and dents
in it.

The next thirty-six hours were a waste. He had nothing
to do, nothing to read, and just as important, the places he
could go to kill the time were paralyzed by summer's end.
At odd moments, what had happened Saturday night came
back to fling its little dart at him, and it was early in the
proceedings that Cal realized that he was going to have it
with him for a little while to come.

The girl, if she could be called that, whom he had been
dating and sleeping with all summer, had finally followed
through, she had stood him up. "If you don't treat me
with a little more respect, Cal Torrenson, I'm going to
leave you wondering what happened to me." It was more
than a standup, it was one of the cheapest tricks he had
ever seen: she had made a date in the full knowledge that
she would be gone back to school two whole days before
the time of their appointment.

He had treated her terribly, of course. He had met her
just after the breakup with Elaine and he had been working it off on her, playing the old situations with the better
endings. He had known it all along. The girl had seemed
to like it, but toward the end he had overplayed his hand.
Hooking her panties onto the aerial of his car and driving
through Mystic had been just too much. It had been a
wild bit, though.

Naturally, Saturday night had been a fiasco. He had
gotten completely blotto and, if he could remember correctly, had tried to pick up some slovenly matron only
slightly more sober than himself. Here he had overplayed
his hand literally. "Get your hands off the candy, sonny,"
she had said out loud in the bar. Now that it was past,
however, he could see that the situation—and the tagline—
were screamingly funny.

The rest of Sunday and Monday passed without incident. Tuesday morning, early, Cal loaded the trunk and

rear seat of the Plymouth with the cartons his mother had prepared the day before. Next to him on the front seat he set his own luggage. There was just this one trip to make—a new arrangement—and then he was going on to Cornell. There were no protracted farewells, he was glad to get away.

It was a clear day, the highways were empty, and he made good time to the house in Darien. When he rolled the car up the drive the big building seemed to project its emptiness, the windows were like blind eyes, and the bits of clutter out on the lawn seemed more like dust mice rolling across an empty floor. Inside, the place was damp and the eerie feeling of being alone settled almost at once in his bowels. He worked quickly, putting the cartons on the dining room floor as he had been told. Then he went up to his room to get his fresh-water gear, his New York State fishing license, and a few books, which, when he saw them, made him think they might be useful.

But out in the car again he sat there a moment, not starting the motor, just staring at the white shingles of the house. He got out and walked up the path and unlocked the front door again. This was really the last time. The thought that this would no longer be his home resounded in him until he could have shouted it. His visions of New York took on an intensity he could hardly bear; June became the month of calamity rather than achievement. Growing up was the calamity, being cast out by himself rather than by anyone else. And it was inevitable; there were no choices, even if his mind seemed to seek them out. Aspects of his childhood poured into him like the brilliant beams of a colored revolving lantern. He ascended the kitchen stairs to the second floor and ran through the corridor and exploded into his room.

Silent ... silent. The debris of boyhood perched and hung from its mountings with such utter stillness that he might have been looking at a photograph. Toy yachts and model planes, puppets he had made, battered copies of boy's classics—they were there to touch, but beyond his reach. The splendid days they evoked. He wished he could heap them up, run his hands through them as though they were glittering golden coins, but they were beyond him. He backed out almost respectfully, as though the room belonged to another little boy, one who still lived.

When he got to the Bear Mountain Bridge he could not really remember having driven there. The radio was on, the quart of milk and the box of cookies were beside him. Perhaps it was the final realization that he was in New York State that brought him around. This was part of it, he had not made the trip so many times that the feeling of newness had worn off. This was different country, different people.

After his freshman year when he had stopped feeling like the little boy on his first trip away, he had toyed with the idea of taking the trip more leisurely, stopping a night in one of the hotels in Sullivan County. The stories he had heard intrigued him, but he did not like the thought of being a lone Gentile among so many Jews. The idea was with him this time too, but once he got on Route Seventeen he stayed there, straight through, until he reached Binghamton and dinner time.

He began to feel more chipper. A senior now. A year, no, three months older and wiser. And harder. He could not avoid seeing Elaine. That pleased him. It tickled his sense of the dramatic.

It was easy to picture her: tall, just a little plump, her hair a fine reddish brown, her skin the color of rich cream. She had the most beautiful, best-tasting skin he had ever known. That in itself was enough to draw him to her. Oh, it was going to be something jolly, to see her again. How many had she slept with since May? She had lost her virginity last year—she said. Cal had been number two. He had been her reaction to the first—that was the way she had explained it, their last night—and it was easy to see her explaining to herself the third and even the fourth as "reactions" to those who had gone before. Like a pinball, "reacting" from one score to another. Sure, with the little bells ringing.

How many had he slept with? Less than ten, on that he was clear. He had given up that counting stuff. Driving across the rolling farmland of middle New York to Tompkins County, he did not want to think about the past. The past was rolling back, especially this oppressive hot summer. The summer was dissolving, yes, sweetly, like the pall of a dawn at sea.

There wasn't going to be a fishing trip. Bix sent a telegram of regrets, something at home had come up. The others who had promised to attend, four sophomores and juniors, were at the fraternity house when Cal arrived, but the liquor they had in them as he came through the door already had them thinking of other game. They wanted to go to the beach. They wanted to go over to Cortland Teachers College. They wanted to go up to Syracuse. One even had the idea of taking in the wrestling there, at the arena. Finally it seemed that anything was all right, except fishing.

Early Wednesday morning Cal left the house with his gear in hand. It was a great morning, the air fragrant, the mist clinging to the treetops. He hurried down the hill to the place off the campus where he had parked his car.

The southern end of Skaneateles Lake was desolate and flat. The creaking of the oarlocks echoed back to the dock and past the scarred earth of the clearing to the trees. He could see birds in the blue sky in the distance. He was not really happy. A morbid emotion was penetrating him, like the air from the bottom of a well. The sounds of the oarlocks grew louder and filled his mind almost as the toll of bells. He listened to the creakings in time to his rhythm of rowing, driving in, driving in. He passed out beyond hailing distance. He pulled in the oars and let the boat drift.

Drift . . . back with his tackle box was a bag of lunch he had bought in downtown Ithaca, like the lunches he used to carry to public school years ago. The milk in the school cafeteria had a taste different from what his mother made him drink at three o'clock. He could remember his legs not being long enough to reach the kitchen floor. Some of the kids had gone away to private school and he had wanted to, but no, he belonged at home. They let him go to camp one summer and he did not like it. The other kids played tricks on him because he was new—frenching his bed, putting rocks in his knapsack. He would not have been new if he had gone every year. Maybe it was the stillness of the lake that was making him remember these things. In camp once they took his pants and his underpants and switched his behind while he screamed at them and cursed.

That sort of thing happens to everyone at least once, he had decided long ago. The really older kids had told him that later, by way of consolation. Those things were universal, like worrying about being an orphan. For a long time he had worried about being an orphan, perhaps when it first occured to him that he had no recollection of his very early years. He had stayed awake and wondered about his real parents, his real father, his real mother. Which was all ridiculous, as a psychology text later revealed.

He drifted some more.

Elaine. There were times when he was sure he loved her. He had never known anyone like her, any feeling like the one she had stirred. Even now he wanted to recall and examine how they had made love in her car, how she had held him tightly and said things that dazzled and frightened him. He had never *surrendered* to a woman before. That last night hurt him yet. He wanted to think about the good and forget the bad. He wanted to go on and think about her, *her,* but he could not, really, not without falling the rest of the way. Pain and desire still mingled to the last recesses of his awakened heart.

He fished a while, caught a catfish, and went home.

He spent the next two days reading *Crime and Punishment* in his room. The "fishermen" drifted in and out, discussing conquests on the beach, where they had ended up. It was not until Friday night, when most of the rest of the thirty-odd brothers of Theta Kappa Omicron had come in, that Cal participated in the fun and games, which on this night consisted on an impromptu party with one of the sororities. He finished the night parked at the edge of the lake with a Rochester sophisticate who thought petting was the perfect adjustment to physical wants and social pressures. He had been tipped off to her in advance by one of the other fellows, and he put her through her paces like a matador handling a cow.

The next morning he went shopping downtown and ran into Elaine outside Woolworth's.

"Hey, you're in an awful fog."

He stopped and raised his eyes. She was standing right in front of him, smiling brightly. She was wearing a dress he had not seen before—very smart, with a neat, open collar. "You would have walked over me," she said. "Say hello. Come on."

He grinned. "Sure. Hello."

"You're looking well. Very tan."

"I spent the summer as a lifeguard. I told you I was going to do that. You look well, too. You've lost weight." Actually more weight than his eyes would believe. He was stunned. The new narrowness of her waist made her bosom seem even larger. The dress showed her wonderfully. He knew he was gaping, but it was not something he could help. He tried to concentrate on her eyes, but the intense and, he knew, innocent pleasure in her gaze intimidated him. He asked, "What are you doing here so early? You don't register until—when?—Tuesday."

"I could ask you the same question," she said.

"I wanted to do some fishing."

"Are you having any luck?"

"Not really, but never mind that. You still haven't told me what *you're* doing here." They were being jostled by the crowd moving around them.

"I came about a job—part-time, you know, Saturdays."

"A part-time job is so urgent?" He chuckled.

"Oh, I've been writing letters for three weeks. It's at the radio station, not a very good job—I think all I'll be doing is running out for coffee all day long—but it's some experience, anyway."

A woman ran a wheel of a shopping cart over Cal's instep. He glared at her, then took Elaine's arm. "Maybe we'd better walk, it's safer."

"But *my* car is this way."

He felt annoyed. "Sure." He reversed their direction.

"I'm in no particular hurry. But why radio?" he asked abruptly. "No more B.B.D.&O.?"

"I decided I like radio and television better. I was in their television department this summer—I was just seething with envy for the people we were working with, producers and so forth. I have to give it a try."

"That made up your mind?"

"I guess so," she said brightly.

He shook his head in wonder.

"Well, also, I decided I didn't like advertising after all."

"Okay. No further questions."

"No, really, I got sick of it. Nobody willing to take a chance, everybody doing what everybody else has done. *And* minding everybody else's business, like so many old ladies—"

"Well, that's part of the business world," he said. "There's nothing so small as big business."

"Mm."

He had hoped she would laugh, and now he felt even more antagonized. "You know," he said, "television is not a hotbed of initiative."

"I know."

"Well?"

"Maybe I'm wrong, but it seems like a field where a good thing is more liable to get done."

"That really is impossible to say offhand, and you know it."

She smiled at him. "You're quite the tiger today, aren't you?"

He grinned. "Am I?"

"Yes, definitely."

"Are you pleased?"

"Oh, I don't want to go into that." Her tone was so flip it was a complete rebuff.

"Well, tell me then," he said, "am I right or am I right?"

"You're right—maybe. But there's still another thing."

"Okay, but it figured."

"You're having fun with me, Cal."

"Oh, I don't want to go into *that*," he said, mimicking

her. He paused. "Okay, I'm sorry. What's the other reason?"

"Well, maybe it's the fact that they're nearer honest creation, but the people I met seemed happier and had a better opinion of themselves."

"I pass," he said. "I really do. When you get down to it, you made the switch just because you wanted to."

"That's right," she said.

They were at her car, the three-year-old Pontiac convertible. He got in on the passenger side. "Are you going to drive me to my bus?"

"Okay, lazy bum."

"You had me walk you here," he said.

"That's right," she said.

"How is your family? Your mother?" That was a dig; she didn't like her mother, though she never said so.

"They're fine."

"Good. How's the car holding up?"

"Listen." She turned the ignition key. The motor boomed to life.

"You have a hole in your muffler."

"I sort of like it. It sounds like a hot rod."

"Okay, let's see you dig out for the nearest Plymouth."

"Roger."

It was a good car. She had worked at a dozen jobs since the age of sixteen, or possibly fourteen, to save the money for it—and it was her baby. Jobs: dollar-an-hour jobs, salesgirl, file clerk, messenger girl—he could not remember them all. It was easy to imagine her working, her complexion was such that that color faded with her strength. And her hair drooped, the difficult-anyway pageboy falling into a mess. She was going to get somewhere. The pathetic thing was that she was just as liable to get married, pregnant, tied-to-dirty-diapers, and all this effort would have been for nothing. And maybe her husband, some fat and balding jackass, a Jew, of course, would make her sell her car.

That was the other thing: Jewishness. To Cal, Elaine's mother was the fount of *her* Jewishness, and it seemed to him that maybe Elaine did not particularly care for being a Jew. She could have chosen him for her "reaction" to that Marv character on the basis of his Christianity. She had made it a point to tell her parents, especially her mother, that she was seeing a Christian. No, a Gentile. Non-believer: Jews and Christians both seemed blind to the insult. Were the Jews blind to it? He didn't think so.

"How is everything at Theta Kappa Omicron?" she asked. "Has anyone sobered up yet?"

"You know. That isn't going to change."

"And Bix. Is that his name, your friend with the Thunderbird? How is he?"

"I haven't seen him yet. I was supposed to, but he didn't show up."

"Oh. Are you going to be Chancellor?"

"What?"

"Chancellor of that frat. You haven't forgotten, have you?"

He didn't want to answer. He hadn't forgotten, but his confession about that passing ambition had been a deeply personal thing. He wondered if she was trying to be cute. When he did answer it seemed to him that he stumbled over his words.

"I was just fooling around with that."

"I thought you were pretty serious at the time."

"My car is around the corner here. Make the light and then I'll walk back."

She stopped the car on the opposite side of the intersection. For a second as he held the door open he regarded her, and she looked absolutely bland. Of course she knew she had needled him. Now he could settle up. "Tell me, did you hear from what's-his-name?"

"Marv? Oh, no."

"He hasn't called you?"

She shook her head. "Mm-mm."

"If I were you I'd be bitched straight to hell for not getting the satisfaction of nailing him back."

She smiled quietly. He hesitated before getting out, because it was obvious that she had won, but abruptly and awkwardly he did it, slamming the door after him. As he crossed the street toward his car he realized he had done more than lose, he had conceded defeat without a struggle. He would never get her to admit to feeling what he felt. In this instance she chose to have a skin as thick as that of a walrus. Or at least make him believe it. He did not believe it. He would not. The defeat was not perfect. There would be the chance that he could make her confess to what he felt, and then submit. Once. Dear God, once.

Or was he kidding himself? She was hurting the hell out of him, that bitch. It hurt to holy hell, but it was just as easy for her as picking a thread from her dress. Every day and every way, and just as easy as she could pick a thread from that well-filled dress.

chapter two

I

Charles David Cumberland, Jr., was born on June 25, 1932, in his parents' bedroom in a frame house off Route Thirteen, north of Ithaca, New York, as his older sister had been born three years before and his younger sister would be five years later. He was a horribly fat baby who refused bottles by the following winter and who, by the next summer, found he enjoyed eating flowers—roses and forsythias, morning-glories and marigolds, all of which grew in profusion around the house and at the front of the yard, cultivated by his mother, who also tended a small vegetable garden in the back. Charles David, Jr., however, had no taste for vegetables.

His father and his uncle owned a gas station on the highway, and it could be seen from the house—far up the hill, where the cars passed and then curved out of sight. During his first years the boy would sit and play in the front yard under the black walnut tree and watch both the house and the station, which was small in the distance, and glittered when the air was hot. Later, after the younger girl was born, Buddy would trudge up and down the hill as he chose—but not across the road. He would stand on the side and yell over, *"Come and get me Uncle Floyd or Daddy!"* and one of the two would come to get him. Sometimes one or the other would take him in the Model A Ford pickup truck into Ithaca, or all the way up to Syracuse, for spare parts, and other times they would put him to work counting the soda bottle caps, which was a very important thing. He would play with the caps a while, stacking them up or putting them in lines, then he would sweep them into the pail under the soda cooler, where he had gotten them. He would got out and make his report, "There are twenty-seven eleventeen soda bottle caps," he would say, and stand rigidly at attention.

"You better open three more then," his Daddy would say. "We have to have an even number."

His Daddy was killed when Buddy was just past his eighth birthday. There was no effort to delude or frighten either of the other children—little Nora was still too young to know what had happened. For his part, Buddy knew all there was about dying: people and animals went to sleep, and their souls floated up to Heaven. It was very nice, and it made sense, too: after all, the soul floated down and into the mother's belly when the animal—or Nora—was about to be born. The feeling of order the ideas gave was pleasing to the child, though he was sad about his father never coming back.

It had been a violent, sudden death, and once it was possible, the two children were taken up to the gas station to see what had happened. A bumper jack, all that was available at the moment, had slipped from under a Chrysler Airflow on which his father had been working, and the rear axle had come down on the man's chest.

His uncle was crying. Buddy's sister was standing back by the highway, which was understandable to Buddy, because this was something really between men—but Buddy had been curious; he had to see the thing *exactly*. The place on the cement had been scrubbed clean, there was nothing but the cement itself.

"Like a bug, huh?"

The man nodded.

"Gee, it must have hurt!"

—Which was the most excruciating memory about it Charlie had. At the time there were things that were strange, like the funeral, the ceremony over the sealed box in which his father was sleeping, and the long slow ride to the cemetery. It came to the boy in the car how serious the moment was, and so he became serious and manly, just as he had three years before, when Nora had been born.

The other mysterious thing was the Uncle Floyd moved out of the frame house, and came to work in the gas station all the way from Ithaca. Buddy did not hesitate to ask his mother about it.

"Some people think it's not right for a man and woman to live in the same house if they're not married."

"Why? Why ain't it right?"

"I said, some people *think* it's not right. We don't know who they might be, but they might not let their children play with you, and that *would* be wrong, wouldn't it?"

"Oh, to hell with them."

"Don't use that language."

"Uncle Floyd does and so did Daddy."

"You have to be grown up, to."

"Oh. But what could you do that ain't right, make babies?"

"Oh, God. Yes, that's right. They would think we were trying to make babies, and they don't think that's right, whoever they are."

"Well, why don't you make babies with Uncle Floyd? God likes babies."

"Dear, dear God. First, you're right, God does like babies, but most people are nowhere near as good as God and so they might not like our babies just because Uncle Floyd and I aren't married. Second, we're not going to marry—we don't love each other enough for that—or babies, as much as God loves them. And third, I personally—do you know what that means?"

"Yeah, you alone by yourself."

"That's right. I personally have had all the babies I ever want. You personally alone by yourself would have been plenty for ten women."

"Oh, Mommy, you're teasing me."

"That's right. Come and give me a kiss."

He went over and kissed her cheek. "Can you do me a favor?" she asked. "A big one. It takes a man to keep a secret a woman tells him."

"Sure, what's that?"

"Don't talk to Uncle Floyd about this. Our talk."

"Why not?"

"It's very simple. I asked Floyd if he would marry me to keep me company but he thinks it would be better if we did what we're doing, with him living in town and all, because we don't love each other that way. If you talk to him about it, he'll think you're trying to shame him with it, or embarrass him—you know what that word means—and make him, you know, like he had a bellyache. You must keep the secret or I'll be hurt. Do you understand?"

"Yeah, I think so."

"And you won't blackmail me? You won't make me give you candy and all? That wouldn't be the manly thing to do."

"No, I promise."

In a week he had forgotten it and he did not recall if for another dozen years, when he was standing at her grave in the early summer of nineteen fifty-two, a month after she had been buried. He stood there in the creased twill of his Army uniform, sweating, looking down at the bleached squares of turf laid on the mound of dirt. Between the headstones he could see a small ragged flag fluttering, and from the trees beyond the cemetery came a buffeting hot wind, and the singing of insects. His uncle, who had driven him from the Ithaca airport, stood behind him, and after a long while his uncle spoke, his voice faint because the wind carried it away, "Your mother was a good, noble woman, Buddy. I'm going to tell you something now, not because I want to hurt you, but out of a want to lighten your grief—it'll be done through the pride you should feel. After your father died I asked her to marry me. Of course she refused. She didn't love me that way—she loved me instead in the way a worth-while human being cares for any living thing—and I'm sure, too, that I didn't let enough time go by. After your father's death, I mean. I was stupid about it—I don't want to go into the details, but you're old enough now to apprehend what I mean—but she did not try to hurt me in return. She could have. She could have deprived me of the only family I had—you kids. But she knew I needed you. I'd watched you grow. And she knew, too, that maybe you in return needed me, to fill the terrible gap. She remembered my feelings, even though I may have forgotten hers.

She made allowances, Buddy. Think of that now, if you can."

She had died suddenly of a heart attack, at a moment when, around the world in Korea, her son was at last boarding the ship to come home. The war had started on his eighteenth birthday, and the suggestions of fate and prophecy that fact evoked, coupled with the confusion of his immature mind, had prompted the boy, a month later, to have his draft number moved up. He went, and despite the offer to play ball for a Class D team in the southwest, and above everyone's normal hopes that he would not be hurt, the move was regarded by all as the best thing he could have done. He would be finished with the service, they said, and he would come back stabilized and more of a man.

In the first months he knew nothing but tortuous boredom; during basic training in Georgia and then afterward, crossing the country and the Pacific, he knew defeat and hate. He wanted to scream it out. And it was the same in Japan those few weeks in the fall; but for the weekends in Tokyo and Yokahama when even then there was only drinking and Oriental wenching, it was a kind of agony he had never dreamed existed: nothing, doing nothing, watching the time dry up under the pale sun, staring at nothing in the black night.

But then it was over, Japan shrank and disappeared in the glare of a glittering sea, and with the same suddenness that the war had changed—in the landing at Inchon some weeks before and in the rout of the North Korean Armies—his life had changed. It was more than what met his eyes as, among hundreds, he marched down the gangplank of the ship, alone with the loneliness of one molecule in the monstrous burgeoning organism of the Army. It was more than the natural *I may die here* thinking, of the same emotional depth as the thoughts of a man who, traveling, enjoys his body functions in one new place after another. It was as if he and everyone else in sight had been veiled with the vapor of the devil's bad breath. They looked marked, inscrutably but inescapably, by more than *I may die*, by the certainty of death, the utter dissolution of even the evanescence of life. The desolation of the port, the muddiness of the river that piddled into the basin, the savage browness of the knolls beyond the town, imbued the deafening activities on the docks with a stark insanity.

And the insanity progressed, over the frozen roads, riding north, sitting silent and cramped in the truck and cursing the vile outrage of the cold. It went on: when the convoy turned about, went south, more maddeningly, more terrifyingly, and still sitting in sullen quietude and in contemplation of the new enemy, the Chinese, and all this unending shunting about. The winter had settled into him like a cold ball of ice in his stomach.

Then this, too, was changed, and in a sudden: first he saw a dead child frozen in a ditch, its eyes half-open and coated with frost, the lips parted, the stomach bloated and the limbs frozen woodenly up from the dirt. The fury hit him like a williwaw. And he saw more as they went south: children rooting in garbage cans, running after the trucks, wrinkled old women begging for scraps. In the night in dreams they came to him, unaltered, eternal in their hopeless mad need. The women and the children shouted him to consciousness for potato peelings. Awake then, lying stiff and still in one of the tents the unit had at last moved into somewhere below the parallel, he would rub his full stomach and try to force crying, as if that would purge what he felt, absolve him of his responsibility, so that, when it was time for him to leave this place, he would go clean and free and saved from it.

The front was stabilized and his unit, an artillery battery, went into action. His hearing went; he had only the promise of the others that it would return when he got away from the sound of the guns. With the thaw the unit advanced a little. The guns went on. By summer, when he had to strip to the waist to do his work with ease, the entrances to his intellect were so clogged and dulled that he was nearly resigned to this state. It was never going to end. The idea of escape from it was only an illusion, the misery of the cold of the winter just brought to sharper focus the torment of the summer.

In October he was sent back to Japan for five days of Rest and Rehabilitation. But his anger and malaise boiled so hot in him that, on the third night, in a bar in Kobe, he lashed out, irrationally, stupidly, and to his own immediate sorrow.

He was drunk; he had been drinking steadily since the early afternoon. He was incapacitated, knew it, and yet he had convinced himself he needed a woman for the night. He had one, too, though she was annoyed with his drooling and whining. She kept pushing him away, and when a Negro sergeant asked her to dance, she smiled happily and eased out of the booth where she had been sitting with Charlie.

Charlie sat there a moment, then got up and followed them to the dance floor. He tapped the Negro on the shoulder. "You're dancing with my girl," he drawled sullenly.

The sergeant, as big as a John Deere tractor, gave him an amiable grin. "Sure, sonny, you sit down and I'll bring her back at the end of the set."

Charlie shook his head. "No, you stop."

"Sonny, you go sit down."

Charlie reeled a bit and pawed the girl's shoulder. "Do you *like* dancing with coons? What's the matter with you?"

Others nearby had been watching him gravely; now they stepped away. The sergeant said, "I think you ought to sit down."

"No! Nigger!"

"I think we should step outside," the sergeant said.

"Fine! I'm going to kill you—nigger!"

On the sidewalk, Charlie raised his hands to fight, but did not get a chance to throw a clear punch. Later he had to think that, if he had acted honestly, apologized, walked away, or even after the first punch cried out that he was wrong, that he had not been brought up that way, that his uncle and his mother both would have beaten him for what he had said, he would have gotten off with less than he had received. But no, he lifted his hands to fight and walked on in. The sergeant, with one open hand, slapped

Charlie's hands down, slapped him twice across the face. Charlie came in again, swinging wildly. The Negro caught the punches on his arms, grabbed Charlie's collar and lifted the boy, one hundred and sixty pounds, onto his toes, and then buried his right fist deep into the solar plexus. He let Charlie go, and as the boy sunk to the pavement he hit him again, squarely on the eye. He stood over Charlie who was doubled up on the cement. "Now, boy, you'll have something to look at and think about for a time."

He did think, and not just about that night, but about all the nights and days that had gone before, across the Sea of Japan. He thought about himself. It was not enough to nod and admit he had behaved disgracefully, or that what he had been seeing had been too much for his child's mind. It was not enough even to resolve to do something about himself and what he had seen. This speared down into the soul of him, and no simple formulae were going to rinse away the scar.

He carried it like a wound, in silence. He did not understand it, but he carried it, and finished his tour of duty.

He was going to tell his mother about it. It was not enough to be a good kid in a good family and be a sort of a success at things. He had to meet the horror of the world and then get reacquainted with the truth of individual justice. All his reacting and carrying-on had not been wrong, but he had gotten what he deserved.

And two for flinching. It was waiting for him in San Francisco: an envelope from his older sister. His mother was dead and buried.

My mother's death has nothing to do with me. It doesn't. She died, that's all. Her heart stopped, like losing a tooth, growing a sty or developing a hangnail. If I had won the Silver Star she would be just as dead.

Still, he could not remember coming east. He remembered changing planes at Buffalo and catching the Mohawk Convair for Ithaca. His uncle met him at the airport and they threw the duffel bag in the trunk and drove out to the cemetery.

It was Floyd who suggested he go to college. Charlie's mother had died intestate, and after the payment of taxes, loans on her life insurance, and the mortgage on the home, there was just enough to give each of her three children a very small amount of cash. For a dozen years Charlie and his sisters had lived on half the profits from the gas station; it was his suggestion that the three of them now sign over their shares to their uncle. There was no argument. It took a few years only because it was necessary for each child to attain legal age to sign the transfer.

Charlie arrived in New York with a pocketful of traveler's checks, a letter of introduction to a horseplayer friend of Floyd's who could get him enrolled at City College, and one suitcase loosely packed. He took a furnished room in the Bronx, a job during the day, and spent the first year of college in the evening session. The next summer he moved to day school, gained the credits he had lost the first year, and made the final decision to become a teacher.

Alice's descriptions of her room at the hotel raised such a curiosity in him that he had to see it for himself. It was no problem getting past the desk, they just entered through the basement and went up the fire stairs. Her room was a miserable thing, so small her suitcase was still on top of her dresser. The bed was against a wall on whose other side was a semipublic toilet; the valves in the pipes did not sit properly, and the water trickled down constantly.

"We'll have to get you a place of your own," he said. "That's for sure."

"I've been making calls, but by the time I get out of work, somebody else has already made a deposit."

They were sitting on the bed, the one chair in the room was a straight-back, not worth sitting on. He looked at her and grinned. "Well, now I know why you picked up with me."

"Why?"

"Any port in a storm. You must have really needed your sleep."

"Oh, how can you say that?"

"It's easy. Stands to reason. I couldn't sleep here."

"Come on, honey, stop it."

"Or what?"

"I don't know. Something. I'll think of something."

"Listen. Seriously, why don't you come in with me until you get a place? This is a rathole. What's the point of paying rent for this?"

"Well, my folks are sending mail here. And if I moved in with you—I mean, got my clothes in your place—I might never get out." And she laughed lightly, nervously. He looked at her.

"Do you feel comfortable yet?"

"A hundred per cent," she said.

"Good. Let's get out of here. We'll get a cup of coffee."

"Would you like me to bring my toothbrush?"

"I was afraid to ask," he said. "It will make two nights in a row."

"Do you have work to do?"

"Reading. An hour or two." Then, "I'd like you to stay tonight, Alice."

"Okay. Let me get my things."

It took him two more weeks to get her an apartment. It was on Eleventh Street, west of Seventh Avenue, and it needed work, but he thought it could be made into something. Finding it had caused him to fall behind on his work, and he apologized when he told her he would be able to help with the shopping only a little. No, it was all right. She wanted to surprise him.

He had wondered how she would react to the independence the place forced on her, but that proved to be no problem, either. Now she could return his hospitality, she said. In kind, he corrected, teasing; she had been plenty hospitable already. It was a game to her, and he was just as glad; the burden was no less off his shoulders.

She continued to be his week-end guest, and on other nights when it suited them both. She was interested in his work and seemed to be able to understand what it meant to him. Whether she did understand or not, she left him alone most of the time when he needed it. She would stay in the front room and supply him with coffee as he blasted through the papers and reports and projects. But then sometimes—even when they were having coffee could be a wrong time; he wanted to keep his mind focused— sometimes she would want to tell him something in which, for the *moment*, he had no interest. He would have to listen, for he felt they said little enough to each other as it was.

On the other hand, he had little to say. She made him quiet, so quiet he had to wonder about his own basic nature. Was he really quiet? On the surface, it seemed not worth worrying about. The silence between them, though, made him think. There were things—about childhood, for instance, or the Army—that might interest her, but he just kept still. He was curious about it, and if he found specific reasons to explain the individual instances of silence— tiredness, for example—he could find no general reasons for the long runs.

More than once he asked himself if he was not so comfortable with her that he could not even be stirred out of that comfort just to talk with her.

Comfortable he was. He had a mountain of work, and he was going through it with a speed that surprised him and with a quality he found perfectly acceptable.

Once the pressure was off, he promised himself, he would be more attentive to her. She did not know how little of him she actually had. What time he had after his work went in the nights to them alone in the dark, in the days to doing those things that had to be done, like getting her apartment. She knew little about his other interests, his friends, or even simply that he knew how to enjoy life. He tried to tell her once, and she said she understood, exactly the thing he thought was not possible. She could not imagine how bad a time this was for him.

If they had had one undistracted evening for them-selves, he could not remember it. They made love often, but it was always after—something. Another thing she did not know: how good a real night could be—or how much he wanted such a night with her. What they had was good, but it was more pleasant and relaxing than it was the thrusting toward the ecstasy he *knew* was possible.

It wasn't love, but it wasn't infatuation, either. He thought of her during the days, often at first, yet when she was not around he felt no deep sense of loss. He could work up a sense of loss, but that was not the same thing. That was intellectual, and that wasn't love.

For her part, she did not have to pause a moment to know that this was the first time she was deeply, emotionally *committed*. She loved it. She loved having a reason for doing all those things she had been doing for so many years for no reason at all. Staying attractive. Alert. Being willing to learn. She had always been a reader, but in the past month she had read more good, important books than she had read in any previous two years.

She was not in love with him, but she was getting there. When she was going to his place to spend the night, she hurried more than he could possibly imagine. Certainly she was getting there. Her actions were proclaiming it: she was answering his telephone whenever it rang, even after midnight when some of his crazy friends called; she left the building with him in the mornings, not, as in the beginning, a few minutes after. Once she had answered his doorbell clad only in a slip, stockings and blouse. That the caller had been a Mormon missionary just increased the fun.

She loved sex. He had awakened her. He did not know it, but often his little touches and pinches were enough— all she needed.

She enjoyed being his. He did not know this, either, but he owned her as much as he owned his car. He was just in his demands on her, and sometimes she wondered if a little injustice wouldn't be fun. The thought of bending completely to his will had its fascinating aspects.

She enjoyed the whirl. Out of his own energy he created an existence more busy and useful than any she had ever known. He was in Brooklyn, uptown, downtown, stopping off in midtown to have dinner with her. "Are you doing anything after I leave you now?" he asked her once. "No, Charlie." "Well, here's a sawbuck. Buzz across town and get tickets to a play or something, for Saturday night." He had no idea how thrilled she was to be so busy.

She did not enjoy some of his friends, whom they met everywhere in the Village. He knew a great number of people, actors, sculptors, dancers, many of whom were very strange and difficult for her. John Murillo, the fellow she had seen from the window that Saturday morning and had hoped—vainly—that she would never see again, was a writer. He had had stories printed in the Village magazines and even some poetry in little reviews, in various places throughout the country. She had seen Murillo twice since that Saturday morning, and as best as she was able to tell, he could not identify her with the girl he had seen in the window.

She tried to accept Charlie's attitude about Murillo, that he had a vicious side, but a pathetic one, too. Murillo was terribly afraid he was not going to "make it," and he confessed his fear to people who were strangers. He had spoken of it in front of her. It had seemed somehow so calculated, for in the next breath he had acted fully recovered, perfectly confident.

He was quick to announce that he had been to Harvard, that he *had* been published, and that somewhere, remotely, he had connections. In Chicago politics, for whatever they were worth. He let things fall, as though one had to know them to estimate him.

Charlie knew the turth about his "connections" anyway. They were Murillo's own father, who had left his mother when John was three or four. He knew his father about as well as he knew the Bishop of Valparaiso, but he persisted, at least among acquaintances and not his very close friends, in claiming this little absurdity. The father had remarried twenty years ago, had another family, and cared only inasmuch as it could affect his pocketbook how his first son fared. Once in a while, usually around Christmas, he sent the young man a check.

Alice wanted to know, why did he have to lie? He was so transparent. How did he keep his stories straight? If he would relax and stop posing, she said to Charlie, maybe he

would see that his real self wasn't so bad; maybe . . .
something. She didn't know what she really meant.

Charlie knew. She wasn't to expect that Murillo and
other people would be like *her*, under their pretenses. It
wasn't so. They were different from her; she was different
from them. She might be sorry if she found out what
Murillo was really like. Charlie wasn't saying that from
experience, he didn't know. But just as likely as not, what
was under the show could be something the rest of us
could not live with. Understand?

She nodded yes. She understood the reasoning, but she
did not think it was so. It couldn't be. There wasn't that
much difference among people.

She didn't have a say about whether they were going to
Murillo's party, the second week in October. She didn't
want to go. But Charlie did—people he had not seen since
the spring would be there. He wanted to keep in touch.
Just as important, Murillo had placed another story in a
magazine. Charlie, for one, was going to show he had at
least that much interest in Murillo's life and career.

As the party came closer, Alice tried to act eager about
it. She even bought a dress, which she felt would tell
Charlie how much she cared.

It was a madhouse. As they climbed the stairs they had
to climb over the other guests, too, who were using the
stairs for a parlor. It was exactly what Charlie had expected, and he took it in good humor. Holding his pint aloft in
one hand, pulling Alice behind him with the other, he
threaded through the crowd. It was a typical party; he
excused himself past people he had known for years and
had not seen for months, yelling hello's and how are you's
as though he had seen them yesterday.

She was not at ease, and further into the room they
advanced, the more uncomfortable she became. In attendance were too many with beards, too many women
without brassieres. She was out of place—too clean. Col-
lectively they smelled bad. She wanted to do a good job
for him, make a nice impression, but these people needed
rewiring. If she smiled hello to someone to whom she had

already been introduced, he or she looked at Alice as though she had committed a *gaffe*.

When Charlie found a clear space he turned to her. "How are you doing?"

"All right—I hope."

"I don't know a lot of these people," he said. "They look just as strange to me as they do to you."

"I'm glad to hear it. I thought I had followed a rabbit in here."

"Hm? Oh, Alice in Wonderland. Very good. What do you want to drink? You don't have to drink this, it's only my contribution."

"Give me a good jolt of it," she said.

"No expression of opinion, please."

"Why not?"

"Because *I* brought you here. I'm taking the rap."

"No, you're not. You're not responsible for the armpits of these people."

"Okay, I'll be right back." He disappeared in the crowd like a man stepping into a cornfield. She lit a cigarette. It wasn't going to be bad. They would be out quickly, and home.

Someone prodded her shoulder. She turned around.

"Excuse me, are you the girl who just came in with Charlie Cumberland?"

It was a girl, a Latin, a pretty girl with dark eyes and long wavy black hair. She smiled warmly. "The reason I ask is that I'm not sure. I saw him when he came in, but all I could see of you was your hair, just for a moment. I was over there, on the other side." She gestured toward the windows. The place was so jammed, it could have taken her just this long to get across.

"Yes," Alice said, "I came in with him."

"I've heard about you. You're very pretty."

"Heard about me? Heard what?"

"That Charlie was going with a very pretty brunette."

"Oh? W-what do you want?" Stammering. The fear was slicing through her.

"To talk, that's all."

"Talk? I don't know you."

"My name is Connie. Your name is—?"

The girl seemed to surround her. She smelled. Alice wasn't sure. She could feel herself being pushed, the rage going up. "I thought you knew me," she said stridently.

"Not your name. What's the matter with you?"

"I don't know you. Why did you come around now? If you want to speak with Charlie, he'll be back in a minute. Please—" Alice wanted to hit her, now. The thought went through her mind like someone running across a stage: hit her. The girl just smiled.

"Do you think you'll marry him?"

"That's not your business!"

"Look, I was just trying to be friendly," she said.

"Don't kid me, you know what you're trying," Alice said.

"How primitive," the girl sneered.

"All right, fine, goodbye."

"You have a lot to learn," the girl said.

"If you don't mind—"

That did it. The girl smirked and turned away. Alice stood there a moment, then tried to draw on her cigarette. A shower of sparks descended on the back of her hand. She dropped the cigarette and ground it into the rug until the tobacco was spread and squashed into the fiber.

Now Charlie came up behind her. "Here we go, children. —What's the matter?"

"Nothing."

"Yes, there is."

"—Connie. She says hello."

"Oh. Here's your drink."

"Did you know she would be here, Charlie? You know *about* her. Why did you do this to me?" Her voice was down to a whisper; the more she said, the softer it became.

"Take it easy, Alice. I didn't know she'd be here. What did she say to you?"

"She started—she wanted to know about us. She doesn't know anything, does she?"

"Of course not."

"It's our business. Ours."

"Okay. Drink you drink. We'll get out of here."

"What's between you two now?" she pressed.

"Distance."

"No, really."

"Really. Distance. I went around with her last spring, okay?" And he looked down at her, whether he knew it or not, as though she were not worth hitting, just pushing out of the way.

"Oh."

"What is it?"

"Get me out of here."

"Alice, what is it?"

"Get me out, Charlie, *please!*"

He felt like an idiot. He had pushed her over the edge before he realized what he was doing, and now she was hysterical. He passed the drinks into the nearest hands and steered her through the apartment to the hall, down the stairs to the stoop, stepping over people and guiding them aside as he went.

There was no place to go. In the doorway he stopped her and turned her around and took her head to his shoulder. Her body shook. Passers-by below on the sidewalk looked up, but he ignored them. She cried a long time.

At last she sniffed and looked up. "Can I have a cigarette?"

"Sure."

"You've just had an unsolicited testimonial to my feelings."

"It's not funny, Alice."

"You don't know the half of it."

"I am the half of it."

"Are you?"

In the half-light her face was blotched, streaked and ugly. "You want me to say it now, don't you, while I'm not trying to get something out of you."

"That's right, just as if we were parked on lover's lane. I want to know I'm loved for me and not my body." She giggled and sniffed again.

"You are."

"But my body's okay, too?"

"You said it."

"I love you, Charlie."

"I love you, too."

"Can we go home?"

"Sure."

"Now?"

"Sure."

They walked along. They crossed Fourth Avenue and walked past Wanamaker's on the north side. They were going slowly. She held her cigarette out before her and tapped the ash to the walk. "It's funny," she said. "I *know* you've had other girls. I know you had her. I don't know why it should bother me so."

"It shouldn't." Maybe he should say more, he thought, assure her that he had cared for Connie no more than for one of the Mama-sans in Tokyo. It was not true, though there were things about Connie he had thoroughly disliked. He wanted Alice to keep talking. He wanted to understand this side of her. She stayed quiet a moment, and he found himself thinking that he would tell her later that he had never been involved with her. It was true. This was important to him.

"You're mine now," she said, looking ahead. "I don't want anyone breaking into what we've woven between us. I'll do anything for you, but I have—I *guess* I have to have something in return. Maybe it's wrong. I don't care. I'll never meet anyone like you again. I know I won't. I have to have you—" She stopped, waiting. "You can't say anything like that yet, can you?"

"No, I can't. Not like that." He wondered *why* he was not involved like that. He had never been, with any woman. Maybe he was just incapable of it.

"All right," she said. "I wouldn't have believed you, anyway.

"I won't abuse you, Alice. I swear it."

"That's fair enough. All I want is a chance.

The next day, Sunday, they drove up to the Bear Mountain Inn for dinner. It was a fine, crisp day, and everything went perfectly. After dinner they drove on to

West Point, which neither of them had seen before, and there they took pictures, mostly of each other. The fresh, clear air tired them much too soon. They went back to the Inn, had coffee and then crossed the Bridge to drive back to the city down the east side of the river. The sun was setting. The river shimmered through its own mist. The spectacular vistas opened and closed quickly as the car followed Storm King Highway around the edge of the mountains. The singing of the old Chevy six was the only sound through the quiet. Soon, as the sky darkened, Alice fell asleep and Charlie pushed the car a little harder, eager to get home.

They were awakened near midnight by the ringing of the telephone. He did not have the strength to move. She crawled over him, went to the telephone, and snapped on a table lamp as she lifted the receiver. Charlie blinked his eyes to focus.

"Hello? Oh, yes, John, you have the right number. I recognize your voice. This is Alice . . . No, that's all right, you weren't interrupting anything." She looked at Charlie and smiled. She was wholly unconscious of being nude, and she had never looked lovelier. She had a splendid, slender body. "Oh, no, John, we were there last night, but only for about five minutes. I got sick and we had to leave. I am sorry. But I'm glad you called. When will your story be printed? . . . In the spring. Good. Let me say congratulations now. Would you like to speak to Charlie? . . . All right. But that's the answer. We were there but my stomach had been upset and it kicked up again . . . Oh, no, it's something that happens once in a while. I know the explanation for it." She laughed. "Now you have the idea. Be glad you're a man. . . . All right, I'll tell him. Maybe we'll see you in the Limelight before then. Thanks for calling, John. Goodbye." And she put down the receiver.

"I'm really proud of you," Charlie said. "That was a beautiful job."

"I felt sort of funny."

"Well, you were saying things you've said only with me."

"Did it bother you?"

"I was surprised." Now he got it; he should have been shocked. She had moved beyond his control. No, he had been delighted. He was feeling too good from the whole fine day to start up. She would have to achieve an understanding of him this time. He reached to the night table for a cigarette.

His face must have shown every thought, for as if she could read his mind, she said, but in a tone that had no joy in it, "Well, I was still feeling giddy. Would you like a cup of coffee?"

"Okay." She got up. As she reached the door, he said, "I'm ready for dessert, too."

"The cake is all gone."

"I didn't mean that." And he eyed her wickedly.

"Oh, you." But she went into a little pose for him.

There. He felt better, too.

II

Cal Torrenson was sitting on the curb down the block from the house in Darien. From around the foggy corner the bicycles careened insanely, and he could hear the fiendish laughter of their riders. The riders passed, pedaling furiously. Abruptly they banked into a turn and disappeared around the farther corner. It was quiet. Cal knew it was a dream, but he could not stir himself from the curb where he was sitting, gazing at his dirty knees. *What do you know? I'm wearing shorts.*

The laughter came at him again and the boys pedaled madly into view. They came down on him at full speed, as if to smash into him. He could see the spittle running down from their lips ...

"Come out of it, Cal, you've been lying there an hour."

"—Huh? What? Leave me *alone.*" He tried to roll onto his side, but there was a hand on his shoulder restraining him.

"Wake up, Cal! Come on!"

He opened his eyes. It was the downstairs parlor of the fraternity house. In the front room the freshman brothers

were clustered about the punch bowl, laughing and singing
wildly. Cal's first thought was of the laughter, of the
dream, and that the laughter had come from that room.

> *"Whether at Dartmouth or at Yale,*
> *We leave the other bastards pale . . ."*

He squinted up at Bix. Sunken-cheeked, his eyes red-
rimmed, Bix smiled his unhealthy smile. He was holding a
cup of the purple punch. "You didn't last long," he said.
"We were counting on you to go the distance."

"I was drinking on an empty stomach. I didn't have any
dinner."

From the other room the drunken voices howled:

> *"Sons of Theta Kappa Omicron,*
> *The best there is in this old rotten world!"*

There was a shout of approval and scattered applause,
followed by a tremor of laughter. Cal twisted his neck to
see over the arm of the couch. The freshman brothers
were draining their cups. There was another shout of
laughter as one of the younger brothers backed out of the
circle, fighting to get a handkerchief for the purple drool
running from his chin.

Bix said, "Some of them are going to be really out
soon."

"To hell with them. Hey, how many did I have? Seven
or eight tall glasses—not those little things—on a dead-
empty stomach, and I feel fine now."

"Well, sure, it already took its toll. You passed out."

"Oh, shit," Cal said, "I just racked out and took a
snooze." He sat up, his head hammering. "Come on
downtown with me while I get some breakfast. I want to
clear my head." As he stood up he felt the floor roll a
little, but he kept his balance. He brushed his jacket down
smooth and followed Bix out through the front room. He
walked as if he were fighting his way out of a tattered
quilt.

"They asked me how I knew
Raccoon shit was blue. . . ."

They passed through unnoticed to the porch. The singing pushed out against the outdoors, coarse and indecent.
Before the profundity of the darkness Cal's mind began to
work again; he thought first and quickly of the dream,
then of what Bix had said. He backhanded Bix's shoulder
lightly. "Anytime you think you can outdrink me, you just
let me know."

"You have the vanity of a woman."

"Ho, the expert."

"I'm alive, anyway. Look." Bix was pointing to the
house across the street, where a party was in progress, the
music issuing faintly, girls passing before the windows.

"We'll stop in later," Cal said. "Let's wake up first."

Bix nodded, finished his punch, set the cup on the porch
railing and preceded Cal down the walk. Cal drove slowly
down the hill and across town, aware of his slowed
reflexes and poor coördination. The punch, a mad combi-
nation of wine, gin and rum, made him feel that he had
swallowed a frog. Yet the lunatics in charge persisted in
serving punch at these damned, unbearable stag functions.
Tonight's smoker had had no purpose; some freshman
brother had thought a smoker a good idea—it would build
"house spirit."

On the other side of town Cal wheeled the sedan into a
parking lot outside an all-night diner. It was the place they
usually went to. Inside at the counter, they ordered juice,
muffins and coffee, then waited in silence until they were
served.

"What time is it?" Cal asked.

"Just after one."

"If we knock off the food in a hurry, we can get in
some licks at that party. My enthusiasm is up now."

"Well, this was your idea. Say, why didn't you have
dinner tonight?"

Cal shrugged.

"Look, what's bothering you? You're very touchy
tonight, you know."

"There's nothing the matter with me. I was having coffee in Pop's with a friend of mine and I forgot about eating, that's all."

Bix snorted. "Aren't you being a bit cagey?"

"No, it's just that I was engrossed in the talk. What's cagey about that?"

"Who was she? Come on, no *guy* engrosses you. Who was she?"

"All right, if it'll make you happy, I was having coffee with Elaine Sellman."

"I thought that was finished last spring," Bix said.

"I knew you'd say that."

"Well, was it? Is it?"

Cal shrugged.

"Can I ask you a question, then?"

"Shoot," Cal said.

"Are you humping her?"

"Was. I admit it. It's the past tense now."

"She doesn't look like the type."

"Oh, come on."

"No, I mean it," Bix said. "She never looked like the type to me. She looked as if she didn't need it."

"You're being absolutely simple, now."

"How is she?" he pressed.

Cal laughed again. He waited and then, "Are you really curious or do you want to enjoy your food?"

"Oh, Christ, no!"

Cal grinned happily, enjoying Bix's aghast expression. He tucked the last half of the muffin into his mouth. He sucked the butter from his fingers. "She could make a success of a school in Hong Kong."

"You're a bastard," Bix said.

"They said the same thing about Jesus Christ. He told the truth, too." He was still grinning. "Later, if you want—I mean when we're in the room—I'll tell you stories about her you can pull your pecker by. But for now eat up."

"I have to say you had a good thing. What are you trying to do, get back in?"

Cal shrugged again.

"You know, she's almost the perfect Jewish type. Her coloring just has to be a little bit darker."

"I think you have a hard for her," Cal said.

"Would that gratify you, vain one?"

"Dung on you."

"Well, for the record, I have a hard for all women. But I love those big, heavy breasts of hers."

"Virile Bix has spoken."

"What's it all about, though? What are you seeing her again for?"

"I guess I just want to dip my wick again. Now, shall we talk about something else?"

"Tell me this, though, does she go easy? That I want to know."

"For me, it was easy. Now will you talk about something else, please?" *Dope,* Cal thought. *You have nothing. You dream, that's all.*

"All right. There is something I wanted to talk to you about. I got a letter from the City College chapter—you know, official—inviting us down for their initiation during intersession. I thought you might like a trip to the city with room and board paid. Something to do, anyway. I'm thinking about it."

Cal didn't answer; he sipped his coffee.

"I was thinking we could get a few good guys and go down straight from school," Bix said. "It could sort of cap a week of just relaxing around the house and enjoying life."

"Why don't we go to Florida? If we have to go somewhere, why don't we go to Florida?"

"I don't know. I thought this would be cheaper. There are a few of us who haven't seen much of New York."

"Oh." It was the money that counted, Cal was thinking. Bix was about as open as an eighty-year-old tit, and it was one of the most unpleasant things about him. Bix had been on Cal's nerves lately—little things—and neither his questions about this afternoon, about which he wanted to know the whole, distasteful truth, nor this idea of his, motivated by his own cheap habits, were making Cal feel loose and easy in his presence.

"Well, what do you think?" Bix asked.

"Let me have a few days. It doesn't sound too promising. We'd have to be polite to those guys and they're a creepy lot. City College. I don't see how we could get out of their dinner and initiation."

"Well, the letter says they initiate on Friday and have a dance on Saturday. They'll get us dates."

"A twitch of life." Cal wiped his hands on a napkin and stood up. "Come on, let's get back. I keep thinking of that party. I'm ready to go the rest of the night."

During the ride back Bix did not ask again about the trip—he had read Cal's mood correctly. Cal wanted quiet: his stomach was bothering him, burning now; the dream of the boys coming after him kept returning, and so did this afternoon with Elaine—which hounded him more than Bix's hounding, with more ferocity than he was putting into the effort to think about the party they were headed for. It would not be over. It couldn't be.

When he had first caught sight of her coming out of the History Building this afternoon, Cal's first thoughts were of nothing, that utter, startling blankness that carved through him like an air-conditioned knife. He chased after her—running, he later realized in anger—and when she heard him call she swung about, smiling happily as she saw him, as if it were now last spring and those few weeks in the beginning.

"Hello," he said. "I haven't seen you since—when? the middle of September? Is this where you're hiding out?"

"Hi. I'm not hiding out."

"Well, where are you going now?"

"Back to the dorm."

"How about some coffee?"

"Mmm, all right."

"This is sociable," he said, taking her arm.

"I'm in a good mood," she said.

"You *look* good," he said. She was wearing just a blouse and skirt and a light cardigan, but it was so perfectly right. Everything else was perfect for her, too; the sun going down, the red in the brownish trees, the cool and dusky quality of the shadows far off—they all served to heighten the red of her hair and the fine whiteness of her skin. "Why a good mood?" he asked. "Did they give you a show of your own down at the radio station? I wouldn't be surprised."

"That's nice to say, but no, I'm still running errands. I made a sale, just now. I talked myself into a course on the Reformation in the spring. I don't have the prerequisites, but I convinced the Professor. A medal for me."

"I'll have it coined. But what did you do it for? The Reformation. Jesus."

"I wanted to. Now I have books to read in advance, to prepare me. It doesn't sound too bright, this extra work, does it?"

"No, it doesn't." He remembered something. "Are you still interested in Christianity?"

"Oh, yes."

"You'd look like hell in a baptismal font."

"Oh, not that way."

"I know. I'm just being a horn."

"I'm still interested in Christianity, in Christ himself and the way his religion has developed. I know I have a blind spot, I know how it got there, and I want to get rid of it."

"Nothing could be more admirable. Of course your mother doesn't know the Reformation from a hole in the wall."

"I have to live with myself first, Cal. I believe in what I'm doing."

"More power to you. I think you'll do very well."

"Thank you. How is everything with you?"

He told her: nothing had changed. Apparently she had forgotten the substance of their meeting downtown, but then, so had he forgotten when he had seen her. This was good; there was no point in lousing it up. He was holding her arm, he could smell her perfume, he could feel through her arm the rhythm of her body. Maybe this was going to be it, the just once.

And maybe it was going to be more. He had to play it well. Everything he did had to endear him to her, show her how good it was to be with him.

They had their coffee and talked politics. She was going

to work for Stevenson again. Kefauver had no appeal; there was no chance of his being nominated. Cal told her he did not know how he was going to vote, but that he really thought the election was already decided.

"I know," she said dejectedly.

"Buck up. You never can tell."

"That's right."

"Want to go for a ride?"

She shook her head, looked up, smiled nicely and said, "Thanks, but I don't think so."

"Okay. Listen, how are you making out with your personal life?"

"Why?"

"I'm still very fond of you, that's why?"

"I'm getting along."

"That's pretty secretive."

"We're not that close, Cal. We weren't even close last spring."

"That hurts."

"It's true. Face it."

"Sure."

"I'll bet you've made love to three girls since me." She was smiling. "Now isn't that the truth."

"Close. Two.—But what the hell, you know how that is. This is all bullshit, anyway. Even if I had you in my hip pocket it wouldn't do any good. Your mother would only pee on the parade again."

"That's right." But she was smiling, and he read it as a total disbelief in what he had said. They were dead because *she* wanted them dead. She could be so pleasant about it only because she had not cared in the first place. *Bitch, if you think what we did together was not close . . .*

Now, as he parked the car on the darkened hillside, the emotion he had felt sitting in the restaurant echoed back just as powerfully, just as fresh. He was helpless against it. Beside him, Bix was singing one of the fraternity songs in his high nasal croon. There was a wind; the voice faded in the black rustle of dry leaves. Cal could see the branches swaying and tossing against the lighter sky beyond, and here and there through the thick blotches and shreds of darkness a light glowed, a streetlamp, or perhaps, fainter, yellower, a lamp in a window. The air was dry with a dry smell, and cold against their faces.

The house across the street was blacked out. As soon as he saw the dark windows Cal thought of all the cars parked on dirt roads around the lake, or off highways behind trees. It was like the scoring of a nail across a sheet of metal. He had missed out. He needed a woman now.

At the door of their own house Bix hesitated. "The glass. I left it on the porch railing."

"Hand it over," Cal said.

"What for?"

"I want to heave it."

"Why?"

"Come on, for Christ's sake. Hand it over."

Bix gave it to him. Cal went down to the walk and threw the glass toward the other house. He waited, and heard nothing.

"You're in bad shape," Bix said. "You just made the other lawn."

"It went clean over. What do you think I am?" *As weak as you?* he thought.

"I'll be you a dollar."

"All right, it'll be there in the morning."

"Not if it's on the lawn it won't. Someone will pick it up."

"Which will be proof then. I mean, if we can't find it, it'll have been on the lawn. If it's around in back, it will still be there."

"Let's get the glass anyway," Bix said.

"Anything to make you happy."

They could not see the glass out in front. They went around the house, where it was darker and the ground was thick with leaves. They circled the house twice. "Come on," Cal said at last, "I'll *give* you the damned dollar."

"What about the glass?"

"It's a ten-cent punch cup!"

"All right." Bix grinned and they turned back.

Cal stopped. "Let's have some laughs."

"How?"

"I don't know. Think. Do you think anybody is in there?"

"Somebody," Bix said. "Hell, they wouldn't all be gone. Somebody ought to be upstairs asleep."

"Let's empty the garbage cans on the porch."

"Can't you do better than that?"

"I don't hear anything out of you?" Cal said.

"Okay, if you think it will start anything. Life has been dull around here lately anyway."

"If you've been wondering why, ask yourself again the next time you're scouring the earth for a ten-cent punch cup."

"Can't you be decent?"

"No. Help me with the garbage cans." Cal laughed as he turned again toward the kitchen door.

The next day was Sunday, long and slow. Nothing happened. At dinner someone mentioned that the pledges across the street were out early in the morning cleaning up garbage, and someone else said that it would be a good idea if Theta Kappa Omicron instituted the same program for its pledges. There was some laughter but that was all. By Monday night, when he thought of it again, it seemed to Cal that the stunt had been a bust.

But on Tuesday morning the porch of the Theta Kappa Omicron fraternity house was painted purple and lime, and the lawn was done in diagonal orange stripes. On the door, in purple and lime letters, was a sign: *"Pledges of Theta Kappa Omicron: the Avenger has struck!"*

Walking up the hill, Cal hoped that someone with free time would have sense enough to take color pictures of the house. A feud like this could go on for months—years. It could make the papers—oh, *The Cornell Sun* and *The Ithaca Journal* with ease—but maybe even the New York papers. It was exactly the kind of thing that made *Life* magazine. He was delighted.

But then, when he returned to the house in the late afternoon, the freshman brothers and pledges were re-painting the porch, and some were out on the lawn with shears and scissors, snipping the orange grass and putting it into paper bags. On the second floor bulletin board was a notice:

Brothers and Pledges:
Today's incident is to be forgotten. There will be no reprisals. Neither the house nor the men can afford the time and money such projects consume. Those juveniles who ignore this note—even to engage in only planning—will meet with a month's suspension of social privileges. I mean business, so don't try me.

Don Ewing, Chancellor.

Cal went to his room and lay down. There was nothing to be done, of course. Ewing, who was a sober citizen, did mean business. Under the constitution of the fraternity, the Chancellor was more than a figurehead of the house and its representative outside; he had full control. The fraternity had been founded during the heyday of Bismarck's Germany, the constitution had been based on that system, and it had never been changed. Ewing exercised his control—all the power and prestige and symbol of the office. The common opinion was that he was using the office to advance himself, but that had nothing to do with anything. Cal lit a cigarette and looked out the window of the darkened room to the leaves that were gnarled and shabby against the fading gray sky.

Someone knocked on the door.

"Come in."

It was George DeYoung, a crude lummox of a person. He had quick small eyes which now scanned the room and then went back to Cal. DeYoung smiled. "A bit dark, wouldn't you say?"

"I'm communing with the spirit world, for Christ's sake."

"How's everything in the garbage business?"

"Did you get that from Bix?"

"Shit, what do you think I'm going to do, tattle to Ewing, king of the social climbers?"

"Bix has a fat mouth," Cal said. "What do you want? I'm trying to rest."

"Drop by my room at about eleven o'clock. Since you were the start of this, I thought you might want to buy a piece of the rest of it. We have something going."

"Who?"

"Mannings, myself, little Pete Fuller and Bix."

"Ewing will make you all sit on his Phi Bete key and rotate."

"We're going to discuss hotshot Ewing. You've been out all day. We've been discussing right along, the four of us and some others."

"All right, I'll see you."

George Mannings was DeYoung's roommate; he was the same height as the other, but dark, lean and quiet. He had a quick mind. He was in the Aggie school and was one of those practical, mechanically-inclined people. There were times when he spoke a language—in regard to things around the house, the construction of it, and so on—that Cal could not understand. Mannings lived in the part of the world that fed and housed the rest of the world.

Pete Fuller was a freshman brother, seventeen, but already he had shown himself to be a character. He had gone to a prep school and he spoke the prep school language. He had a thousand stories to tell about school and the upper east side of Manhattan, where his family had their home. No one believed him, but he insisted that a couple in his apartment building paid him to watch them have intercourse. When he felt like it, he smoked fat cigars.

They were there, DeYoung and Bix and Fuller—Fuller clouding the room with cigar smoke—when Cal entered, a little after eleven. Mannings was at work on a contraption at the desk and the others were sitting on the two beds, passing among them a gallon bottle of wine.

"Hail to the chief!" Fuller exclaimed. He started to chant the song.

"Have some wine?" DeYoung asked.

"What, are you all crocked?"

"Not at all, my boy," said Fuller. "We're getting brave."

"What for?" Now Cal took the wine.

"Mannings has it," DeYoung said. "It's a bomb. Shit, an automobile bomb. Actually two of them hooked up together. It whistles and yells and then it explodes. It doesn't do anything, just makes noise. We're going to set it off."

"They're probably waiting for us over there," Cal said.

"We'll be careful."

"We have to be sober for that." Cal took a straightbacked chair from against the wall and moved it to the center of the room. He caught Bix's nod, but he said, "What's the catch? I have to hear what you plan to do. It sounds like a good idea, but if you louse it up it isn't worth a nickel."

"First, it'll cost you three dollars," DeYoung said.

"Why?"

"To cover your share of the bombs and the battery we had to buy. A car battery."

"You have it all worked out how I'm going to be in on it."

"Not at all," DeYoung said, and grinned. "All right, we're going to wait a while longer, oh, for two or three hours, until they're asleep or groggy or whatever, then we're going to go over and set it off in their living room. Mannings has been working on a timing device—these bombs are supposed to go off when you turn the ignition key—so we should be back here when the thing does go."

"All right. Three dollars? Who gets it?"

"I do, noble father," Fuller said, stogie in mouth. "Just slide it to me."

"What's this noble father stuff, something new with you?"

DeYoung laughed. "It's something else we've been talking about today. We need a new Chancellor—"

"Stop the presses."

"Right," DeYoung said. "We've been talking about you. Bix mentioned your name. He thinks it might be good for you."

"My keeper."

"We don't give a crap about that," Fuller said. The stogie bounced up and down like a loose diving board.

"Quite right," Cal said. "Neither should he."

"It would be criminal to elect a man for whom the office would be bad," Bix argued.

"Who voted for Ewing?"

Bix said, "He's a sobersides. We knew that when we elected him. We thought he would be a stabilizing influence."

"A lead ass is always stabilizing," DeYoung said. "I didn't vote for him, either."

"Let's kill him," Fuller said. "Maybe he'd loosen up a bit."

"Me personally," DeYoung said to Cal, "I like you for the office. You can handle yourself with people. I mean, with like the alumni and the deans."

"If you want your kind of Chancellor," said Cal, "why don't you run yourself?"

"They wound't vote for me," DeYoung said, a little ashamed. "They think I'm irresponsible. I mean, completely irresponsible."

"Oh," Cal said as if he didn't know it. "Mannings?"

"I don't want it," Mannings said into his contraption.

DeYoung said, "And Bix knows he doesn't present the right image. Fuller is out of the question—any question."

"Oh, now wait a minute—"

"Isn't it true you sleep with your sister?" DeYoung asked.

"Not during Lent, I don't."

"Okay. But do you see my point, Torrenson? And the others figure 'out' for a variety of reasons—they're too young; they'll be busy next semester. There's only seven or eight you can really trust, and you have to ask yourself if they can beat Ewing, who'll be going for a second term."

"He think's it'll look good on his job applications, the prick," offered Fuller, and sent up a gallon of cigar smoke.

"Well, it will," said Cal.

"What do you say?" DeYoung asked.

"Let me think about it."

"Shit, do you have to?"

"Yes. Let me think about it. I don't know if I want to or not." He wondered if he had ever told any of them that he did want the job. He thought of Elaine. Now, thinking that he had told her, and so many other things as well, he had a sick, nervous feeling. He said, "I have to figure out if I can win or not, for one thing. If I stand a chance. I have to think about how I should go about running, whether I should come right out and start defying and opposing Ewing—you know what I mean."

"Would you like to hear our ideas?" DeYoung asked.

"Do I have a choice?"

"No, I guess not. We were thinking that it would be a good idea if you let us just talk you up privately for a while, say a couple of weeks, so the guys could get adjusted to you as a possibility. Then we'd boom a little louder. By next term you'd be set. You wouldn't have to say a word. We'd let it out to those we could trust and who would take it the right way that you were the instigator of this—the garbage and tonight as well, I mean. And if Ewing catches us—that sounds stupid, doesn't it—well, you'd be a martyr."

"Did you ever have a prefrontal lobotomy?" Fuller asked him.

"What?"

"Skip it."

"Idiot," DeYoung said. Of Cal, he asked, "Do you see my point?"

"Yes. Still, let me think about it."

"Oh, one other thing, I've seen the letter Bix got from New York about their initiation. It would be a good idea if you went, if we all went, to show your heart is in the right place. House spirit, and all."

"You know what I think of that house spirit crap. And as for New York—" He glanced at Bix—"That's one of the most unwholesome ideas I've heard in a long time. Do you think you could *stand* one more initiation than you have to?"

"I know," DeYoung said, "but those who went could have some fun—I suppose."

"Let's shelve that for the time being," Cal said.

"Then you'll run?"

"I'll let you know in—three or four days." He had been going to say a week, but even to him, it seemed like stretching the point. He saw he would have to outsmart this DeYoung; he was full of ideas. Cal said, "There's nothing more to discuss for now. Let's pass the wine around again."

"I think we have ourselves a candidate," Fuller said.

Cal knew just how well he had done. He tried to look as if he were in possession of himself. He reached into his shirt pocket for a cigarette, and as he lit it he saw Bix staring at him in awe, in stupefaction. He gave Bix a quick wink.

In a few minutes, Mannings turned from the desk and announced that the timing system was ready for the test. With great care he took the mechanism from the desk-top and lowered it into a cardboard box that had been at his feet. "It's just a matter of setting the alarm," he said. "When the alarm rings, the hammer of it pulls this cord, which trips the mouse trap. A good thing the trap is copper, so we get a good circuit. The trap comes down onto these wires tapped here, establishing the circuit that works the electrical triggers in the bombs."

"*Sure* it does," Fuller said.

"How fast is it?" DeYoung asked.

"When the alarm goes off, instantaneous."

"What if they find it before that?"

"It's delicate. The wrong kind of juggling will trip it, too."

"And somebody has wet drawers as well," DeYoung said proudly. "I forgot to tell you, Torrenson, this thing smokes like a bitch."

"Oh. You need two bombs?"

"For effect."

"Oh."

The system worked well enough. The alarm clock setting dial was off by three or four minutes; it took several tests to determine the extent of the error. When they were satisfied they sat back and finished the wine.

After a while they began to feel safe and Mannings went out to check the hall. He came back with an all-clear sign and he and Cal carried the rig down the stairs. The five gathered on the porch. Cal whispered, "Bix, go across and see what's up."

Bix scuttled down the walk into the darkness. DeYoung took out a cigarette to light it. Fuller reached over and broke it in half. "Allen Dulles needs you."

"Who?"

"Said the owl. Why don't you get a neon sign and a brass band?"

"Oh."

Bix was back. "It's quiet," he breathed. "There's a fellow sitting in the front room with a paddle in his hand, but he's asleep. They have a wire strung across the porch, oh, about shin-high, and it runs in under the window. I don't know if it's attached to the fellow's toe or what."

"We'll see," Cal said. He turned to Mannings. "This thing can't go off until you set the alarm, can it? I mean, if we jiggle it too much?"

"No, it's safe now."

"Let's take it over and snoop around. This shouldn't look like a relay race."

"Very good," Fuller said.

The wire was as Bix had said, but faint, eluding the eyes. The two set the box down and Cal climbed over the porch railing to peer in the window. The wire ran to an electric fire alarm gong set on the front room floor. Cal went back over the railing to Mannings. "It's a bell as big as a dinner plate. Go back and tell the others to get all the clothesline they can. We'll trip it from our place—a pull would do the same as a kick, wouldn't it?"

"I would guess so."

"Good. And tell them a ladder, too. We can set *this* off on the second floor."

"You'll make a good Chancellor." Mannings grinned, but not in a way Cal appreciated.

"Are we going to *do* something or aren't we?"

"I'll be right back with the stuff."

"—And another man," Cal said.

Mannings came back with Fuller, who had the rope coiled over his shoulder. He had a fresh, unlit cigar in his mouth.

"Speak, oh Phantom."

"Loop the line around the wire and run it back to our front room. Lightly, though, for Jesus' sake. If you trip the alarm, I have a fish-hook in my room that's just right for your scrotum."

"You *will* make a good Chancellor," Mannings said.

"Fuller has to be treated like cattle," Cal said. "Right, Fuller?"

"The Master speaks and I obey."

"Humbly," Cal said.

"Reet."

While Fuller went to work on the line the other two put the ladder up against the porch roof. Mannings carried the box up, then Cal followed him. He was waiting on top, sitting there.

"Where do we put it?"

"Don't you know your way around over here?" Cal asked.

"Not on the second floor."

"You should meet more of the women they have over. They take them up here. In the center is a hall, running the length of the house. A window looks over the porch."

"Come on, then."

Through that window they could see one small light glowing at the far end of the corridor, casting a sombre pall. The window raised easily. Mannings set the clock, looped the cord over the bell clapper, and gingerly lowered the rig onto the floor inside."

"Ten minutes."

"Maybe five," Cal said.

"You may be right."

They scrambled down lightly and carried the ladder around behind their own house. The other three were waiting in the front room. Fuller was holding the rope that ran limply over the ledge of the open window.

"When do I pull this?"

"After."

"Reet."

Cal looked across carefully, staring; he wanted to see the thing happen—but in a minute he thought again of being Chancellor. A shiver ran through him. It was like an orgasm of the mind. Chancellor. Jesus.

The whistle started; his ears stiffened in response before they received the sound. The sound was terrific—a dozen times louder than he had conceived it—an enormous, shrill-pitched scream, piercing, even at this distance deafening, like some great bomb falling, the biggest, most fantastic bomb, falling, dropping, curling down the register. Then there was an explosion, exactly like a bomb, a deep-sounding, reverberating boom that caused the windows to rattle and the floor beneath them to shake. The roar echoed and faded up and down the hillside gorges until it was almost gone, and then, coming back— probably from far across the blackened valley—it repeated, softly, diminutively, a tiny distant sound, like a cannon at a midnight flag-raising. A deeper, newer thrill coursed through Cal. He laughed, he yelled.

From the center window across the way a huge cloud of yellow-white smoke billowed forth. There were shouts and yells. Lights went on. In the blinkingly-bright windows Cal could see the fellows running, and suddenly, from around the side of the house, three barefoot, pajama-clad figures came tenderfooting over the shingles of the porch roof. One had a fire extinguisher and began to spray it in the smoking window. In his exaltation Cal thought of the bell, and looked over at Pete Fuller. Eyes glittering moronically, Fuller sat entranced. Cal pushed him aside and took up the rope and pulled at it violently. The bell shot off, baranging out at the night. He started to reel the rope in when, from above, he heard footsteps.

The others were already moving. Still holding the rope, Cal followed them in a run back through the parlor and the dining room to the kitchen, and on out to the back yard. The five stopped beyond the lawn, waist-high in shrubbery. Cal coiled up the rope while the others, breathless, laughing, congratulated each other. He was thinking of being Chancellor again; it seemed almost assured now.

Bix grabbed his hand and shook it, Cal mumbled some-thing pleasant in return. Chancellor! Who to tell? Elaine?

Elaine. Like a black stain the thought of her spread through the liquid of this golden moment. This, this stunt, was beyond her. If he told her, so would only moralize.

It seemed safe to go up the back stairs. The five went to their respective rooms—as Cal suggested. The others would catch on if someone went down to watch the commotion with his street clothes on.

"It was great," Bix said. "Wasn't it great?"

"I thought so. Leave the light off. If someone comes around to this side of the house he might get wise."

"You were fantastic. I didn't think you had it in you. I mean with DeYoung."

"Well, there you are. I'm going to run—and win, too. I'm going to win so well Ewing won't know what hit him."

"I think so. You have a tremendous amount of con-trol."

"Mm."

"Say listen, I have a bone to pick with you. What was the idea of that crack about the trip to New York?"

"I was saying what I felt. I think it's a lousy idea. Don't consider what we'd like to do. Face what we'll have to do."

"Yeah, okay, but why did you have to put it on so thick? It was like spit in the eye."

"Nah."

"You do it all the time to me now, Cal."

"Jesus, what are you, my girl-friend?"

"Listen, we've been friends for three years now. We've kidded each other, sure, but this is different. I don't think it should go too far."

"I think you're imagining things. I had a point to make tonight. DeYoung is going to try to control me. I was putting him on notice that I was my own man."

"Well okay, then."

Cal paused. "Say, you're not turning queer on me, are you?"

"What the hell gave you that idea?"

"I'm just kidding. I wanted to see how you'd react."

"Well, don't worry about it," Bix said. "The next time you think of it, though, remember you brought it up first."

"What does *that* mean?"

"Just getting even. Goodnight, Mister Chancellor."

"Go scratch yourself," Cal said, annoyed. Already he was thinking of something else: who to tell. His father. First he thought of including it in his next letter, but then he was thinking of giving his father a ring at the garage in Hartford. The old man would enjoy the story about the bomb. It would be good, telling *him* a story for a change. But Cal would keep still about the incident that had started it all, strewing the garbage about on the porch. It had no originality or class.

"That's right, operator," Elaine said. "Brooklyn, collect."

"One moment, please."

She drew on her cigarette and shifted her stance as she listened to the intricate beeps and buzzes signaling the call going through. She was in a stand-up booth; the discomfort would keep her aware of the cost of the time.

The operator gave them the go-ahead.

"Hello, Elaine?"

"Yes, Pa, hello. How are you?"

"Fine. Is anything wrong?"

"No, I just called to ask if it's all right to come home this weekend."

"Sure it is, baby. What happened, did you quit your job?"

"No, the boss asked me if I wanted the day off. I *am* a luxury there, you know. He thought I should go home one weekend. It was nice of him, wasn't it?"

"It's nice of you to think of us. The house is like a tomb without you."

"Thank you. Where's Mama?"

"In the bathroom. She'll be right out. So what time will you be home?"

"Friday night, for supper. I'm going to cut my classes in the afternoon. I've been saving them up."

"Can you do that? Take the afternoon off?"

"Oh, sure."

"Sure?" he asked.

"Yes, Pa."

"Be sure to have the car checked," he said.

"Yes, that, too. And enough air in the tires."

"I was going to say that."

"I know," she said, laughing.

"I must be getting old. Do you know what I'm going to say often?"

"No, not really."

"How is your money holding out?"

"Fine. Please don't give me any when you see me."

"We'll see. Here's Mamma.—She's coming home Friday," he said away from the phone.

"It's about time," the woman said. Into the telephone, louder than necessary, she called, "Hello? What's the matter, dear?"

"Nothing, Ma. I'm getting Saturday off so I'm coming down for the weekend—"

"What? Shhh, I can't hear.—Your father wants to know what night you have a date, or is it both? I might say the same thing."

"No dates. I have work to do."

"What kind of work?"

"I have to go to the library."

"Oh, why?"

"Why did I go to college?"

"You didn't answer that one, either," he mother said, and laughed herself.

"You're in a good mood."

"I worry about you, that's all. Have you seen that what's-his-name?"

"No."

"I hope not," her mother said.

Elaine kept still. She drew hard on her cigarette.

"So when will we see you?"

"Papa will tell you," Elaine said. "I have to get off now.

I don't want to waste money. They don't tell you at three minutes on this kind of call."

"I know. I wasn't born yesterday."

"Give Papa a kiss for me."

"Yes, sure. I wish you'd think about quitting that job, Elaine."

"We've been through that already. I have to get off. I'll see you this weekend."

"All right. Goodbye, dear."

"Goodbye, Ma."

In the house in which she had grown up, the room whose furnishings she had selected, Elaine could truly relax. It was good to know that somewhere in the world a place of security and love existed, a place to which one could retreat, breathe freely and rest.

He bed was firm and the sheets were cool, from beyond the door pushed shut came the familiar sounds of the television set. Elaine stretched and pulled the sheet and quilt up about her neck. She could be fourteen or thirteen again, for as much as this place had changed.

The door opened. In the frame of light her mother's plump stooped body was silhouetted. Her grey hair glinted steely-blue. "Elaine, are you awake?"

"Yes, Ma."

"There's a good picture just starting, *The Great Gatsby*, with Alan Ladd. It's about the twenties."

"No, thanks, Ma. I'm very tired. I know the story, anyway."

"All right. How do you know the story?"

"It was a book I had to read for school." which was a lie, but a kind one. Elaine had read it on her own, but her mother would have taken that news as an assault on her.

"Oh," the woman said coldly. Then, "Was it good?"

"Excellent, Ma. You'll like the picture."

"Oh." Again. There was no way to touch her. Now she simply stood there, waiting for the chance to leave. She did not have the confidence to say, "Well, goodnight," and pull the door closed after her.

"Ma," Elaine said, "don't forget tomorrow. Early. I

have to be at the library and I want to have breakfast with both of you."

"Yes, dear."

"I love you, Ma." She said it on impulse, without thinking, and she was glad as soon as it was out. But then her mother smiled weakly, her arm moved nervously in the way that showed she did not know what to do, and at last she backed out as the word, "Goodnight," was uttered, half-spoken, half-choked. The door closed and in the darkness Elaine lay there in the moment of failure, the vacuum between them.

After a while she sat up and lit a cigarette. There *was* a vacuum between them—but that was not going to stop Elaine from loving her mother. It was urging her to show her love more. No part of her mother's life had been easy, she was one of the millions caught between the old and the new—and so much, much more.

Elaine did not know everything about her mother's life. Simple facts were missing: the woman had been born and brought up in Poland, and when Elaine's father—a young man then and having saved carefully for the trip— went back to that country, his birthplace, too, they met and were married. He took her to his new home; the accidents of courtship and marriage had made her an American. Elaine knew nothing about her childhood, schooling and friends. Her mother very rarely talked about her past, but recently Elaine had learned more details of the family history—one of the details being that her mother's cousin had married a Christian. Of all the people Elaine's mother had known who had faced the Nazi extermination, only that cousin still lived, still in Poland, still prosperous and still not communicating with the only other trace of the family left on earth.

The fact had a specific relation to Elaine, but she was not inclined to think about it now. Cal Torrenson was a dead issue. He awakened other thoughts that were just too unpleasant and unimportant to waste time on now.

But Cal was the only Christian she had every really known, and he did not care that much about his religion. It was now more *her* religion, in that she had become so

intensely curious about it that she retained more facts than
he did, and was more involved with what those facts
meant. He was, however, firmly anti-cleric and anti-
church. He was also anti-history, if he did not know it,
for he was far more interested in the world as it was
than in the reasons for that state of being.

Partially because of him, then, Christianity remained
shrouded to her. It seemed to loom over her like a schiz-
oid young giant, partially corrupt, partially pure, with
layer upon layer of depth, meaning and interpretation.
The giant within, of course, was Christ Himself. Everything—intensified, diluted, transmogrified, glorified and
even perverted—emanated from Him. On one side, rising
out of the past, glowed darkly the fire of Catholicism,
harder and more fierce than all the souls who had built
it, baroque and splendid, sublime in its reach for timelessness. On the other side, ruddy with the health of the
American way, peopled with scrubbed faces, smelled sweetly, and often too sweetly, the essence of modern protes-
tantism. But not far from the twittering togetherness and
the plump smiling shepherd of a minister was protes-
tantism's past, the dark, morbid horror of Puritanism
and John Calvin, the anti-semitism festering in the bril-
liance of Martin Luther.

All this she had to understand. Her ignorance fed her
alienation from the Christians, and while she was still
possessed of shreds of hate, she could not be redeemed
before herself. The stain of prejudice would stain everything she did. She could not be a good Jew while she
still resented the Christians.

She awoke almost whimpering, and opened her eyes to
the glare of the day. From the other room came the os-
cillant whine of the vacuum cleaner. Knowing her mother's
system of doing things, Elaine threw back the covers and
ran into the other room.

"What time is it?"

Her mother did not look up from her work. "Calm
down. Look for yourself."

The clock on the fireplace showed ten to eleven. "Why
did you let me sleep so late? You knew I had to get up!"

"Wanted to, you mean. We decided you should sleep. You should have the time off."

"Daddy decided it, too?"

"Yes."

"It wasn't fair!" she cried. "I had things to do!"

"So? You told us yourself it's for next term."

"Whose idea was it?"

"What difference does it make?" her mother asked.

"It was yours," Elaine said.

"So?"

"Forget it!" She went back to her room. In half an hour she was showered and dressed. Her mother was in the kitchen. At the door Elaine called, "I'm leaving, Ma!"

"No breakfast?"

"It's time for lunch. I'll eat in the city."

"Are you taking your car? There's no place to park."

"I'll put it in garage and pay for it."

"Oh.—There was mail for you today. It's under the clock."

Elaine went to get the envelope. It was her state scholarship check from Albany, one hundred and seventy-five dollars. She put the check back in the envelope and returned to the door. "There's nothing I can do about it on a Saturday. I'll take care of it next week."

"You don't want me to do it?"

Elaine paused. "—All right."

"We'll see you at supper," the mother said, content now.

"Yes." Elaine went out quietly. On the sidewalk she looked up at the living room windows on the second floor of the two-family stucco house. Her mother could hurt Elaine and then turn around and be hurt herself—all in blindness.

Little things, incidents manufactured: this state scholarship check was the perfect example. When she could, her mother made Elaine's bank deposits—although she disapproved of Elaine having so much money, or having held so many jobs to earn it. Taking the money to the bank was a way of staying part of things. But when Elaine said just now that she was taking the check to her other account in Ithaca, she had meant no hurt by it. She had forgotten. Her mother had concluded though, that Elaine had been trying to punish her for letting her sleep late— and for all the other little recent assaults. Even in their views of the differences between them, the two women were on opposite sides: Elaine wanted to minimize them; her mother cast their shadows over absolutely uninvolved happenings.

Her mother still brooded about Marv. Somehow she had made impossible connections and saw a repudiation of herself in the breakup of that affair. Elaine had let Marv get away because her mother had thought he would make a good husband. It was pathetic in that she was trying to become part of that thing after it was done, and more important, because she was crediting Elaine with far, far too much power, and showing what she thought of her own power in relation to the girl.

As if Elaine had any control at all over her affair with Marv. She crossed the street to her car, got in and started the motor. She sat looking at the house across the street.

Marv. Even now thinking about him was like being drawn to some horror her instincts warned her not to look upon. Why had she thought of him at all? So past, so dead, yet the chilling sense of sickness and shame he brought upon her was as natural as exhaling.

Marv had come along at the perfect time, Elaine's third year of college, her twentieth of life. He had manners and conversation and the kind of eyes that gave the impression that his mind was at work. But, by the third date even Elaine knew there could be no love here. By the end of the first month the pleasure of romance was irretrievably gone. When the Christmas holidays began a year ago, both parties went home to Brooklyn—not to revel in their continuous proximity to each other—but to entrench and strengthen themselves for the long emotional and psychological attrition to come.

She had embarrassed him in a class by taking apart an argument he had put forth, and had sought him out afterward to say that nothing personal had been intended. He was pleasant and accepted what she said and invited her for coffee. They began to go out. He was straightforward and upright in the company of other people. He was so quiet respectful with her parents that both of them mentioned it. Yet in private he played a game of egos, self-assertions and frustrations, all petty, witless stuff—but stuff at which he was so clever, so subtle, flamboyant and then cautious, that it took her months to realize just that it was a game with him.

He would comment unfavorably on her clothes, or comment favorably with such a reservation that the hurt was just as deep. He would flatter her at seven o'clock and then at eleven ask her to type a paper for him, correcting his spelling and grammar along the way. He kept her wounded and soothed, never settled. Like a professional he had read her reactions correctly: she thought he was as handsome a man as had ever paid attention to her. He told her he had never cared for her physical type, but that there was something appealing about her—her eyes, her neck. He played on this difference in their opinions of themselves, complimenting her and yet making sure she knew how very attractive his former girl-friends had been. More than once he pointed them out, in Joe's or some other place, bringing to the forefront the threat that they were.

Before it was done she had lost not only her virginity, but her self-respect. In the beginning she had presented herself honestly, with hope, telling all. He knew the depth and quality of the emotions she had already reached, and more, what she had yet to learn. He anticipated her when she could not anticipate herself. He turned her lack of knowledge from a pleasure for him into another weakness in her. Before it was done, he had led her up from relative innocence and through the sub rosa world of acts for which she was not yet ready, which for him and between them were reduced to acts of meanness and degradation.

Meanness and degradation were the last things she saw in him, the night she announced carefully and softly that she was not going to see him again. It was outside her dormitory, in his car. He had been very calm, but then, with a suddenness that terrified her, he reached across her lap to the door handle, twisted it, then pushed her out onto the ground. He grinned as she got up. "So long, pig," he said.

Now, as she pulled the car out of the parking space, Elaine realized she had dreamt it all last night—that confused, unhappy nightmare in the mood of which she had awakened this morning. Thinking of Cal Torrenson had done it. It had done it before. But the dreams of Marv were not all that thoughts of Cal Torrenson evoked; Cal himself had his share in her old misery.

Once she had pitied Cal, and had been sorry that she had used him so obviously to ease the hurts the other had caused, but the pity had turned over the weeks into something she loathed feeling: although he knew about her, about Marv and what he had done, and why she had come to sleep with him, Cal, he had denied it in himself and had chosen to think that something else was true. Last year, after his first real hurt, he had resorted to a kind of semi-adult tantrums. They had gone on for over a week.

There was still no reasoning, no logic. He was too immature to be able to love, to receive love, so it was not love. He wanted something he could not name—nor could anyone else. Elaine was sure that if another girl had done the same thing to him, *she* would have become the object of his attention. Because of him, Elaine was eager to have school end, to have June roll up and the ritual of commencement spew them out of Cornell in wholly different directions.

She missed having sex, but she did not want to think about it. But her mind always turned to one, Marv; two, Cal; three, her husband someday. And how many years to marriage, how many times would it look and feel like love and be natural and innocent and understanding all at once and just long enough? The male narrow-mindedness a virgin could admire and a woman with one affair behind her could forgive was now contemptible to Elaine. But only slightly could she wish for virginity again. Virginity was ignorance. She wanted to get married; she was sure she would marry in a week if she met the right man, someone with respect for human worth.

She should have married Marv, for her mother's part.

Of course her mother could be told nothing near the truth, and so she thought Marv had been fine and generous and would have made a good provider and father. She could not accept Elaine's word alone that Marv had been sick, vicious and perhaps even psychotic.

But if Elaine had erred in not giving her mother more to know about Marv—that last night might have been enough—she had definitely erred in telling about Cal at all. There, too, she had shown her inexperience with real emotions. For weeks, to Elaine, who had been humiliated in the first affair, the new one *had* seemed like love. Cal had had fine, charming ways, a ready smile. In a sense, he had been the innocent in this one. She had taught him some things, yes. And gladly, for he had been almost beautiful to look upon.

For her mother, associating at all with a Christian was filthy. It was better not to marry, although that was bad, too. But from Elaine's point of view, the alternative, the one that caused her to withdraw from her friends, was as heinous as never doing anything, never aspiring, never hoping, never working. In truth, the alternative her friends were taking was all those things. Her friends were picking husbands, *picking* them, herding them through the use of their sex into lives that were not living, homes in the smarter Jewish communities, like it or not, vulgar cars in which they could be chauffeured—how Elaine hated to see a woman riding in the back seat while her husband drove; it looked as if she had him saddled! Some of her friends were already moving toward the conspicuous vacations in Sullivan County and Miami Beach, mink stoles on shoulders, oozing jewels, make-up so thick they already looked like wraiths ...

And her mother, Elaine's mother, having never had the money or mobility to tell class from glass, thought all this was splendid.

As she turned the car up onto the parkway, Elaine wondered if she could ever make her mother understand that she, too, wanted to be a mother, that having a child or children and raising them properly was one of her highest ambitions. But no, her mother could not grasp that being different could also mean being good. It was part of the heritage of having been persecuted so long, this herd instinct of the Jews. They had to stay together, right or wrong, and they actually *feared* someone who went off on her own. Judaism was imperiled. Nonsense. It was safer in Elaine's hands. While her friends were studying the travel folders, she was struggling with Martin Buber, in an attempt to *understand* ...

All she wanted, at the bottom of it, was love with a man and respect from one child at least, and the chance for the rest of her life to be useful to the world.

"Try to understand her, Elaine," her father said.

"Yes, Pa." She was behind the wheel of the car again, and he was on the sidewalk leaning in the window. There had been a fight upstairs at breakfast because Elaine had said no to a request by her mother to come home again in two weeks—for a wedding of one of her father's distant relatives.

"Family is very important to her, you know? She worries about you."

"My only wish is that she express her worry in another way, instead of just yelling and sulking."

"Try to see her point of view, though. She's all alone during the day and she'd like to be sure of the future—in here, in the heart. A woman—I think she loves suppertime, when the family is all together and eating—which is an important thing, you know? She can sit back and realize that the family is getting somewhere together and she's a real part of that getting. Her love is when the family comes to her at the end of the day. You don't come, Elaine. You're different. You don't believe in it. It's tough on a woman in your mother's situation. All I want you to do is understand."

"Yes, Pa. I know you're right." She wanted to say more, tell him that he did not know his daughter as well as he thought, but they had been down here a long time. Her mother would be beginning to wonder what they were saying.

Elaine stepped on the accelerator to race the motor and open the automatic choke.

"It sounds all right," the father said, nodding at the hood.

"It's my baby," she said proudly.

"Be sure to have everything checked."

"Yes, all right."

"Do you have enough money? You won't be able to get at that new check until you can make a withdrawal yourself."

"I know. I have plenty upstate."

"You have the first dollar you ever earned, you know?"

"I'm *not* cheap! I bought this car, didn't I?"

"Sure," he said laughing.

"I just don't burn money up. I don't even think about it."

"Well, I better get upstairs." Elaine turned to kiss him. "Don't forget to wave to your mother after you make your turn," he said. "Be careful."

She kept the window down until she was on the avenue headed toward the parkway. After a dozen blocks she wheeled the car into a gas station. It was deserted and inside the office, the attendant was sitting with his feet on the desk and a book in his lap. He was facing the car, so she did not blow the horn. He did not get up and after a minute he did move, but only to turn a page. She tapped the horn. Very leisurely he ambled out, the book under his arm.

"Sorry to wake you," she said cheerfully.

"Oh," he mumbled. "Well. I mean, I'm sorry. Have you been waiting long?"

"No. It must be quite a book."

"It is, but I'm behind and I have to catch up."

"It isn't a novel?"

"No, a textbook. Here, hold it while I take care of you.—What do you want, by the way?"

"I have the feeling that if I hesitate, you'll fall dead asleep right on the spot. Are you that tired?"

"No, I'm always lousy in the morning. I've only had one cup of coffee."

She smiled and gave him the order, then settled back to look at the book, *Imperialism,* by a man named Moon. She had seen it before, on a library table at Cornell. Leafing through it, she could see that his was a new copy, but that it was well marked, underlined and bracketed methodically. She read a few paragraphs: he had underscored the right lines, the important ones, the keys to the rest. She came to a section about the Congo, and King Leopold of Belgium. She read a paragraph about Belgian overseers killing the wives and children of the natives who had tried to escape the plantations. When the attendant returned, she passed the book back to him.

"What did that book cost?"

"It's not for sale," he said.

"I know that. I want to buy one for myself, I think."

"Oh. It's six, maybe seven-fifty. I forgot, but you'd better write to the publishers for it, though, it's—"

"I think I can get it at college," she said.

"Oh, sure, the Cornell Sticker."

"What do I owe you?"

He told her and she gave him the money. "Look," she said, "would you like me to get you a container of coffee? You're going to show withdrawal symptoms in a minute."

"Would you do that? It would be very kind." His face lit up as if he had been told there would be a Christmas after all. "There's a place about three blocks back." He was reaching into his coveralls for change. "See if they have a bagel or breakfast roll that's fresh. I know they probably won't, because it's Sunday. But give it a poke, you know? If they have one, I mean. Preferably a bagel. But just get coffee if all they have is cakes and Danish and that other sweet crap. Get some coffee for yourself as well. We can make a party of it. I open up like a flower after my second coffee."

"Or just the thought of it. The process is starting already. But I can't stay. Thank you. I have to drive to Ithaca today, and it's a long trip."

"I know, my home is up there. So stay, we have a lot to talk about."

"No, really I can't."

"All right," he said, "but next time."

"We'll see. You go to college down here?"

"Yes, City College."

"We ought to change places," she said.

"A thought. Your car is newer than mine."

"You wouldn't look so good in my clothes," she said.

"See, you're staying already. Why don't you get the coffee and make it official?"

"Oh, I ran out on my parents to get back to school. Do you want me to feel guilty?"

"Ten minutes. That much guilt won't sear your soul."

"You know, if I listen to you much longer you'll have me in the coveralls working the gas pumps while you sit at the desk with your feet up reading and sipping coffee."

"Another thought—"

"—But get the coffee?"

"Yes, that's right. Thank you."

"I'm not doing it for you, now, you know. It's just that I can't stand to see a case of shock right before my eyes."

"Go," he said. "Every second is a guilty second. Each new minute is a new neurosis. Go, before you're a psychotic."

"Yes, sir."

He made a little bow as she put the Hydromatic into reverse.

chapter three

I

From the radio unobtrusive music drifted through the darkened room, undertoning the pleasant treble clinkings of the dishes in the kitchen sink. A soft fall of light spread itself from that doorway until it shone, faintly, without line or real illumination, on the farther wall. Charlie felt a breeze, a sudden harsh one, enter through the windows that faced the courtyard; it accentuated his thick, logy feeling, depressing him further.

From the kitchen Alice called, "Are you asleep, honey?"

"No." He did not even want to speak.

"Are you feeling better now?"

"Yes, a little."

"Can I get you anything?"

"No, thanks."

She came to the doorway and peered in. "Are you sure, honey?"

"Yes, Alice. I'm all right."

"Gee, I hate to see you like this. Listen, if there's anything—"

He just shook his head, hoping to signify that he was really all right. She nodded and went back into the kitchen.

She thought that working on Sunday had upset him, but it was what he wanted her to think. He had worked Sundays in the past and, though this one had been particularly inopportune, he had long ago developed the resistance to the little extra load. But this one had come at the wrong time, a time when returning to the place where he was expected, where he expected himself, was in itself and alone an unbearable task.

Here at Alice's apartment, where he had been due and

he had come out of respect for himself, he had to sit
straight and hold his fork properly and attend to her. Not
like a stud horse attends a mare, but in a convoluted,
insipid version of it. He attended her, marked her words,
not because she demanded it, but because of late she was
so damned uncertain and fearful that, lest he set her off
the way a man unleashes a trauma-ridden lunatic with the
magic word—the lunatic screaming and yelling through
the streets and finally throwing himself under the wheels
of a truck—he had to be cautious, obscenely so, politic,
concealed, entombed. Because she did not have the understanding, he could not tell her all the things that happened
to him, everything he thought, all the fantasies and mad-
nesses that accompanied a human mind, a tired mind.
Because they had, together, passed some silent second on
a clock after which all that had gone before was frozen
forever like emotional Jello, they were committed, inextri-
cably suspended, to doing the same things over and over
again, day after infernal similar day. He tried once to
break out of the Jello of their sex life, and she asked,
"Where did you learn that? When did you think of it?"
And he could see in her eyes that saying he had known it
for years and had remembered it during the day she
would take to mean he had been dreaming of the one he
had learned it with—not true; what and with whom had
detached themselves from each other years before. And
then for hours or perhaps days after she would wear it
like a scab, as if all his past was grievous unto her—which
it was—as if all the things he knew, learned beyond her
company, were grievous. A discussion of the techniques
involved in good historical research had ended, to gratify
both, in a session on his couch; *that* she could understand—
so that it came superbly clear that instead of him leading
her carefully into his wider world, she was dragging him
back into the chintzy room of her late adolescence. And it
was almost entirely intellectual, for she was kind and
decent all the time, not pettily decent in the way that
allowed no berth for anger or argument, but deeply so,
out of her heart. She had met him once in midtown with a
new fountain pen, because she had noticed his old one was

scratching and running dry. It was that sort of thing, bubbling up from the fine broth of humanity itself, that was so painful to him. Their relationship had to end, and in no way but completely. He had known it for weeks; he had it polished to an epigram in his mind, but he could not bring it up out of the nowhere it would be to her, because she gave no hint of anticipating the break.

For her it was the opposite. Last night, which was probably the beginning of his newest wave of resentment against her, she had asked him to go to her parents' home for the Thanksgiving holidays. Impossible. He told her to go alone, but no, she would stay in the city with him. She asked about Christmas. He had to say something affirmative, because he was expected at least to pass through Tompkins County to pick up his uncle before driving on to Syracuse to see his sister.

He cut the conversation short, but at the end she understood that at some time during the Christmas week, he would be at her parents' place. *God bless us,* he thought, *every one.*

He had to end it long before December, but he could not muster the overt savagery it would take. It was going to be a holy mess: she did not have any idea of what was going on in his mind. Or she did, and was running away from it. It was this possibility that turned toward her the rage he should have felt toward himself. *He* should have known better. He.

She came out of the kitchen again, drying her hands on the towel. "You look comfortable and relaxed."

"I'm going to get up now, I think."

"You're not leaving, are you?"

"No, not right away. But I'm not really satisfied with the lesson plan I have for tomorrow. I'm not going to be able to get anything out of the kids."

"What are they up to?"

"The Era of Good Feeling—you know, the seventies, eighties and nineties." He did not know if he had to explain it, but he felt he had to. He said, "The country was getting stronger and the modern era was about to— well, just burst. Everybody sensed it in a way; the country was unified for the first time. It's an interesting period but the kids can only spend two classes on it. They have to get the basic facts for the Regents but I want them to *feel* the era, too. They should get the mood of the people, but they shouldn't miss the injustices that were building up."

"Oh."

"For example, industrialization, in which some men were building great fortunes while thousands were jammed in the mills and mines and factories. I want to show how a thing can go along buttering the world but increasing its injustice, too. This wasn't slavery. It was difficult to point out the injustices when the country itself was gaining so much."

"Want some more coffee?"

It was like a sign over a door, bright red: EXIT. "Sure," he said, "then I'll have to go." *Good Feeling. I'm in great shape for it. But why can't I speak out? Goodbye, Alice. We're not going anywhere. We might as well face it. Goodbye and I'm sorry.*

And then, as he stood at the kitchen door watching her pour the coffee, he thought, *Ten minutes' guilt. Where?* He remembered: this morning and the redhead—and allowed himself a little smile, because Alice's back was turned.

It was Saturday again and they were going out to dinner. He sat uncomfortably at the end of the couch, his eyes fixed in an unseeing stare at the bathroom door. Not wanting this, he had trudged over from his apartment sullenly. It was late now only because he had cleaned up and dressed so slowly. Just a moment ago she had been telling him about her week—he had not seen her since Tuesday—but because of the door, he had called to her to keep still until she could come out. It had been maddening, of course, to have discovered she was not ready to leave—but she had been busy too, she said.

She opened the door and came out. She was wearing a dark blue cocktail dress with a low, rounded collar. It was very attractive, but he did not want to say it.

"How do I look?" she asked.

"Very nice."

"What's the matter?"

"I'm tired, that's all."

"How is your paper on Lake Chad coming?"

"All right." He rubbed his eyes. "I think it's going to run fifty pages, with the material I have."

"Good.—I'm ready if you are."

"Sure." He got up. *Now. Tell her now!*

He helped her with her coat and they went down the stairs to the black cold street. There was nothing to describe what happened on Tuesday: they met uptown near her office, during his up-city trek to night class. They sat in a restaurant and ate—lightly, he was never hungry lately—and gazed out at the sallow November dusk. Now he could remember nothing he had said, and his mood had been so intense it had slugged her senseless. That he was torturing her was a fact far from lost on him; every minute he let them both endure this was an addition to a debt he would have to pay somehow on another day. Ten minutes' guilt. The phrase he had worked up with the redhead Eleanor or Elaine clung to him like a virus—odd, that it should be twisted to this, when Sunday morning, the fastest half-hour he had known outside a classroom in months, had been such fun. It was likely that he would not see the girl again. He could fill a city directory with the names of interesting people he would never see again. When he put that fact against this, the one of Alice and himself, it came up a lousy life. It was a non sequitur but it was difficult to elude. And it was just this kind of thinking, so childish, that made situations like this continue and worsen.

He thought, *Tonight's the night,* remembered the joke, and laughed aloud.

"Booby hatch for you," Alice said. They were crossing the street.

"Soon. What were you trying to tell me before?"

"I was talking to my mother on the phone Thursday night, and she said that whatever we wanted to work out in regard to Christmas week would be fine with her. You could spend the first night with us and then go on up to your sister's the next morning, then pick me up for the trip down to the city again, after the holiday—"

The intricacy of her planning was like a knife slicing the air around him, carving him out of the reality he could see; he looked ahead, then over at her, but it was as if he would be unable, if he reached out, to touch anything. But even if his fingertips met any substance, he knew it would feel fantastically strange, as though someone had hooked up the nerve circuit in his arm in a new and frightening way—yet legitimate, for the mood he felt, whose center was worming towards his stomach, was intensely, grotesquely clear: everything, even distance, was in uncommon focus, with lines so sharp they dazzled his eyes. But when his mind tried to settle again on the older, more familiar conception, it rested at once on the particular idea of the Christmas trip, which resulted in a kind of shock thrumming straight to the center of him. He was sure that in a moment he would begin to tremble, but his first reaction was not fear, it was revulsion: that he could have allowed this situation to attain this point caused a cold slow wave to issue through him, the beginnings of real physical nausea. He stopped still in the middle of the block, and wished he had something he could grip with his hands.

She looked around. "What's the matter, dear?"

"No." He wasn't looking at her. "Listen," he said very quickly, "let's just forget everything—all of it. Right now. You turn around and go back to your place and I'll go to mine. I don't care what you do—I didn't intend the cruelty in that—but let's—I want to break this off now, right now. We aren't going anywhere. We're just wasting our time. Let's just—admit we've been wrong."

He turned his eyes to her. She looked stricken; her hand was coming to her mouth. He could not fail to see that he had hit her so hard, so suddenly, with this, that she did not know how to react.

"Look," he said, "I don't want to hurt you. I didn't."

She took a step back; tears were already in her eyes. He could not think of any physical thing that would have had a more punishing effect than what he had just done. He hated it. He wished he could find whatever it took to turn away and run.

"You've never loved me?" she whispered.

There was not even a thin line between him and speech, yet he could not do more than open his mouth and stare, wishing he could tell the truth with a touch, a gesture, or an expression on his face, and still not hurt her. He began to hope that *this* expression would do it—which was impossible, he knew, because he had no idea of what it conveyed. But it was not in him to walk away. He could not determine what quality he would be displaying if he walked away. Courage?

"I love *you*—"

"Alice, I—"

"You haven't felt anything!" she cried, as if he had pushed her at last to the final wall of strength.

"That's not true, I—"

"Do you know what I feel inside?"

Again that less than thin line; he stared helplessly.

"You fuck," she said. "It's the dirtiest word I know. It's what you are." And she was walking away. He couldn't move, and stood still and watched her go. But she was right; he felt nothing, now he felt nothing but the shock of the word. And worse, he did not want to feel anything. He wanted nothing at all. She was almost to the corner, walking near to the buildings. He kept watching her until, coming to the end of the block, she turned and was gone.

He waited a moment, then looked about and started in the other direction, the collar of his overcoat turned up, his hands in his pockets. This was the best way, he was thinking already. The ugliness had been quick; time and clever preoccupation would dissolve the residue. In a few months both of them would look back on it and feel pangs, but know the right thing had been done.

But the word clung: in spite of its meaninglessness, through it what she felt had been perfectly given over to him. And she was justified, for he had been obscene in a very real way, and not even his insider's knowledge of what had been the currents and flows between them could dissuade him from thinking that the affair had been a callous use of one person by another. But his effort had been, all along, in the direction of sparing her grief. No—himself. In the direction of sparing himself. The machine-like stamp of what he should have done from the start was the thing he had tried to evade. He should not have let the first night happen; afterward, his sole recourse had been in telling her what the first night meant—in bald, unmistakable terms—and saying goodbye, taking no chances with the future. No real love ever began in bed. The fact was, despite his thinking he wanted to spare her, he had not admired her. His efforts had had a contempt built in. There had been one or two good moments, sure, but his contempt for her and for himself for fooling himself had finally risen to the surface.

He did not want to think. It was finished; he wanted to get away from it. Right now, where was he going? He was just walking. He had not eaten, but he was not hungry—naturally. Yet he had to do something.

Coffee.

Charlie walked down to West Fourth Street and then across to MacDougal, going at a good pace, trying to enjoy the cold of the air. He entered Rienzi's, but saw no one he knew in the smoke-hazed front room. But he did not want to troop through to the back, and he took a small table near the center aisle and opened his coat. The place was fairly crowded and he could see other people passing outside, headed for the other coffee shops up and down the block, or the bookstores that were open until late in the night, or the parties that blossomed on the weekends like wild noisy flowers. Charlie was too busy to come here often now, but he did not feel out of place. If something was out of place, it was the night; the night itself was disordered.

When the waitress came he gave her the order and then, to get rid of his nervous energy, he went over to read the bulletin board. The usual things were for sale—cameras, phonographs, motorcycles and scooters. Classes in modern dance, painting and sculpture were being offered in various places. People looking for rides or riders had notices up; the destinations were Mexico, Florida, San

Francisco and Los Angeles. There were post cards from those places, Europe and North Africa. His curiosity appeased, he went back to his table and poured a cup of coffee from the pot that had been set there.

The front door opened, and John Murillo, bulging plump under a tweed overcoat, came in, accompanied by two young men Charlie knew well. Seeing him, they came straight up the aisle, pulling empty chairs from nearby tables. Charlie shook hands with them all. Murillo set his chair in the aisle and the waitress came over to ask him to move. The four of them, Charlie, Murillo, and the others, whose names were Hal and Skip, were crowded around three sides of the table.

To Charlie, Murillo said, "Well, old sock, where've you been keeping yourself? I haven't seen you in weeks—or heard—since the night I talked to Alice."

"Well, I've been pretty busy." He remembered ten minutes ago. The way she had looked at him. "Have you placed anything new?"

Murillo shook his head.

"Well, when this one you just sold is printed, maybe you'll generate some interest."

"How is Alice?"

Skip laughed. "What is this, old home week?" He had lost some more hair at the temples since Charlie had seen him last, over a year ago. He was wearing a starched white dress shirt, open at the collar, a V-neck sweater, and over that, a bright grey topcoat. Though he was the same age as Charlie, and long out of college, he affected collegiate dress, which made Charlie wince, though he never showed it. Skip did not know Alice. Charlie said, "No, not at all. They're good friends."

To Murillo, he said, "Alice is fine. She went upstate for the weekend."

"Oh.—Well, tell her I said hello, will you?"

"I'll do that."

Then, as though aware he was pushing, his voice nervous, Murillo said, "Whenever you're ready to give her up, you know, old sock, just give me a ring."

"Um, sure." If Charlie looked at him now, what he

really felt would come through. Still, remembering that morning when Murillo had to know who was in the apartment, he thought, *you turd*. He saw the waitress and motioned her over. Skip and Murillo gave her their orders, and she looked at Hal, a Nordic type with sunken cheeks, a prominent nose and a big chin. He was leaning back, his hands clasped behind his head. He had his eyes squinted for some reason.

"Bling me cup of fulm," he said.

"What?"

"Fulm. F.u.l.m. Comes in flevvic tin." He was the last one who should want to try this; his voice sounded as if it came from the bottom on a well.

"Oh. Well, I'm sorry, we don't—" Seeing the others laughing, she pulled herself up, and snapped, "No fulm!"

" 'S'all ligh'," Hal said. "Have no camla." Placing his hands prayerlike before him, he bowed low.

Scarlet with anger, she turned to Skip. "What does he want?"

Skip looked her up and down. She had a terrible face and skin the color of the belly of a fish, but her body was good, maybe a little too fully shaped with baby-fat. Under a black sweater and skirt she was wearing nothing but a slip. Skip said, "What he wants and what you'll give him are two different things—right here, anyway. Better bring him a cup of American coffee, too. That makes three altogether."

Diligently, scrawling slowly, she wrote it on her pad, then said it almost proudly, "Three."

"Er, and slice me off some of that stuff," Skip said.

"What stuff?"

"Forget it."

When she'd gone, Skip said, "She must have just come down from the hills, a-scratchin' and a-smellin'."

"Maybe," Charlie said angrily, "but what were you trying to pull? You weren't being funny."

"Don't worry, I was way over her head."

"The noise was coming from the wrong place. You would have had to use English to angle it so high."

"Very good," Hal said, laughing.

Charlie looked away. He had done the right thing, calling Skip on it, but he had done it out of a vicious mood. What a collection with him: two bums and a first-class sickie. He had work at home to do. He wondered why he didn't get up and walk out of here.

Murillo said, "She *is* scurvy looking, you must admit."

"I must admit," said Skip snidely. He was turning on John now, whom he detested.

"Peace, brother," Hal intoned.

"What you have to understand, Hal," Skip explained, his eyes narrowing, "is that John here is about to bring his great message to the world, and he needs criticism every step of the way. What's to be your message, John, how much you hate your mother?"

Murillo was taken unaware, and his face masked over. Charlie wanted to break Skip's nose. Murillo said, "That may be so, but it'll be talent that'll—" Charlie didn't hear the rest of it; John had been hurt, and he was trying to answer out of the same feeling a child has when he is losing a fight to an older, bigger boy: he was incoherent.

To Charlie, Hal said suddenly, "I'd say they weren't fit for the company of decent young ladies, wouldn't you?"

"Yes, I'd say that."

"You look like someone who would take both their places."

"Get a yardstick and we'll measure."

"Very good. Seriously, I promised this gash in the Bronx I'd help fill her party. You're a reasonable sort and you know the score. Do you want to join us?"

"By 'knowing the score' I take it you mean that I don't react violently to deviant behavior. Well, I don't—when it's at a reasonable distance."

"Well said. Live and let live. Deal you in?"

"I don't go all the way to Bronx to find everyone flat on the floor from pot. I have to tell you that. Live and let live is one thing, but I don't want to be the only one conscious by midnight."

"That grieves me deeply," Hal said.

"You, too? By God, when the next depression comes, marijuana will be so widespread they'll be selling it on street corners instead of apples."

"I like my pleasure big," Hal said, with a flourish of the hand. He could probably tell from Charlie's talk that Charlie's experience with junk was limited strictly to the observation of people who, in Charlie's world, were really few and far between. Charlie wanted him to know this. Now Hal said, "There'll be a lot of college kids at this place, Cumberland, so things will be well below boiling."

Charlie looked at Murillo, who was no more capable of living dangerously than he was of flying around the room. Charlie said, "All right, I'll come along."

"Fine," said Hal. "You're the squarest guy I know, Cumberland, but you're fine."

"Well, whenever you're ready."

"After our coffee."

The coffee came and they drank it and then went out to Hal's car. It was an old Buick sedan, dirty and dented. When he had the doors unlocked, Hal turned to Charlie and asked if he still had his driver's license. Charlie nodded. Hal gave him the keys. "Do me one, will you? I want to sit in the back."

Charlie was confused a moment, then he said, "But keep the windows rolled down, unless you want a mellow chauffeur—Oh, can I try out the car?"

"Run it into a wall, I won't give a shit. But I knew you had a vice."

"Oh, balls."

The radio was turned on and there was little talk. The sweetish, dirty-socks smell began to rise faint and cold from the rear seat but it never became strong. Though it had been a year and a half since his last encounter with it, Charlie could recognize the odor immediately. He would know it in a hundred years. When he looked into the mirror, he could see nothing but the tops of their heads—Hal's and Skip's; Murillo was in the front—and the reflection of the orange cigarette glow on their foreheads. The very surreptitiousness of the act made it repugnant to Charlie—something he was sure he could not explain to them. He told Murillo to roll down the wondow on his side, and in a few seconds it was very cold in the car.

As soon as he had the feel of the mushy steering, Charlie played with the gas pedal a little, then, turning from East Sixteenth Street onto the East River Drive, he pushed down until he'd built what felt like the car's easiest speed—a little under sixty. He noticed that Murillo was tense and glassyeyed. The road ahead was almost empty, but the few cars on it were scattered in all three lanes, presenting the challenge of weaving through them. Charlie pushed the pedal to the floor; the passing gear of the Dynaflow snapped in sharply, and the car lurched forward, sloppy and soft, the motor droning up. When the needle touched seventy Charlie slacked off a little, beginning to work the pedal, threading the car methodically through the traffic. The dark water on the right was going by very quickly and the lights on the far side were throwing straight shimmering lines over it. There was a wind ripping in and the car shuddered, but held fast, locomotive. As it moved into the tunnels under the U.N. Building and Sutton Place, the wind roar grew deafening and in the mirror Charlie could see the lights of the Fifty-ninth Street Bridge lowering back. Overhead was the clouded murky yellow sky, reflecting the city light.

"Oh, go!" Hal exclaimed.

"I wish to hell he'd slow down," Murillo whined.

"Shut up," said Skip, "you ain't dead yet. Let the man have his fun."

Charlie said nothing, concentrating on the road. But he was thinking that there was no "fun" involved and now, since the word "fun" was uttered, all his aims were lost. He could see he had been wasting time from the start, and these seconds' thought had reawakened it all. In asking how many minutes had passed while he had not thought of Alice he *had* thought of her. He wondered if there was anything ahead that could make him forget, but then just as quickly he was asking himself how she could be doing, now, alone. How was she going to do over the longer run, the weeks and months?

A car ahead moved to the right and gave him an opening. As he slapped down on the gas he was stopped inside, dead, by another question: why this berserk flight?

Why was he running? It could almost make him believe he could not endure the aftermath. It wasn't true. He had done the right thing, and he was prepared to take the consequences. He was forced to think of Korea and the way he'd acted in that circumstance; had it been to his ultimate advantage, he probably would have fled then. Had it been possible, if he'd had the strength, he would have raced ten thousand miles over sea and land to safe and mild Tompkins County, New York. Now, in a situation meaning so much less, he was running at the fastest speed he could devise. From what? To what? He didn't know either answer, and he was afraid.

In the back seat Hal and Skip were sublime. Hal bawled the directions over the Dyckman Street Bridge and through the twisted, hilly streets of the Bronx. Charlie had not lived far from here, his first year in New York; it had been years since he had been in the neighborhood. The sight of it brought back all its dingy memories, the drab days and the sombre nights, but after so long it was like someone else's past. Yet it was not remote and cold inside him; it was a probing warm needle gently turning back the layers of better times, exposing that year like a hidden scar. And it was as if it had a life of its own and had been dormant all this time; it pulsed into a kind of reality until the pride and sorow with which he remembered it was a magnified thing, bright and almost living itself. He had a sensation of his own private journey down the woven corridors of life; a feeling of secret history was revealed, a history which was never recorded and offered no meaning: the paths of all the small lives, lives like his own, down through time, participating now and then in the great events, but nearly always crowded into anonymity, toiling through the days and nights from private beginnings to private ends, responding to and reflecting the phases and the rhythms of life. Rarely in wrinkled, well-noted history did one glimpse the sheen of sweat or the shine of a smile, but now, in a startling, maddening flash, it was all he saw. The two kids kissing in the fourteenth century, a knife slipping in in the ninth. Suddenly it was covered over again, as if by clouds. He was antagonized;

he wanted to yell. It was as though he could believe his presentiment that he would never see it again, and that he would have to crawl after it, studying its reflections in the landscape for the frantic want of the real thing.

The party was in an apartment in a garish old sandstone building squeezed in with dozens of others. The streets intersected in no pattern, and one was directly opposite the house; it ran downhill to the elevated line. In the glow of the yellow light, the scene had the stillness of a painting and was almost pleasant in the dim running of lines and angles.

The four could hear the party-noise in the elevator. On the fifth floor, where they alighted, the noise was louder, even jarring. Hal walked directly to the right door, touched the bell, and entered without a blink of hesitation.

Charlie was the last inside and, over the heads of the others, he could see the usual party image, the crowd and the dense pall of smoke. A woman in her forties took their coats. She was tall and dark-haired and heavily made-up, and trussed in a dark dress that fit her badly. Hal disappeared with a plump girl—the woman's daughter, Skip told Charlie. Skip had been here before, and steered the other two to the card table in the hall on which liquor, glasses and ice were set. But then he excused himself, saying he wanted nothing to drink, and pushed into the crowd in the living room. Murillo looked at Charlie and shrugged, then offered to fix drinks.

The woman came back, saw Murillo at the table, told him to go ahead, and turned to Charlie. "Hal told me you were going to be a teacher—you're the one, aren't you?"

"Yes, that's right."

Murillo passed him his drink and made a kind of "so long" gesture.

"Dear," the woman said in a distraught tone, "why should *you* want to be a teacher? It's for those who can't *do*, you know."

"I heard the joke," Charlie said. He sipped his drink.

"You have a lot of confidence," she said.

"What makes you say that?"

"You didn't grin stupidly when I put the screws in. How old are you?"

"Twenty-three." She reeked of perfume. Her upper lip was flecked with tiny vertical gouges, as if she did a lot of arguing. She certainly seemed to want to argue now. He sipped his drink again. She had no deep creases in her face from smiling or the weather, only tense shallow lines—on a skin that was soft and discolored from disorder and late hours.

"So?" she said. "Why?"

"Excuse me?"

"Why do you want to be a teacher? You really could do much better."

"You'll have to give me an example."

"Oh, business, for one."

"Which business?"

"You'd have to decide that for yourself," she said. She was trying to push the burden on him. She did not know it, but she was talking to someone who could wait for the slowest and most inarticulate of thirty-five youngsters to state *all* the issues of the election of 1896. He said nothing and kept staring at her. Finally she gave in. She said, "You still haven't given me a reason why you want to teach."

"It explains itself. I want to."

"Don't you ever question yourself?"

"I beg your pardon?" He could think while she was repeating herself. If he let her in just a little bit, she would hammer at him all night. The next time around, instead of an answer to her question, she got, "You know, we don't even know each other's names."

"Call me Harriet," she snapped.

"Charlie. How do you do?" And with an amiable grin, he gave her his hand to shake.

"Well, listen, when you have an answer to my question, you look me up. I really have to tend to my other guests."

Charlie smiled again and let her do the retreating. She had paused a moment, to see if she could make him back away. He was still smiling when she looked around from halfway across the room, but this time he let a trace of satisfaction show through. She did not credit him with that much subtlety. She sneered, concluding he was an idiot at last. She could think what she wanted, for he had gotten rid of her. *You self-important shit*, he thought.

He went into the living room. There were a few people here he knew from City College and the Village, but most were strangers, young, but not very young. He could hear music, but could not make it out, and no one was dancing. As he moved through the crowd he discerned that the piece was *The Firebird*, splendid incidental music, cheerful and uplifting. Near the phonograph no one was paying serious attention to it. Everything was conversation, loud, yammering and distorted. He moved out to the foyer again. There was laughter coming through the corridor from the private part of the house, which was dark. Charlie could see into the kitchen from where he stood. Hal was not there. He was still missing with the woman's daughter. Charlie did not want to think they had gone into one of the bedrooms. The girl's mother was in the house. That was all Charlie needed, to have the woman catch Hal fooling around with her daughter.

Charlie looked back into the living room. Skip had found a chair and had dissolved into it, his face in corpse-like composure. *Let him have his fun*, he had said while Charlie had said it himself, after Hal. Of course Hal was fooling with the daughter; they weren't playing Scrabble. And he had to know the mother felt as he did about it, or had no opinion. It was hard to believe she could be without an opinion about any subject, but it had to be so.

Off in a corner, Murillo had a girl boxed against the wall, and he was talking with that earnest, purposefully wry nonchalance of a man at work. She was going for it. She brushed a speck of lint from Murillo's lapel.

Charlie had had enough. The coats were in the bedroom. He could not ask the woman, nor wait for the daughter. He went down the hall to the closed door. He knocked.

"Who's there?"

What the hell, who knows me? He said his name.

"Who?"

Hal's voice: "He's the one I brought. The teacher. It's all right."

"Just a minute," the girl called. Then: "Come in, but don't turn on the light."

There were twin beds in the room, the coats on one, Hal, and the girl on the other, a sheet drawn up over Hal's back. The girl peeped out from under Hal's hairy armpit.

"I came for my coat," Charlie said.

"You couldn't wait?" the girl said.

"Man, you're too much?" Hal boomed, and started to laugh. "Turn on the light, for Christ's sake. You may as well. If I have trouble now I'm going to sue you for non-orgasm."

"You'd never win. How could you prove it wasn't the stuff you have in you?"

"Jesus, I could demonstrate on the judge."

Charlie nodded. To the girl, he said, "I was talking to your mother. Fine woman."

"I should have warned you," the girl said oversweetly.

"What about you?" he asked.

"What about me?" she said.

"Sure. Well, I have my coat. Goodnight, and have a good time."

"He's ridiculous," the girl said as Charlie shut the door. She sounded constrained, as if Charlie had caught her at precisely the wrong moment. He grinned malevolently, wishing she had been her mother instead.

In the foyer, Murillo saw him and waved him over.

"Leaving so soon, old sock?"

"I've changed my mind. I have a lot of typing to do in the morning."

"Oh?" said the girl. "Are you a writer, too?"

"Sorry, no."

"There are a lot of writers here tonight," she said, and smiled at Murillo.

"Can I speak to you alone, Cumberland?"

"Sure."

The two went toward the front door.

"You lived around her, didn't you?" asked Murillo. "Is there a drug store open nearby?"

"Probably. I don't know, my place was a good distance from this one."

Murillo glanced back at the girl. "You wouldn't believe it, would you? She asked me to go to bed with her. She has a room around the corner. She looks pure and innocent. That's the horrible part of it, you find the innocent-looking ones parked in cars or in hotel rooms—you can't believe what you see, can you?"

"Or what you hear, John."

"What? Oh, if you don't believe *me*, go and ask *her!*"

"I'm not really interested. What are you trying to tell me by it, anyway?"

"Nothing. I don't know. She's a kind of a symbol to me. What can you believe in or trust any more? Take a woman, *any* woman—even your Alice, I'd imagine, please don't be angry—and before long she'll disgust you with some story about what she's done. But it's like that with all life, every part of it. People—they just make you sick."

"Listen, do you know the story about the boy who followed the whore to her hotel?"

"I'm not much good at jokes," Murillo said.

"Well, they made their arrangements. Then, in her room, she undressed and suddenly caught him staring at her. He wouldn't take his eyes off her. She spoke to him; he didn't seem to hear her. He just stared. Finally she shouted, 'Well, kid, what did you expect feathers?'"

Murillo snorted. "You're no help, Cumberland."

Charlie put his coat on. "I don't know what I meant to be, John," he said tersely. "Goodnight. I wasn't kidding when I said I had work to do."

He did not look back as he headed out. Sick or not, Murillo would return to his girl. And drug store or not, he would flop her onto a bed somewhere. Charlie should have told him that, instead of holding back, as he always did. Damn it, if Murillo wanted help, he should see his doctor. Charlie shifted his weight impatiently from one foot to the other while he waited for the elevator to make its groaning ascent from below.

The dreary ill-lit streets, one after another in their sterile sameness, flowed quickly by. There was no way to kill the mood. Though he had come aware of himself in the car, he had still hoped for escape up here. Escape. Hope was an integral part of escape, but the people here were in a wallow of hopelessness he did not have the ambition to resist. Hal, Skip, Murillo, the mother, the daughter. Charlie could see the gouge marks on the mother's upper lip. So she was a little more subtle, but in her way, she had intended to use Charlie for her private trampoline. He had the feeling he was doing the right thing now, leaving. These people were a danger. Murillo. A violence seethed under his actions and words. There was no telling how it would burst out. Just for safety's sake, Charlie would have to stay away from him.

It was easier, suddenly, to think of Alice and himself: it was so simple and isolated. The party and Hal and Skip and the mother and the daughter each showed Alice and himself in a newer, cleaner light. The barrier between them was human, not depraved. Now, as if the contrast was too much for his mind, it sealed over everything. A disquiet sizzled in him through a sudden light-headedness he felt. He was tired. It seemed he had run to the end of his energy.

In the luncheonette below the el station he bought the newspapers and a magazine for the ride downtown. He was glad he did not have the car. This was the kind of night his preoccupation and anxiety could run him into an accident. The subway was better: the long drugging ride, reading to drown himself in; it was good, he would get a chance to rest.

At Grand Central, to avoid the two-block walk through the tunnels to the shuttle, he went downstairs to the Queens line, which crossed town to Times Square in the same way, but on which trains ran less frequently. He felt he would rather stand waiting than walk. But the train came quickly and he stepped in and sat down.

A crowd was waiting to get on at Times Square. He moved through and started up the stairs, when the noise registered. He had been hearing it since the train doors opened, but only now did it emerge from the surrounding din: voices—yelling in Spanish, and drunken. Charlie had to look about him, other people, mostly middle-aged men, were standing at the foot of the stairs, looking up, their mouths agape. A man Charlie's age was at the far side. From upstairs came the sudden, chopped report of metal and glass in impact, then more laughing and shouting. Charlie saw that of the crowd that had swarmed onto the train, about half had not taken seats; they were standing at the open doors, their eyes uplifted. He turned to the nearest man.

"What's going on?"

"Spicks, they're breaking everything up, the bastards."

Charlie did not answer, but looked up again. There was another explosion of yelling, crashing—explosion: did it remind him of the war? He could feel his stomach tightening.

The man, who was near sixty, said, "Somebody ought to lay a soldering iron on their gonads, the spick sons of bitches."

Charlie went down the steps to him. "Get out of here. Get out of my sight."

"What? Why? It's a free country."

"And I'm free to kick you in the backside for spewing that kind of filth. Get out of here before I do it. I'll kick you so hard you'll be buried with three shoes."

"What are you, a pinko or something?"

"Go on! *Go on!*"

The man moved back. Charlie closed his fist and feinted with it. The man turned around and walked more quickly, glancing over his shoulder.

There was another crash upstairs and more voices, some in broken, heavily accented English. Charlie could hear them coming from another place, the adjacent staircase, and he went around to see. There were about ten, all Puerto Ricans. Four went into the train and sat down, trying to ignore the others, who grouped on the platform. One strode to the door and said something to those on the train, and then he laughed drunkenly.

One sitting down cried, "Do you want to get os in

trouble with the paleece?" He glanced timidly at the people who had moved to the ends of the car. The one outside laughed again and went back to the others by the staircase. Charlie tried to get a better view of them. They were jostling each other, laughing and talking rapidly in Spanish. One who was wearing a natty blue topcoat stepped out of the group and walked up to a gum machine and stopped before it. He called to the others and when they turned to him, he lifted his knee to his chest and thrust his heel at the clear plastic window of the machine. It gave and the metal frame bent in and the mirror above it shattered. Laughing, he pulled the plastic out and began to fill his pockets with chewing gum.

Charlie bolted forward, then stopped. He had to stop them, but then, just as suddenly, he couldn't. He didn't want to move. He looked around, no one had taken a step; everyone was standing motionless, afraid, trying to look away.

From within the car one of those sitting down ran out. "Do you want to get os all arrested?" He pushed the one in the overcoat. "Stop eet! Look what they think of os!"

The other turned halfway from him, then wheeled suddenly and punched him in the middle of the face. The man staggered back on the platform, his nose spurting blood. Women in the train screamed. The other three came running out and the first ran into a pointed shoe that caught him full in the stomach. He doubled over and a knee came up to his head. He fell down, and two who had been on the platform started to kick him.

Charlie moved; it was as if something caged in him had burst out. He let his newspapers fall and grabbed the nearest one—one from the group on the platform—by the back of the collar and threw him down. The man could not have weighed more than a hundred and twenty pounds. As he struggled to his feet Charlie grabbed his coat and lifted him again, this time into the air, and threw him down again. Now he hit the concrete solidly, did not stir for a second, then rolled over and heaved for air. Charlie looked around, recognizing the young white man who had been at the far side of the stairs. He had one in a hammerlock and was trying to twist him to the floor. Charlie felt a curious mild elation: it was getting to be a fine fight. The crowd was scattered to both ends of the platform; people were yelling and screaming. It was odd. None of the men were helping. This was fun, in a way, yes, but did they think that he and the other fellow had started fighting for that?

Right in front of him two of the platform group were piled on the one who had had his face bloodied. Charlie pulled at the top one until he was loose. Charlie waited for a clear swing, then hit him in the face. Another from the car grabbed the man around the neck from behind and pulled him down, flailing his face with both hands, spreading the new blood about. There was another crash; Charlie spun around, someone had gone head-first against the wired glass of a newsstand, and the glass had a perfect hemisphere dented into it. The man who had made it was on the cement below with another man on top of him.

The fight spread out. Inside the train the one in the natty blue overcoat was on top of one of the others. Charlie ran in and pulled him off. The other slid off the seat onto the floor, holding his head. The fellow in blue grabbed Charlie around the waist to start punching at the kidneys. Charlie took his ear, twisted and punched down with his left hand on the back, at the neck. His knuckles hit the skull and shot into pain, but the man let go and tried to run. Charlie reached for the back belt of the overcoat and pulled. One end snapped loose but the other held and Charlie, taking a better hold, spun him around. The coat had come down past the man's shoulders; he could not raise his arms. He blanched at the thing he could see coming, but Charlie had to forget the moment of charity he felt; the man's own handiwork was pumping all over the station. Putting his weight behind it, Charlie sent his right fist into the man's nose. The man reeled back, but then, gaining his balance, he returned with a wild overhand right that caught Charlie on the ear. His left came in, too, but he was off-stride and it had no force as Charlie caught it on the arm. The man was cursing in Spanish. Charlie jabbed a left into the mouth; he could feel the teeth cut into his knuckles. The man's guard went down and Charlie rushed in and slammed him against the side of the car. The wind went out as if the man were a bellows. Charlie gathered up the folds of the coat and slammed a second time, then a third, letting the man's head whack against the window. A police whistle blew. Charlie looked over his shoulder; a Transit Authority patrolman, a man at least sixty, was coming down the stairs, swinging his right stick. *Shit, a candidate for a cardiac!* He could see the crowd still huddled toward the ends of the platform. *Here's your reason to help, pigs! If this old man dies, who's to blame? Where does the blame end?* But in a moment Charlie smiled happily. The old man let the stick fly, holding the leather thongs; the stick crashed into a man's calves and the man collapsed, howling, reaching for his legs.

The one Charlie had was pushing to get away, but Charlie grabbed him by the throat and pushed him toward the floor, then swung up at the man's stomach. The overcoat softened the punch and Charlie could see nothing was going to be done this way. He clawed at the back the coat and pulled it over the man's head. The jacket came with it, ripping like paper. The man was trying to lift a knee into Charlie's groin. Charlie brought both his hands, locked together to the size of a mace, down on the man's back. The man relaxed, softened, and slipped to the floor, gasping. He looked up, his nose and mouth full of blood.

"No more, meester. Please. I won't fight."

"I'll kick your head off if you're lying."

"Yes. No fight."

Charlie pulled him up and dropped him into a seat. The blood was running down his chin and splattering to his shirt. Charlie looked around and picked the other man from the floor and let him fall beside the first. He looked outside and saw the patrolman and the other fellow lining them up against the newstand. Charlie called, "There's room in here. I have one who's losing some blood."

The patrolman nodded and began to direct the others into the car. When the eight were seated, the patrolman turned to Charlie. His face was deeply creased and florid now from the strain. "You," he gasped. "You tell me what this is about."

But everyone started talking at once, appealing for the patrolman's attention. The patrolman told them all to shut up but one did not. He stood up and began to chatter a story. The other fellow who had fought barged over to him and slapped his face and pushed him into the seat. Charlie, nearer to him than the patrolman was, grabbed the fellow by the arm. "Calm down! The fight is over!"

"Who the hell are you?"

The patrolman said, "You'll keep your hands to yourself. I'm the law." He turned to Charlie again. "Okay, you try once more."

Charlie recounted what he had seen and heard, pointing out those he had seen on the platform. The crowd was gathered outside the car now and was looking in through the windows. Some people were wincing at the blood. There were four Puerto Ricans with split lips and bloody noses. The fellow who had been hit by the stick was doubled up holding his calves like a trapeze artist in a somersault. The patrolman asked Charlie if he wanted to press charges.

"For assault? Oh, no."

"What about the gum machines?"

"I saw only the one do any breaking. I'll sign a complaint, but only if you think anything's to be served."

The patrolman nodded and turned to the other fellow. "What about you? What did you see?"

"I saw it all. I'll go down with you and sign a complaint. But I don't want to make any charges for my own sake. I didn't get hurt."

"That's good of you," the patrolman said.

"Officer!" Someone was pushing through the crowd. It was the man Charlie had threatened at the foot of the stairs. As he stepped into the car and saw Charlie he drew himself up, startled. Then, to the patrolman, he said, "I saw one of them do it. I had a perfect view from where I was. It was that one, there." He pointed to the one in the blue coat.

Charlie said, "This man is a bigot, officer. I heard him make several remarks before the fight. I told him what he was, and not politely. He may be trying to settle the score with me, or maybe he's just psychotic about these people."

The patrolman studied the man's face, which now registered complete astonishment. The patrolman asked, "Did you see anything? Really?"

The man was looking at Charlie. "Oh, I saw, all right. I've been a witness before. This bastard communist here is trying to stir up trouble. I've seen his kind before—"

"You watch your dirty mouth," the patrolman warned. He turned to Charlie. "If he saw, he saw, and there's this other guy to corroborate it. There's not much you can do about that."

"Yes, I know. I saw the thing myself. But these people got their lumps already—that's the way I see it."

"I know. The best thing you can do is give your name to them in case their lawyer feels you can discredit this fellow with what you heard him say earlier. But he doesn't have the final say, by a long shot. The vending machine people have to be notified. They may want to make an example, or maybe they want to forget it. You can go any time you want, now."

"Is that all you're going to do with him?" the man asked.

"Did you see *him* do anything?"

"No, but—"

"Shut your mouth!"

To Charlie, the man snarled, "You cocksuckers always get a break with the law! That'll change, you wait!"

The patrolman faced him. "He could have you arrested now, do you know that? I want you to shut your mouth and keep it shut!"

"Why, I ought to take your number!"

"Say another word and you'll be in for obstructing an officer!"

The man stepped back, horrified.

Someone was sent to call the wagon. The patrolman took all the names and told the two witnesses who were going down to the station that they would have to take the train; there would be no room for them in the van. They looked cheated, but nodded and turned to go. Charlie waited until they were out of sight, then went out of the door of the car and prepared to push through the crowd.

But several people backed off. He looked at their faces, but they turned away. One of the women masked her mouth to say something to the man next to her. The man put on a grim look and said—his words carried clearly— "He had to. It's like the other guy said; they have all the laws on their side." Charlie glared at them, set to demand they speak up. But for a second, the vital second, he did nothing, and they took the chance to move away, averting their eyes. As he looked around at the others he saw that they were blank, of no opinion. Unsteadily he moved through toward the stairs, almost ill. It was one thing to read about this in the newspaper, but another to see it. In the presence of the man's clever suggestions, these people were powerless. But for the patrolman and the lack of the idea and a leader, they could have turned on Charlie.

On the downtown platform, the man and the young fellow were waiting, on their way to the station. As he passed, Charlie regarded them with contempt. But he faltered in his stride and grew nervous as he felt their hate turned back on him. He wanted to face them down, but he kept walking, actually afraid.

He had been stupid at the staircase, threatening the man. His stupidity had come back, not to him as much as to the Puerto Ricans. They were responsible for what they had done, but it was this extra insanity he had evoked that could mean the difference between justice and revenge. The old man could have his say in court, and there was no guessing how he would be heard. Judges were human, too.

The downtown express rolled into the station. Charlie entered the first car and stood at the forward window looking down at the tracks which had began slowly to glide beneath the wheels. The darkness of the tunnel caused him to see in the glass the reflection of the other passengers behind him, sitting and staring passively. He thought of the behavior of the crowd. *Live and let live.* The right or half-right thing Charlie had done was lost not only in the rantings of the old man and the behavior of the dunce who was now his ally, but in the ugly vacuum in the mind of the mob.

Where did it begin and end? Where was a man's responsibility to himself and his world to rest at last? How was he to exercise his duties once he found them? It was fatuous to believe that his own absence at the party or his refusal to attend could have changed the events there even one minute of one degree. Or what would some overt action on his part mean, say, a year from now? People did not change so easily.

Yet the questions that were unanswerable in one context were inane in the other, for down in the subway Charlie had felt the hot noxious breath of the mob. He had had to act. He had to act now.

A man who was really alive could not ignore even that small flit of violence. He could not be afraid—and he could not fortify himself with idiotic dogma. It was his duty to search out, just as it was his right to be free. He had to know the truth, where both freedom and duty began.

But one thing was clear: there was no difference between the people at the party and those he had confronted on the platform. He could not even say who were more violent. The people at the party thought they were in revolt. Nonsense. What they expressed, at the heart, was the bourgeois ethic they were running away from. Smugness. Self-salvation. Self-glorification. Maybe that was at the center of their desperation, the fact that they could not get away from their bourgeois selves. Or maybe it was the knowledge that it was exactly the failure of the bourgeois ethic that allowed them their ignoble flounderings. Nobody cared. Everybody believed, but nobody cared. The people at the party had, in their own way, lost their belief in the ethic. But because of their weakness, they were still pinned with it. They were mounted now like a frieze upon the columns that made the rest of our society. The whole thing was a temple to self.

The train slowed into the Fourteenth Street station and Charlie stepped out and went up the stairs to the access to

Twelfth Street. It had started to rain, a fine soft mist in a cold wind. He turned up his collar and started to cross the street toward his building, but then he stopped. The row of brownstones, black against the dark yellow sky, windows glowing a dull yellow, conveyed to him a mood of loneliness and desolation. The rain whirled brightly underneath the lamps. The feeling oozed over his thoughts and made them more burdensome and oppressive; the futility of his thinking suddenly smashed at him. None of the people he had seen tonight could be convinced of anything. Each had his own set of rationales and justification. What was he to say and do when he could see nothing worth the saying and doing? A quiet, the quiet of the dead, lowered about him; even through the cold and the rain he felt the escape from him of his own desire to be free.

Talk. To talk, speak, express his ideas and seize ideas, hold them in his hand like glimmering jewels.

He thought of Alice again and then, slowly at first, then rapidly, the thought of her rolled in on him, swirling darkly in his dark confusion. He looked down and up Seventh Avenue. It was only after midnight but the rain and cold had driven people indoors. He began walking again, but in a different direction, down the Avenue and across toward the theater and, farther down, toward Eleventh Street. Her building was well off the Avenue, past a stand of thin naked trees. He started to imagine her, what she looked like: small and slim, black-haired, pretty blue eyes. Tonight must have been terrible for her. He did not want to think about that. He did not want to think at all. She would be glad to see him, really she would. What they had had so far had been better than all he had known before. He imagined her smile again. She would understand things if he explained them to her. She was not stupid. He had never thought the two of them out. Or given her enough time. They wanted each other. He had taken out his overwork on her. He had treated her terribly.

He went down Eleventh Street to her house and up the steps to the narrow vestibule. The inner door was ajar. To the walls of the corridor clung a musty odor. He could hear the resounding of the rainwater above, running off the skylight which spread a dim light down the stairwell. He ascended the stairs.

There was no light beyond her door. He was asking himself now if he was really going to ring the bell, of if this was not some morbid joke on himself, a madness of his own to cap the night. What was he doing here? A touch, a push of a button, and turning back would be impossible.

He could hear his breath and the rain pouring above and his heart thudding in his ears. His palms were soaked with sweat and rain. He wanted to turn around and go back down but instead he reached forward the pressed the bell.

"Who is it?"

"It's me."

"Charlie? Just a minute." There was a squeak of the bedspring, a wait, and then the close snap of the doorbolt. The door came open and she stepped into the hallway light. She was wearing pink silk pajamas and her hair was wrapped in a kerchief. "Is anything the matter? Are you all right?"

"Yes—I don't know. I'm sorry about before. I didn't mean it. I blew my top, that's all. I've been working hard, I'm not like this."

"I know." Her hand was under his chin, trying to life it. "You can't look at me, though, can you?"

"No."

She put her head against his chest. "I don't make things easy for you. I should. I know you don't love me, but you may someday. I'm smart enough for you and I don't care if you don't love me. I love you. It's all I care about. It's all I should care about."

"Alice, I—"

She looked up at him. "Will you stay tonight? I've made myself pretty—not for you. I just had to, to feel good. But will you stay?"

He nodded. "I wanted to. I wanted you."

"I'm sorry I called you that word."

Five weeks later, they were on their way to Tompkins County.

The old Chevy convertible flung its headlight beams over the road past the glowing curve markers and the gray birches into the dark woods beyond. Here and there nestled patches of luminescent snow. In the silence the motor sang and the wind flapped through the canvas top. To the left the trees fell away and against the clear sky at the top of the hill Charlie and Alice could see a barn and a silo and, farther back, a house with lights cross the lower floor. There was a moon and in the field below the buildings the moonlight glowed coldly in the brown stubble of cornstalks. In some of the furrows were traces of snow. The trees folded over again.

"It won't be long now," she said.

"About an hour."

She reached for a paper bag on the seat between them. "Do you want something to eat?"

"No, thanks. You go ahead, though."

She left the bag undisturbed and looked ahead at the road. The road widened to three lanes and there were fields on the right side, empty and dark, flowing down to a black stand of trees. Past the trees the hills rose sharply to the skyline. Now and then a light shined. The car rolled over a single-track railroad crossing and on the right a wooden fence suddenly rose. The fence ended at the side of a barn and on the weather-worn wall of the barn was a red metal sign which, in yellow letters, said, *Red Man Tobacco.*

Charlie drew on the cigarette. It hissed up, made an orange spot on the windowpane before him, and went out. Outside, against the black shadow of the mountains, the dim images of the freshly whitewashed farm buildings glimmered and eluded his burning eyes. The moon was low behind the house and overhead, in winter's hardness, stars shone down through thin clouds coasting beneath. In the yard far to the left of the house the topmost branches of a sycamore, thin and leafless above the mountains and against the sky, caught the low moonlight and glistened ice.

He turned from the view and made his way in the darkness back to the bed. He drew again on the cigarette and tapped it out in the ashtray on the night table. He pulled the quilts up about his body. It was an old bed, soft and sweetsmelling.

The clock on the dresser indicated three-ten. He had been here, awake, more than two hours, since they, Alice, her brothers, her parents and himself, had said goodnight to each other and the joking and laughing and drinking and talking of shared events.

It had been one mistake to come, a mistake all his. He should have cut if off as soon as it was clear it had been a mistake to return to her—that it was hopeless. Some maudlin emotion had stopped him, the same that had seized him at her door that night and had caused him to think that he was there, and thus had to give it an honest try. What he wanted to know was how he had convinced himself after the realization had worn in that this was the best, and—for her—gentlest course to follow. How had he concluded that this was the right thing, letting it run right through Christmas?

He threw back the quilts again and swung his legs around to the floor. The roon was cooling down now and the air felt almost solid on his bare skin. He reached to the night table for his cigarettes.

Why had he gone back in the first place? *Jesus Christ!*

He got up and walked to the window and looked out upon the dim landscape. Through the glass came the frigid falling swoon of the wind around the eaves, and to the left, where the top branches of the sycamore had reflected the moon, there was little but darkness. He could hear the branches faintly thrashing. He could see them faintly dipping and bobbing.

Now he was just waiting until they were back in the city. It had been his plan in the beginning to wait until after New Year's. He couldn't do that now. Their emotions did not even have a cleanness to them any more.

Oh, they had made their honest try and had even

achieved a kind of warmth, but it had not lasted long. The scene in the street had killed it in advance. His one hope was that she felt it all, too, and had the same twinge of shame looking at him as he had when he looked at her. It was his one hope, but it was not a very big one. He knew now how it would go at the end, four days from now.

Tomorrow he would drive over to the gas station to see his uncle. Depending on how much talking they did, or whether they wanted to kill an hour playing Spit in the Ocean, Charlie would return here for supper, or call, or something. Christmas morning, he could pick up his uncle again and they would drive to Syracuse. He was not expected back here until the morning after. Alice had not asked to meet his family—Charlie tried to see that as a basis for his hope.

But he was looking forward to the holiday itself, to seeing his sisters, to his mad brother-in-law who always wanted to know how things were doing in the history racket.

How was the history racket? Barely moving, Charlie thought; it was the slow season. Not that his work wasn't moving, because it was, or that he was having trouble with his classes, because he wasn't—it was that he had lost touch. His sense of order had been subverted. He had been looking, these past weeks, not on a particular time and place, one which had evolved out of the times and places past, but on an utterly bewildering chaos. Since the night of the party in the Bronx and the fight in the subway he had gone back to that feeling of unrecorded history, that moment he had had while driving the car. It was too big and his efforts were too desperate. It had come to him recently to try to add to it, take the people around him, what he knew of their lives, and pile them up—but he felt uncertain, as if the whole world would be more than all the parts he could ever put into it.

Still, he had thought of everyone in his mind's reach: his father, his mother, his uncle, Murillo, Alice. In the moments at night before sleep was extracted out of him like the devil's pence, he would relive whole episodes of his life. At times he wondered if he were going mad. He had never heard of anyone having done this, not anyone at all. There was none of the giddiness he had felt about getting home when he had been in Korea. No, this was something new. This was earnest. When he had a moment and remembered it, he turned to it with the diligence of a beaver building a dam.

Korea: one of the things. The road and the frozen children. He had gone through it again and had seen it in inflamed technicolor.

And after, at his mother's grave, what he learned about her and his uncle. It filled him with a sweet pleasure of which he was ashamed, for it was his place, he was sure, to fell nothing at all.

He thought of his father and his sisters and the life down across the road from the gas station—he would see the house tomorrow—and all the intricacies that developed into the joy in his heart when he thought of those years.

He thought of the name Buddy and the relentless crooked ploddings of the personality it denoted, unimportant but to those nearby and important then only by proximity. He could have been born not at all and the vacuum thus created would not have stirred a leaf. Yet that did not make him unhappy. He felt there was no morality in his being or not being.

He stood at the window and drew on the cigarette.

Something was happening. Slowly, diffuse, the lost insight commenced again unfolding: he could see his mother and father again together, not clearly, and his sisters as children—all so vague. Disturbingly, he thought of Skip and Hal and the party in the Brox. Lives overlapped and connected, collided; what each wanted made sense only in itself. Taken together, all ran wild. There was a pattern, he felt sure of it, but it seemed impossible to discern. Worse, he could not put himself in his proper place.

His eyes were drawn up toward the mountains: through the barren trees coursed a glow of headlights. Slowly, from left to right, they turned in and out of view, approaching. Over the silence built the soft steady drone of a motor. The lights curved in among the branches, still

visible through them, then they swung back, shining for a
brief instant directly at him. They turned away a last time
and beamed up a slight incline of the road. He could see
the red points of the tail-lights trailing in the darkness behind. Up over the crest of the hill the car vanished, and
the sound, following, fading, passed after it. He was alone
again.

It was funny, really. He was not expected back at
Alice's for hours, but because his uncle had something else
to do, the time allotted flopped emptily at Charlie's feet.
At first he felt honor-bound to report back to the McCarthy household, present himself in the kitchen, and confess
the things that had worked the change in schedule. It did
not occur to him until he was on the road again that he
could do what he wanted with the time—the only time in
the whole rotten week he would be by himself.

It was mid-afternoon and the road was empty. He fed
the car more gas and it gained speed as it crested a hill
and the next valley was revealed. The road made a
straight descent to a railroad crossing and then went on up
the other side. The woods had been cleared and the
sunlight spread pink and gold over the straw-swept earth.
The sky above was a vivid blue, and in the distance, small
clouds, bright with pink sunshine, were gathering up. He
thought about turning on the radio, but did not do it.

He could not define the mood. It was something like
waiting, but more. There was a tension, springy, like
hanging on a rubber band. At different moments it seemed
that various parts of his body had become more sensitive
and alert than others. He would notice his fingertips, his
palms, the sides of his face. He would feel his eyes in their
sockets.

"I don't want to hurt her!" he yelled, and felt better. He
deliberately summoned up her face. "I don't want to hurt
you," he said softly.

The good feeling passed like a happy memory at a
funeral. The real feeling rolled over him again.

The streets of Ithaca were empty and cold. Cornell, he
knew, was shut down for the holidays. He remembered

wondering, when he had come into Ithaca on Saturday nights, what all the college students did when they were home. He had been so shallow as a kid he had not been able to project it. It had really puzzled him, and now, on his own last Christmas vacation, he had finally remembered. He smiled at the boy who had wondered, and then saw the long distance that boy had had to travel. It wasn't funny; it was a thing that made him feel honest pride.

Once past the shopping district, he put more pressure on the accelerator. He did not know where he was going, only that he was headed west. The sun was low and he put the visor down. The dust in the car swam in the sun's rays; his knuckles on the wheel could feel their warmth. He rolled down the window so he could take pleasure in the whirr of the tires.

The road wound up around a hill, and as he passed a space in the trees on his right, he looked back at the town. The buildings were sinking into the greyness of the trees; the tower of the University Library was pressing against the thin swath of land behind it and the lake beyond that. The lake spread smoothly into the north.

Soon the high-crowned road was straight, and empty as far as he could see. On both sides for great distances lay fields and pastures, flat, even, and yellow to the farther walls and fences, to the uplands and naked woods. Now and then he passed a farm and people working in the yard, or a woman taking wash down from a line behind the house. The color of the weather was on their faces and bright in their eyes. Out in the open again, the land would at times fall away and there would be, for many, many miles, hills and mountains, with mountains beyond them, in sunlight and heavy shadow, under the clouds building up, or under places of blue clear afternoon sky. He could see over the hills and mountains to the horizon where the land and sky merged in a thin film of grey. He could almost sense the curvature of the earth.

On the road ahead a man was walking, his back bent down. On impulse Charlie slowed the car until it was at a stop beside the man. Charlie leaned across the seat and opened the door. "Want a ride?"

He was an old man with wet yellowed eyes. "How's that?"

"A lift! A ride!"

"Oh! Sure thing! Thanks!" He got in. His clothes were foul with liquor and sweat. Charlie opened the vent a little.

"How far down are you going?"

"Just a ways. You can tell I'm deaf, can't you?"

"It's all right!"

"Well, tomorrow's the big day," the old man said.

"That's right. Merry Christmas."

"Same to you, boy."

They were silent. After a mile, a house came up on the left side.

"This is it, here."

"All right."

The man was out on the road again, looking in the car window.

"Well, have a nice Christmas," he said.

"Thank you. You, too."

"You want to come in for a snort? My old woman won't mind. I was thinkin' you were from the city for a while, but I guess you ain't."

"No, I guess I ain't," Charlie said, using the word for the first time in years. "But I can't stop in. I'm sorry."

"Too bad. I wouldn't mind talkin' for a while. Well, I'll be seein' my son tomorrow—he's got kids of his own, you know—and it ought to be a high old time."

"I'm looking forward to the same thing."

"I better get in the house," the old man said. "I'll see you."

Suddenly Charlie extended his hand. "Again, Merry Christmas."

The man shook hands firmly. His skin had the texture of a brick. "That's right, boy. Merry Christmas."

Soon the road was lifting and lowering in long undulations. The steep hills passed, and ahead over the rolling fields, it looked as if it all suddenly fell away, for past the next rise, he could see for what seemed miles—across pale smoky air to a high wall of woods that turned back flat under the sky. As the car pitched forward he could see more: bare tree trunks jutting up from a mat of brown leaves, all along the width of his vision. The space before him brought them incredibly near. To the left the approaching skyline dipped to a notch under which he could make out billows of stone, and then, more to the left, the skyline leveled up again. The car sped through the obscuring final hillock, and unfolding and rolling back in perspective as if the earth itself were in motion—close almost to the touch, and then vast miles distant—the entire vista spread open to him, far more than he wanted to take in at a single glance. Without thinking he turned the car up onto the shoulder, locked the hand brake and stepped out. He was at the rim of the escarpment, and below to the right was Seneca Lake, flat in the grey of still water. It spread northward beyond the lip of land. At this, the southern end, there was a bridge, and on the opposite side, cars and buildings and roads. A car was going over the bridge. Where before he had glimpsed the notch it was now a great bowl formed out of rock and earth and he could see hollows in the boulders hewn by the water's spilling rush. It was Watkin's Glen; now, unexpectedly, it called up the memory of a visit here—some lost summer's afternoon. He felt a sudden cold wind and his attention was drawn back to the lake. It was smooth. Over a part of it a breeze cast tiny ripples, then let it lay still again. There were waves farther up, then just below. His eye caught another car turning from the other side onto the bridge; the car came over and then curved to pass underneath him, out of sight below the out-crop of rock. The wind was like wet ice; it pierced his thin woolen trousers and his light jacket so that he had to think of going back to the car, yet he couldn't leave, not just now. He was urged on to what was here all around him, and what he could sense his body quickening to. It was beyond his five senses: he wanted more; his intellect struggled to tell him what it was.

But then, as if he heard something at his back, he wheeled about. There was nothing to see; behind the quietly vibrating car with its puff of exhaust steaming up, the road curved back through the last hillock. Only half-assuaged, he turned back to the Glen. Now, because something that had occurred to him before returned, a chill raced through him. That he had been here before and had forgotten it caused the chill to forge deeper. In his mind—as they had been that summer—appeared his mother and father and the child-ghosts of his two sisters. As if they were bedroom echoes of a thing that had happened this afternoon, he could hear their shouts and laughter through the torrent of cool water below him. The loveliness and fragility of the memory made him surrender to his fear; for a second he seemed to stand at the precipice of time, and what had been so firm and strong in him trembled, as though the disgorgement of this one forgotten thing thing heaved the foundation of what he was. This beautiful and terrible rolling earth somehow reflected what had trooped across it almost from the first: small, unstately, humanity itself, in grubby grandeur. He knew he was not up to it, that he was trying to hold back a flood with his fingers. He wanted to turn to the chaos of written history, but his sensibilities were drawn back by his primeval parent. Uncontrollably, he kept seeking out visions of his own parents. Of people. Individuals. The great tide of souls spilling through all the nights and days on the first steaming dawn. He went back to the old man on the road, even to Murillo at the party in the Bronx. He wanted to reject something, anything, and stand clear and aloof. He wanted to hate himself for this, for being swallowed by this desire to swallow and accept and comprehend. He wanted to make a reservation about something and he grabbed at the nearest, stongest thing, his own treatment of Alice. But, in this strange detachment—or this final involvement—he could only pity and mourn himself, in the high sense.

It grew dark. The evening star came out, steadier, brighter, than the others. He had an hour to get back to the McCarthy place, and there was no point in delaying any longer.

It was raining outside, a cold wintry drizzle, and from

here, the window of Alice's apartment, he could see down
to the narrow yard—the dust settled over the garbage
cans and the newspapers scattered about, soaking filthily
in the gray rain. He knew he was letting his mind wander,
and that it was wrong. But it was natural, trying to run
away. He could not understand how he had come to hope
for a better time. That he had hoped at all seemed absolutely criminal.

"Why?" she cried again. "Why are you doing this to me?
What do you want from me?"

"I don't want anything—" Keeping his back to her, he
let whatever he was going to say trail off in a noncommit-
tal shrug. Her questions had been the same five or ten
minutes ago, but in thinking of the right, honest way to
answer them, he'd let himself escape. He had not the
slightest notion of what words, sign language, pictures or
Coast Guard signals could possibly express the raw, hurting but tedious emotion he felt. He raised his eyes to the
dreary afternoon and wondered why he had not simply
told her over the telephone that it was over, it was nice
knowing you, and click. But no, somehow he wanted her
to realize that it was nothing she herself had done, that he
had infinitely more to do with the blame than she did. But
there was no way, not both honest and painless. He had
really wanted the impossible. No scars. No anxieties.
Clean. The sun would come up and they would both never
have to work again.

He turned around. She was still sitting on the couch,
her face blotched from crying. There were no lights in the
room. "It was a mistake," he said. "There isn't any more
to it than that. It was simply a mistake."

"You said that an hour ago."

"I'm not lying to you."

"But I want to know *why!* What have you been doing
all this time? If sleeping with me isn't lying, I want to
know what is!"

"I was wrong. I'm sorry. I told you it was my fault."

"Oh, you're so cute, telling me I was a mistake! What
am I supposed to do, just take it? You're walking out on
me! Don't you realize that?"

"Alice, be reasonable—"

"You don't like it! You've got a guilty conscience. Well, I'm sorry for you, I really am."

"Can't you pull yourself together?"

"Do you know what I feel like doing? I feel like killing myself, that's what!"

"Don't be silly."

"What are you trying to do, torture me?"

This was idiotic. He had to get out. "I'm leaving," he said. "Goodbye."

"Go on, get out! Get out!"

The door was open now, and he could hear people coming up from below. He felt a stab of the coming embarrassment—he would have to pass them, whoever they were, on the stairs.

"Go on!" she screeched.

He pulled the door shut behind him. The couple on the stairs was on the landing just beneath him. The sound of the door caused them to lift their gaze to him. They were trying to appear unconcerned. But through the door, as it began, came the sound of Alice's crying. The girl coming up sneered visibly. As he started down past her and then past the man Charlie tried to keep his face hidden, but he could feel their stares. The shame he felt made him want to turn on them, but he kept going, faster with each succeeding stride.

II

During Christmas week Cal worked on papers and reports. It was not that he had that much to do, for on his wall beside his desk he had a time schedule which allotted one day for each four hours' work. He moved along easily, reasonably, rising at ten in the mornings and pacing himself so he finished at dinner-times. He worked, took a break, worked, napped or read a novel. He read *Andersonville*, a book he had received for his birthday in August. He did not touch his Christmas books for fear he might not be able to put one or another of them down.

Once, for a half-hour, he counted the votes of which he

was assured in the election for Chancellor of the fraternity. He had fourteen our of thirty-four, with the rest undecided, uncommitted, and a few definitely for Ewing. At this stage, Cal's chances were excellent. Among the undecideds and uncommitteds were three or four who did not know he was running, and another four or five who did not know that their best friends and mentors were going for Cal. Cal took the list he had made and put it in his wallet.

The week was very pleasant, really. He worked virtually undisturbed. When his mother's cleaning woman came into his room she worked around him, chattering about the fine Christmas everyone seemed to be having, or that he was working too hard. Cal's father was in Hartford at the garage; his mother was in New York the first two days, exchanging gifts and visiting, and the third and fourth days she was still out, in the neighborhood but still visiting.

On the fifth day, Cal drove up to Hartford to meet his father for lunch. His father had asked him to come, explaining that the Christmas rush was over at last for him, and that they could spend an afternoon talking and telling stories, as they had not done very often in the past when they had had the chance, and would not be able to do in the future, when Cal completed school and moved to New York.

It was a good day, about what Cal had expected. He had gone prepared to talk about his plans, which hinged on the responses he received to the letters he would write in the spring, about the Army, about the "future"—meaning his attitude with respect to situations, his own marriage for example, which had yet to occur. His father wanted to hear about those things, but just as much, as they lingered in the restaurant and then drove slowly through the busy streets back to the garage, he wanted to hear about Cal's social life, the election, even his thoughts. As Cal had anticipated, his father wanted to talk about himself—about the old days, what he had done, what he should have done. A lot of it was familiar stuff, but some of it was new. There was a lot, Cal was sure, that he was

never going to hear. It made no difference. He knew all the
had to, to know how much he cared for his father. One
afternoon, during which he would do nothing, walk
around, get shown off to the dispatchers and the stewards
at the garage, was little enough he could do for his father,
helping him who was trying to close the gap between the
generations, who was trying to do something for Cal
himself.

Cal saw his father as a typical American success story,
and he was, of a kind. As he had told his son in the
back yard of the summer house at Groton Long Point that
Sunday in September, he had everything a man could
reasonably want. And more—though this had gone unsaid
but clearly not unstated—he had earned it all himself. He
had started with almost literally nothing, taking a chance
when he was young, working and then working harder,
pushing and building.

When George Torrenson took a position with one of
the Hartford insurance companies after his graduation
from Colby College in nineteen twenty-two, he felt as if
he were being interred alive. It worked on him physically.
He developed symptoms of asthma. He stayed awake
nights, his supper burning and knotting in his stomach. He
was unable to swallow his breakfasts, as though his throat
had rotted. He hated going to work, being on time,
hello-ing the idiot boss, applying himself at the stroke of
nine to the mass of routine paper-work on his desk, like a
man scratching his soul out of his fountain pen, bit by
sacred little bit. He was not allowed to leave his desk
without signing a sheet. He was allotted ten minutes "personal" during the day, and he had to hoard it. He could
look around and see men older than himself, parched and
sterile, their juices blotted up by the paper on which they
scrawled. For a while, for many, many weeks, George
considered abandoning it all, fleeing across the wide,
bright, unknown United States, maybe interesting himself
in one of the social or political organizations he had read
about. He read tracts on the martyrdom of the Wobblies
and in his heart he worshipped them, not for their hero-

ism, not for their cause—for he was undecided on that, but for flinging them selves against the great system, the sucker of souls.

When in nineteen twenty-two he thought of his boyhood he could remember it in fine detail: what he had done, who he had known. One long night he counted up the number of people who were gone, dead: a boy drowned, a girl dead in childbirth, an old man down the street whose life faded one afternoon into the prissy sheets of his disintegration. George thought of these things because he wanted to be realistic. He was only going to live once.

He dismissed his old daydreams. As a boy he had read Horatio Alger's stories, and at night, listening to katydids and crickets, he had lived them. In nineteen twenty-two, of course, they embarrassed him. But eight and ten years earlier—spliced between wonderings of women, recollections of ballfield triumphs—the wheeling-and-dealing George Torenson, the country's youngest success, sold and bought, made and broke, and won, always won. He stode through his factories and offices, snapping orders, flicking ingenious sweet changes in his organization. He blushed and stammered at functions honoring him. It was a swell dream.

In the summer and fall after his graduation from college, he could hear the rolling knell of futility and loss. Only a prostitute he knew gave him escape. She sustained him in the warm blubber of her breasts. He would lie back and weep softly and she would take care of him. His parents, who were over sixty, thought he was at the Y.M.C.A. playing handball.

That November in the restaurant where he bought his meal tickets, George overheard the conversation that changed his life. He had stayed away from the stock market because he did not know enough about it and he was afraid. But a lot of people were making money and everything was beginning to climb in price. But it seemed logical to him that if some were making money, others were losing—money couldn't be cut out of thin air. He did not want to be one of the losers. The two men talking worked for George's company, in the investment section.

George had heard they had made money on their own, and it *was* possible, for they appeared to be living beyond their means, living like hundred-dollar-a-week men. One of them sent his family to Portsmouth in the summers. George listened, borrowed five hundred dollars from his father, bought the stock he had mentioned, and watched the listings as in three months the stock raced up to twenty-four hundred. He sold, repaid the loan, followed the advice of one of the columns he had begun to read, and ran the money up to four thousand. It was like a symphony to him, rising and building like a tide. He quit seeing his prostitute. But the following summer he had eleven thousand dollars—and in was in cash, *cash,* because he was afraid with the fear of man going too far.

The money had to be put into something durable. It had to be something he could slap with his hand or sift through his fingers. It made sense. He dreaded going back to that woman and her "Come on, dearie, what have you got for me this time?" He wanted something *real.*

It was his father who supplied the idea of buying a bus. There was a need for them. Soon the field would be closed. Buses represented the public transportation for the future. There would always be some people who could not afford cars, and the railroads and trolleys did not always go exactly where people wanted them, or at the right times. Eleven thousand dollars could fill part of the gap. And he could always get part of his money back by selling them, if he failed.

George bought a Yellow Coach. It had thirty seats, a V-12 motor, a four-speed transmission and a turnstile. He took out liability and collision insurance, secured a permit, bought advertisements in the local newspapers, and started running his bus in through the suburbs to downtown Hartford. He worked from six-thirty in the morning until one-thirty in the afternoon, and then after lunch began again at two o'clock to work until nine. On Sundays he started at noon and quit at seven. The fare was a nickel. On the first day his gross was two dollars, on the second, two fifty-five, but in two weeks he had standees on nearly every trip. In two months it was time to go to a bank for a loan, to a lawyer to protect him from the bank, and to his father's friends to protect him from the lawyer.

By nineteen twenty-five, George had ten buses on three routes, and still owned seventy percent of his company. He bought an abandoned barn on the outskirts of town to house the equipment, and first he had the barn fireproofed, then he dug his own gas tanks, and finally he had the barn torn down and a real garage put up, the ground all around covered over with asphalt, and a hurricane fence put around the place.

In the early thirties, when the question of franchising arose, George Torrenson had a worth of six hundred thousand dollars, and the ability to satisfy the state that he could meet his public responsibilities. His thirty-five buses, he maintained at a commission hearing, could cover his twelve routes like a shortstop with Saint Vitus' dance. The remark made the newspapers and for a while he was a bit of a celebrity.

He took his first vacation in the summer of 'thirty-two. His parents were dead now and the company ran itself, smooth and well-oiled. It was routine now; even growth, somewhat slowed by the depression, was routine, and a man was justified in standing away a while to watch it hum.

He went to the Haddon Hall in Atlantic City, driving down in a new Buick roadster with the trunk filled with new luggage which in turn was filled with new clothes. He was determined not to scrimp; he had reserved a two-room suite overlooking the boardwalk. On the first evening, as he stood at his windows gazing out to the beach and the lights of the ships on the sea, he felt that quailing in his stomach which said he was spending too much money, he was going past his limit, he could get into trouble. But the feeling was mixed with the trebling of expectancy, and as he slipped on his dancing pumps and brushed the lint from his tux—trying to remember to call it a dinner jacket—he felt he could fly downstairs from the window, that he was capable of anything.

But in the dining room when he saw her, he was

stopped as if by a wall. She was sitting with an older
couple, clearly her parents, some two or three tables
away. He could not stop looking at her, her pretty auburn
hair, her ready smile, and the polished, intelligent but
unpracticed way she could look around at seemingly nothing, take it in and continue with her business. When her
eyes fell on him he was still left in such a doubt as to
whether she *was* looking at him that the desire to go over
to her, or just get up and speak from where he was, was
so powerful and devouring that he thought of running out,
or ordering a newspaper, a hideous gaucherie, just to
relieve himself. But at the precise moment the three of
them got up to leave, he too, was on his feet, hurriedly
scribbling his name on his check. It was impossible to be
discreet; he did not even think of it. She passed within
inches of him, but as if he were a potted plant. He was
frantic and in a rage—but after he had given the trio a
few steps' start, he was in a delirium of study, of her
neck, her back. Her evening dress was cut low, her skin
was browned lightly, gleaming, and under it he could see
the smooth play of a woman's small muscles, from tennis
or swimming. He imagined her on a golf course, and
though he had not glimpsed so much as her toe, he could
picture her slim brown legs under a swirling skirt. He
wished he were better looking, that he'd had more experience with women—despite the thought that he would hate
her wretchedly if she required those things in a man.

In the lobby the trio stopped to talk. She was turned
almost toward him, and he shrunk back a step, as though
they were alone, the two of them. In truth, to him,
everyone else was like a shadow in the whirr of lobby
noise. She took notice of him now, probably out of the
awkwardness of his movement, and a small, deprecating
smile traced her thin lips, which were colored dark because of the darkness of her skin. Her eyes, too, were
dark, very dark, making the whites brighter still—like a
Negress, he had to think irreverently. But that idea made
her more exciting. He wondered how the rest of her
looked. Her dress was very tight; he could detect the tiny
protrusion of her stomach—but then he looked away,

toward the doors, flushing as if his actions and thoughts were open to her.

Then the amazing thing happened; her parents went out through the revolving doors, and she stood alone. He struggled for the courage to go over, even while the others were in view, but he could not. She was moving, going toward the desk. He was horrified. She went on to the elevators. She had a long, straight stride; he could imagine her legs under her dress, slim, brown and muscular. Now, as if a spring in him had been wound so tightly it had had to snap, George was propelled toward the desk.

"What's that girl's name?"

"I'm sorry, sir—"

George glanced over his shoulder; one of the elevators was almost down to the lobby. He snatched a bill out of his pocket and thrust it at the clerk. The clerk smiled with the superiority of an old lady schoolteacher.

"Louise Allison."

George wheeled around. The elevator was open; Louise—it took that fraction of a second for him to embrace the name—was stepping inside. She turned around and looked at him as the doors clapped shut. It was like awakening before the end of a dream.

But the pointer over the doors did not move. He was struck by the fear that something was wrong inside, that something was happening, the elevator falling. But when the doors rolled open again, like a flower unfolding. She stepped out, smiling at him, and winked. He could not move. She came all the way to him.

"I don't know you, do I?"

"No-no."

"You look so desperate."

"Oh, God. I'm so ashamed. I apologize—" He was gaining control again quickly—"Louise."

She smiled. "Would you like to go back to the dining room for coffee? That's a nice public place. You understand."

"Oh, yes, of course. Please don't think badly of me. My name is George Torrenson. I'm not a madman—"

But later he told her that, had she not come out of the

elevator, he would have probably checked out that same evening. *She* brought it to the surface; her manner made him *want* to confess it.

She was from Scranton and had gone to Vassar and was living in New York now, working for a publisher. This was the second vacation she had spent with her parents this way, meeting them at their destination. She was twenty-four.

He did not tell her right away about himself or what he did. That she lived and worked in New York unnerved him; he was afraid it would brand him a bumpkin. More, that she was twenty-four and still single, had gone to a really smart college and worked in something chic like publishing disturbed him very deeply; he was sure she might have such a shabby personal story to tell that he would never hear the full truth of it. That she could have had many, many lovers, all greasy and grotesque types, made him want to cry. Within two hours he was wishing he had met her years ago, before it could have happened. Finally he asked her to go for a ride.

They headed south toward Cape May. He could no longer control himself. "What kind of girl are you?"

"That's a new one."

You've heard a lot. "No, I mean it."

"Well, you just take you time finding out."

He hated the implied threat, and thought now that perhaps she was some kind of frigid old maid-to-be. The two-lane road was empty and dark, and the sultry air buffeted over the windshield. He wanted to pull off to the side, but he was afraid. "Listen," he said, "I want to be friends more than I want trouble. I don't like to talk like this, but I want it to be clear. I'm not a nut. How long are you going to be down here?"

"Another week."

"All right," he said.

"How about you?"

She had come to him; he felt faintly satisfied. "I don't know," he said.

She took his hand and squeezed it. "Stop being an old sourpuss."

"I'm not a sourpuss."

"You don't know how much you are. In the lobby there, you looked like one of those Union Square communists with the mad hair and all, the way you glared at me."

He said nothing; he was too hurt and ashamed. He wanted to tell her why he had seemed that way, but he didn't want to give in. "Will you go swimming with me tomorrow?"

"We'll see," she said.

"You're holding my hand."

"Can't I keep something in reserve? You come at me the way an angry child would—I don't know. You just want to consume me, or something. Must you have and know everything at once?"

"Do you want me to take you back to the hotel?"

She was quiet then, "No."

"All right. We'll find a roadhouse or some place to talk in."

In the six remaining days they went swimming and played tennis and he took her dancing and for long walks or rides. By the end of the week he knew she had never been in love and, worse, that she did not love him. At best, he was good company for her—at the very best. Most of the time they were at a stand-off. He wanted her badly, but did not want her to know it, and so he was sure she knew it better than if he had told her outright, in one curt sentence. He was sure they were both clinging to the delicate attraction between them. She *was* attracted to him, because she never refused the simple, safe demands he made on her. Before falling asleep each night, he felt sure he could seduce her at any time. She did not mind dancing close, or wearing clothes that revealed her bosom— several times on the beach and on the dance floor, because of the cut of her clothes and the attitude of her body, he had seen her nipples. Oh, she was aware of what she awakened in him. Yet the rest of the play they engaged in forbade sex, just as much as the horribly hot weather. Sometimes he was sure that if it had been cooler they would have been lovers almost instantly, despite what they felt. But the heat was the last veil that made the sum of all the veils impenetrable. He went downstairs to each new lobby-meeting in a hateful, anguished rush.

He drove her back to New York. She softened to him. She smiled more, as if to say the artificiality of the resort was really behind them, and they could love each other openly the way people in real contact should come to do.

The rest of their courtship had to be brief. Her apartment was in Brooklyn, a terrible distance from Hartford. She came up three times for weekends, and he drove down the other times until late October, when he brought her a ring. He had not proposed; it had not seemed necessary. The hardship of the distance pulled them closer together, they exchanged letters during the weeks, the constant unsatisfied sexuality of the first six days swam into the deeper, broader base of their communication—on Fridays his eagerness to see her turned like warm pinwheels of delight. He saw her in a different way, as someone splendid and tender and thoughtful. On those weekends in Brooklyn he would stay at the Hotel Saint George, though later on, when they were very late getting to her place, she suggested that he sleep on her couch. He did not accept because he did not want the temptation, even if it seemed implicit that if he knocked at her bedroom door, he would be welcome. Now he wanted to keep their affair thoroughly pure, just because they were heading into marriage. It was his secret pleasure that she was weakening, but he interpreted it to mean that the base of their relationship was stronger, that his own feeling was truer. The slackening of their sexual attraction gratified him. He wanted his marriage to last. He wanted his home founded deep in bedrock.

They were married on the first Saturday of November, in a judge's apartment on the upper west side of Manhattan. Because George had been in Hartford preparing the house he had rented, she had made the arrangements. Her parents were there, seeming pleased to see him. Her father could accept George's word that he could not get away from business at this time of year, so close to the holidays, but her mother appeared slightly unhappy about being

cheated of a big home-town church wedding. The party
went to the Waldorf-Astoria after the ceremony. Louise
had given over her apartment to her parents for the
weekend—George had been thinking *they* would be going
there—and at seven o'clock, the celebration was over, the
participants full-stomach tired. At seven o'clock the, the
first night began, the disjointed, out-of-pace night, aritifi-
cial and hotel-room bleak, unhappy—scarred in their
memories by a nervous, sweating, struggling failure.

Their return to Hartford the following afternoon
marked the beginning of the most miserable months of
George's life. Though she did not say it, Louise did not
like the house; it was dim and dismal and out-of-style. Not
even the hours she had waited to mention eventual moving
could hide from him her deep displeasure. That second
night, as he lay awake and staring at his lighted cigarette
because she had denied him—she was hurting, she said,
did he mind so much? She would make it up—he felt
off-balance, pushed, about to be pushed again, poked,
prodded and herded into a way of living he did not want.
His hate for her was fierce. Looking at her—she made a
disgusting snoring noise when she slept—he could understand how men less reasonable than he had come to
murder and dismember their women. His own urge to
smash her as she lay there was immense.

He did hit her later on. The pattern they had built
caused her to sulk when she was angry. She would go for
days without speaking. He did not know what she wanted.
He bought he a car, let her run up a bill at the bookstore, submitted to her friends who kept inviting them to
parties in the city when he hated the city and her friends
and their cheap bright talk. He even met her for lunch
three times a week, dressing neatly to meet her, going to
the better restaurants. But in the evenings, if he tried to
speak to her when she was reading, he would have to
yell—even scream—to get her attention. A polite
"Louise?" meant nothing; she ignored him. She would say
she hadn't heard him; she had been absorbed in her book.

It was after some trivial thing—he was never able to
remember what—that he struck her. He was yelling, tell-

ing her that she did not care about him, that she cared
nothing for his work or the fact that he had built what he
had out of nothing, when she yelled back, crying, "Do you
know what's the matter with me? I'm bored! I'm bored
stiff! And you're right: I don't care! Not a bit! And do
you know something else? You're the dullest man I've
ever known! Absolutely—!" He slapped her face, hitting
her only with his fingertips, and then he stood over her,
slapping her arms and her sides, hoping to wring some
satisfaction out of his brutality, but thinking he had seen
his father slap his mother once, and thinking how sickening the act had been. He stormed out, then, quivering with
unspent anger, and went for a drive. He went to every
place he had ever heard of as being a hangout for prostitutes or pickups, but he found only one woman—an old
Negress who wanted more money than he would have
spent on even the most beautiful girl—and he sped home
disgusted with himself.

Louise was awake in bed, sorry. She wanted to repair
it, and though the rage was past, he took the moment of
this advantage, and hoped calmly as she did what he
demanded that it would satisfy him, that he would wake
up whole, that somehow out of the continuing dirt something solid would be established, something worth-while.

She became pregnant three months later, and the tran-
quility was over. To his impending fatherhood he had no
reaction. He did not know how to react. It was something
strange and tasteless to him, but because her discomfort
was immediate, he strove to be kind, bringing her little
presents, telling her his thoughts and ideas about the child,
about being a parent, trying to have her believe he
thought of it always, when in fact he thought of it rarely,
like a debt he had to pay.

It was later that he reacted, when he could see what the
child was doing. He could not stand to look at her. Her
belly grew monstrous, even her pores were dilated, her
navel was as large as a fifty-cent piece. Her breasts
swelled, the nippled enlarged and turned brown, and the
brief moments he saw her unclothed he saw how the
breasts drooped flatly on the swollen stomach. Her slim

body would never look the same again. She would look flaccid and loose and he would not be able to stand her. It came to him one day just why prostitutes did exist, that a man had to be attracted to sex if he was going to have it at all, that the perfume and the mystery were good things, as much a part of the civilization as—as insurance.

The night she invited him to feel the baby kick was the night he moved out to the living room couch. The jerking thrust under her skin chilled him.

The changes worked in the six months following the delivery were not lost on him. He was delighted to see her return to almost exactly what she had been before. He had talked her out of breast feeding Cal because of the permanent damage the kid might do. Breast feeding was not very popular, anyway. She agreed to using formula, and thanked him afterward, when her bosom was high and small again, exciting in a new way, a maturer way. The marks on her stomach near her pubis faded so much he had to look to find them. He was very happy, very happy.

Over a period longer than six months he learned another thing—that they would be happier with each other if they were not always around each other's necks. Separation, for them, at least, and for short durations, was a good thing. More actively than ever he took part in hunting and fishing and allowed her the trips to Scranton. It seemed to him that both profited from their different interests; the routine of the household ran more smoothly, and all but one of their arguments were petty and easily resolved.

Their final struggle took place when Cal was eight or nine. Louise had gotten pregnant again, but on the third month spontaneously aborted. She was sick for weeks afterward, and did not regain her proper strength for half a year. It was after that interval, when she brought up the subject one night just in passing, that an idea came to him. He had heard recently of similar incidents, and how many people had solved the problem.

"Listen, do you want any more kids?"

"I don't know. I'm not sure at all now, George."

"Well, you're almost thirty-five. It could be tougher on you than before."

"I know." They were in bed and the lights were out.

"There's another thing, I'd be sixty before we could get another one out of the house, if you had him tomorrow. Do you know what I mean? I want to have some time for myself, and I don't want to be old when I get it. I mean, we're entitled to some time of our own, don't you think?"

"You don't want another child, then, do you?"

"No, to be honest."

She was quiet. He thought that was as good a moment as any to bring up his idea. He said, "Some of the drivers' wives had just the same trouble you did. One was in her forties. He—her husband—was telling me about it. He was scared to death of losing her—you know. He had her into the hospital for that operation, what do you call it, a hysterectomy—"

"No."

"What?"

"I won't do it. I don't want to be turned into a female vegetable."

"That's a lot of nonsense. It's nothing like that at all. You're just the same as before."

"What, did you hear that from your drivers? How would they know?"

"Oh, come on," he said. "Nothing happens to you as far as sex goes. They don't touch that part of you. But you don't have any more periods—I think."

"No. I don't love menstruating, but I don't hate it, either. Besides, I like the risk involved. I like taking a chance. Sex wouldn't be two beans to me if you were sterile. Or to any woman, I'm sure. All that huffing and puffing for nothing would be ridiculous."

"I'd like you to think about it," he said in the cool tone he had always used with her.

"I'm thinking about something else, just what I was thinking before I miscarried—that I wouldn't mind having a baby again. A baby. Holding it and fussing over it and giving it a bottle. I would like that again."

"Not me," he said.

"I know. I know all about it."

"Well, I want you to think about what I just said. *I* want you to."

He mentioned it again, and she refused a second time. He forgot about it. But then a second time she became pregnant, within a year of the first miscarriage, and again, after three months, she aborted. Now he began to believe she would die if she conceived any more. Perhaps she didn't know her own mind; perhaps she really didn't want another child. He remembered Gary Cooper and Helen Hayes in *A Farewell to Arms*. It was very dramatic and romantic, but he didn't want anything like that to happen, not at all. There had been no kid to be stuck with in *A Farewell to Arms*. When Louise was well again he pressed the subject of the operation, and he kept pressing it until she gave in. She made sure he knew she was going against her will, and when he visited her the first time in the hospital she looked around from the window, pale and haggard, and said, "Are-you-happy-*now*?"

In his anger he was glad he had left Cal with neighbors; he believed she would have said it even if he had been in the room.

Cal was a simpering, whiney child. He had been a whiney baby. George's first idea of what parenthood would mean came in the hospital, when he first saw the child; the baby was nothing but a squealing ball of reddened flesh and he, George, felt absolutely nothing for it. When Cal was brought home the new father did not even try to feign interest in him. The truth was that he nearly loathed the child—there seemed to be nothing likable about him. George had been hoping that the sleeping on the couch would come to an end with the delivery, but on the first night, a night of continual crying, it was clear that it was not; the baby, of course, had to be near his mother, and George needed his own sleep. It was months, therefore, before he could get back into his own bed.

Luckily enough, Cal slept in the early evenings the first few years, so George did not have to endure him for more than an hour or so every suppertime. Now and then he would try to be friendly toward the child, but he would do something wrong or clumsy and Cal would start crying. George would yell to Louise to come and take the baby away from him.

Naturally Cal was closer to his mother, but the only thing George resented in it was that he had to hear at the day's end whatever Cal had done, or gooed, or said, from crawling and walking all the way up to his first achievements in school. It was not until the kid was older and more reasonable and better able to listen to what was being said that George awakened to him. Still, through his childhood, Cal was whiney. George took him fishing and hunting, and at least in the beginning, Cal showed no interest in those things. He felt sorry for the animal and fish, which was the woman's attitude. After a while, however, along about his twelfth or thirteenth birthday, Cal changed. George did not know if it was some kind of minor miracle, or the new friends Cal was making—they had just moved to the big house in Darien—or the new, wider scope of the boy's vision, due to puberty. But Cal began to take part in sports and read the sports pages. He asked for a bar bell set—and got it; and more, he used it—and he started to take an interest in cars and photography. When George suggested they subscribe together to magazines both of them like, the boy leaped at the idea. The change was both amusing and startling; George wanted to ask about it, but he did not know whom to ask, or what. In time, he quit wondering.

But he took note of the eclipse of Louise. It was as if Cal were rejecting and disowning her because he had discovered she was not preparing him properly for the world he had to deal with. Whatever Louise's reaction, she kept it to herself. She accepted her consignment to Cal's emotional trash heap, and withdrew again to her books, her girl-friends and her shopping. She intruded only rarely. For the next three or four years, until Cal began to manage his affairs for himself, he was the exclusive property of his father. George took him hunting and fishing, and told him stories of life and the world of business and men.

But then at seventeen it was time for Cal to rebel

again, and for a long period he was no one's property. Most of the time he simply kept to himself. There were fights and tantrums, but they were never serious. He stayed unresolved about his career, but that did not impede his progress toward manhood.

Cal had shaped up. Of course, he had inherited his mother's talent for analysis, and, to George's thinking, he tended to be intellectual and bookish, but they would all be assets in tomorrow's world. A man needed more and more tools, just to get by. George had always wanted to see Cal make it on his own. A sizeable estate awaited the boy, but what was that without the strength to manage it? George had wanted Cal to be a man, and more and more, it looked like the kid had made it. Yes, and George was ready to say it aloud, the kid was going to be all right.

Cal had learned one real lesson from his mother, and it was that it took a long time to know a person. All the years of his early childhood, when she had had him for herself alone, she had been a saint. She had been reasonable and kind, and she had never resisted him when he crawled onto her lap and nuzzled into her bosom. She was the beautiful lady: she was in King Arthur and Robin Hood, and she could pick him up when he fell in the yard, put his helmet on straight and load his gun, kiss the sore spot better and wink at him. While she was sitting under the tree reading her book his world had a beginning and an end.

She changed when he changed, around eight or nine. She was sick for a while, and when she came out of the hospital, she was different. He want to play with the other kids and at first they came to his yard or he went to their yards and all the mothers gave them cookies and milk. It was good for a while, but when he had a fight with a kid he would forget it soon but she never forgot so that it put him in bad with the other mothers—they blamed him because of her.

She made sure he was always outside after school, or, on rainy days, on the first floor where she could see him. Sometimes the kids would visit on rainy days but she always called while he was at someone else's house to tell him to get bread or milk or something, on his way home. She kept pestering him. She said she wanted to make sure he was all right.

His father stuck up for him once and wanted to know what she was worried about, but all she would say was that boys ought to be watched. His father said she was nuts and walked out of the room.

She didn't trust Cal, and he learned it soon enough. One of the other fellows' mothers even said it to him after she telephoned him at the fellow's house, "Doesn't she ever give you any privacy, sweetie? Doesn't she trust you?"

Cal just wanted to be like the other fellows. Like going away to private school. They were all doing it. The kids who had more freedom had more adventure, too. It was so. *He* had to stick close to the house and listen to the stories the other kids told, about what they had done and seen. Sometimes he even thought about *being* someone else, changing places with him. But he couldn't think of anyone who wanted to be *him*.

His father was always in the background—too busy. It was all right. Only the boys with older brothers had fathers who took them to ball games and places. Cal went with his father a couple to times, no more or less than the other fellows, he thought. You couldn't expect a man to work all week and then devote all his time to his son. He had to have time to devote to himself, like everyone. *She* had free time all week, when Cal was in school.

Then, as Cal got older and started defending himself, she got bitchy. She shrieked at him. Finally, when he was thirteen, she walked into the bathroom while he was taking a bath. She got all the way in, too, and took a good look. He saw her. He was beginning to grow hair. Soon after, she asked him if he was playing with himself. He could have slit her throat.

The old man, though—he was different. He wasn't as clever as she was, but he knew more about people. He had bided his time, waiting for Cal to come around. Suddenly they clicked—like that. His father didn't push him. He made room for Cal. He brought Cal into his affairs. To show how much confidence he had in his son, he took Cal down to the playroom one night and spent hours tell him about sex. How it worked. He told him about menstruation. And menopause.

He was honest, too. He hadn't been a great lover. He had been afraid of women. But he guessed he had done all right. He didn't know. He didn't have many stories to tell, he said.

As Cal moved further into his teens his mother became a genuine, garden-variety shrew. She opened her mouth only when it suited her, or when she felt guilty. Cal starting calling her "The Madame." She made little forays into mother-love. If Cal kept up with the articles in her silly magazines, or her novels by those ridiculous women with three names, he could have spotted the forays coming, but it wasn't worth the effort. As far as he was concerned, his mother was a dead issue.

On New Year's Day, nineteen fifty-six, Cal received a long-distance telephone call from fraternity brother George DeYoung, who was at his home in Watertown, New York.

"Happy New Year!"

"Sure, George. What do you want?"

"You sound like you have a head."

"What do you think? And I'm typing up a paper as well."

"Then I won't ask you how many times you've written nineteen fifty-five."

"Thanks for sparing me." Idiot, Cal thought. Cal had been awake two hours, since noon, and he still felt as if he had stepped on a land mine. He was in good company. His father was on the couch in the living room, his feet on the ottoman, his hand to his head. He looked like a silent movie actor trying to express tragedy. Now, of DeYoung, Cal demanded, "What do you want, George? I haven't got all day."

"I just got a call from Mannings in Boston. He's at the convention."

"I know. Thanks for the flash. Is he having fun?"

"No."

"Give me his address, I'll send him a card."

"This is no time for funny stuff, Torrenson. The election is at stake. Ewing is there and he's buttering up the guys for another term."

"You called to tell me *this*?"

"I think you ought to go up there. Put in an appearance. You could drive up and be there tonight—an hour is all you'd need. Just show up. Say you changed your mind, something like that."

"Just a minute." Cal put down the phone and walked into the living room. "Dad," he called *sotto voce*, "do you want a laugh?"

"No."

"I mean it. Go out to the kitchen and pick up the other phone and listen to this fellow. It's George DeYoung, the one who's supposed to be the political mastermind."

"Couldn't you tell me about it?"

"You wouldn't believe it."

"All right." Cal watched the man struggle up from the couch and shuffle past him toward the dining room and the kitchen beyond. He waited a proper interval, then went to the hall telephone.

"George? I just wanted to get a cigarette. Let me have that again, will you?"

"Is somebody on the extension? I just heard a click."

"That was me. I found my cigarettes in the kitchen and I didn't want to walk back."

"Oh."

"Let's have it again, then, will you? I'm not too on-the-ball today."

DeYoung repeated his idea. "Don't you think this isn't serious, Torrenson. Mannings told me that Ewing had a brand-new face on, he's one of the boys, just so he can get elected again. He's been buying liquor and everything."

Cal wondered what "everything" could include. He could see Ewing guiding the Cornell boys into a whorehouse, introducing them to the girls, and waving bye-bye as the couples disappeared. "And this is all so he can have it on his job résumés, eh?"

"I guess so," DeYoung said, sounding like Henry Aldrich.

"To hell with him. He can have it."

"You're not serious!"

"I should have asked you the same question. I'm not going to Boston, particularly for a fraternity chancellorship. You ought to have your head cleaned and blocked, George."

"Are you going to New York anyway? I mean, between semesters?"

Cal was tempted to say no, or just hang up, but he said, "Yes, George, I'm going."

"Good." DeYoung let out a lung-collapsing sigh. "But you have to get on the ball, Torrenson. We can't afford to lose this. We have to *win*!"

"Not we, George, me. *I'm going* to win."

"What does that mean?"

"It means your three minutes are up. Goodbye."

"Hey, wait a minute. Who's been talking you up for the Chancellorship all these months? Who's put in the work?"

"Thanks for reminding me."

"Don't you think you owe us the little effort it takes to show some house spirit?"

"I'm going to New York, aren't I?"

"I think we ought to shop around for a new candidate. I don't like the way you're slicing this."

"It's a little late for that now, George. You've done everything but carve our names together on a tree. Wouldn't you look silly talking me down at this point?"

"It could be done."

"If somebody else wins, George, you'd really be out. This way you're in—a little. I have to figure out just how much you're in. But why don't you go back to the Rose Bowl game on television and forget about Boston and Ewing and have a fantasy about being house treasurer or secretary or something?"

"You're a prick, Torrenson. I was trying to do you a favor."

"Impossible on the morning after, George. And don't swear over the telephone, it's against the law."

"Is it?"

"Yes. Goodbye, George. I'll see you tomorrow night." And he hung up.

"Boston!" his father said, coming out of the kitchen. "Why, the boy has absolutely twisted his cork!"

"He's lucky. I could have talked *him* into going."

"You should have."

Cal lit a cigarette. "It's sad the convention isn't in Los Angeles. You would have had the pleasure of hearing him ask me to fly."

"You were rough on him at the end."

"Some people like to be beaten," Cal said. "Who am I to argue?"

"Sure, like some women with belts and so on."

"I've been watching this bird DeYoung for months. He's been giving it to me in his own subtle little way. I've just been waiting to see which way I could get the best of him. This was a time I could experiment."

"Want some coffee? Your mother made fresh before she went back to bed."

"All right. Come on, I'll heat it."

"That's what I had in mind." He grinned and clapped his arm around Cal's shoulder. They walked out to the kitchen. "You're all right," his father said, "But right now I want a little service. I'm your father and I'm hung over, so what do you say?"

"I say okay," Cal said and grinned, and then blushed.

The Pontiac convertible wheeled up to the gas pumps and in the office the signal bell gave its familiar two rings. Charlie waited a moment, then went out, hunching against the cold. The redhead rolled down the window. "Hi. How are you?"

"Fine, Red. Just gas?"

"No, I'm having trouble and it has to be fixed. I'm going back to school today—I hope. The motor is boiling over."

He frowned. "Did you check the radiator?"

"No. It happened just now, on my way to the parkway. And it hadn't been running more than ten minutes."

"All right, let's take a look." He opened the hood as she got out of the car. "Did you ever have anything like this before? These old buzzards are famous for overheating."

"No, never."

"Say, listen, I forgot your name." He was using a rag to remove the radiator cap.

"Elaine."

"Elaine," he said. "There, you have no coolant. It's stone empty. There's a leak somewhere."

"What does it mean? Will I be able to leave today?"

"It means you can't move the car until I find the leak." He was standing up again. "It could be serious or it could be simple—and cheap. It'll be as cheap as I can possibly make it, in fairness to the boss.—By the way, my name is Charlie."

"I remember. I remember City College, too."

"Let's have another look," he said, turning again to the open hood. The lower radiator hose was loose at the engine block, and the block, of course, was hot. "Say," he called, "did you hit a bump or something just now?"

"No."

"How about yesterday?"

"—Yes! Yes, I did, just before I got home."

"You have a loose hose. Do you want to see it?"

"May I?" She stretched over the fender beside him. She was wearing slacks and a heavy jacket and on the cold air he could smell her make-up and her hair. "No, I can't see it," she said.

"Down at the bottom. There—watch it, it's hot!" But she had pressed against him even more to see and he had lost his balance. His hand touched the block a second and in reflex he pushed back, almost knocking her down. They faced each other.

"Oh, I am sorry," she said. "I didn't realize—"

"No, forget it. Are you all right? I didn't intend to shove you like that." He examined his hand: a two-inch welt was forming across the back of it.

"You'd better put something on that to keep it from drying up."

"I guess so. Wait here, I'll be right back." He walked

back to the office where the mechanic was now sitting at the desk, tilting a bottle of soda up to his mouth.

"What did you do, teach, burn yourself?"

"Yes, is there anything for it?"

The mechanic pulled open one of the desk drawers and slid a jar across the desk. "Have some Vaseline. Take all you want, it belongs to the boss's wife."

"You're a scream."

"That's some piece," the mechanic said, pointing the soda bottle toward the window. "A big job, just the way I like them. It that how you got your hand burned, teach?"

"Lay off."

"Try to control yourself now and don't make any anti-Semitic remarks. She's coming in. Nice walk, too."

"How is it?" she asked, closing the door.

"I think I'm overacting, to tell the truth." Charlie turned to the mechanic. "What time is it, Skeezix?"

"Eleven-thirty—teach." He looked surprised; perhaps because she was present he had thought Charlie would forego the nicknames.

"Listen," Charlie said to Elaine, "either way you cut it, it's going to be a wait. You can't put fresh cold water in that block. I would rather wait myself before slipping that hose on again."

"How long?"

"Long enough for lunch, if that's all right with you."

"Oh, look at him go!" the mechanic exclaimed.

"I hope you were listening," Charlie said to him. "There'll be questions later." He began to unbutton his coveralls. "Well, are we, or aren't we?" he asked her.

"We are." She winked at the mechanic. "Didn't you know? He's the American representative of Speedy Gonzales."

"Holy Christ!"

"Steady," Charlie said to him, and grinned. With an elaborate gesture he hooked Elaine's arm.

Outside, she said, "My remark was strictly for him. I didn't care for that 'teach' stuff."

"All right, but you rocked me, too. It was completely unexpected."

"Oh, I'm no recluse."

"I didn't think you were. You'll have to wait again. I have to move your car away from the pumps."

"I'm not really hungry," she said.

"All the better. I'll be right back." He went to move the car. He walked back from the side of the station. "Where would you like to sit, in a delicatessen or a regular restaurant?"

"Well, I *am* going to have coffee."

"Restaurant it is, then." He took her arm once more, without thinking. When he did think of it, he did not move his hand. But it did not escape her notice.

"You *are* speedy, you know."

"I don't like eating alone."

"You could bear it once in a day."

"Oh, but I live alone."

"That's your own fault. You could move back to Tompkins County—see, I remembered that, too—and eat with your folks."

"It would be a hell of a trick. They're both dead." He had put it so bluntly that she reacted as if he had punched her. He had wanted to get through it quickly, but he had overdone it and now he regretted it.

"I'm sorry," she said.

"So am I.—But listen, the next time you plan a drive like the one you're doing today, have your car checked first, will you?"

"Yes." He had been obvious, and she showed it.

"They've been dead for years, all right?"

"All right," she said.

"I didn't want you to think you had said something."

"I know. It was kind of you."

"And amateur, too. We cross the street here."

They settled in a booth in the lunchroom and Charlie ordered and then excused himself to wash his hands. He had begun to dislike what he was feeling; it was six days since he had last seen Alice. He had not thought of her all morning—nor yesterday afternoon, either, though New

Year's Eve, the night before that, spent in a saloon on Sixth Avenue, had been a little more difficult. But now, as if just because he was really enjoying himself, his mind had turned to Alice three or four times. The thoughts had no particular shape or clarity; they rang softly in him, like a distant bell. He returned to the table.

"You're a history major, aren't you?" she asked.

"That's right," he said.

"I've been working on the Reformation, and—"

"Two dollars an hour."

"What?"

"I charge for tutoring."

"Stop it," she said.

"Okay. Go on."

"That's it, I guess. I'm working on the Reformation."

"It's a lot of subject."

"Well, my major is psych, roughly, and I wanted to learn something about Christianity. I'm Jewish, and—"

"You don't say? I'd have never guessed."

"You're terrible. Are you always like this?"

"No. You seem like a lot of fun. But let me get this straight: you're going to do a hatchet job on Luther or Calvin or somebody, like the one that idiot did on Hamlet."

"He's not an idiot! He's one of the leading men in the field."

"Hitler was a leader in his, too. It means nothing. You be careful you don't make his mistakes. If you can't learn enough, forget it. Do a paper on the role of women, or something."

"Oh, boy, is your mind closed to psych majors or something?"

"No. I have an open mind. I was able to accept the atomic bomb, wasn't I?"

"I don't know, were you?"

"Yes," he said. "It's not my dish of tea, but there it is."

"Well, we can both get agitated about it some other time," she said.

"Talk about closed minds," he said. "How subtly you inject your opinions."

"I was just trying to get us back on the topic. You agree with me about it, don't you?"

"That has nothing to do with it," he said. The waiter came with his sandwich and the coffee. Charlie kept trying to look very grave.

When the waiter turned away, she whispered, "You're hopeless, you know that?"

"Well, I have something to tell you. That Sunday when you went out for coffee—remember? I enjoyed it for days afterward. I'm not kidding you. It was a very pleasant half hour."

"Speedy Gonzales."

"Nothing of the sort. I don't want you to be angry with me, that's all."

"Then you'll have to help me with the Reformation."

"Be careful. Keep *your* mind open. Don't go in with preconceptions."

"Oh, I've been in a long time now. I've been reading for months."

"And?"

"And nothing. I'm still gathering my material. Who knows what I'll read tomorrow?"

"All right," he said. "You have me at my own game. Tell me about yourself. What are you going to do with your life?"

"Do you want to hear?"

"Why, is it bad?"

"No, it's just long."

"All right, then."

"Well, I started out wanting to go into advertising. Then I wanted television. I tried that last summer—a little, anyway; I worked in B.B.D.&O.'s television department. Then, thinking that all broadcasting was the same, I got a job in one of the radio stations in Ithaca." She stopped, flushing. "But now I've had enough of that. It isn't creative enough, free enough. Everything is sell, sell, sell. It gets sickening after a while. I'm quitting radio this Saturday."

"What can you do? Can you write or something like that?"

"No. That's it. I don't know what I want to do. Nothing satisfies me."

"What about teaching?"

"No."

"All right."

"It's just not for *me*. You understand."

"It's all right. I have a thick skin."

"You're a rat."

"Have you thought about getting married?"

"Of course. I have to do something in the meantime, before I have children, and after, when they're going to school."

"Oh." He smiled. It was so orderly.

"I don't want to just drift along until I meet someone. I don't ever want to look back and think that I was on the prowl."

"Then you're wholly without prospects."

"Not wholly. I know some men."

"I know some ladies," he said, with deliberate insipid phrasing.

"All right. No prospects." She sipped her coffee. She had the kind of hair the sun set ablaze. But it looked just dark, indoors. She asked, "How old are you?"

"How old do I look?"

"You could be any age," she said.

"I'll be twenty-four in June."

"You were in the Army."

"Right."

"Were you in Korea? Or is that the wrong question to ask?"

"Yes, I was, and no, it isn't. I was in the artillery, but I was just there. I couldn't fight my way out of my own peach fuzz—at the time."

"You weren't court-martialed or anything, were you?"

"No."

"Then you were probably no different from the rest. How old were you, eighteen, nineteen? That explains everything."

"How old are you?" he asked.

"Twenty-one. But fear isn't such an abnormal thing."

"War is, though."

"I'll believe you," she said.

"When can I see you again?" He was asking on impulse, and it amused him, because he had felt gratified with what she had just said.

"You can't. I'm going back to school."

"You won't be there forever."

"I don't want to see you, anyway. I don't want to get involved with you."

"You're taking a lot for granted," he said. "I could find you loathesome on our first date."

"You wouldn't, I assure you."

"What does that mean?"

"Let's—just leave it at that."

"It sounds bitchy. I'm not kidding now."

"I'm sorry. We were having fun."

"All right," he said calmly, not knowing what else to say.

"We could write," she said suddenly.

"And see each other during intercession."

"We would have to see about that. It's not my doing, it's my parents'—my mother's. She's from the other side. So is my father, for that matter, though I never think of it. I guess it's my doing, too. I broke the rule a year ago—with a waste of time, at that."

"You're asking for trouble," he said, more to himself.

"I know, and I'll write you first. I won't be bitchy or anything like that. I won't do that to you, I swear."

"As long as we're on the subject, we might as well get the exchanging of addresses over with. If we do it in the office, Skeezix's carnal wishes will all come true."

"And that must never happen," she said, and then smiled.

"Never," he said.

Her first letter arrived in three days. She had written it the morning before, her first chance, she said. She was studying for her examinations, as he had to be, too, and it was running her down. This was by way of an apology for the letter's brevity.

But by his standards, the letter was not brief. He was very pleased with it, although he felt slightly rebuffed by its formality. When he thought of it, however, he saw he had not realized what to expect, and when he thought of it more, he realized what a fine job she had done, under the circumstances. He was able to see himself trying to say something to a stranger, thinking that that something had to be engaging but not deliberate, thoughtful but not too personal and not at all chatty. He could see himself sitting at his desk and weighing these things, staring at blank paper. When he answered her that same night he began by relating these thoughts and complimenting her for having started them off so well. With these lines done, it was easy to go on for three double-spaced pages. He quit writing only when he saw that he was struggling to be interesting. The letter was in the mail that night.

There was an answer before the end of the week, on a greeting card whose line was, "I don't mind being ugly—do you?" She had written on the second and fourth pages and in the blank areas around the drawings, signing it finally on the first page, at the bottom. In a neat upright script she said that she had begun to wonder about childhood in Tompkins County—what did a boy do to fill his time? Charlie felt she had gone to the bottom of the barrel for that one, either out of a lack of something to say, or in an effort to get him to open up. It was Friday evening when he read it, and he was tired. He wanted to be clever and acerbic in his answer, but his good sense caught up with him as he faced the typewriter. She was not stupid; he owed her the recognition of an intelligence at least equal to his—he had the feeling it could be higher—and, therefore, a proper answer. He wrote four pages on what he and his friends had done, mentioning at the end the dances at the Grange in Marathon and the movie houses and Ithaca's pool room. He quit typing only out of weariness, and carried the letter down to the mailbox just to get the cold air, which he hoped would refresh him enough to allow an hour's reading.

Her answer came on Wednesday, and it was not, as he had hoped before he saw the thinness of the envelope, a match to his letter. He wanted to know about *her* childhood, but she had not realized that. Her letter talked of books, her frustration with studying, her frustration with careers. She wanted very much to do something "worthwhile." Her trouble pivoted on that word, but he was not sure she knew what she meant. He waited until the next night to answer, and then he had to keep his letter short. His tests were due the following week, and he had to study. He was going well enough, but he had to know his facts for the final in the Imperialism course. He explained all this in his note.

But on Saturday night, when he returned home from work, he felt, as he opened the text, that he was close to studying himself stale. He was conversant with the major facts, and it was only seconds before he could call up the details of each campaign or issue, and it was just minutes to his phrasing, in wholly acceptable language, their ramifications and influences. He wanted to get away from it for a while, but he did not want to escape completely.

He took the cover off the typewriter and wrote the longest letter of his life. The greatness of Moon's book surged through his imagination like a flood tide, churning up what he had been wanting to express for weeks. There was no meaning to history, he wrote, but then he followed it with that Santayana had said—"Those who do not remember the past are condemned to relive it." But that, Charlie was sure, was all that could be said. The imposition of a system or a formula to history was just that, an imposition—on the people who had to deal later with the material the imposer had mauled. There was no dy/dx to history; there were too many variables. A system worked well in history only when it was broad enough to cover all the situations, and then it was not a system, it was a platitude. One of the problems, he thought, was that some people had begun to regard the study of history as a science instead of what it was, an art that required talent and diligence.

It was not even good science, though, to lock oneself in a museum or a library and clerk up ten volumes or just one thick one which did nothing more than argue in favor of a pet moral—not even a whole sentence, just a phrase. The ascensions and collapses of various societies could not be checked off as "challenge and response," and the internal heavings of those societies could not be dismissed as part of the "class sruggle." Both were impositions, both were platitudes, and both mocked the difficulty of the past.

He sat thinking a while, then started writing again.

To impose even so basic a concept as that of a beginning, a middle and an end to the study of history was to force upon it a part of our heritage. Western culture was captivated by storytelling, and in life, things happened formlessly. The simple gratification of the esthetic sense could distort history. The esthetic sense had real meaning only in relation to the structures of our minds.

Moral judgments rolled in like a fog. The concept that the spreading of our society and its values was a good thing stemmed in part from the Christian belief in prosyletizing. A century ago, Christianity had made the exploitation of Africa, Asia, even the Pacific islands, easy for the European empires.

The belief in growth was more important than many people realized. Athens considered the quality of its democracy to be more vital than its counterparts to the political and economic problems through which the Twentieth Century viewed that city. Athens died, western politicians pronounced, because it had failed to grow. But perhaps the sacrifices in democracy the western nations have made for the sake of growth have already killed them. They have already moved far from the ideals that once evoked the labor of honorable men for their sakes.

If we are dead, we cannot know it—for now. But because we have fallen a little, we cannot assume we are going to fall the rest of the way. Not even gravity is a law in history. The possibilities for redirection are endless.

There was no morality in history. If a God directed the course of human events, men would never know it. The success of the West so far came not from the strength of morality or the strength of God, but the strength of belief, in itself, through things the West deemed worth believing ...

After he mailed the letter he went to bed. He was tired and he had enjoyed himself.

The next Tuesday night he received a long-distance telephone call from Ithaca.

"This is a surprise. How did you get my number?"

"Out of a book. This isn't the sticks, you know. We have phone books."

He laughed. "Did I sound that way in that letter about what I did when I was a kid? I didn't mean to."

"No, I'm just teasing you. Would you like to talk?"

"Sure. What about?"

"Anything. Just talk. I thought it would be nice."

"All right, when do I see you?"

"I don't know," she said suddenly, quietly.

"When do you come home?"

"A week from today. I'll be home all that week and into the next. Can I come around to the gas station that Saturday for lunch?"

"Sure, but I think you can do better."

"Must I? Do you want me to?"

"I won't tell you that," he said. "You have to make the decision yourself."

"You're so smart. You know just what I want to hear. Well, what if I tell my parents I'm meeting someone in Manhattan that night and I walk around to see you? It's only about six or seven blocks from my house to where you work. You have a car, don't you?"

"Oh, do I have car? I ought to hang up. I have a nineteen forty-eight Chevrolet, and it's in better shape than that Flexible Flyer of yours."

"What's a Flexible Flyer?"

"Weren't you young? A Flexible Flyer is a sled. You know, for snow."

"Oh." She giggled. "But is my car as bad as that?"

"I ought to know. I'm the one who fixes it."

"Now I know you're teasing. You only fixed it once."

"That's right. You have a fine car, peaches. You go on thinking that."

"What did you call me?"

"Peaches. It slipped out. I call them all that. Don't you like it?"

"It sounds like a chorus girl. Do you go out with chorus girls?"

"Not really."

"Say, you're not accusing me of having an empty head, are you?"

"No, not at all. Why?"

"I read that letter of yours today," she said.

"So?"

"You were tired, weren't you?"

"What the hell, I was just fooling around—!"

"Still," she said blithely, "you're not much of a logician."

"All right, are we going to duel with Phi Beta Kappa keys?"

"You're not in it already, are you?"

"No, and I won't be, either," he confessed.

"Well, there you are."

"Which means you're up for election?"

"That doesn't make you angry, does it?"

"No. I'm very proud." He was pleased with the tone of his voice; he *was* proud, and it hadn't been necessary to act.

"I did like your letter," she said. "Every single ream of it."

"You're making me blush. I mean it. I hadn't given the length of it a thought."

"Well, the letter was the reason I called."

"To see if something had happened to me? To see if I was all right?"

"No," she said, trying to be serious, "I was impressed. You're so exacting. You seem to be in the middle of something inside yourself. I think I got the gist of what you were trying to say, and I *was* impressed. Does that please you!"

"Very much, because you impress me, too. What are

you going to do during your time off next week? Tell me something fantastic."

"I'm going to read and make clothes."

"You sew? I *am* impressed."

"What are you going to do during your time off?"

"I don't have any. They abuse the poor student teachers. I'll have a day or two, but that's all. There's a lot of paperwork."

"When will you have those few days?"

"I don't know—two weeks from now. Why?"

"I was wondering if I could meet you after school one day next week—for supper or coffee. Or is that against the rules?"

"No. How about next Wednesday?"

"Fine."

Now the operator cut in to tell Elaine that three minutes were up. She wanted to go on talking but he would not let her. He told her he would say in a letter where and at what time she should meet him. But when he hung up he was sorry about it, in spite of his common sense. And something else bothered him, too—his utter willingness to meet her, the thing he had done with Alice so reluctantly after the beginning. A twisted feeling, one that felt like someone trying to cross the wires of his brain, was upon him. He was sorry about Alice, but what more was he supposed to do? They had been making each other miserable. It had taken him time, but he had done the right thing by that girl at last—one would think that would be the end of it. What more *was* he supposed to do?

That Saturday night after work he drove uptown to Forty-Second Street to a movie. Despite his interest, he nearly fell asleep in the middle of the second feature. He stopped off at Grant's for some oysters, then drove home.

He heard the telephone on the stairs, but was not sure it was his. At his door, after the ringing had stopped and then started again, he was certain, and he hurried to grab it, though he was convinced it could not be Elaine.

"Hello?"

"Charlie?"

It was impossible not to recognize the voice. "Just a minute," he said, and set down the phone again, turned on a light, and lit a cigarette. "All right."

"I've been trying to get you since seven o'clock. I—"

"I've been out," he said.

"Oh." She was silent.

"What is it, Alice?"

"Nothing."

"Come on. Why have you been calling, then?"

"It's nothing. Really."

"You don't spend four hours trying to reach somebody you haven't seen in almost a month for nothing. What's on your mind?"

"I—I wanted to ask you a favor, but I can't if you're with someone."

"I'm not with anyone, Alice. I was just uptown to a show." He wanted to say, "Are you reassured now?" but he kept still.

"Charlie—can I come over? I'd like to. I want to talk to someone."

"Why, Alice? You have to tell me why."

"Can I tell you when I see you?"

"What's the matter, can't you talk? Aren't you alone?"

"I am now."

"Then tell me over the phone."

"Charlie, *please!*"

"What is it? What's the matter?"

"What did you tell him?"

"Who, for Christ's sake?"

"Murillo! What did ou tell him about us?"

"Murillo? I haven't seen him since before Thanksgiving. Why? What's happened?"

"Are you sure you didn't see him?"

"Of course I am." He wanted to hang up on her; his anger was far more intense than his curiosity.

"I met him on the street today. He invited himself up here. You know how I dislike him. He said things— innuendoes. He asked me to go out with him and I told him no, and then he said he'd come by later next week, just to see if I'm all right. But he said things, Charlie, about me not being a virgin and having slept with you—"

"Look, did he ask about us, whether we were still seeing each other?"

"Yes."

"What did you tell him?"

"The truth. But how could he know what we did? Unless somebody told him, I mean?"

"He saw you at the window that time, don't you remember?"

She was quiet.

"And the night after the party," he said. "You talked to him on the telephone. Remember what you said? You were in my house then. Only a fool would think there was nothing between us after that. He's not a fool—"

She remained quiet.

"—Look, would you like me to talk to him? I'll tell him to keep away from you. That's the best way. What do you think of that?"

"Yes, all right. When will you do it?"

The question gave him the feeling that he had just stepped into a strait jacket. He realized that he wanted nothing to do with it—but he owed her this little thing, at least. "I'll do it now," he said. "Did he tell you where he was going?"

"He said something about having to write tomorrow. I think he was trying to impress me with his need for sleep."

Charlie thought of the *New Yorker* line, "Just give the news, please," but again he kept still. "All right, I'll take a ride over to his place and see if he's there. I'll call back in an hour."

"Thank you."

Without waiting for goodbyes, he hung up. He looked about the apartment: if he put the thing off even for a minute, he would never move. He put out the light, locked the door, and went down stairs again. He drove across town to St. Mark's Place.

This was the first time Charlie had seen the apartment

house without a crowd in it. It looked abandoned. Its sour smells swam out of the hallways. Stains blotched the walls; obscenities were chalked on the stairs. Charlie ascended softly.

A typewriter clacked beyond Murillo's door. Charlie knocked heavily, so the sound would carry over the noise. There was quiet suddenly, and then Murillo opened the door. His sallow loose flesh swept up in a wide smile.

"Old sock! Hello! What brings you over here?"

"I have a message for you."

"Oh? It sounds very serious."

"Shall we go inside?"

Murillo nodded and led him into the living room. The typewriter was set up on a card table and around three sides of it were scattered half-used sheets of onion skin. Through the rooms drifted the thickly sweet odor of borax, the roach inhibitor. Charlie said, "I just got a call from Alice."

"Oh? I thought you weren't seeing her. That's what she told me."

"I'm not. I'm delivering a message for her, though. Do I have to spell it out for you, or will you tell me?"

"If she has anything to say to me, she can say it herself." Murillo had pulled the chair away from the card table and had it turned around. He was straddling it with his arms folded across the top of the back.

Charlie said, "She was sure she had said it, but she wasn't certain that you had gotten the point."

"I don't want to discuss this with you, Cumberland. This is strictly between her and me."

"Let's not be thick, John. She's asked me to tell you to stay away from her. She told you that herself. She doesn't want you around. She wants to be left alone."

"That wasn't the impression she gave me at all," Murillo said, and smiled. He looked at Charlie in mock innocence.

"Listen," Charlie said, "don't try to bullshit your way through this. She was hysterical when she called me. She wants you to stay away from her!"

"I fail to see how this is any of your business." He shook his head and chuckled. "The door is that way. Close it on your way out."

"What's the matter with you? Jesus, you're not a bad guy. She wants you to leave her alone. Can't you do that? Do you have to make yourself so damned obnoxious?"

"I'm wondering now who's really doing the ordering— you or her. You're some messenger, you are. You're really getting worked up. Well, I'm not going to rearrange my life because you feel guilty about taking the cherry of some little pussy who's turning into a tramp anyway—"

Charlie hit him. Murillo saw him move and he tried to back off, but his hands were down and Charlie's fist caught the side of his face just under his eye. Murillo stumbled away, one hand up to his face and the other outstretched, trying to keep Charlie at a distance. Charlie pushed the chair aside and Murillo, stepping back, tripped backwards against the couch. As he struggled up Charlie grabbed him by the throat and using all his weight, forced his head against the wall above the couch. Murillo fought to get loose, and Charlie leaned his weight on the heel of his hand.

"You're choking me!"

"Are you going to see her any more?"

"Let me breathe!" His nails were clawing the skin off Charlie's hand.

"I'll keep you here until you're too weak to fight, and then I'll kick you to pieces. Are you ready to leave her alone?"

"Yes, I swear!"

"Look at me and say it!"

His eyes rolled down, grotesque, bestial, and he gasped, *"Please!"*

Charlie let go and stepped back to watch Murillo fall on the couch and draw for air, his heavings mixed with blubbering sobs. Waves of revulsion rolled up in Charlie's throat and, in a spasm of nausea and weakness, he stepped back again and turned for the door. He hurried out,

leaving the door pen behind him. What had he done?
Why? What were the police for? He had done it again
with his own stupidity and temper, just as on that Saturday
night in the subway. He stumbled down the bleak stairs.
He had to learn before he did some irreparable damage.
Why had he done this? Murillo had been right: a little
guilt, a fresh guilt. He would have to remember. No—he
was so sick and disgusted with every part of the whole
business that he did not even want to think it was worth
remembering.

The cold street air burst over him as he came out on
the stoop. He looked down the block to the place where
he had parked the car, but then he remembered that he
was supposed to call her. He wanted to get it done. He
looked forward to it like wiping dog dirt from his shoe.

"Hello, Charlie?"

"Yes, it's me. I just talked to him. He promised he
would stay away from you."

"He agreed just like that?"

"More or less. I had to tell him that you were sure you
didn't want to see him. He said he really knew it; something came over him when he was with you. He has a lot
of problems."

"Yes."

"If he bothers you again, though, call the police. I can't
do any more—there's a limit. The threat of the law would
keep him away. But I don't think you'll see him again."

"Would you like to come over for coffee? We could
talk—"

"It's late, Alice, and I have things to do. Thanks just the
same."

"You weren't ever going to call, were you? You could
have. I've had a lot of time to think. I was wrong, I know
I was—"

"It's been settled, Alice. We were making each other
very unhappy."

"All right," she said. "I won't bother you again." It was
silent through the line. She had not hung up. He had

nothing to say. There was nothing more to be said. He was sure, for a second, that he could detect her breathing. But he did not want to utter a syllable to her. Someone had to sever this. Carefully, as if he were trying to say something to her by the action, he put the receiver onto its cradle.

chapter four

Through the dusty windshield and beyond, through the angled girders of the bridge over the Harlem River, Cal could see the dusk settling between the buildings, thick and dark, edged with the light of the sun below the horizon. Coming at him, headed north, were the streams of commuter traffic, bound for the winter weekend. Some headlights were already lit, shining yellow on the cobblestones and the steel mesh of the bridge. Cal's Plymouth, mounting the bridge's center, whirred over the steel, then bounced onto the bubble-de-bump of the cobbles again, sinking into the violet haze. Next to Cal, George DeYoung came awake and looked around. He wiped his face with his hands.

"Where are we?"

"Near the Polo Grounds, just north of Harlem."

"Not by me. I see niggers all around us. We is inked out." He slid down in the seat, below the window. Either Bix or Pete let out a short laugh. Cal could not see them in the mirror. DeYoung said, "These niggers are getting mighty popular, is all I got to say."

"How far is it now?" Bix asked.

"Not far," Cal said. "We just have to cross town and then go down a little bit."

"You know this town pretty good, don't you?" De-Young asked.

"A little."

"Too big for me. Let's see what they got on the radio." He turned the dial.

Cal looked at the time. They were still early, with more than three-quarters of an hour to spare. He was tired now, having driven the distance from Liberty to New York. DeYoung had driven the first leg, from Ithaca, but he had

183

slept and he would go in fresh. Cal was ready to explode. He had not wanted to come. It was not even necessary. The election was in his pocket.

They found the New York chapter house easily enough. Cal parked the car and they carried their luggage back up the block. The house was an ordinary brownstone, shoddy and needing paint. The four trooped up to the entrance.

The door swung open and their hosts swarmed around them. The cocktail party, as much a part of the initiation as the mumbo-jumbo at the altar, was swinging along. Someone shouted for drinks. Someone else shouted for freshman brothers to carry the bags. The first voice shouted a change of order—drinks in the bedroom.

The bedroom, the only one in the building, was too small for a child to use, but it contained four bunks, uppers and lowers, squatting with the functionalism of toilets. The sheets and blankets, though tattered, appeared clean. A dozen hosts crowded in, jubilant and drunk. Cal shook hands and heard names and answered questions about the trip. At last someone jostled in with the drinks. Instantly he was sent down for more.

The pledges, Cal was told, were down in the cellar, going through the final bit of hazing. They could be viewed in a moment. Dinner would be served for another hour, and in the meantime, the pledges would provide amusement.

"Fun for all!" someone shouted. Cal didn't laugh. The second round of cocktails was muscled through. Cal reached for another glass. Someone noticed he had drinks in both hands. Cal shrugged and said nothing.

DeYoung and Fuller were perfectly acclimated. De-Young called for a community piss and there were four volunteers. In a moment a voice from the hall stated that someone was standing on the sink and aiming from there. "He isn't hitting anybody, though!"

"Get a fan," Cal shouted, "and work up a mist!"

There was general laughter.

The party moved downstairs to the bar, where two more rounds were served. When the chatter subsided a moment and someone suggested it, the pledges were brought up from below.

There were five of them, dirty, exhausted, blindfolded, in dungarees and heavy flannel shirts. The sweat coating their skins was smeared with a thick black dust. It was explained to Cal that, for the past six hours or so, they had been shoveling coal around, from one pile to another, back and forth across the cellar. They had been wearing their blindfolds while doing it, naturally. It was the ritual. Even at dinner the blindfolds would be raised just the slightest bit, enough to allow sight of the necessary plates and silverware, and nothing more.

The City College stunts were quite routine. The pledges were paddled, then used as tennis balls, a variation of paddling. They were fed cold canned mussels, into the syrup of which had been introduced a foul-smelling chemical to induce vomiting. All five spat out the mussels before the chemical could act on them.

They were led, one at a time, up to the bathroom where they were knelt before the toilet bowl. They were ordered to reach into the bowl and eat whatever they scooped up. Bruised and mushy bananas, cut to suitable lengths, floated in the bowl, which had been rinsed out with CN. Each pledge ate and, in the effects of his assumptions and the mussels of the moment before, he gagged, vomited and cried, but not until he had been hustled away from the bowl, which had to be saved for the next pledge.

When he had recovered sufficiently, the pledge was led downstairs again, where his blindfold was removed. He was told to drop his pants. A short heavy cord was tied around his penis; the pledge was given a cinder block to hold while the other end of the cord was fastened to a hook driven into a block. The blindfold was resecured. The pledge was told to drop the block. Of the five, three broke down and cried and another let out a stream of helpless profanity, but, of the five, five dropped the block. They had heard the snipping of scissors and felt the cord give. One actually sighed and smiled, and Cal was able to laugh for the first time honestly and well.

With the games at an end, the pledges were led upstairs to wash for dinner, then down again for more paddling. Cal, along with some others, withdrew to the other room, where Fuller and Bix were telling some of the City College fellows about the variations to the ritual the Cornell chapter had worked in. City College followed the book precisely—Cal was not surprised. He sat there sipping his fifth drink, wishing he could find a place he could crawl into, curl up and sleep.

He was not going to have any time for himself the entire weekend. Tomorrow night would be their silly dance. The Cornell men had been fixed with blind dates from a school for stewardesses. Sunday afternoon it would be over. But it was tomorrow and Sunday morning that had Cal unnerved; the company of the other three, as well as those New Yorkers floating in and out, made him sick. He contemplated getting halfway in the bag and staying there. It would be new to him, to be drunk several days in succession. It would be worth trying. Now, sitting in the room and listening to Fuller bark out orders, the omnipresent cigar flagging, Fuller reveling in the attention he was getting, Cal giggled. Sure, drunk all weekend.

Dinner was served on the first floor at a series of tables lined end to end and covered with cloths in a way that was supposed to mask the dissimilarities among them. There was confusion about the seating order—some of the hosts were too bombed to remember their rank—and finally everyone was left to find a seat for himself. Cal took a seat between a tall, rugged-looking character who introduced himslf as Gus Eberly and a younger fellow—Eberly introduced him, too—named Jerry Matthews. Matthews was thin and brown-haired, no more than eighteen.

"Jerry here," Eberly said, "has the most luscious baby backside. Some one of these days he's going to let me have his cherry."

"Is that right?" Cal asked. The kid did have a girlish quality.

"That's right. He's the fairest of the fair."

"Lay off that shit," Matthews said.

"That's right, Ace," Eberly said. "We have to be nice to you. You have a blonde."

"Is *that* right?" Cal asked.

"Oh yes," said Eberly, "he has a really healthy animal, don't you, bubby?"

"Quit it," Matthews said, trying to sound menacing.

"Oh, he's thrown me over," Eberly moaned. "Maybe I'll use that as my excuse to bug out tonight."

"You do that a lot? Bug out?"

Eberly gritted his teeth and nodded. "Have to. Can't stand watching these kids go through their games." But abruptly his manner shifted. "I understand there'll be something special tonight. You men are going to show us something new."

"I don't know. That's up to you. You'll have to decide if you want it."

"What's it all about?"

"Come to the meeting and find out."

"A little close to your vest, aren't you?"

"You'll see."

Eberly leaned over to Matthews. "You better watch this one, bubby. You might learn something." Then, to Cal, "Seriously, what's this about? I came late and I heard only that you were planning something."

"You stick with it tonight," Cal said.

Later on, Fuller came around from the other side of the table. Cal introduced him to Eberly and the other fellow. "Oh, Master, I was wondering if you would explain the mock blackball to the chapter when we go into conclave. You speak better than I do and you can keep it brief. I was thinking that maybe you would like to drop the ball."

"That's up to them."

"They'll swing. They want to see how it's done."

"All right, it'll give me something to do."

Fuller went back to his seat. Eberly said, "That sounds like it's worth waiting for."

"That's what I've been telling you, sport." Cal noticed the look of admiration in Matthews' eyes. He was obviously very inexperienced. It was difficult to imagine him with a blonde—a healthy animal. Perhaps Eberly had overstated it. But this Eberly had awakened Cal a little; he was a curious type, all affectation, a kind of deliberate composite of movie stars. With regard to his type, women fell into two groups: one which loathed him, and the other, which would lick the salt from his pores. Cal had to think that the groups were about equal, so Eberly did all right. He probably needed rest cures.

The chapter room was like the one at Cornell. The walls were black, the floors well-polished—the cleanest in the house—and the chairs, ordinary folding chairs, were arranged theater-style before the altar. The altar was draped in black, and behind it, two steps higher than the rest of the room, were the Chancellor's desk and the speaker's lectern. The four guests were guided to the front row, and Cal began to wonder about the difficulty of making his presentation from his seat—he could not face both the Chancellor and the rest of the chapter at the same time. But the back of the room was wrong, too—in the last row he would appear too much like someone who had just drifted in. He had to suggest to the Chancellor that he be allowed to speak from the lectern, and he could use no more than a motion of his hand. He had to be invited up; more would be presumptuous and maybe offensive. The lectern was used but once during the course of a regular meeting, for a portion of the ritual, a talk by one of the brothers on a provocative and enlightening subject. For the most part the talks were just rehashings of lectures the brothers had heard in classes. Still, the lectern was a special place, and to be invited to speak from it was a visible sign of the Chancellor's favor.

Cal was awake now. There was a sense of fullness in him, as if some emotional stoking-up had been going on. He felt ready, not so much to play the part in the ceremony later, but to stand up, speak, and convince. It was a small but pleasant challenge, and there was a real satisfaction to be derived.

When the room was filled the door was locked and the Chancellor rapped for order. He was a mild, intellectual-looking boy with horn-rimmed glasses. But he had the attitude of command. As the brother who tended the door called to the front the names of the brothers who were down in the cellar with the pledges, Cal startled himself with a spontaneous thrill of anticipation, as though what he was to do had genuine meaning, as in a job—as in succeeding in a job— earning the admiration of superiors, winning a promotion and increased power and importance.

"Okay, fine," said the Chancellor. He squinted out to the brotherhood. "I understand that our guests from Cornell have a suggestion about the ritual. Could one of you give us a quick run-down?"

"Go ahead," DeYoung said to Cal.

"Take it easy." Cal stood up.

"Brother, uh, Torrenson? Just go right ahead." The Chancellor settled back in his chair. "Oh, by the way— welcome." He smiled. "It's official now."

That's better, Cal thought. During the polite laughter at the Chancellor's remark Cal pointed toward the lectern, looking deferential. The Chancellor said, "Come on," loudly and distinctly. He smiled again. Cal realized he could not have wished for more.

He moved cautiously, almost reverently, behind the stand, where the light was on him and the audience could see his clear respect for the paraphernalia of the ritual. He rubbed the top of the lectern with his finger a second, then, after nodding first to the Chancellor, he spoke. "The think came up accidentally before dinner, when some of the fellows were discussing the ceremony. Up at Cornell we've introduced sort of a ariation just to kill the tedium of the ceremony, which can become pretty difficult after five or six semesters. Our night club brothers are more apt to stick around, for one thing, and we think that that's important—don't you, Eberly?"

There was a roar of laughter and some applause.

"The fact is, though, the ceremony takes some twenty minutes longer, but it gives us all a chance to be Barrymores—you'll agree that that's important, too, Gus, won't you?"

There was a scream of laughter now and more applause. A boy in the back called out, "He's got you pegged, Gus!"

Eberly stood up, grinning. "I wish to protest—"

"Okay, okay," the Chancellor said, laughing, too. "Go on," he said to Cal.

Cal turned to him. "I couldn't help it. I had to sit next to Eberly during dinner.—But really," he said to the audience, "our variation wasn't just pulled out of a hat. A number of our boys thought it out and put it together, to make sure everyone had something to do, a part to play. The lot of us usually sit for an hour or two, remembering our last dates, or looking forward to the next one, when we promise ourselves we'll bring on a moment of truth.

"—What we do is blackball one of the pledges on the last vote. We usually pick the best of the group so the action looks even more irrational. After it, we give the pledges a chance to decide whether they're going to stick it out together or come into the fraternity without the one who' I been blackballed. Also, the pledge in question gets a chance to defend himself against the charges made, which are always absurd. They have to be absurd, or else you would be exposing his weak points to ridicule. You can't foster that kind of resentment.

"That's about it. You have to decide whether you want to try it—" He hoped he hadn't hit the word "try" too hard; he had only wanted it to hook into their minds. "You talk it over and we'll answer your questions. I don't want to go over it step by step because I'll only have to do it again if you choose to try it. Okay, and thanks for your time."

As it developed, there was only one serious objection— the idea was too cruel. But the objection was overruled by the boos of those who were eager to try it. Their curiosities had been whetted; they called for a vote.

The arrangements were quickly made. Cal was selected to play one of the two major parts and Eberly was picked for the other. The victim was chosen, a Freddy Blake. The pledges all looked alike to Cal, but he was told that Blake was the youngest, sixteen, the most zealous, and the least experienced. The description made Cal think of the boy he'd met at dinner—he had trouble remembering the name—J Ferry Matthews. At last the pledges were brought up and into the room.

They were lined before the altar facing the brotherhood, their blindfolds secure. The Chancellor, on his feet behind them, intoned the opening lines of the ritual. The pledges looked very grave. The Chancellor instructed the Pledgemaster to carry out the final vote. A couple of the pledges had their fists clenched in nervousness.

The voting box was toted from the back of the room to the front, across the rows, so that each brother who could be bothered could lift a marble and drop it down the chute to the tally side of the box. The Pledgemaster went up to the altar then, rolled the marbles around a little, and announced, "Candidate so-and-so has passed."

This was done four times so that, by elimination, Freddy Blake was the last. Cal could feel the knotting of expectancy. The Pledgemaster passed through the rows the last time. The room was so quiet Cal could hear the hissing of cigarettes.

At the altar the Pledgemaster took an extra ten seconds. "Candidate Blake—has failed."

On cue, the shout went up. "Who did it? Who did it?"

The Chancellor, rapped for order. "Quiet! Get the pledges out of here! Who did it?"

Cal stood up, his arms akimbo. "I did."

"Do you want to tell us why, you son of a bitch?"

"Watch your mouth—"

"Get the pledges out of here," the Chancellor shouted. The five boys were being trotted to the door. The Chancellor came around the altar, his teeth revealed in an enormous smile. "I'll kill you, you hot-shot! You come down here and get drunk and think you own the damned place!"

They scuffled, knocking the chairs about. The rest of the brothers were hooting and cursing, their eyes on the pledges being herded through the door. The door slammed behind them and the yelling went on, not in words now, but in sounds, gutteral and loud, mixed with escaping titters. George DeYoung, true to form, climbed on his chair and jumped off, screaming, "My eye! My eye!"

"All right," Cal said.

The room was silent. The Chancellor asked, "Now what?"

"Have a cigarette, then send down for what's-his-name, Blake, and bring him up to answer the charges." He sat down. "So far, it's as good as we ever have upstate. Does anybody have a dirty movie to run to fill the time?"

Blake came upstairs again. His blindfold was in place but below it on his skin could be seen the red welts of crying. His lips were parted and dry. The Chancellor rapped his gavel for effect. "The meeting will come to order," he said sternly. "Er, Blake, the charges against you have been made by Brother Torrenson of Cornell and you are up here to answer them. You needn't get worried, because as soon as the son of a bitch is gone we're going to initiate you."

"I object!" Cal shouted. "If anything goes against the constitution of this fraternity, I'll report it to the convention at the end of the year. I'll see that this chapter loses its charter!"

"Ah, shut up!" someone yelled.

"Order!" the Chancellor said, and pounded his gavel. "Now, *Brother* Torrenson, if you'd be so kind, would you state the charges against Pledge Blake?"

"All right, I will." He swaggered forward. "I *first* met this Blake two years ago at a dance here in New York, I don't remember exactly where. I was with a girl with whom I was then going steady. This person, Blake, cut in on us during the dance and caused me great consternation. Of course, nothing came of it—or so I thought—but tonight at dinner, this person recognized me and gave me a big grin. When he and the rest of the pledges were being taken down to the cellar, I followed to speak with him. The first thing he said when we were alone was, 'How are you, you old bastard? And how's that whore you used to go out with? I went out with her the next night, you know, and I got in with no sweat at all.' I don't think I have to say any more by way of charges. His conduct speaks for itself."

Someone in the rear shouted, "That's what you get for running around with whores, Torrenson!" There was laughter and applause.

"Let's have some order," the Chancellor said. "Now, what about these charges, Blake?"

He was crying. "I don't know a thing about them, sir. Two years ago I was only fifteen—no, fourteen!—and I didn't go out with girls. I have an older brother who looks a lot like me, sir, but he was married two years ago, so it couldn't have been him——"

"Why not?" Cal asked, smiling.

"Oh. Oh, I'm all confused. I never did anything to offend Brother Torrenson and I'm *sure* it wasn't my brother two years ago. I could even call him, if you want——"

"That won't be necessary, Blake," the Chancellor said.

"But I know I didn't do it, what he said," Blake cried. "I'm sure of it. I know I didn't. And I know I didn't talk to him before, I know that much. I'm sober, I swear I am, sir. If Brother Torrenson thinks I've done him wrong, I'm very sorry, and I'm sorry if my resem-resemblance to someone else has caused him any—you know. I'd be glad to make it up to him. I want to be in the fraternity, honestly I do, sir, please——"

Cal turned toward Eberly, who was already on his feet and moving toward the front of the room. Cal sat down quietly. Eberly said, "May I have a minute, please?"

"Brother Eberly has the floor."

He came up to Blake, stood before him, then walked a full circle around him, close enough, Cal thought, for Blake to feel Eberly's breath upon his neck. Eberly was gritting his teeth and nodding gravely all the while, perfect in the part. Almost in a whisper, his voice throaty and full of feeling he said, "Son——" and stopped. Swallowing, he started again, more steady, "Son, I don't know how I'm going to say this to you, but I'm surprised, and, yes, shocked, that's the word, at your deportment. Audacious.

Presumptuous. Nothing else can describe it." He stopped again. "To think that you could hope to enter our secret order, conducting yourself the way you do. You stand here and take these insults from this, this drunken *swine* and don't even defend yourself! *What do you have for a backbone?*" He put his hand on the boy's shoulder, breathed deeply, and resumed in a low tone, tremulant. "I'm sorry, Freddy, but I can see that we should all be thankful to Brother Torrenson, who, in his wisdom, has seen this. He has seen fit to do us a great and noble service. You're on your knees, Blake, and crawling, and we can't cotton to that. It would never do. I've tried. You'll admit that, won't you? We've all tried—to toughen you up these past weeks, help you along, but I'm sorry. I'm very sorry, but I have to meet the demands I make on myself. I have to change my vote—"

Freddy Blake collapsed. Eberly caught him as he fell and hefted him up over his shoulder. His arm around the boy's thighs, Eberly made for the door, brushing by those others already standing. Cal, rising slowly, watched helplessly. He started after them, but Bix grabbed his arm.

"Stay here, there's nothing you can do."

"I ought to see how he is."

"No, stay. It isn't your fault. They picked the man, not you. They picked the kid who couldn't take it."

"Then you saw the look on Eberly's face?" Cal asked. "He looked as if he wanted to kill me. The bastard, I didn't tell him what to say."

"Then to hell with him. You know it isn't your fault."

"That's right." He sat down, not feeling consoled. He lit a cigarette, trying to hold his hand still. His mind went to the election—it was next week, just next week, the first week of the new semester. *Oh, Christ!* Though this could have no possible effect, and he knew it, for the first time he believed in the outside possibility of losing. *Christ!* He wanted to cry it out of his soul.

The fellow who first had lodged the objection came around in front of him. "You guys are pretty cute. That's playing rough, don't you think?"

"Get the fuck away from me before I pitch you out the window!"

Bix took the fellow's arm. "Leave him alone. You guys picked your man, not him. It wasn't even his idea in the first place. He's just as upset as you are."

A moment passed and Eberly appeared behind the altar.

"All right," he said. "Blake is fine and we're going ahead now, so let's have everyone quiet. Quiet everyone, the pledges are coming up again."

The ceremony moved to its conclusion, and during the tumult of congratulations, Cal slipped out and down the stairs. A keg of beer had been set up in the front room. Cal took a mug, filled it, and moved off to the side, where he could see the others, who came down the way rain starts, slowly at first, and then in a rush.

A circle formed by the windows and someone started a song:

> *"In ancient days there lived a maid,*
> *Who plied a very ancient trade;*
> *Her trade was one of ill-repute:*
> *In fact, she was a prostitute."*

The objectioner came over to him. "I want to apologize."

"Okay, forget it. But where's Eberly? I wanted to talk to him."

"He left. He slipped out during the oath."

"Well, *he* certainly has no right to be angry with me."

The other fellow laughed. "You know what he said to me as he went out? "Well, Ace, I got me out in a hurry, didn't I?"

Cal said, "Don't let him kid you. It upset him just as much as it upset the rest of us."

"That's where you're wrong," the other said. "He's always like that. As soon as a thing happens, he can twist it to his own purposes."

"You're dramatizing. I saw his face—"

"I saw it, too. *That* was part of the act. He wanted to zing you while he was at it. He's that way—very fast. *I* know him."

Cal shrugged and turned away and sipped his beer. The fellow had come over to apologize just to find another thing to argue about.

"I still think it's a lousy idea," the fellow said suddenly. "I think it's a terrible idea. There's a lot of psychology in it, but is that what psychology is for, torturing children?"

Cal turned back to him, glaring. "Are you kidding? It was just a stunt."

"I'm very sure psychology is not for one's own amusement and gain. I'm very sure of that."

"Look, stupid, if you want to argue, find someone else. I'm in no mood for you."

"You're pretty free with the name calling too, aren't you?"

Cal sipped his beer, watching the fellow over the rim of the ring. *A fight,* Cal thought. *By God, that's what I need, a fight. I'll cut your heart out!*

Jerry Matthews came up, but did not say anything. To the other fellow, Cal said, "Just leave me alone, will you?"

"Sure." he walked away.

"You look like you got it," Jerry Matthews said.

"Yes, what's the matter with him? Is he some kind of nut?"

"It's the way he is. He'll argue you into your grave, then raise his voice as the dirt muffles your hearing. He's not a bad guy, really. You should see him and Eberly going at it, sometime."

"That's interesting."

"What, Eberly and Alex? It sure is."

"No, what you said. All that grave stuff."

"Well, that's the way he is.—Look, I came over to ask you something. You're a psych major, aren't you?"

"Yes, but are you going to fight with me, too? That's the way your friend began."

"No, this is a serious question. The way you make it sound, the mock blackball, it was as if it were all worked out in line with some—I don't know—natural law. Is that right?"

"Well, it's pretty basic. If you think about it, it'll come to you."

"Oh. Um, are you going on with psychology—I mean in graduate school?"

"No, I'm going into advertising or personnel work. I'll have to see. How was my talk?"

"That was good. Those cracks about Eberly won the guys over."

"They were supposed to. I figured he was the house wierdo. I didn't know you had two."

"Hm. But I'm still wondering about the blackball thing."

"Well, it's simple. Give people something to do, and they stay with you." The kid was pressing, and Cal's curiosity was again evoked. He had given him a straight answer because he wanted to hear more, maybe even about graves.

"Do you think that would apply to church groups? I mean, the rituals are on the same order."

The suddenness, the lack of subtlety, were things Cal said, "I suppose it could apply to church groups, but there could actually feel in his ears. Measuring his words, Cal said, "I suppose it could apply to church groups, but there are other factors involved."

"Like what?"

"Well, they're fairly obvious."

"I don't know a thing about it," Matthews said blandly. "Really, I don't."

Did he or didn't he? One thing, though, Matthews was not going to speak out and expose himself. If Cal wanted to get inside him, he would have to give a little. "Take a look at a church," he said. "Look at the interior of it. It's all so very cryptic and mysterioso." He grinned at Matthews and thought of the blonde animal. She had to be a kid, too. Eberly had overstated her. As far as Cal could see, this kid had nothing to offer a woman. "What's on your mind, kid?"

"Er, nothing really."

"Then why do you have such an interest in the church?"

"I don't. It's just sort of a passing thing."

"Don't shit me."

"I'm not. Really. There's nothing to it."

"All right. Suppose I told you that the human race has a susceptibility to ritual. It's part of us, part of our subconscious life. The human mind seems to need something bigger and more incomprehensible than itself. Some of our oldest applied psychology is bound up in the dogma and tradition of religion."

"Mm."

Cal kept waching Matthews, who looked away evasively. From the other side of the room came a shout; someone had tossed beer on George DeYoung, and now he was retaliating. The crowd pushed back as the beer splashed out.

"There they go," Matthews said. "Childish, isn't it?"

"Certainly. You know," Cal said, still watching him carefully, "a man needs something inside him to fill the vacuum of terror."

"How's that?" It was very quick.

Cal repeated it.

"That's very interesting. I imagine that's true." The kid was trying to be dilettante and was doing a poor job of it. If he did not want Cal to know something, he could walk away—but he was not doing it. It was as obvious as hell that he was trying to maneuver Cal into telling what he wanted to know. He didn't have a chance. Cal was giving no free samples today.

Cal said, "You know, there's such a thing as the psychology of the confessional."

"I've heard of it, I think." He was still looking away. Now suddenly, "Everything is so easy for *them!*"

"Our fraternity brothers? Of course it is. It isn't for you, though, is it? Do you want to talk?"

"N-no."

Something in the way the kid said it caused Cal to feel an oozing of pleasure. He pushed on.

"You can talk all you want, you know. You'll never see me again after this weekend."

"I know that, but go away. Do me a favor."

"You have two legs. Use them. You're bursting with the desire to spill something, so why don't you face it? Do *yourself* a favor. You'll probably not have an opportunity like this again."

"I know," Matthews said.

"My guess is that it might just be something I can help you with."

"Why do you care?" he asked angrily. "Yeah, why *do* you care? You're the guy with the big cruel ideas. I voted against you, you know."

"Do you want to know why I care or do you want to make noise at me?"

"All right, go ahead. I'm listening."

"I'm curious, for one thing, and for another, I'm bored here, just standing and drinking beer—"

The raw voices chorused up:

> "Hi-ho Cathusalem,
>   The harlot of Jerusalem.
>   Hi-ho Cathusalem,
>   The daughter of the rabbi!"

"All right," Matthews said. "But not here. There's a bar on Amsterdam Avenue, the Emerald. We all go there."

Cal smothered his grin. "Sure."

They got their coats and went out to the street. The wet city wind swept through their clothing. Cal had an uneasy feeling, an unsettling in his stomach. Suddenly he thought again about the election, about losing. It was so irrational; he was going to win. It was in the bag. Ewing looked too desperate; he wanted to win too much. The fraternity liked its candidates aloof and assured. Cal was those things. He was in control of himself. He pushed the thoughts away and walked faster, causing Matthews to break stride in the effort to keep up.

In the bar the booths were separated from the counter by a wall, a remnant of the time when the place was two small stores. It was an Irishman's bar, but there was a perfunctory acknowledgment of the fraternities of the College in the paddles and emblems mounted on the walls. Matthews motioned toward the booths and Cal nodded, then went to the bar to order. Matthews joined him as the bartender was bringing the change. "I can't afford to buy rounds of liquor," Matthews said.

"It's on me," Cal said. "Happy days." They went around to the booths. "Now, what's on your mind?"

He shrugged. "I can't talk about it just like this. It's—I don't know."

"Drink your drink. It'll loosen you up."

"I don't feel like drinking."

"Okay, suit yourself." Cal slumped back in the seat. The eerie pleasure in this was warming in him again. He said, "I was saying back there that ritual had a hold on people. They have a need for it."

"Yes, that's right," Matthews said.

"What religion are you?"

"Episcopal."

"I'm a Presbyterian, but I haven't been near a church since I was baptized or christened or whatever the hell it is. But Episcopal is something like Roman Catholic, isn't it?"

"Something. The amount of the difference depends on the individual church. It's pretty close, though, on the whole."

"On the whole doesn't interest me. What about *your* church, the one you go to?"

"It's pretty close, I guess. But it doesn't have closed confession in the telephone booths. It has open, general confession."

"You go regularly?" Cal asked.

"I used to, but not any more. In the past month, though, I've been twice—two successive weeks—but that was two weeks ago now, and I haven't been since."

"Why? Why did you go?"

"I went. What's the difference?"

"Cut the crap."

Matthews looked away. He was seventeen or so, and his

face was changing, losing its softness. He had wavy brown hair. He was still a good-looking boy. Maybe that was his charm. Cal thought of the blonde again.

"You want to know something," he said. "Why don't you come right out and ask it?"

"All right," Matthews said. "I want to know about the psychology of religion, if there is such a thing."

"There is."

"Well, tell me."

"There's more to it than just that."

"No, that's all."

"I'm not telling you anything then, kiddo. I'm not going to let you pick my brains. I want to profit out of this too. I want to hear what made you go to church—"

Matthews was looking down at his drink.

"Go ahead," Cal said, trying a new gambit. "You can leave."

"It isn't that."

"What, then?"

"I was thinking that you're no dope."

"I never said I was. But I will tell you one thing: I'll take five-to-one odds that your trouble has something to do with your girl-friend."

Matthews looked stunned. Cal decided to follow it up quickly.

"Want to know how I know?"

The boy nodded.

"It was a lucky guess. But now that you've admitted it, it isn't too hard to put it all together. You're sleeping with her, aren't you?"

"Let's forget this. Let's go back to the house."

"Why?"

"Let's just go back."

"Goodbye."

Matthews didn't move. After a long moment he said, "I can't talk like this. It' something wrong. There's something wrong about it."

"Look, I told you before that the chances of us seeing each other again are one in a million. On Monday I'll be two hundred and fifty miles from here, and glad of it.

I don't give a crap about you or your girl-friend—yet there's a chance I can do you some good. You've admitted that by coming out here to the bar. But you have some silly half-assed notion that not talking is honorable. Because of it you'll go right on feeling miserable. You'll deserve it.—You can't talk to her about it, can you?" he whispered suddenly harshly. "She doesn't feel what you feel, right?"

"I don't know."

"I'm right, though, aren't I? Everything I've said has been absolutely correct?"

"Yes."

"Where does it start, with the girl or the church?"

"The girl, I guess. I hadn't been to church since the beginning of high school."

"What's her name, by the way? I can't go on calling her 'the girl' and neither can you."

"Evelyn," he said.

"Evelyn what?"

"What do you want to know that for?"

"For Christ's sake. 'Evelyn' just hangs there. It doesn't mean anything. Only little kids use only first names." He paused. "Remember?"

"Yeah." And he grinned. "Evelyn Hillyer, her name is."

"It's very nice. There. Let's get back to it. You *started* sleeping with her, didn't you? There was no one else before. What about her? Were you the first?"

"Y-yes."

"You love her?"

"Oh, yes." He said it very clearly, deeply, as Cal had never imagined hearing a fellow say it. It was almost funny.

"What is it then, you feel guilty?"

"Yes—I don't know if I can explain it to you. Right afterwards, the next night, I don't know, my mind started to go on me. It was as if I were going to die the next day. A thing opened up in me, the most enormous terror, like one of those dreams when you're falling, but it was as though it was going to keep spreading in my stomach. It was like dying itself. It *was*. I was going all to pieces—it was all I could think of. It was as if the thing drew me to it."

"I've never had anything like that," Cal said, truly impressed.

"I hope you never do. It's horrible. But let me tell you the rest. The next couple of days I was sick—"

"What kind of sick?"

"A cold. Fever, stuffed nose, you know."

"Okay."

"Does that mean anything?" he asked.

"I don't know. I don't think anybody can know. It *could* make you sick. Let's leave it there."

"All right. I was too sick to think anything for the next couple of days. But then, after, I resolved to go back to church. I didn't tell Evelyn or anyone. I was ashamed to tell her, because she felt so good about everything. But I had to go back. I felt such an awful burden—"

"What are your people like?"

"Let me tell you the rest of it, please. There's much more."

"All right." Cal sipped his drink again.

"First I went to this young people's fellowship. It meets on Friday nights. I gave Evelyn a story about going up to the fraternity. I never met such a collection of goons in my life. They showed a movie about a drunk, and the powers of reform. When he stops, he's suddenly in a new home and has a new car—just like that. And then they had a discussion about what they could do about alcoholism. As Christians. They actually talked about going into bars and that kind of stuff, like in the movies."

He stopped and waited. Cal said, "All right, we'll start with this group, then. These people live in a dream world, and they're quite as sick as the very worst, but since they don't do anything illegal and they're quiet, nobody bothers them. The same kind of people develop faith in psychology, if they don't have a background in religion. They withdraw into a world of artificial order, the only kind they can cope with. Did these people argue and then settle nothing?"

"Yes, each had his own point of view."

"There. But there was no venom. There was no issue. and they knew it. They were doing their little bits, their little acts. Let me say this. If the thing that's got you now had started earlier, or if other things had not made an impression on you—for instance, the fraternity—you might have gone their way. At least for a while. You see?"

"I see. They have an easy time of it, and they can still think they're good. Well, I didn't go again. But I did go to church on Sunday, that Sunday and the next. I went at eight o'clock because my mother teaches Sunday School at nine-thirty and stays for eleven o'clock service. I didn't want her to know that I went, because she would want to know why. She wants to know everything, even if it just upsets her.

"Well, the first Sunday I came away unsatisfied. I wanted to talk to someone. The same feeling happened the second Sunday. I had to talk—"

"The power of the confessional," Cal said.

"You said something about that before."

"It was one of the ways I drew you out."

"People want to talk, don't they?"

"People have to talk, when the situation arises. It's very complicated. I'll try to explain it later. To whom did you talk?"

"The minister. After communion the second time—I didn't receive because I didn't want him to see me; for one thing, he would have said something to my mother, and also, I didn't feel right about receiving yet—anyway afterward, on the steps outside, I asked if I could talk to him. We went back inside and he said he was glad to see me and that it would be good if I got back into the swing of things. Finally I spilled it out to him, and he said something that was like a kick in the stomach. He said, 'I'm glad you've come to your senses. A cheap girl with her pants down for every boy can do more damage—' It was something like that. I hadn't told him the exact situation, but it was too late then. He had fixed me—"

"What about Evelyn? What is she like? How old is she?"

"She's seventeen. It was the most natural thing in the world for her. I'm sure her parents know about us. They're good people. They've been very kind to me. I've had good Christmases, but this past one was the best of my life. They made me so welcome in their house Christmas night."

"Okay, let's go back to it. You've never told Evelyn about any of your doubts, and you didn't want to talk to me tonight. That's a fair statement, isn't it?"

"You know it is."

"Well, isn't the same thinking running through your mind tonight as when you were talking to the minister? That you're betraying her? You didn't want to hurt her good opinion of you?"

"Yes. But I keep going back and forth! I do!"

"What are your parents like? I already know your mother goes to church, but are they live wires? Do they swing? Do they go out much?"

"They're not gregarious at all."

Cal was set back. "New word?"

Matthews flushed. "Evelyn's been improving me."

"She sounds all right."

"She is. She really is."

"What kind of a guy is your father?" Cal asked.

"Very quiet. So is my mother. They never even go to a movie."

"But your girl and her family are just the opposite. That's a fair statement too, isn't it?"

"Yes."

"Do you want to hear about the psychology of religion? Briefly?"

"Yes."

"Now, we mentioned the power of the confessional. Now, in confession, if I understand it correctly, people just pour off their sins. The pressure builds up in them and they have to let it out. Why does the pressure build up?"

"In me?"

"No, George Arliss, for Christ's sake."

"I know," he said, "but I can't say it."

"You said it before. The burden. The burden of sin.

You felt you were doing something sinful and you had to expiate it. There was a conflict in you, a tugging of forces that hitherto, had seemed unimportant. Now, because of your recent action, you were made to see how very important one of them is. Your action made them both important."

"I don't follow you."

"Let me ask you this: why did you feel the burden of sin?"

"I don't know."

"Where were you every Sunday until you got to high school?"

"Church."

"Are your parents adulterers? Is your mother full of lust and ecstasy?"

"Of course not," he said stiffly. "I just told you."

"All right. Let me tell you: you felt the burden of sin because you had been taught to. You were supposed to feel the burden as soon as you had broken the vague code your parents and the church had set up. It's epitomized in the church—the code, that is. The church, it appears in your mind, is the very best place to unload the garbage that's been heaped on you. Do you want to know why?"

"Yes, naturally."

"Because the church taught you years ago to come running back every time you got caught in a little snare— but the snares are church-made. Evelyn feels no guilt, does she? If your feeling of sin is valid, why doesn't she feel it? Is that the wisdom of an Eternal Being? Not in a pig's ass."

"I thought of those things."

"So use your head, man! The church *tries* to scare you! How do you think it's arrived at that very strange shape in its architecture. It was designed to give you a feeling of infinity and timelessness more than the human spirit can bear. The garments, the ritual, even the lifting of the altar above the eye-level of the—what do you call the people who go to church? To hell with it—above the eye-level of the people, all these things were done to incite respect and fear—" Matthew nodded. "We were over to the Metropolitan Museum and we saw El Greco's portrait of the Cardinal. All those things came through in it, I mean the conscious attempt to incite and arouse—"

"There you are! What's the matter with you?"

"I just this minute thought of it. I had forgotten."

"The churches don't have any special knowledge about a way of life," Cal said. "They've made no substantial progress with the human situation since they began. They've only bent it a little to suit their own ends."

"I don't understand them, then. Why do they do it?"

"There are a lot of reasons. For one, it's a vicious circle. Ministers are zealous about their flocks for the same reason you felt your guilt. They would feel guilty if they failed. Some ministers and priests back in the old days were just mercenary and power-mad. But now it's different. A lot of them earnestly believe what they say, even though what they say can be shot full of holes by any good logician. Let me tell you something about religions: once you accept their first premise, they have you, because they can prove anything by it. They've spent centuries dreaming this up, just to box you in."

Matthews was quiet.

"Don't let it frighten you," Cal said.

"I'm not. I'm just thinking about it."

In the interlude Cal's mind doubled back to another thing. "Um, do you have any pictures of your folks? I could see a lot in a photograph, I think."

Matthews passed over his wallet. Cal went through the snapshots, looking but not really seeing. He came to the ones of Evelyn Hillyer. She looked just wonderful. There was something really exciting about her, in a bobby-sox sort of way. She was small, with a good, young figure. Her hair was curly blonde—real blonde. Cal handed the wallet back, not saying anything about her. He caught his breath.

"Well, do you think I've helped you?"

"I don't know," Matthews said. "I really don't."

"I think you'll be all right."

"I hope so."

"You haven't slowed down with her, have you?"

"What do you mean?"

"I mean your sex life."

He shook his head no.

Cal wanted to find out more about it, but he did not know how to go on.

"It's getting late," Matthews said. "I have to ride the subway to Queens."

"Have another drink."

"No, thanks, really."

"Okay."

Matthews got up. "Well, good night. Thanks for the conversation and the drinks."

"Don't you shake hands?"

"Sure. Goodnight." He smiled pleasantly but mechanically. "Thanks again."

Cal nodded goodnight and sat down again as Matthews left. The boy had a small, delicate hand. Cal could see him on top of that girl. She was the kind that laughed and talked and then smiled tearily when it was done. Cal could see her tomorrow night. An exhilaration ran through him, but a confusion, too. Consciously he turned away from it to thoughts of his own date. A stewardess, smooth and slender, he hoped. They had fine skin, all of them. They knew how to use make-up and dress well. He felt a shudder as he pictured her. He sat there a moment now.

He hoisted his glass. Something was wrong, but he did not know what it was. As soon as he thought of something it turned sour, like snow turning to water as it hit a street. Maybe the election had him upset. Anticipations and anxieties seemed to be ripping across him in a fast-running, extremely bitter tide. There was nothing he could do about it. He finished his drink and got up. He would be better off back at the fraternity house now, in the crowd.

The next afternoon he went out to a drugstore and tried to call his father. He got The Madame.

"He's not here, Cal. He went up to Hartford. Is there something wrong?"

"No, mother." He closed his eyes. "I just wanted to talk a little bit."

"How is it going?"

"Terribly. Right now they're all sitting around looking at each other, about half a dozen of them. They don't even want to get up a little game of cards. It wouldn't be right, nor some reason."

"Oh. Well, maybe your friends are afraid that the City College boys don't have enough money."

"We all know better already. They have enough for this. No. It's something else."

There was a pause.

She asked, "How is the campaign going?"

"All right. It's in the bag." He detested that word "campaign." She had to use it when speaking of the election. One didn't campaign for a thing like this; it was something more subtle. She didn't know this, but the effect was the same as if she did know it: the word twisted and diminished what he was trying to do."

"Do you want your father to call you?"

"No. Just tell him I called. Don't bother him."

"I know you wanted to let off steam——"

"I feel a little better," he said, cutting her off. "Thanks."

"Why don't you take in a matinee? You could still make it from where you are."

He told her he had already thought of it, but there were too many things that made it impossible. Some of the City Collegers didn't have *that* kind of money, and others had to stick around to help decorate the house for the dance tonight. It wasn't in the fraternity spirit to go off and enjoy oneself when others could not afford to, or had to work. Under normal circumstances Cal would not care about their criticism, but today he did not feel like begging for it alone. He did not feel like being alone at all, which would be the case if he went to the theater, because the others who could go would vacillate and fret over the opinions of the rest until it was too late to make a matinée, or even the second half of a double feature at a local movie.

She went on about the theater while he thought to himself that that was the explanation for the fact that there could be no card game. Both groups played cards so much that, when it was suggested this morning, two or three fellows—Bix among them—put forth the argument that they should do something else. Couldn't they talk? They did not even know each other. They were all better than just a bunch of poker players; they were capable of much, much more.

Well, they weren't, Cal thought. What he had told his mother had been the truth. Bix and the others were in the fraternity house now, looking at each other. There wasn't a good story teller or conversationalist among them, except Pete Fuller, and he had wanted to play cards, too. When Cal had left, Fuller was alone at the pool table, letting them suffer, as he had put it.

Maybe he could pick up a novel, Cal told his mother, and spend the afternoon with that. It seemed like a good idea to her. She told him not to worry and he said he wasn't going to, and then she said he should not hesitate to pick up the phone later on, if he wanted. He would remember, he said, and they hung up.

He buttoned his coat and went out of the store into the icy drizzle that had begun to fall. He knew what he was going to do. He was going to keep his promise to himself and get drunk; not falling-down bombed, just high, and not so high he would not be able to enjoy a book if he found one on a shelf of that God-forsaken fraternity house. He had learned something from this trip. He could feel his anger rising. He had learned never to go on with a plan made in weakness after he had become strong. He would settle with Bix and DeYoung. The trip was a wreck and they had insisted on it. When he thought that this was his last college winter and that he could have done something good with it, his anger went through him like a charge of electricity.

Even the thought that he would see that girl Evelyn tonight was not sweet; it unnerved him: he wanted her, he would talk to her, but he would not be able to have her.

He wondered unhappily now how long he would think of the image of freshness and innocence she presented.

Before he returned to the fraternity house he stopped in a liquor store and bought a fifth, and then at a delicatessen he got a couple of bottles of soda. When he entered the house he went straight back to the pool room, where he flashed the bottle to Fuller. "Ready for your vitamins?"

Fuller put down the cue. "You're the doctor."

"Where are the others?"

"Upstairs decorating," Fuller said. "Bix is helping them. DeYoung is out having the beer dry-cleaned from his suit."

"Okay." They went upstairs and while Cal went into the bar Fuller rounded up the others for a drink. Cal had judged them properly, no one wanted seconds or thirds when there was no ginger ale. Except Fuller. He knew how to drink, and Cal had counted on him for company. The two settled at the bar for the afternoon. DeYoung came in, had a drink, another, found the talk too high-toned, and went up to the bedroom to nap.

At seven o'clock the group cleaned up, shaved, dressed and piled into two cars to cavalcade over to the east side to a restaurant Pete Fuller recommended. The bottle was far from empty, and it was passed back and forth by George DeYoung and two of the hosts. By the time they got to the restaurant they were quite loud, and the meal was just above the level of a shambles. In trying to make himself understood DeYoung succeeded in having the waiter bring him a plate of spaghetti with absolutely no sauce on it. DeYoung made the waiter take it back.

Cal learned something new about their dates: they were not stewardesses-in-training at all, but girls who *desired* to become stewardesses. It could mean anything. Such a school was in business, and it could let the world's worst pig take the course to get her fee. It could even argue, with certain logic, that it had no right to pass judgments on a girl's looks or charm. To Cal, it had been a cheap trick; the one thing that might save the weekend could develop into the crowning disaster. As he looked at the City Collegers grinning and laughing over their wine, and later, as it took them twenty minutes to compute their shares of the check, Cal wanted to tip the table over on them, walk out, get in his car and leave the whole stinking bunch where they were. Fuller was only a few blocks from his home. The others could struggle through the dance as best they could, and Bix and DeYoung, who deserved this, too, could ride back to Ithaca on a groaning and drafty day coach.

Cal did nothing. They went downtown to get the girls. Cal's date was a brunette, tall, very thin, with light eyes. Her face was thin and freckled. She was nervous and had a way of looking to the side when she was speaking. She wasn't ugly, but she was no stewardess, and that she had not seen it herslf marked her, in Cal's mind, as a dreaming, brainless, overgrown daffodil. Still, she was not the worst of the lot, and Cal hoped she had some surprises in her, such as sex. It did not seem likely, though. Her name was Gloria Lou.

The house was crowded when they got there. The band, set up by the door, was playing a slow tune, and twenty couples were shuffling to the exhausted rhythm in a gloom that wholly obscured the decorations. Cal and Fuller led their dates up to the second floor. The girls wanted the powder room. Cal found out what they were drinking, then directed them upstairs. He and Fuller went into the bar. He asked Fuller how he had made out.

"I'll trade her for your string bean," Fuller said. They got their drinks. "Bottoms up," he said.

"That's going to be the tone of the evening," said Cal.

"You aren't going to get far," Fuller said. "Neither am I."

"We can try. What difference does it make? Drink up."

They finished their drinks and got two more and the girls came down from the bathroom. With a drink in her hand, Fuller's date was a Queen of Society, and she proposed a toast to the fraternity. She was a plump, boiled-looking bleached blonde. Cal proposed a toast to airline girls in general, and girls from their school in particular. He asked Gloria Lou how she liked the work.

"Oh, I like it a lot."

"That's good," he said.

Fuller told the girls about the fracas this past fall with the fraternity across the street. He concluded by telling them how Cal grabbed the rope out of his hand to set off the bell. Fuller raised his glass. "Our leader," he said.

"Are you the president?" the boiled one asked.

"He will be."

Fuller was going to get a medal. Cal asked the girls where their homes were. Gloria Lou was from Moline, Illinois. She asked about them.

"Darien, Connecticut," Cal said.

"Cincinnatti, Ohio," Fuller said.

Cal urged the girls to finish their drinks so they could all get fresh ones and go downstairs and dance. He looked at Gloria Lou, who smiled back as if she were falling in love with him. "Come on," he said. "I want to get you high."

"Why?" She arched her brow. It looked fantastic.

"Listen, I'm not a good talker."

"You have to tell me why first."

"I think you're all right. How's that?"

"Mmm." She smiled, showing her gums. She finished her drink.

Downstairs the band as playing another slow one. Gloria Lou liked to dance close. She was very thin and he could barely feel her breasts against him, but she was not afraid to let their thighs touch. At the end of the set Cal took her to the side and as they watched the others Cal took her hand and held it so his hand rubbed her thigh.

"My," she said.

"What is it?" He was not looking at her.

"Nothing," she said.

DeYoung and his date came over to say hello, and the hands were disengaged. Bix and his date came over. DeYoung called Fuller from the floor and proposed they sing a Cornell song.

"Wait till later," Fuller said. "Come on, Cal. You and Gloria Lou need more drinks."

They left the girls with the others and went upstairs. "How are you doing?" Cal asked. "Pete Fuller from Cincinnatti, Ohio. I bet you can't even spell it."

"I can't," Fuller said. "She's not dead, but she's one of those little mothers. She drinks like a fish and then gets cute. 'Why do you drink so much?' she asks. Next thing, she'll want to know if my socks are clean. Well, I'll let her mother me. The thing is, I ain't weaned yet. Come to me, Mamma baby!"

They went downstairs again. It was nine-thirty now and people were still coming in. There was another fox trot and everybody danced. This time Cal touched his lips to Gloria Lou's cheek and she kissed him wetly on the neck and patted his back. It was an old-womanish gesture that made him feel tired of her. But at the end of the set he kissed her again and now she hugged him quickly.

He walked her to the room at the back of the house where the pool table was set up. The room was blacked out but they could hear some people twisting and struggling on the sofas. She was waiting for him. He kissed her. She kissed badly, all teeth and gums, but he put his hand on her breast. It was just a soft little lump. She pulled his hand away.

"What's the matter?"

"No," she said.

"Why not?"

"No," she said, more angrily.

He thought of asking her to sit down on one of the sofas where he could really grapple with her, but another impulse ran the other way and he said, "Come on, let's go back outside."

They finished their drinks and danced again and he went upstairs with the empty glasses. He was beginning to feel the liquor now. He saw Jerry Matthews hanging up his coat and looked around for the blonde, but she was not in view. Cal got the fresh drinks and returned downstairs to his Gloria Lou.

She regarded him nervously as he gave her a glass and

silently bade her to drink. He watched the crowd then, feeling her eyes upon him. She asked him to dance.

"In a minute," he said.

"I'm not used to being turned down," she said with an attempt at cheer. He looked at her coolly.

"Neither am I," he said. It was perfect. He looked back at the crowd. He had put her down twenty-two notches with that one. It had been completely worth the sacrifice of a lump of tit.

Fuller came over again, and then Bix, and at the next chance they all danced with each other's dates. At the end of the set the band took a break and the girls went up to the powder room. Cal stared at the crowd again, sipping his drink. He was skidding with the noise, thinking of what it was going to be like to be Chancellor.

Bix was called upstairs. He was down again in five minutes. Gloria Lou was crying. She was going to be sick. She wanted to go back to the school.

"What did you say to her?" Bix asked. "What happened? Sure she was drinking, but something must have happened."

Trembling with shock, fear and anger, Cal reached into his pocket. "Here. Here are the keys to my car. Do me a double-barreled favor. Take her home and take my word for it that she's nothing but a moronic shit."

"I'll take her home, but—"

"Take her home," Fuller said suddenly. "It's not your business. Cal asked us to take his word."

Bix hesitated, but then he nodded. "You're right." He looked at Cal. "Maybe you ought to be in the bar where she won't see you when she's putting on her coat. She'll be ready to come down in a minute or two."

"Sure. Okay."

"This has been a rough weekend for you," Bix said. "You've been under a lot of strain."

"I'm glad you're beginning to realize it. This trip was your idea."

"Thanks," Bix said, as though slapped.

They went up to the bar and Bix continued to the bathroom. Fuller's girl wanted to ride downtown with

Gloria Lou. Alone, Cal worked himself into a good position at the bar rail.

"Gee, you're hanging onto that rail like it was a lifeboat."

Cal looked around. It was Matthews. "Hello, Kid, I guess I am. How are you making out?"

"Okay. Where's your date? You didn't get stood up, did you?"

Cal made room for him at the bar. "No, but the effect was the same. She got sick. Somebody else took her home."

"You're in no shape to drive," Matthews said.

"Not now, I'm not. Where's your girl? Evelyn. I saw you before but I didn't see her."

"She's here. She's in the front parlor."

"Well. I haven't been in there tonight."

"Want to come in and say hello?" Matthews asked. "I just came in for refills and she's waiting."

"Fine. Get your drinks and lead the way."

Evelyn was waiting alone by a bookcase, fully as pretty as the picture had led him to believe. She was as tall as Matthews, with bright blonde hair and, when she saw her lover, an even brighter expression. Matthews gave her her drink and stepped go her side to make the introduction. He told her about Cal's date.

"That's a shame," she said. "I hope it's nothing serious."

"I think she began to feel better as soon as I was out of sight," Cal said.

"You shouldn't say that. Don't knock yourself down that way."

"I don't usually." She had caught him off-guard. Her reply had been so gracious, well-meant, and completely naïve that it could not be laughed off. She had lovely eyes, with a great capacity for expression. They appeared curious and unhappy now, as she regarded him from the reserve of her good manners. In her eyes he could measure how drunk he was—very drunk. She was dressed beautifully, her dress the color of champagne, the collar rolled, the neck low enough to give a hint of her bosom. Her skin was very smooth. "The truth is," Cal said, glancing over at Jerry now, "is that she drank too much too quickly. I—I've gone on a bit since she left."

"That's all right," Evelyn said. "You're allowed, once in a while."

"Thank you." There was a pause. "Well, don't let me hold you two up. It was a pleasure to meet you, Evelyn."

"No," she said. "Stay a while."

"I'd like to, but I don't have anything to say." He laughed. Getting away from the bar and walking had let the liquor really take hold. He felt flamboyant. He wanted to say good things—how radiantly lovely she was. He held it in. "What school do you go to?" he asked her, ignoring Matthews.

"Hunter College. It's just across town here."

"Isn't that also a high school?" Cal asked.

"Oh, yes," she said. "I went there, too."

"I know somebody who went there—but she's quite a bit older than you."

"What's her name? I might know her, you never can tell."

"Elaine Sellman."

"No," she said. "No, I don't know her."

"There." Downstairs the band started up. "A heavy, Jewish girl," Cal said. They didn't hear him because of the noise. Matthews said something to Evelyn and she smiled and Cal looked at him questioningly. Matthews shook his head to indicate it was nothing. Cal nodded and sipped his drink. He watched other people moving out of the room to go downstairs to dance. To Matthews he said, "Please. Don't stay here on my account. You're not responsible for me."

"Come with us," Evelyn said.

Cal shook his head no and moved aside in an invitation to go by him. They said goodbye and when their backs were to him Cal looked at her legs. Good. Fine, smooth ankles. In another moment he went back to the bar.

She was a wonderful girl. Matthews probably didn't even know it. He was just a boy—and she was ready for man. She was giving him too much. Too much for *him*.

She had to really love to hump, Cal thought. Sure, she was one of those who really loved it. No hint of that part of her life showed, she was so polished. So young, so fine; he could throw himself at a girl like her.

He had his glass refilled, took a good swallow, paused a second, and headed downstairs.

They were dancing at the edge of the crowd on the farther side—quite near a wall, which, Cal thought, made his job simpler. He moved around to a point six or eight feet from them, keeping his eyes in another direction. He looked back. They had seen him. Matthews gave a little wave and she smiled. Cal nodded pleasantly and then carefully let his attention be drawn elsewhere again.

As the set ended he looked back and they came over to him as if hypnotized.

"You've changed your mind," Evelyn said.

"Well, there's practically nobody upstairs now."

Another couple came up and Matthews introduced them to Cal. Evelyn knew the girl and started chatting with her. The fellow said something about the dance, but it was lost as the band started up again. In the noise the five stood there looking at each other.

"This is silly," Cal said. "Why don't you dance?"

Matthews shook his head no.

Cal shrugged, took a sip of his drink and handed the glass over to him. "You don't mind if *I* dance with your girl, do you?"

"No—no."

"Would you like to?" Cal asked Evelyn.

"All right." And a smile.

He escorted her to the middle of the floor, being careful about the way he walked. When he turned to her she let him take her with reasonable comfort, his right arm not so extended as it went around her waist that it would grow tired quickly. "This is very kind of you," he said.

"It was kind of you to ask me."

"Well, I don't want Jerry standing there while I keep you to myself. After a minute or two I'll wave him over to cut in. He showed me your picture last night. I was very impressed. You're a very pretty girl."

"Thank you." She smiled warmly.

"I'm still impressed," he said, "but by something more important, the obvious depth of feeling between you two. One doesn't see it often. Even between two people just a couple of years older all kinds of malicious undercurrents come through. What you have is a very excellent thing. How long have you been seeing each other?"

"Not long—six or seven months. I know what you mean. I've seen it myself. People lose their trust, and often it's because they aren't honest themselves. I think we've tried to be honest with each other."

"You know," he said, "that tells an older person quite a bit." He was phrasing it carefully. "It says you're moving out of the stage of puppy love into something—something more profound."

"There comes a time when you have to give up suspicion," she said. "I think we're all suspicious and it works against us."

"That's right. But at the same time—" Again he as groping. "At the same time you have to use some caution. A person's motives may not be things to suspect, but sometimes his weaknesses are. He may mean well, but just be incapable of doing what he means."

"I understand." And she did, too; he could see it working on her.

"Hell," he said. "We shouldn't be talking like this. I shouldn't. After I saw my date tonight, I thought I had about as much choice of dancing with a girl as pretty as you—well, as of getting to Africa next week." She started to blush. "I mean it," he said. "She as so ugly it was pathetic. And she was going to be a stewardess. Sure, on the *Titanic*."

"Stop it. You're being cruel."

"Okay. I'm going to call Jerry over now. But why shouldn't I be bitter? After being with you these few minutes, I feel like I've been cheated—"

"I'm beginning to suspect *you*," she said from her deep embarrassment. Cal saw Matthews coming through the crowd. He turned back to her and winked.

"Maybe you should," he said. She smiled again, pleasantly, he thought, but still embarrassed, still not his equal. The next dance, Cal realized as he went back to his drink, was going to be even better.

The liquor was working intensely now. He was feeling dizzy but his legs were still solid, very solid. His tongue was staying loose, which was good, because it was serving him well. He did not know what he was trying to do, and he doubted that he could be very effective with her because he was so terribly drunk, but whatever he was trying, he was going to go through with it. It was almost an experiment; he was going along with his associations. Whatever happened would be as much her doing as his because it was her conversation he was rolling with. He was thinking seriously about her now. If she gave him a chance to connect, he would take it all the way. Now he looked at them: they were dancing silently, closely. He figured it was all right to go up for another drink.

They were still dancing when he returned. He took up the same spot. He took a sip of his drink and as he brought the glass down some of the liquor slopped on his wrist. The music came to an end. The couple started over.

"Somebody danced into me," he said as he finished wiping himself. The handkerchief was soaked. He looked up. "Well? Any complaints?"

"None whatsoever," Matthews said easily. "As near as I can tell, you were a perfect gentleman."

"On that basis, then, I'll ask for an encore. Just one."

"All right with me," Matthews said.

"If you can keep off my toes," Evelyn said to Cal.

"I never—" The music started again. "Come on, I'll show you." He took her by the hand to the center of the floor, faced her, and slowed his movements very suddenly. "No kidding now. This will be my big charge of the the evening." He held her as he had done before, then in a moment, leaned back and looked at her directly. "A little closer?"

"I do suspect you now, you know."

"Don't worry. I mean it."

"Okay, then, just a little. If it gets too much I'll push you right back."

"That's telling me."

He got her close enough to feel her breasts pressing his chest, she didn't seem to object, and it was simply terrific. He closed his eyes. Her breasts were very firm and felt even bigger than they had looked. He did not have to think about what her nipples were like. They were pink and large—not dark like Elaine's, but shaped like them, big and pink, with a smell and taste of their own. He could almost feel one in his mouth, his tongue touching it. He thought again that she loved sex, this child he felt himself now rejecting furiously as a child. Yet not a woman; he could seduce and remold her, he was sure. The presence of her sex, in the press of her body and the odor of her perfume, was more than he could bear. His excitement pumped and surged through him, fouled by his drunken desire to urinate. He considered rubbing himself back and forth across the front of her, but he was too drunk to accomplish so delicate a maneuver.

He moved away from her a little. She did not look up at him. Her face was very still, as if she could not wait for the dance to end.

"Listen," he said quietly, "I know I'm drunk, but please don't let that distort your picture of me."

"Hm? No, don't think about it?"

"That sounded very cool," he said.

"It wasn't meant to be," she said in the same level tone. "I'm not angry with you."

He decided to take her at her word. "I'd like to see you again—"

"I think we'd better go back."

"No, I know how it is between you two. If I thought it was going to last, I wouldn't try to interfere. But we had a talk last night, he and I, and I don't think he's old enough for you. He can't resolve some of the things that are bothering him—"

Her body went rigid in his arms. "What are you talking about?" She pushed back from him, but he held her so she would not break away from him completely. "What do you mean?" she demanded.

"You know."

"No, damn you, what did you talk about?"

"Watch your language, young lady—"

The tears were already in her eyes. "Did he tell you about us? Why?"

"Control yourself. Yes, he did. Because he's a kid. Because he means well, but it takes more than that—"

She seemed to go limp. She as looking away from him. He took her more tightly and pressed himself into her. She could feel it; her eyes glazed with shock. Even through her girdle her belly and thighs were marvelous and round. For a moment she did nothing. He thought he got a whiff of his own sex odor.

She shuddered. Tears spilled onto her cheeks suddenly. "Get away from me. Get away." She tried to twist away and push his arms down. "I want to go back . . . I—I won't tell on you, don't worry. Go upstairs. Don't come back with me." She was free of him and going across the floor. He saw he could not reach out for her. Would she tell? He wanted to warn her, but it was impossible. He started for the stairs. Nothing would happen. She would keep her mouth shut and nothing would hapeen; even if she told Matthews nothing would happen because the kid would have to explain his own failure. He was afraid of Cal. Of what Cal knew. It was more than a simple case of a pass having been thrown, and they all knew it. Cal was safe at least from the phony moral censure of the group and the beating some phony people would want to give him. Sure, he was safe, but as his hand went out for the bannister, it was shaking violently, and he thought his bladder was going to empty into his pants right there.

"Come on, Cal, let's go. Please." Bix, standing behind him, tried to take Cal's arm. Cal stiffened upright and faced the top of the stairs; he reared back and almost fell, but Bix braced and pushed him up.

"Get your hands off," Cal shouted.

"Sure, I'll let you fall."

Cal did not know how much time had passed—an hour, though; at least an hour. He had positioned himself at the bar, waiting for someone to come up, but no one did. No one gave him a glance. H saw a couple of coats get carried downstairs. No doubt Matthews had asked someone to run the errand for him. The kid was scared that he would not so much as look at Cal.

The band stopped and the people got quiet and sprawled out on the couches in the dark rooms or went home. Cal scrabbled once among the half-empty bottles on the bar and came up with a very bad drink; he drank it anyway and passed out, almost sick, on a couch.

Now they were at the top of the stairs, the light bulb of the ceiling fixture directly overhead. He could feel the oppressive heat. Bix seemed to hold his arm more tightly. Curling his free hand into a fist, Cal swiped at the bulb as if it were a punching bag. The glass exploded and shattered on the wall.

"What did you do that for?"

"Will you shut up, you lousy fag?" Cal lurched into the bedroom and fell across the nearest bunk. The light in here was obscene, like a cheap public toilet. The shadows of the bunks climbed the dirty pink walls in brutal black angles. Cal turned his eyes to the large, antiquated window panes down which a cold and steady rain ran jaggedly. The light went out, the door closed. He was alone.

A gust of raindrops splattered against the window, sounding like pebbles flung up from below. It was pouring now, sharp and cold as sea water. The house seemed to shake. He could smell the sea everywhere. He breathed it in deeply. He was on a beach in his drunkenness and being drenched by the rain and the waves intermixed, the waves rising high and green against the gray rolling sky.

He felt a discomfort, a minute, eerie terror rising through the flannel of is drunkenness, as if he were suddenly cut off from the land . . .

Did he fall asleep just now? He was awake again, and far more sober than he had been. The house was even quieter. How time had passed? He listened for the rain again, but it was too soft to hear. He opened his eyes and saw it trickling down the window. There seemed to be no one else in the room. Probably only a few minutes had passed.

Tomorrow would be the trip back. Again he was tempted to leave the others here and head for home. He had a few days. A few days relaxing in the good company of his father and he would be fine. He should have taken the opportunity at the beginning. No trip, no complete waste of time. If only he had talked to his father this afternoon.

Now even if he could convince the others to take the train he did not dare. He did not know what had been spread around about tonight. If anything. He could not take the chance. He had to stay close now and head off the stories and the rumors, the reconsiderations and finally the connivings. DeYoung would connive to beat him and so would Bix, just to keep Cal humble. Well no, they were going all the way with him.

Just a few days. Just a few more days and he would be Chancellor of the fraternity. Oh, but dear God, what was the difference? His life would not change so much, and there would be something new to wait for: graduation, the Army in two years, then getting out of the Army. In the end, at the bottom of himself, he might be waiting just for death.

He waited . . . he wanted. That was it: he wanted. We all wanted, he thought. There was no end to wanting, and no beginning to satisfaction.

That night Evelyn Hillyer was sick. As soon as she was home, out of the cold air and in the warm house, the stuff was in her throat and racing toward her mouth. Her hands to her lips, she ran to the bathroom. She had never squealed before. She squealed then, running through the dark house, hitting into furniture. In the bathroom, she kept the light out. That was that, anyway. She could do it in the dark.

No explanation. He wouldn't speak. Mumble, cry; there were things about being wrong and sorry. At last at the door she put it to him in a threat: he had to tell her

exactly why, or she would not see him again. She had
gained the illusion of control of herself. Her voice was flat
and even and low. Other illusions had worked so deeply
into her that she was wondering if it were not all a
nightmare, if—and she seriously thought this, too—if it
were not happening to some other girl. She did not want
to believe she was threatening him, who had actually
owned her until this night. As she watched him in the
moment that followed she could feel the illusions quickly
and silently, being torn away, layer by layer. It was cold
again, so cold. The sense of shock returned, altered. It
meant not just discovery, but change, too. She was changing. He was changing before her eyes. He just stood
there, his mouth open, staring at her appealingly, hopeless-
ly, like a boy, a dirty little boy. In this terrible moment in
her life he did not know enough to give to her. It was when
she thought this that she let out a noise and ran into the
house.

Later—the next day, and the first few days that followed—she looked ruefully over what she had thought,
after they had left the fraternity house and were going
home. The first shock was done; she could do no more
than just choke out that she wanted to leave. She could
tell him what had happened and she did tell him, begging,
wanting to know why she had been treated that way.
Treated like a whore, she thought when she was remembering, remembering too that she had not even been able
to think the word that night, in the first car of the subway
train, rushing home to Queens, alone with Jerry—except
for an unconscious drunk—and thus able to talk. She was
still begging then, and thinking—and it hurt in the days
afterward as much as anything—thinking: *I'll be wise.* She
would not judge him too quickly. He had had his reason,
she was sure, and it would come out. But nothing came
out, and there was nothing in his life that justified the
act—not anything. At the doorstep, then, when the layers
were being ripped off, she could finally see what it really
meant; he had been bragging, drinking and bragging with
that filthy drunk Torrenson. It was terrible to believe, but it
had to be so—he had been bragging about his conquest.

His one conquest, she thought finally, bitterly. He had said that she had been first, and, in a dozen fumbling and painful ways, he had proved it. At that time, they had been a source of her happiness. At that time.

Even toward the end of the second day she was realizing that the happiness could never be brought back. He had killed it for them, and she would never have it with anyone else. There was only a once for such a thing. She was not thinking of anyone else, but it was beginning to come to her, dimly, like an approaching voice, that if she was to have any kind of love, it would have to be with someone else. She hated the idea. Someone else, and the act of loving would be reduced by just that much. All those things Jerry had made hollow and dead would disappear completely. Sex would become a qualitative thing, like food.

Jerry did not call. She did not know that she expected him to, but he didn't. She had things to do. She had to register for the spring term and buy her books. She did not miss anything in the routine, but it was as if everybody were running and she only walking. It was as though she were in a trance. The shock was going on. The weather was mild for the end of January and the start of February, but each breeze chilled her, and she felt herself recoiling from the fresh air.

She did not want to think about anything. If something released a memory—Central Park, say last summer at night, petting under a tree; or a beach party, also at night, sleeping in his arms—it was like a butterfly with a sting. Other things would flutter up, bitter and hurting, until she worked her way through all of them to Torrenson, drunken and leering, trying to press himself against her on the dance floor. She would wish then that there was some satisfaction in vomiting; she could vomit finally and it would choke out of her and she would never think of any of it again. But no, it stayed down. Nothing came up that stayed up. It came up to her throat and she would think about it and it would slip back down again.

And Jerry. She could remember herself on the bed in the fraternity house, naked for him, her legs up, the thing going in at last, and she *was* ashamed now, because it still excited her, just the thought of it, and so much that she was not sure she would not do it again with him, if he asked her. Even with him; strange, with all the reservations of no longer loving, she was still vulnerable to him there, though she would fight him now, to punish him. She *had* loved him, and he had put out the real light in her with his dirty act. Maybe in his own terrible appetite he thought her part was easy, but it wasn't. A girl couldn't wake up in the morning in love and then that night realize that she was starting to hug a pillow that was just a pillow again. If she got a twinge, a thrust of delight, she did not want to believe it didn't mean anything. But it was so; the boy wasn't going to fill it any more. It was like sneezing oneself out of a dream.

They had met last July at a party at the fraternity house, and had begun to date right away. They would meet in Manhattan after the days at their summer jobs; they would get a hamburger and then take walk, or go to a movie. There was always something. There were enough people in the city during the summer to keep the fraternity house open, and there were plans being made, parties being arranged. Jerry became her one true friend; they could talk and argue and he would still do tender things: a telephone call at the right time, a small present. He was quiet and under that, shy, and under that, awkward, and they went very slowly. She knew where they were going perhaps before he did, but she let him do the leading. He was still afraid she would stop him, but she did not hint at the truth, that she was ahead of him. She let him make his own pace, honoring him that way, she thought. After the quiet Friday night in October, she believed that he had been right, for when it was done the experience was complete—there was no more in her reserve, no more of her inner self to give. He had taken her up perfectly. In a finer way than he imagined, he had mastered her. His house was around her.

He did not change much; he remained quiet about himself and his family, but in some ways he took on a happiness she had hoped for. After the first few weeks, when for some reason it was even more awkward for him, he took her more easily, with humor sometimes. He wanted to play more, and then finally, experiment.

All these things were a sham now, because he had made fun of them to impress Torrenson. She could not even understand how he could have misjudged the fellow so badly. Torrenson was no one's friend. She avoided thinking about it, but as the days passed it became more difficult to stay clear of any of it. Things popped up, there were new twists, questions. Who else knew? What had he meant by a remark he had once passed, one she could not even remember properly? His little gestures and games—how much a part of them had been the attempt to humiliate her? Now these were things she wanted to know, but would never know. The earth seemed to be sliding beneath her. And at the end, if she had been so wrong about him, when would she be sure she was right? How could she be sure? And if she submitted to a man's games again, doing what he wanted, how could she be sure she would not approach them with disgust, expecting another bad outcome?

She had been raised to think of herself as a person, not a toy. She was an only child, her parents had centered their lives on her, had always been honest, and had answered her questions not just adequately, but in the attempt to give her new things to think about, from the strength and safety of their love. Now she was treated as an adult, given the privacy she wanted, never questioned. They had guessed about what she was doing with Jerry, but they had not spoken out, trusting her.

They had believed she could be intelligent. She could not gather herself up and run back to them now; she had not done it when she had really needed their advice and did not know it, at the start. She had to manage, so not to make them ashamed as well as unhappy. Oh, they had guessed this, too, that something new and bad had happened, and they were being warmer and more sympathetic with her, but she wanted to prove she could manage, so they could wring out some pride. But it all ran more deeply than that for her; *she* needed something bigger than the pleasure she could get from their pride. She needed something to end her own unhappiness, her own shame, which was real.

She could not get going. Everybody was running, and she was walking. Once the necessities were done, she slipped into gray malaise that kept her from work, and denied her rest. She should prepare her clothes for the new semester; she didn't do it. She should be building herself up on sleep; she couldn't sleep.

She started taking pills she bought over-the-counter in the drugstore. There was supposed to be nothing harmful in them, but they had said the same thing about cigarettes, so she began her tapering-off at once. She took three and then two and then three and then two and two and two and finally one. What they gave her was not rest, but the time was pushed behind her, and she was keeping up a kind of pretense. It was easy to follow the schedule of withdrawal, because her health was at stake.

For the rest, though, her clothes, her personal cleanliness, the habits that made the difference between a neat, clean girl and a pig, she could feel herself letting go. And she did let go, as much as she could stand. She did not wash her stockings every night. She did not clean her shoes. Once she tried sleeping in the nude, which she had never done, but she did not do it again for fear of her parents' reaction if they discovered her. She did not want to be discovered.

One night during the second week of classes, she awakened for no apparent reason, wanting to go out. She was off the pills now. She was awake and full of energy, but she was afraid—again, of what her parents might think. She sat by the window of her room, staring down at the empty and silent street. Her personal freedom of choice was now very important to her, and she contemplated moving out. But she had no reason. As the night began to break she went back to bed unresolved, still in the backwash of things.

It was after that night that she discovered why she had slept in the nude the week before. It was the first of a chain reaction of demands for little sick thrills. Every now and then she had to gamble something, if only to pass the time or make a humdrum thing more amusing. She was aware that her bathroom faced the street and that, from the house opposite, everything could be seen—yet she took three of her showers with the window fully opened. She did not dare look to see if anyone was watching, but that was all right. That someone *could* see was enough.

In the subways she took to looking at men, secretly and very carefully. With the milder weather they were wearing lighter clothing, higher coats. She would look and imagine and wonder. Sometimes it was fun, just as often it was disgusting, but she did it just the same.

The girls in her sorority went to a dance, and for that entire evening, the first one out alone in over half a year, she flirted and teased. She danced with the fellows who were obviously on the make, letting them get close, rub themselves against her. She played dumb, and tried to get them more excited as the numbers ended, and then let them get off the floor as best they could. She did not dance with the same fellows twice, and when they came around again, she gave them "No, thank you's" that were pretty, polite, and utterly innocent.

It was wonderful, watching them squirm. They were far less powerful and knowing about such things than she had imagined. She could control her own excitement, and when she went home that evening she was sure that the little thrills added up to a big one. And the way she slept vindicated her; she slept well, just as if she had had intercourse.

For a while she wondered if Jerry would call. She hoped for it, for an explanation that would satisfy her. She would be less demanding now. They could be back together again, in the same way. There would be no punishment and no reservation, but the comfort of each other and of each other's bodies.

After a time those thoughts stopped and the gray void moved on without them, almost easier now because she was familiar with it.

The reaction was resounding in her like the report of a gun in a hilly land, echoing and rolling, repeating and deepening and covering her like an odd rain. It went into and past her senses and plunged inward and downward; when there was nothing, just silence, the world looked the same, but it was not: something had made a mark.

The sorority arranged a party with a group at Cooper Union, and Evelyn put her name down. The night for the party came up, a Friday, a bad night for her for some reason; she was depressed again and confused and upset. She did not really want to go to a party, it called for too much of her. But she got ready anyway, and when she was out of the house she was glad. She could not explain this gladness any more than she could explain the depression it was covering up; her feeling was light and strange and tense. But it was not really pleasant, either, like the taste of some exotic food.

The party was dull. The men were all new to her, arrogant and smooth and soft. They seemed too sophisticated to smile sincerely. When one of the girls suggested that they leave to find something better to do, Evelyn was eager to go. Between the two of them, Evelyn and Joan, there was enough knowledge to get them around the Village.

Outside, Joan suggested they walk up to St. Mark's place, where some of the Villagers lived. They could start there and work west, looking for things to do. Evelyn did not know Joan well, and she was just as pleased; she did not want to talk, only be out in the open and on the move. Her feeling was similar to the one she had had that night she had awakened and had wanted to go out. She understood her mood less now, and the tense confusion was back of her. She was physically nervous, too; her palms were wet with perspiration.

There was nothing to do, no place to go. They walked up and down the street twice, listening to the din coming from so many apartments above. She was depressed again and not really ambitious enough to hike all the way over to the west side. Joan was ready to go. They stood together on the corner of St. Mark's Place and Third Avenue, just looking at nothing.

"Well," said a voice behind them, "here are a couple of likely-looking young ladies."

"Beat it," said Joan, who turned to them first. There were two fellows, a tall blonde one and one shorter, who was cute in a hard-boiled way, a sort of a scarred Andy Hardy.

"Let's see," said the tall fellow, "you girls go to Barnard."

"No."

"Not possible," said the cute one. "No camel's-hair coats."

"Right, right." The tall one turned to the girls. "My name is Hal, and this is Skip. How do you do?"

"We're chicken inspectors," said Skip. "We have a flask and a Stutz Bearcat around the corner. Want to go to Roseland?"

Evelyn couldn't help smiling.

"Hunter College," said Hal.

"Right," said Evelyn.

"Well, a live one. What's your name, little girl?"

"Wait," said Joan. She drew Evelyn aside. "Excuse us," she said to the fellows, who were smiling as if they were at a clambake given by a volunteer fire department. "I don't know about you," she whispered to Evelyn, "but I want to."

"Get picked up, you mean."

"What you do is your business."

Evelyn was alarmed. "But it's just between us. You don't tell anyone."

"You like the short one, don't you?"

"Yes. They don't seem so bad, do they?"

"Better than at that party. Okay." They turned to the fellows. "Hi. I'm Joan and this is Evelyn."

"Now that wasn't so painful, was it?"

"What wasn't?" asked Joan blithely.

"Right," said Hal. "Well, this is it: we're headed for a party down the block and you're invited—by us."

"You're invited by me," Skip said to Evelyn.

"All right."

"Will you blaze the trail, Hal?"

"My pleasure, brother."

Skip took Evelyn's arm and steered her behind the other couple. "You're not brothers," she said.

"We belong to a secret order."

"Oh. Where's the Stutz Bearcat?"

"I left it double-parked outside the Hippodrame."

"Don't be surprised if it has a flat tire."

"You're a hip kid."

"Thank you."

"Pretty, too. Come down here often?"

"No—you live here, though."

"That's right.

"What do you do?"

"Nothing yet. Let's not get into that. I have my prob-lems. I'm trying to get organized. What about Hunter?"

"What about it?" she asked.

"Yeah, what about it? And why don't you have a date tonight?"

"I've been given the ax," she said suddenly, impul-sively.

"That's the first time I've heard it put that way. It sounds as if you worked for him."

"No, but yes. Does that make sense?"

"No," he said.

She said nothing. In the effort to be flip she had told so many half-truths and outright lies that she did not know what she had really said. She was stunned by herself. Almost as if she had planned it she had placed herself in a low and submissive position before this fellow, a Green-wich Village bum. He had already killed most of his appeal for her, yet she had demeaned herself anyway.

Hal and Joan turned up a flight of stairs into an apartment house. It was a sickening place, full of smells. The hall was a riot of noise. The four hiked up the stairs.

Hal wedged a path for the others to follow through the mob in the hall into the apartment toward what had to be the kitchen. "We have to pay our respects to the host," Skip said to her.

"All right."

"Oh noble host!" Hal boomed.

A plump, sallow-skinned young man turned to them. He smiled uncertainly. "Hal, Skip, how are you!"

"Sweet maidens of Hunter College, meet your host, Mister John Murillo. Say hello, girls." They did, smiling and blushing. "John, this is Joan, and the lotus blossom with Skip is—a thousand pardons, my dear, such beauty is conceived as beauty alone and I forgot your monicker."

"Evelyn Hillyer." She smiled prettily.

"We found these sweet things traipsing around the street downstairs. We didn't think you'd mind if we brought them."

"Oh, no, the more the merrier." He hesitated suddenly. He was not sure of himself at all. "Well, you know where the drinks are."

"Right, brother."

"Another member of the secret society?" Evelyn asked Skip.

"Not really," he said quietly. Murillo was attending one of the others and had not heard. Evelyn thought it was a cheap thing to imply. "What do you want?" Skip asked.

"Rye and ginger—whatever is there."

"Okay."

He excused himself and now, because Hal and John had moved away a little, Evelyn was alone with Murillo.

"Um, listen," he said, "I'm going out for a breath of air. If anybody looks for me, tell them I'm downstairs?"

"All right."

"It's been nice meeting you. Enjoy yourself."

"Thank you."

He left and Skip came back with the drinks. "What do you think of the party?" he shouted.

"So much noise."

"Well, Here's looking at you."

The drink was terrible. There was an impasse now, for she was not curious about him and he was saying nothing. After a moment she was thinking that nothing was going to happen. She had simply changed parties, but as if she had traded clean underwear for dirty.

She wanted to leave. She would let a few minutes pass.

She would play stupid and maybe he would let her go. She looked around at the crowd.

He asked her what her major was. She told him. He asked where she lived. She told him. He asked how old she was, and she lied, saying she was twenty.

"You've got a good-looking body. Is it all yours?"

"I ought to slap your face."

"Don't try it." And he grinned in a way that told her he would hit her back—with his fist. She looked around again, this time more urgently. Where was Joan? Finding her would not help, anyway. Evelyn could explain later. she put her drink on a table.

"Excuse me, I'd better leave."

"I didn't mean to offend you. Stay."

"No, I'd better not. Sorry." And she was moving away from him.

"Evelyn!" he called. She turned around. "Up your ass!" he shouted, and laughed.

She pushed through the people and went quickly down the stairs. On the stoop she nearly fell over John Murillo, who was sitting in the middle of the right-of-way.

"I'm sorry. I'm leaving. Could you tell me where the subway is?"

"Up the block and across the street to the triangle," he said. He turned around to her. "What's the matter?"

"Nothing."

"No, there is. You didn't know Skip, did you?"

"No." She started down the stairs again.

"He's a dope addict, you know."

She stopped, "A what?"

"A junkie. He uses marijuana and he's on heroin, I think. I don't know. I heard that recently."

"I just met him."

"You have to be careful these days," he said old-maidishly. She felt sorry for him.

"What about you?" she asked.

"That stuff? Oh, no."

"You're a bum, are you? He's a bum."

"No."

"What do you do?"

"I'm a writer."

"Oh." The February air was getting to her. She tucked her collar closer to her neck.

"I invited him to the party," he said, "but I don't know why. He's filth. I'm beginning to think I'm drawn to filth. I'm attracted to it, like a moth; I don't know."

"Mm."

"Want a cigarette?" he asked.

"No, thanks. I have my own. Have you had anything published?"

"A few pieces in the little magazines. There's not much money, but—"

"At least you're doing what you want," she said.

"That's right," he said.

"Can I talk to you?" She didn't know why she asked; she didn't want to talk.

"Sure. Sit down, if you don't mind the stoop. It's cold." He made room for her. He laughed nervously. "I'm not as handsome or as flashy as he is, but I'll try—"

"You don't have to be," she said suddenly. "You'll do fine—" She stopped. It was out. All right, him. He was pathetic to look at, but he was going to purge her of Jerry. This fellow.

He did not answer her. He sat staring.

"What's the matter?"

"Nothing," he said.

"I'm sorry. I—I didn't mean to upset you."

"Then you meant it the way it sounded? You want to? You want to go with me?"

"Y-yes. And just the way you think, too."

"Do you do it for many men?"

She nodded. Automatically; somehow it was right.

"How many?" His voice was thick.

"I don't know."

"When was the last time?"

"Oh, a while ago—I don't have any diseases," she added quickly.

"You really like it, then."

It was getting more and more darkly pleasant, moist, liquid, running like a spring shower speeding down a curbside. There was a thrill in it, a deep, dirty thrill. She could imagine the way it was going to be. "You'll see how much I like it," she said.

"There's a hotel down the block. Come on."

She took a taxicab home, staring out the window at the pavement rushing by. She hurt. She wanted to be sick again. It had been disgusting, and she felt dead inside. Oddly, she thought she would be able to do the necessary things more easily than before, but they wouldn't mean anything. She had had the soul snatched out of her. From here on, and for a long, long time, it was all going to be wasted motion.

In her room she prepared herself in the dark and crawled into bed. Her body felt like so much wet, dirty wash. She slipped into a light and weary sleep.

During the next two days, it came to mind only now and then, while she was brushing her teeth—*this mouth . . .* she would think—while she was watching television—*I did it. Me.*—When she was sitting down to dinner—*My parents couldn't have any idea.* It would stop her, like a movie projector stops, but only for second, and then she would start up again. The view would be changed, a little worse, a little more remote.

On Sunday night after her shower she made the mistake of stopping and looking down at herself. Her skin was still glowing and firm from the hot water and the towel-rub. She looked as she had always looked. Her vision failed suddenly and she thought she could feel her eyes rolling back in their sockets. The breath ran out of her. She reached out to the towel rack for support. She closed her eyes. Her legs were shaking.

She stood up straight and kept her eyes closed. She was thinking of hurting herself down there, but she couldn't. She couldn't even hurt herself enough to cry.

The next night, three weeks and two days after he had last seen her, Jerry Matthews called. He wanted to explain, and apologize, he said. He wanted to tell.

She was quiet, thinking of Torrenson. He had reminded her instantly of Torrenson. Her heart was beating and she could barely grip the phone. She thought of Friday night and for some reason particularly of kissing that fellow. The taste. The taste of his mouth.

"Please," Jerry said. "I've been thinking it over."

She looked quickly around the house. Neither of her parents was within earshot. She took the receiver with both hands. "No. No, you can't see me, ever. You did this and you live with it."

"Did what? What happened, Evelyn?"

She could feel the catharsis coming. She would feel purged now. It would be worth it.

"Y-you listen and I'll tell you. I'll tell you good. This is going to hurt you, Jerry, and I won't be sorry, I promise you."

II

If Charlie knew what she did with his letters, Elaine thought, he would stop writing to her at once. She saved them, each one opened neatly—the bundle of them stacked carefully in the corner of her dresser drawer. If he knew the rest of it, he would go into shock. She had thought of buying a ribbon, but had given it up—a ribbon to untie and retie would be too much trouble; she had thought of using a rubber band, but had given that up, too—it would wrinkle the paper. So the letters, well over a dozen, were stacked in the corner of the drawer, neat, perfectly neat, there to reread or even just to look at.

In the beginning she read them in public, in the cafeteria in Willard Straight or in one of the soda shops, the way one read a newspaper; but lately she was taking them back to the room, reading them seriously and carefully while sitting on the edge of the bed. She knew that the waiting for them was almost as important as the letters themselves, and that writing answers was as delightful as anything about *him,* for she felt she was talking to him, and he was listening—though, too, she could picture him dropping off to sleep under her unending dull chatter.

Only his first letter after the intersession had any word of their one real date, that Saturday night, and that comment was just a repetition of what he had said on the telephone. She had called him. He had had a wonderful time, he said, and he meant it. In the letter, with very nearly the same words typed out, his sincerity seemed to take a step away. But she did not question it. It was there for her to see, and she believed it.

The letters had produced more of an intimacy than either of them had suspected. She had wondered about the way they would conduct themselves, and when he came down the steps of the school that afternoon they had arranged to meet for coffee, it was obvious he had wondered, too. Some of his students were with him, tough-looking boys. He introduced them to her and they said hello nervously and then excused themselves. The easy, comfortable way he handled their respect was a new and intimidating thing for her. The boys approved of her; he could tell it that easily. They stood talking a while. A vague formality remained between them. He said it, but it didn't really help. They tried to relax, and finally most of their uneasiness did disappear. They laughed about it and he teased her gently, which was as far as they could go. Seeing him as a teacher had done it as much as anything; she had the feeling that she had been writing to another person.

Their reserve carried over to their Saturday night. They went into Manhattan for dinner, then to a play in his neighborhood, and finally to a place on Third Avenue where there was dancing. They talked for hours, about the play, the arts in general, politics, jobs they had held. They were at her door at three, both terribly tired, and after a few fine, mutually respectful kisses, they made plans about the telephone call the following week. She went inside with a mixture of feelings, happy about them, about him, that he had not failed the promise of his letters, but unhappy about having to bring up the idea that he could not meet her parents, unhappy about insulting him that way. But that night she dreamt the whole evening again, and when she awakened Sunday it was with a feeling of refreshment and satisfaction that made her smile, roll over in her bedclothing, close her eyes against the pillow, and remember the kissing, his lips on her lips, his tongue touching her tongue.

After the second week of the new semester, he began to write without waiting for her answers. His letters came steadily every other day. They were not more personal than before, but they were more full, more diverse, and their tone indicated—to her at least—that he was not having to reach for things to say. He did not mention this change to her, but she picked it up herself, and followed his lead. It was very easy to write about what she did and thought—even the most trivial things. At times she would hesitate—afraid she was boring him, but then she would plunge on, as if he were down at his mailbox before dawn, waiting to read about her troubles with her index cards on the paper about the Reformation, wanting to know about the impatient way she was waiting for the Spring.

On the first Monday in March she received two letters— one, dated the previous Friday night, was of normal size, typewritten; the other was written in ink, very thin, one small sheet of paper folded in half. It was postmarked Saturday night. She was late, so she tucked them into her purse.

Later in the cafeteria over a cup of coffee she began to read them, in their order out of fairness to him, in spite of her curiosity about the second note. The first was about the way his classes were developing and then, on the second page, about a novel she had recommended to him. He did not read much fiction, but he had enjoyed this book, and he thanked her.

She put the letter down and sipped her coffee. She opened the second envelope.

Elaine—
Don't be upset, but I've lost my job at the gas station. The wife of one of the mechanics is expecting her third baby and he needs the extra money. The boss was very kind, giving me two weeks' pay to help me understand. But this is . . .

"Hi. Can I sit down?"

She looked up. It was Cal Torrenson, coffee cup in hand, already putting his books on the table. "Sure, go ahead."

"Thanks. It looks like mail call around here."

"It is." She put a protective hand over the first letter.

But this is the point, if it's all right with you ...

"Don't worry, I'm not going to pick it up and read it."

"I'm sorry." She put the note in her lap and folded the first letter into its envelope. "I shouldn't have left this out anyway. It looks messy."

"What the hell," he said. "How've you been?"

"All right."

"I was down in your town the other week, during intersession. You know, it's really dismal in the winter."

"No, no, it isn't."

... if it's all right with you, I'll come up this week-end. I could stay with my uncle, I suppose, but it would be easier all around if I went to a hotel in town. We could decide ourselves about whether you want to meet my family. But that's hardly the idea at all, I've been thinking all day that I need ...

"Jesus, that's some letter. I just stuck my tongue out at you and you didn't so much as bat an eye."

"I'm sorry, I didn't see you."

"I *know* that," he said.

"What did you say?"

"You'd better finish the letter."

... that I need a vacation. If you don't want me to come for any reason, call me Wednesday. This is strictly spur-of-the-moment and I won't be offended if you say no. I realize that you may have made other plans and so on, or that my coming up was more than you bargained for. Please let me know if

*you have any objection. But I would like to see
you.*

And it was signed. "There," she said. "Now, what were
you saying?"

"That must have been one hell of a letter."

She shrugged.

"You look very good," he said.

"Thank you."

"Do you want to hear the end?"

"All right," she said, "tell me the end."

"I was elected Chancellor of the frat."

"That's what yo uwanted, wasn't it?"

"I don't know. It was kind of off and on. Well, now I
have it—or it has me."

"It's a lot of work, then."

"Well, I'm glad for you."

"Oh, yes."

"You're in a good mood, do you know that?"

"No, I didn't. I'm glad about that, too." She was thinking that she had nothing to say to him. She wanted to
finish her coffee and get away.

"Would you like to go out this weekend?"

"Oh, no. Thank you anyway."

"You're not busy both nights, are you?"

"As a matter of fact, I am. I'm busy all weekend."

"Say, are you thinking of getting married?"

She smiled. "I'm always thinking of getting married." It
was a perfect getaway line. She got up and started to
gather her books, still smiling.

She was committed to his coming up not just because
she had allowed Wednesday night to come and go without
calling, but because she had contrived not to call, had
planned not just that night but the weekend as well, and
was ready for his letter asking her to make a reservation
in one of the hotels, and to buy tickets to whatever was
worth-while Friday and Saturday nights. But commitment
or no, the dreams ran against her, like an undertow or

even the ocean's full tide, fretful, restless dreams, of things she could not remember upon waking.

She would lie there on her side looking to the window and smoking a cigarette, her mind sifting the things she was sure the dreams could be made of. There were no familiar notes. There was nothing. Half the time she could not form clear pictures of the things or people she wanted to think about: her family, Cal, Marv before him, not even Charlie. The thing bothering her was like a shaft of gray steel jammed down through her brain, and it was not until the cigarette was out and she was trying to sleep again that anything came into focus: what she had to tell him—that ugly story. He might have to know it sooner or later. In the morning when she awoke and had to hurry into the business of the day, it was like being unchained.

The overstuffed chair faced toward the door to the street, away from the registration desk and the stairs. She sat still, outwardly calm, watching the people passing on the sidewalk under the lights of the hotel. It was eight-thirty and she was early, but she had had no real choice; for hours now she had been capable only of waiting. Soon he would come through the door carrying a small suitcase, the collar of his topcoat turned up; he would not see her at first, but then he would, and grin boyishly, and come over. He would have something nice to say . . .

"Hello."

She turned about. He was standing behind her.

"You haven't been waiting long, have you? I got in half an hour ago, so I thought I'd clean up a bit. You look terrific."

She stood up. He had the topcoat over his arm. The smile seemed to dissolve her; she could not really look at his face. He leaned forward and kissed her lightly on the cheek. "Come, on, we'll go to dinner. Which would you like, the College Spa or the Normandie?"

"Neither. They're too expensive. I mean, wouldn't you like to drive to a place? We could talk along the way."

"That sounds fine." He took her arm and they started out.

"How did you get up here so quickly?" she asked. "You must have flown."

"A little. I left right after school to beat the traffic—and I spent last Sunday tuning up the motor. I didn't think you'd turn me down. Just as soon as the boss told me I was through, I thought of coming up. I must have had it in my brain beforehand. I think I would have come even if you had told me to stay home.

His car was down the street from the hotel. When he got in on his side he had a package—it must have been under his topcoat. "Here, this is for you. Elaine, I missed you like hell."

"Oh, I didn't think of getting you anything—"

"Be quiet and open it."

It was flat and rectangular and she could guess the contents almost at once. She removed the white wrapping paper carefully and lifted the lid. There were handkerchiefs, three of them, of delicate linen with very fine filigree work on the edges and in the corners. "Look," he said, "they're not much, but I wanted to get something nice but not common. And I didn't want to upset you with something too intimate. You know."

"They're beautiful, Charlie, perfect. I love them." She took his hand and he turned to meet her halfway, but quickly she said, "Let me, please. I want to do this myself." Before she was finished speaking her hand went around to the back of his neck and brought him to her, his mouth to her mouth. She wanted to keep her eyes open until the last to tell him the full measure of her feeling, but she could not; she had to close her eyes for the intensity of what they said, and for the fear and caution collapsing inside her. Her lips pressed his, smooth, warm, half-parted; she parted them more with her tongue, touched his tongue, tasted the wetness of his mouth. The feeling compressed, intensified to a sound she could hear somehow far off, such as a bird's single long cry against a blowing wind.

He held her hand tightly for a moment, and then turned to start the car.

"I have to tell you how it's been," he said. "I don't

know if I can. The time seems to fly, but for the moments I think about it, and then it slows down sadistically. I try to go about my business and not think of it—not think of anything concerning us—"

"I've been doing the same thing," she said.

"It's too early to think. There's really nothing to think about but a state of mind. We could foul it all up by Sunday morning. We could do it tonight. We knew practically nothing about each other."

"I know," she said with sudden gravity.

He held still a second as if inside him something was registering her answer and the inflection of it. Then, "I enjoy being with you, Elaine."

"I enjoy being with you."

"All right, where are we going?"

"Oh. Go south on Thirteen. There's a place a couple of miles out."

"Not halfway to Elmira, I hope?"

"No." She smiled and touched his arm.

He drove quickly through the gleaming, brightly lighted town, crowded for a Friday-night good time. Soon they were moving over the flats in the southwest, with the far hills and the fields dim brown under a crescent moon. There were stars and a few small clouds. Lights twinkled through the bare trees on the hills. The road was deserted.

He took her hand again. "Relax, will you?"

"I'm trying."

"We have a lot to thrash out—on my side as well as yours. Tell me if I'm presuming too much. You know, all we've talked of so far are ideas, and not even the big ones way down—it's as though we were deliberately avoiding each other."

"Aren't we?"

"A typical Brooklyn answer, a question. Of course we are, and we have good reason. I've been thinking about our trouble, if you want to know the truth. I don't particularly care about my children not being Christians, but I don't think I could let them be Jews, either. They would have to be nothing, nothing at all. I don't care about Christianity that much, any way you cut it—do you want me to stop?"

"No." She touched the package in her lap and looked down at it.

"But I couldn't have my kids Jewish. I couldn't give up my own tradition and heritage—I do have one—for one I don't love more. I admire Judaism, but I admire it for its conceptions—justice, for one. Ethics. The claim any of the religions makes on me is on that level. You feel that way, don't you?"

"Yes." But she was thinking she had never said it aloud. She had never dared.

He was quiet a while, as though he were thinking the same thing she was: that, when the talk and the bravado were through, where would she be? She had no doubt about him; he was not the kind to retreat. She wanted to be cheap and small and think he had nothing to lose, that his people were dead and that he had never had any real training, only what a child needed to make life smooth. His sacrifice would be nothing, compared to hers. But those thoughts seemed to slide out of her mind. Everything seemed to slip away, and she was left to thoughts of how well she had avoided thinking these weeks. His dominance over her was frightening; she wanted to hate him for it, and for the fact—for her it was a fact—that he was never wrong. But it went both ways: he was right in his being right, and not righteous. It melted her. He seemed to be aware of the control he had over her, but his feeling was simple, natural and uncontemplated. She wanted to move closer to him, as close as possible. That he would be gone Sunday morning terrified her for a moment; she wanted to take hold of him, now, immediately. She looked at him a minute. His attention was on the road, and he didn't notice her. The thing that had caused this silence, religion, came back to her, and she did not move.

"What will we do after dinner?" he asked. "Do you know any places where we can dance?"

"A couple. Is that what you want to do? You're not too tired?"

"No, I'm all right.—Here's something for you: I wrote

to you about the dances over at the Grange in Cortland? Well, what I forgot to write was that the couples would wander back to the cemetery and the kids would sneak up on them and throw rocks against the headstones."

"Oh, that's hateful."

"Another one? My mother told me this one. They used to have a schoolteacher everyone disliked so one day they chained his car to the road. They drove a spike into the road and chained down the rear axle."

"That's hateful, too."

"I know. How do you feel?"

"All right."

"You've gotten very quiet."

"I'm sorry."

"Would you like to hear how I almost became a baseball player? I don't think I told you about that."

"You?"

"Sure. I pitched in high school. I had an offer to play class D ball, but I went into the Army instead. That's the whole story."

"I'm glad," she said.

"What?"

"I'm an absolute ninny on sports. I don't know anything and I should know more. My father will come home and say the Yankees won the double-header and I have to stop and think what that is."

"Well, I'll fix you up fine. I like the races and baseball and the fights. We'll take them all in."

"All right."

"Don't put me on. If you don't want to go, say so."

"You're serious, aren't you?"

"Yes."

"Well, so am I. I want to learn—a little." She looked over at him and they laughed together.

He said, "Tomorrow, if you want, we can drive over to the place where I used to live. I want to call my uncle anyway, as long as I'm here. If you'd rather not go, I'll take an hour off and go over by myself."

"I'd like to go, if you wouldn't mind."

"Fine—but I do have to call him first, to do a little

explaining. I was up here during Christmas week, but I was staying with other people, the family of a girl I met in the city." He took a breath. "That's an explanation in itself. In a word, I have to get him squared away on my love-life."

"All right. Um, the restaurant's coming up on the right, just around this bend."

"Tell me about your childhood or something to get me off the subject, will you? We'll talk about it later—it's what we have to thrash out, but I'm not in the mood right now."

A question came to her. "You weren't married, were you?"

"Oh, no." He wheeled the car into the parking lot of the log cabin-style restaurant. The lot was nearly empty. He brought the car to a stop a hundred feet from the building, and when he turned off the headlights, it was dark around them.

She could not talk. She knew he was not really expecting her to begin to blurt out her history, but she was expecting it of herself—and with a subtle, overwhelming difference. As she sat there staring ahead and waiting for the words to come of themselves, she realized the stupidity of her predicament: she had to start soon and get it done or not be able to tell him at all. She would not be able to reach him, then, on any level. Their feeling would dribble off to Sunday morning and he would drive away and it would be over. At first she thought she had to phrase it carefully, not to hurt him. No; it was that she did not want to *see* him hurt. She was so afraid for what she felt that she did not want to chance seeing his weakness. At the heart of it, she did not have enough confidence in him.

He slipped the car keys into his pocket and took out his cigarettes. He offered her one. Her hand went out for it, shaking. He saw it. She kept her eyes down. Her chance was passing, but she could not speak. The burden shifted to him, and she was ashamed.

He said, "Calm down. We can sit here and spill everything out and then go have some dinner. It's not the easiest way. It's the way we're allowing ourselves. Let's just say it and be through with it. You have nothing to tell me—well, go ahead and I'll see."

"I hate this!"

"You like me, don't you?"

"Yes."

"I like you, too," he said. "It's why I'm here."

"Please don't talk to me as if I were one of your students."

"I'm sorry."

"I'm sorry, too. I didn't mean to snap at you." She picked at the cover of her package. "I'm not a virgin."

"I know. I knew it a long time ago. But you told me again tonight, outside the hotel."

She looked at him. "Are you hurt?"

"I don't know. I don't know why that is. I just don't know." He drew on his cigarette. "I'm curious, but not intensely so. The thing that could hurt me—I guess I'm just deciding this—is if you betrayed me now or recently. It would disappoint me. Do you understand? Because you had accepted my feelings."

"I haven't done it."

"I haven't done it to you, either."

She was finished with what she apparently considered the most sordid part in five minutes, and when he saw that she was talking more easily, he cut in on her and suggested they go into the restaurant. They talked quietly across the gravel of the lot, and he thought about what she had told him, and two characters named Marv and Cal. He felt protective about her, wanting, in some way, to avenge her. It was hard to believe she had worked herself into such a situation. She was the young woman whose letters had awed him. She must have been a different person, a year ago.

In the restaurant, after they had ordered, she began talking again, this time guided by his questions. Her voice was sweet and deep, almost musical; he loved hearing it. She seemed happier and brighter now. Once in a while she would stop and look at him, smile, and go on, as if she

could draw a kind of strength from him. She seemed to
have no idea of the strength she was giving in return.

He had never felt anything like this. These past weeks,
coming up in the car today, he had known it would be
good, but it was more intense than he could have possibly
imagined. He would not get enough of her. Sunday was
going to come down on them like a highballing truck.
When he thought that he was going to carry each minute
to its limit, he saw how quickly the minute was going to
run.

"How do you feel now?" he asked.

"Good. Better." She smiled.

"Best?"

She thought it over. "I can't compare this with anything. How's that?"

"Wonderful. You're wonderful."

"Do you think so?"

"Yes. Talk to me. Come on."

She told him about her parents, and more particularly
about her mother. He had heard similar stories from other
girls; still, he felt almost the physical need to withdraw.
He caught himself thinking of his own family, the house,
the gas station. He wanted to interrupt and tell her about
them, but he stayed silent, remembering the summertime
trip to Watkins Glen. He thought of the old man on the
road this past Christmas: *his* family had been coming to
see him the next day. It had been going to be a high old
time. Now, suddenly, Charlie sincerely hoped it had been.
He stopped abruptly. The dread he felt at having moved
himself so far from her grabbed at him. His eyes mirrored
it, he realized, for, even if she could not guess what he
was thinking, she took his hand to bring him back to her.
The love-act caused in him a flood of wanting so real he
could see for certain it was only that kind of unhesitant
giving that was going to solve the distance between
them.

"I started making my own associations," he said.

"I could see it. I don't mind."

"No. I want to treat you well."

"You do," she said. "You don't know how well you do."

"Go ahead. I want to hear some more."

"Daydream some more, you mean."

"Don't tease me when I'm being sincere."

"Okay."

Everything worked at cross-purposes, she said about her parents. Her father had not tried to jolt her mother out of the self-pity she had felt on coming to this country. He knew full well how strange and frightening America was to her. He sought to be kind, and the consequence was that she never adjusted, never developed the ability to adjust. She opposed each move and progression up from the hardlife, just out of a bitter fear of anything strange. Even now he had to placate her when he wanted anything, and as often as not he gave up. He had never bought a car, for example, and Elaine knew he had always wanted one.

As for their feelings for each other, Elaine could only guess; she had never seen more than a dry kiss on the cheek. There were no loving looks in her sight, no gestures, no touches. Elaine did not believe they existed with her parents. She had no conception of what love between man and woman was like.

She stopped, smiling and blushing. "That's not entirely true, any more."

"I wasn't thinking anything," he said innocently.

"You rat." She could not look at him.

The food came. He was thinking that, for as much as he cherished his background, he knew less about love than she did. He was willing to believe that she had always known about it. The truth was that she probably lived more intensely than he did. He was even willing to concede that much to her.

She started talking again after a moment. She was told nothing. When she was eleven, and began to need a brassiere, she had to ask for it. The following year, when her menstruation started, it was a time of terror and rampaging fear. There was no discussion between mother and daughter. The woman gave the girl the necessary equipment and a folder of instructions. It was another full year before Elaine really found out, from a book read in the library—she would have never taken the book home—what had begun that awful morning.

"Elaine, will you forgive me if I ask a question? I have to ask it.—Do you at least know how to keep yourself clean?"

"N-no, I don't think I do, really."

"I'll teach you, then."

"I need things from the drugstore, don't I? I couldn't buy them. I couldn't."

"I'll get them. Don't think about it."

She was quiet a while. "I can't talk now. I'm so ashamed."

"No. Stop it. I was way out of line."

"No, you were right. Give me a minute. Where was I?"

"You were going to tell me about school," he said. "Forget it, if you want."

"No."

"Would you mind if I told you I was very proud of you? Proud to know you?"

"I don't know why. I feel like nothing, around you."

"You're not," he said. "You know you're not."

"You make me so happy."

"Okay," he said. "Go on. I didn't mean to interrupt."

She smiled and touched his hand again.

In grammar school she had been one of the three or four brightest students in her class. Her teachers recommended that she go to one of the special high schools, and it was her parents' Old World respect for learning that made them agree. But it was the special high school— Hunter High, on the east side of Manhattan—that brought about the first real separation of Elaine from her parents, which in turn worked into the deeper separation, the one between her parents.

At Hunter, girls Elaine's age used lipstick, pancake and eyeshadow. They wore falsies. They wore nylons and girdles every day and took the latest novels from lending libraries. They knew popular music, movie stars, and the ultimate in sophistication, the Theater. Some of them used four-letter words with ease and talked openly of sex.

At fourteen Elaine was fat, misshapen and awkward. She had only one pair of low-heel pumps. From the beginning she knew she did not want to imitate the other girls, but staying *so* out-of-place was impossible. The friends she made were both like what she was, and what she wanted to become. Her first demands on her parents were simple and physical, and they were met after only a little opposition from them—her father did not want his little girl to grow up; her mother thought she was being foolish. But clothes and lipstick dark enough for color were wrested from them, and for a while she was happy.

What the girl discovered frightened her mother. Elaine took to reading maturer books, following the lists of her teachers. She spent her baby-sitting money on tickets for plays, and began going to the movies on Friday nights instead of Saturday afternoons. Her mother would make faces when she repeated some of the ideas she had heard in school. But her father was glad; he talked to her about politics and current affairs, he read her textbooks, and tried to help her with her homework.

And this dichotomy of attitudes increased as time went on. As Elaine matured her father took her more and more into his confidence. One time he came up for a promotion; he told her, not her mother, and she kept the secret later, when the job was filled by someone else. When Elaine fought with her mother, which was often, the father tried at first to conciliate, and then, because it was the only course open, he tried to explain the woman to Elaine. In the beginning, it was through him that Elaine forebore her mother's abuse.

Her mother opposed Cornell. She did not want Elaine going away to college. She could go to Hunter or City College, as the other girls were doing. She did not want to understand that Elaine had won scholarships and prizes enough to pay for more than half her fees. She rejected the idea that the change in environment would be good for the girl, in that it would help her grow.

She did want one thing: marriage for Elaine—for that would mean some dependence on *her*, through the first year, then during pregnancy, and later when the children came. Grandmothers were invaluable. She wanted to be a grandmother, to solve the loneliness and the boredom.

"Charlie, I don't want my children suffering her problems. They can grow up clean of all that, and I owe them the chance—"

"You're right," he said. "Now, let's stop here for the time being. Let's just sit here and finish eating this stuff. It's going to be like ice." She was beginning to say more than she had intended, he felt. He did not want to endanger the trust she had in him by letting her relax beyond her own true wishes. She might hate the situations her mother forced her into, but she did not hate the woman herself. He did not want her thinking she had gone too far too emotionally and had given him ideas that were misleading. There was plenty of time to get everything straight. There were other things that were more worthwhile to do and say for now.

As for him, it wasn't possible to judge her mother. Elaine had described the woman too well. Her standards were different. But because of the suffering she had put on Elaine, his opinion simply hung there. He could taste the uncertainty Elaine was living—and making more bitter for the sake of seeing him.

He was still in awe of her, this lovely, lovely young woman. When he saw what she had come from and what she had made herself, he had so little confidence in his own abilities that he was afraid he would not be able to sustain her interest. Yet she continued . . . on the way up he had thought he would be able to seduce her, but he wasn't going to. There weren't going to be any motels in the excitement of liquor and dancing close. Now he could see that even the idea of seduction had nothing to do with them. He found himself reaching eagerly for his obligations to her. They frightened him, and as a result he was making promises to himself he had not conceived of before this moment, and pondering difficulties he wanted to avoid, realizing that lesser ones in his past had tripped him up.

He looked at her and thought of Alice again. Where would be the pride he wanted Elaine to have in him after she knew about Alice? But he had to tell, to attain Elaine's honesty. It was going to be a dubious conversation and the shadow of it depressed him more and more. He tapped her hand to atract her attention. "Would you like to hear my tawdry little drama? It starts in a bookstore."

Elaine sipped her coffee and looked up at him. "You don't owe her a thing, you know. She used you at least as much as you think you used her. She took advantage of your good nature. She spent the night at your place—big deal. All she had a right to expect was breakfast in the morning. The burden of her loneliness was on her; she put it on you. She made you aware of everything she felt, and she's naturally an uncertain, jealous, suspicious person to start with. You knew it. That you thought to call her back that first morning after she saw you with Murillo shows it. But Murillo shows something else: that she's capable of using her feelings and what you know about them to advance herself. When Murillo bothered her six weeks ago, she made sure you knew it, and hoped you would feel concerned enough to want to come around again and, ahem, assure her."

"I think you're being harsh with her now," he said.

"Oh, am I? I know my sex. Even the sweetest of us, meaning yours truly, are capable of the wildest schemes to advance ourselves. Take me, for example. Even while I was going with Cal I thought of what I would do if Mary called me. I was just going to sort of let him know I didn't need him any more—that's the way I put it to myself. I woke up—and maybe she will, too, and see the affair for what it was and you for what you are." She paused, smiling. "Don't you want to know what you are?"

"All right, tell me."

"A louse."

"Okay."

"I'm sorry, honey. I really am. I just wanted to tease you and lift you out of it."

"I know, but I was wrong. I—"

"Of course you were. We all make mistakes. But she helped make sure you would feel this as severely as you do. She knew as much as I know already that you're concerned with the consequences of your acts—"

"You know that?"

She nodded. "Don't ever be afraid to hurt me, you know, if you get tired of me."

"No—no. I wanted to say, I think as much about what I did to Murillo as anything. Of course I can't apologize to him—he would feel he was getting carte blanche to bother her. He would. You don't apologize to people like him."

"Of course not." She sipped her coffee again. What he had done to Murillo had been a surprise to her. She had not thought of him in a context of violence.

He watched her light a cigarette and look out the window. She seemed unaware of the victory she had won over herself: she had talked as easily of Marv and Cal as she had of her many jobs. She was still looking out the window. He tapped her hand.

"A penny," he said.

"I was just dreaming of you."

"I'm right here."

"Please don't make me blush. Tell me something." She was smiling brightly now. "If you had picked me up like that, would you have tried the same thing with me?"

"Damned straight."

"A girl likes to know these things. Are you going to take me dancing?"

"All right." He looked at the check and reached for his wallet.

"Are you having a good time?" she asked.

"A ball. I really am."

"So am I. Don't leave early Sunday."

"I wasn't planning to. Come on."

Sunday night, as usual, Elaine called home. She got her father. Her mother was out to the store, he said; she would be back in a minute. There was a silence. There was nothing Elaine could tell. She had been counting on her mother to have something, even something unpleasant, to sustain the conversation.

"So, what did you do this weekend?" he asked.

"I went out. I had a couple of dates."

"Same fellow? You sound in good spirits."

"Do I? Yes, the same fellow. Friday night we went out dancing and last night he took me up to Syracuse to the fights."

"The fights? You like the fights now? Now I get the picture. Who is he?"

"Just a fellow, Pa. You don't know him. The fights were interesting. A fellow was knocked out."

"Hm. This fellow you're going out with—is there anything we should know about him?"

She hesitated. "Yes. He's a Christian."

"Not the same one?"

"No, Pa. I told you you didn't know him."

"Is he up there at school?"

"No, he lives in New York." She thought of saying, "I met him during intersession," but she wasn't going to lie.

"Well," he said, letting out a sigh, "I won't say anything to your mother. You know what's right—Here's your mother coming in now. It's Elaine!" he said away from the mouthpiece. Now back: "By the way, it takes more than a flashy knockout to make a good fight. That's no place to take a young girl, anyway."

"It way my idea," she said heatedly, but he wasn't there. While she waited she thought, *Charlie was disgusted with the knockout, if you want to know it.* A sick, sinking feeling took hold of her. Her mother came on and, for the next few minutes, the conversation did not seem to make sense. Then her mother started on some petty thing or other, and when Elaine had had enough, she said that the time on the call had run out long ago and she said goodbye and hung up.

In her room the silence screamed. She prepared for bed and then sat a while with her back against the plumped-up pillows. She was sick now, and good. She could not remember anything. But she was not going to tell Charlie, what had happened tonight. There wasn't any need. It was like being punished in class for something the girl in the seat behind had done. Nothing, not even the sudden hate she felt for everything could relieve the pressing feeling in her chest. She was glad he was not her to see this, for she felt fat again, and ugly. She thought of her father and the way he tried to manage his life, with his soft, self-demeaning way; she thought of the pride she had felt these past two days in her desire and hope and suddenly she felt dirty, irresponsible and useless. When it was late and black outside the windows, except for a lamp on the pathway shining through the bare branches, she heard someone walking down below and a good way off, on the gritty path, and whistling—no tune at all. As if they had been signaled, her feelings boiled up all at once. She felt a bitter rage more powerful than she had thought her emotions could be. The spell ended almost as suddenly as it had started, and she was left exhausted and coughing, wishing for real tears and, too, the warmth of another soul.

On Wednesday night when she called Charlie she told him that her father knew about them. "He didn't take it as well as I had hoped, honey."

"How do you feel?"

"Frightened a little, hurt and disappointed. Not too bad. I'm all right."

"Listen to me," he said. "I want you to conserve yourself. Go for walks, do the things you want. Indulge yourself in the things you want. It will keep your strength up."

"I wouldn't mind having you around," she whispered.

"I feel the same way," he said.

"I wasn't going to tell you he knew. I was going to spare you. I'm pretty good, aren't I?"

"You're tougher than you think," he said. "I'm not worried about you."

"Does that self-indulgence really work?"

"How do you think machelors learn how to live so well? It takes the sting out of the loneliness."

"That's good. I never thought of that."

"Feel better?" he asked.

"Yes. Oh, yes."

"Will you indulge yourself?"

"There's a fellow in my psych class. He's on the lacrosse team. He's been giving me the eye."

"I would prefer that you walked, to tell you the truth."

"Oh, I love you for that. You keep away from those modern dancers, too."

"Listen, I've been living in Loew's."

"I know," she said. "Keep writing to me, Charlie, please. I love your letters."

"I wrote last night. You ought to get it tomorrow. I was planning, to get out another tonight—"

"Don't, if you've just decided that for me."

"Oh, no. You'll see."

There was a letter on Thursday, kind and gentle. He talked about their weekend and how quickly it had passed for him. She answered him immediately, while she was eating her lunch, and then later she took his advice, and walked through the quiet afternoon until dark. The air was cold, and she made herself very tired, and that night she slept soundly.

The letters went on, more intense, more loving. He could not hold back, and he pulled her with him. Gifts crossed in the mails, first small pieces of jewelry, then books carefully inscribed, and at last articles of clothing. He came to expect packages—a sport shirt once, handkerchiefs, a wallet. He sent her blouses and skirts and slips. The gifts were expressions of love he could not utter even now; he knew it, and so did she know it. She wrote to wish that he could put them on her. This was exactly what he had imagined, and when she offered herself, he was even more deeply, profoundly thrilled.

They spoke more on the telephone, but the sound of their own voices made their situation that much more intolerable. The letters and gifts impelled them to talk, and the calls impelled them to touch.

He planned another visit, but on the third weekend in March fifteen inches of snow fell on the city. By the next week the roads were still not good—and they had to be good, because he had to be able to make the trip in six hours. He bided his time in the Loew's, scowling at the screen.

They planned for the second week in April. She was coming to him. That Friday afternoon he dismantled the apartment in search of dirt, and by early evening he was nearly ready, the windows and door open, the air blowing away the smell of furniture polish.

He was sitting at the kitchen table, his bare back to the open door, his bare feet planted on the cold floor, while he hunched over a tepid cup of instant coffee and the new issue of *The Atlantic*. He was trying to muster some interest in the Washington Report and the campaign. He had heard footsteps on the stairs outside, and he was awaiting the slam of another apartment door. A pair of hands descended on his eyes.

"Play the game," she said.

His heart leaped. "Er, Harold Stassen."

"I have too much hair. Try again."

"Yul Brynner."

"Do you want to kiss Yul Brynner?"

"Not particularly."

"Don't look around." She took her hands away from his eyes and she bit him lightly on the shoulder. "How's that?" she asked.

"If you're Yul Brynner, I'm going to rap you right in the mouth."

"Stop," she said, and turned him around. His eyes were very bright. "Give me a good kiss."

"Oh, it's *you!*"

"I'm going to leave."

"Come here." Then, "You're early. What happened?"

"I couldn't wait." It was very matter-of-fact and happy.

"What did you do, Elaine? You would have had to cut the full day."

"I took a plane," she said.

"You're kidding."

"I did," she said proudly. "My first one. It was very nice. Give me another kiss." She put her arms around his neck and he held her at the waist with his elbows, to keep his polish- and dust-covered hands from touching her coat. "Show me your place," she said. "I want to see what kind of a housekeeper you are."

"Why don't you ask if I can cook?"

"Well, can you?"

"Sure." He pulled in her suitcase from where she had left it in the hall and shut the door. "Here," he said, guiding her into the living room, "this is it, with the kitchen, but for the john, of course, and a little room in the back where I have a desk and stuff."

"It's lovely. Are you sure all the earrings and empty beer bottles have been cleaned out?"

"Oh, yes. The man came around with the truck just this morning."

"That'll teach me. The place is lovely, Charlie. I like it very much."

"Good." He turned her around to him. "Now—where do you parents think you are?"

"They dont think anything," she said seriously. "Only if they call the dorm, which they have never done, will they be able to know I've checked out for the weekend. And that's all. Sunday night, when I call them from up there, everything will be normal."

He steered her back into the kitchen and sat her down and started to prepare some real coffee. She said something about service, too, and he smiled. He turned around and leaned against the stove and stared unashamedly at her legs. She moved her skirt up and then down.

"I'm just hoping I don't lose control of myself," he said.

"Nothing could please me more."

"There'll only be one first time. I want to remember it, so don't overwhelm me."

"You'll remember, I promise."

"You must have been in good shape on the plane. Lots of vibrations?"

"No comment.—Can I see the back room?"

"Go ahead."

He thought of her parents again. So far, so good, but soon they would be hammering at her. Either her father would tell her mother, or she would, to restore some dignity to herself. This was something to celebrate, and the choking of it the way they had to do was enough to turn a proud young woman's love to hate—for him.

She came back. "You look so sad."

"I just remembered—I don't like sex."

"Goodbye."

"Wait, we can work something out."

She laughed. "See my lawyer."

He reached for her and she backed away. "Come on," he said, "I was only kidding."

"Well, I don't know."

"Take a chance, kid. Come on." He winked.

"That's lewd."

"I know. Come here to me now." He put his arms around her. "I love you, Elaine. I do."

"I know. I love you. I' never been so happy."

She was crying. His dream melted and he opened his eyes. He was still holding her. The bed was moving from her spasms. He stroked her arm and kissed her forehead. "Elaine. What's the matter, Elaine?"

She did not move.

"Elaine. Wake up."

She sat up. "What? Oh. What is it?"

"What was the dream about?"

"Oh—I don't know. It's gone. I'm sorry."

"No. Let me hold you. Come on."

"Do you want to? Don't do it if you don't—or something."

"I want to. I've been doing it right along."

"This is new to me, this part. I'm very happy, Charlie."

"I know. I am, too."

"Don't think about the dream," she said. "It doesn't mean anything."

"That's right," he said. "You have the right idea."

chapter five

I

The road climbed the hill and curved down again toward the lush green valley on the left. On the high side were ramshackle stands, whitewash peeling, almost overgrown with weeds. Their windows were dark. Across the valley a freight train was rumbling through, pouring smoke up past the power lines that swung lightly, like music, through the trees. Charlie pulled the car off the road past the stands and began lowering the convertible top. He stepped out to straighten the folds in the cloth, and suddenly he felt lost; the earth under his feet was spongy and soft, a sensation he had filed away in a dusty corner. He was disappointed with himself deeply, for having forgotten. There was a pleasant breeze carrying the odors of the decaying woods and the new sweet grass. He had forgotten them, too, or had forgotten to anticipate them. He got into the car again, distracted.

This was their last chance for a weekend before the closing of school, which was still three weeks away in the beginning of June. Neither could spare the time to make the trip again. As it was, he was stretching it, taking another Friday off.

Their time together did not amount to a week, strung hour to hour, but it seemed like both more and less. It was blurred. It was spread by the letters and the telephone calls into his ideas and daydreams, which were the spillways of his stopped-up hope. He had thrown himself into this with a great intensity, but it was like walking toward the mountains; the mountains were there, but as he approached them they grew more distant.

He had to take her on her own terms even if the doubt did come swirling in. But if he was afraid, he tried to remember what she had said: that she had never cared for

264

anything as she cared for this. She was still struggling—
she was meaning to try. He was getting a run for his
money, he thought to himself reproachfully. All he had to
do was keep still, so little, and he was having trouble. He
wanted her. For the first time in his life he felt something
more than his own reactions.

The road flattened out. He hit the brake sharply once,
twice, a third time, and brought his speed down to thirty
miles per hour. The car rolled from the asphalt onto
yellow concrete. On both sides, under thick, wind-thrashed
trees, stood old large houses glowing in the swaying, dap-
pled sunshine. Ahead, against the branches, a traffic light
changed from green to yellow to red. He brought the car
to a stop and watched people—school children, mostly;
it was lunch time—cross in front of him. The other end of
the town was just beyond the next block, and behind the
houses diagonally across the thoroughfare was a field of
new alfalfa, glittering and hot.

The light changed and he started forward again. The
tall trees went on past the town and through the fences
below them he could see the fields going back to the
distant woods, the rows of alfalfa still short and neat,
gliding from front to back as if around a wheel. Between
the rows were clods of soil dried hard and dusty in the
May sun, and everywhere was the rich, heavy odor, sweet,
warm and intoxicating.

When his mind went back to what he had been thinking
his hands grew weak a moment. He was afraid again, very
afraid.

He picked her up at her dormitory, and they drove up
Route Thirteen to a motel they thought a suitable distance
from the school. She was feeling better than he was and
just being with her helped him relax, but it was difficult
for him to forget himself. They went back to town for
dinner at the Normandie, and got high on the wine. Still
he had not come through. They walked, then back to the
car. Nothing was going wrong, but nothing was going right
enough to make him really happy.

The next day he took her over to Watkins Glen, which

she had never seen. He came in from the south deliberately, and when he saw the bridge and the bluff on the eastern side where he had stood last Christmas, the entire experience was back on him, and he was glad he was saving that for her for the last.

They parked the car and walked into the Glen, up the trails beside the rushing water, around under the falls and up the other side, almost to the top. Yesterday's drive and his nervousness were catching up with him, and he was quite tired, but they were having a good time and the gap between them was closing.

They walked back down to the car. She was fretting about her hair now, which the dampness had ruined. Did he mind if she set it in the car before they left? No, go ahead, there was more to see anyway. Like what? Be patient, he said.

Her hair did not take her long. She was curious about what was to come. He started the car out of the village toward the bridge across the foot of Seneca Lake. She asked him again and now his attitude was changed.

"Well, maybe you won't think so much of it. When I was up here Christmas week, I drove out here. Up on that bluff you get a view of the lake. You'll see it. You know, as we went through the Glen I could remember more and more of the time I went through with my family. It was bittersweet, remembering, and more."

"May I hear about it?"

"I began to think that it wasn't enough to take *you* there. There was so little I could tell you. But our own children, and drawing them into the world: that would be something. I can't really articulate it. I would like to bring our children here. I'll tell you one thing: if I don't marry you, I won't be able to come back without thinking of you and today. But I have yet to close the circle for myself. Now I'm starting to repeat myself."

"No, you're not. How do you feel? You look so tired."

"I'll be all right."

"Would you like me to drive back? You can take a nap."

"You can drive if you'd like, but I won't nap."

They were going up the hill over the lake. They were silent now, he thought because he had said "our children." First time. He had not thought. If it had been a little torture for her, she had not shown it. He reached for her hand. She took his hand and kissed it. He glanced over: she looked happy. He had misjudged her.

They were at the top and he turned the car onto the shoulder. "Here we go. Bail out."

They met at the front of the car and he took her hand and they trudged over the grass to the edge. The water was a very dark blue, reflecting the deep, clear sky. Below them a sloop, with its sails full-blown, cut along with the waves, peeling off a small white cap. Far to the north, almost out of sight in the distance, was a tiny moving fleck, the wake of a motorboat. In a minute he quit looking and turned to her, but she was too occupied to pay attention to him. Overhead, a twin-engined plane, a Convair, was flying toward the northeast, the fuselage gleaming in the sun, growing brighter. The sound of motors growled over the countryside. Suddenly, as the position of the plane became right, the reflection burst white and blinding in his eyes, so that he had to look away.

She turned to him. He knew at once she hadn't noticed the plane. "Ready so soon?" she asked.

"If you are."

"Give me a kiss first. It's a beautiful view."

They went back to the car and she got behind the wheel. "All right, where do we go?"

"Let's go down to the Loop and grab a flick." He was slouched against the door with his knees against the dashboard. Now he felt like having fun.

"The Loop is in Chicago."

"So, is Chicago posted?"

"What does that mean?"

"Off limits."

"Well, no, it isn't. But why don't you climb in the back and take that nap, virile Cyril? That's what has you tired, you know."

"Don't be silly. And I'll stay here and see the accident from a good seat."

"Wise guy. Let's go into Ithaca for dinner."

"Suits me." He closed his eyes as she backed the car off the shoulder and, as he realized he was going to sleep, he grinned, but did not try to stop himself.

As though only a moment had passed, she was kissing him on the mouth. She stopped and moved aside and he opened his eyes. There were branches overhead and he could feel a cool breeze. He stretched and yawned and from around the car came a splatter of applause.

"Bravo!" somebody shouted.

Charlie looked around: there were four or five collegiate types, all young, grinning moronically.

"Good morning," Elaine said.

"Don't you sweep the streets around here?"

"You should have heard them a moment ago, 'little snookums', and so forth."

"I can imagine. Get them out of here, their faces are worse than fried eggs."

"Scat, everybody. He's a horror when he wakes up, and he might attack."

"Jesus," he mumbled, "they're going to think all kinds of things about you. What are you doing so very close to school anyhow? You're supposed to be away for the weekend."

"I forgot. Don't worry about what they think. I kissed you in front of them, didn't I?"

"That's right." He grabbed for her.

"Oh, no, you're awake now."

"Can't prove it by me. Where's the coffee?"

"Fifty paces away, inside the luncheonette. Do you think you can make it?"

"Carry me."

"Oh, come on."

They went inside. The campus was across the street and from their booth by the window they could see the setting sun behind the trees; the leaves tossed and flowed in the wind and like melted jewels, flung through the liquid light.

"I'll be all right in a minute," he said. "I'll be just great."

"You're great now."

"I've perverted you. You've lost your power to judge."

The goons who had been around the car were sitting at a nearby table. They looked over and laughed.

"They're jealous," she said.

"That's right. Say, you didn't cop any feels while I was asleep, did you?"

"I'm not talking."

"What time is it?"

"After five, why?"

He didn't get a chance to tell her. Her attention was drawn away, and she was looking across the street to the gate from which four young men in dungarees and sweat shirts were emerging. They were upperclassmen, dirty and disheaveled, as if they'd been moving pianos. "What is it?" he asked.

"The one nearest us is Cal Torrenson."

"Okay, you look away while I look. We don't want him to think you're pointing him out to me. He'll know what I know, then."

As she lit a cigarette he glanced quickly out the window. Torrenson fit her description of him, tall, very well-built, blonde and collegiate-looking. His hair was cut Princeton-style, which was the vogue up here.

"Well?"

"All right."

"In a way I was hoping you would never see him, or Marv, either."

He was confused a moment; Marv wasn't here any more. But then he saw she was afraid of even chance encounters in New York, say, or anywhere. It was silly. He said, "I wouldn't think about it one way or the other. You shouldn't let it bother you."

"He'll come over and say hello. Be prepared for that. When he wants to, he can be the personality kid himself."

"So, nu, he'll say hello."

"That's lovely," she said.

"Now, if he has a brain, all three of us will know what the others are thinking. That's your trouble; you'll be thinking that both our minds are going like hell, sizing each other up. Don't worry about me, I've been in this situation before."

"But you weren't—" She stopped.

"That's right, conceited, I wasn't in love then."

The four marched into the luncheonette and across to a far table. Charlie said, "Tell me who the others are, if you know."

"They're his fraternity brothers—excuse me." She turned and smiled sweetly, civilly, to the other side of the room. Torrenson was smiling hello, but then suddenly he pointed to Charlie, as if to ask, "Is he the one?"

She nodded.

"What gives?"

"Quite a while ago, before you came up last time, we met in the cafeteria while I was reading your letters. He asked me to go out that weekend and I told him I was busy both nights. He guessed something from the look on my face and the way I handled him."

"That's gratifying."

"Did I have you worried?" she asked.

"No, but now that you ask—"

"Okay." She took his hand. The coffee they had ordered was brought over by the waitress.

"Here he comes," Elaine said. "Steel yourself."

"Hi," Torrenson said. 'Elaine, I just wanted to ask you a question about something."

"Sure, just a minute." She made the introductions. Because Elaine was there, Charlie was supposed to stand up, but he didn't, because he didn't feel like it.

"Excuse me for staying seated, but I'm just waking up."

"Hm?" Torrenson was trying to find a sinister meaning. Charlie was thrilled. "Yes, sure," Torrenson said, "waking up."

"He was asleep," Elaine said.

"That's logical. But what I wanted to ask you, Elaine—

I'm writing for job interviews in New York, and I was wondering if I should go into detail about my background and schooling, or just say, you know, that I'd like an interview. You know those people, so I thought you'd be able to give me the right idea." He looked at Charlie. "I'm going into advertising or personnel, by the way, Cumberland. One of the two."

"Oh."

"Keep your letter short," Elaine said. "Just say you're graduating from Cornell and you'd like to apply for a job. They handle it the way *they* want, and there's not a thing you can do."

"Except study the right answers for a battery of psych tests."

"You know that depends on where you go. But don't try it unless you can be absolutely sure of yourself and your subject. These people who do the interviewing have been at it for years, and dealing with people who have had good reason to try to outsmart them. They know their stuff, and they'll be able to spot a phony a long way off. And if you *do* get spotted, you may never get a job, because for all we know, there are black-lists going around."

Charlie said, "Honey, black-lists are illegal and have been for years." He wondered if Torrenson had really thought he could pull off a little snooping job with such an asinine question. His own statement had been naïve; anyone who wanted could have a black-list, law or no law. But he hadn't been able to sit still while this turd satisfied himself. He was getting into it because, according to the things Elaine had told him, Torrenson was at the same old stand, wheedling, hanging around. As soon as Torrenson addressed him directly, Charlie would roll clean over him. In his mood, Charlie felt like it.

"These wouldn't be precisely black-lists, dear," Elaine said to him. "They would be lists of the people who failed certain tests, much the same as the lists insurance companies keep of those who fail to get policies. It might hold up in court just as well. And even if you could get a decision against it, it wouldn't do you much good."

"To the barricades," Charlie said.

"Oh, they have a right," said Torrenson.

Charlie looked up at him and grinned mischievously. Here was the chance. "Don't take offense, but you don't really think so. That you'd bone up for the test shows it: the system doesn't apply to you. Take it one step further: everyone objects to the system and tries to defy it, so you have a revolt against a rule that is, for all practical purposes, as powerful as a law. And it's a law with no common good at all, so they don't have a right."

"Come on. A man has the right to hire whomever he pleases."

Charlie said, pouring it on, "No, it depends on his criteria. His criteria have to fit into public policy. This isn't my field, but Elaine and I have talked about it some. It seems to me that these tests are working in an area in which public policy hasn't been formed. When the policy is formed, it will be against the tests."

"You've missed my point. A man can *still* hire whomever he pleases."

"No. Sit down. Make room for him, Elaine." Charlie had satisfied himself but now he was drawn by two things: by the argument itself, which he would have enjoyed any time; and by Torrenson himself, whm was not the genial collegiate he wanted to appear. He was extremely tough and controlled. Chancellor of his fraternity, Charlie remembered Elaine having said. He didn't even know what that meant. He glanced at Elaine in the attempt to tell her, *only a minute, I promise*. "Look at it this way," he said to Torrenson, "some of these tests are built to find out if you're the kind of man to put the company or your wife first. That's the most severe criterion, I know, but it's still one of them. Now when you want to know that, you infringe on a man's freedom. Suppose you have two men, one a fink and the other willing to do a just day's work for a just day's pay. But you've discovered the fink through the test. How do you decide who gets the job?"

"Well, whose interests are at stake?"

"Exactly. At the heart of it, the public's interests." He could see Elaine looking at him proudly. "And no less important," he said, feeling better about the time this was taking, "the interests of the individual. You see, when a company hires someone who'll give his all for the company, it's exploiting a cripple. No one has the right to expect more than a full day's work for a full day's pay. By forcing people to do more than they want—or should— you endanger the society. Take a person who's neither a cripple nor a well man, but someone who is just ignorant of what is being done to him. With this deep testing and so forth, a door is being opened in him so that he can be taken advantage of. Do-or-die can be slowly established as the standard among the ignorant. You could compare the result to labor conditions in the last century, except that everyone would have a smile on his face."

"I think you're overstating it, but what's your idea of a solution?"

"Control," Charlie said.

"That's socialism," Torrenson said flatly.

Not at all,—necessity. Since this knowledge about the nature of people is out and because there are men who are willing to give so much of themselves as to jeopardize the freedom of other men, it must be controlled. The forty-hour week and the minimum wage don't run into socialism, they run into necessity, because history has shown people—on both sides, management and labor—to be other than what we'd like them to be, whatever the reasons involved—"

"I'm glad you hung that on," Elaine said. "May I say something? In the last century many of the evils of company paternalism came out of religious convictions, one of the results of Protestant reform. The employers were sure they were doing the right thing, watching over the workers outside the plants, that it was right to try to keep them free from sin."

"There's your answer," Charlie said. "Write short letters. But why you should want to go into that stuff is beyond me."

"Why, what are you going into?"

"I'm in it now, to a degree. Teaching."

"That's beyond me, too."

"There you are," Charlie said with no warmth.

Torrenson stood up. "Well, nice to have met you.—Say, if you're not doing anything special tonight, why don't you drop by the fraternity house? Elaine knows where it is. We're having our big dance, which explains my condition. We've been cleaning all day."

"We'll see. Thanks." *We're even,* Charlie thought. *I got you and now you got me. "Elaine knows where it is." You're fast, pal, but you're sick, too.* He watched Torrenson go back to his table.

"What do you think?" Elaine asked.

"Oh, he's a cutie. I'm putting together what you told me about him, begging to go out with you, and so on. Just this little contact with him has frayed my nerves. I couldn't resist going after him. I hope he didn't hurt you with what he said."

"No, I was thinking of you."

"I'm all right. I was surprised at his speed and subtlety. I thought he would be just slightly dull."

"I think he is. You didn't convince him with your argument, which was beautiful."

"His kind doesn't convince. They operate on an emotional level."

"Doctor Cumberland and his portable couch."

"Am I right or am I right?" he asked.

"You're right," she said.

He looked at Torrenson again. He was talking with the boys. "I'll bet that club of his is full of people just like him."

"Do you want to see?"

"Maybe for a while. Right now we'll finish our coffee, go back to the motel to change and shower and a few other things, and then go to dinner. I want to have a good appetite when I sit down to eat."

"I'll do my best," she said, and smiled. "'Maybe for a while.' That means we're going. I know you."

"I'll keep it short, I promise."

"I know."

"Listen, if you're not interested in what I suggested for

the time between, I'll get you a magazine and you can read it."

"Stop. How could I read?"

"I'll show you."

"I don't want to learn," she said.

"The thought isn't tempting you, is it?"

"Come on and find out," she said, changing her tone again.

All the houses over the side of the hill were lit brightly and the lights shined out into the darkness against the branches and down onto the lawns. From a dozen places close and distant wildly cacophonous music crashed out into the spring night. He held her hand as they walked up the road, and he could see over the lawns to doors and windows thrown open, and verandas crowded with people. Their voices mingled with the music, and across the damp and perfumed air the two were one, chaotic and disquieting. He could see people dancing and others talking. From one house far back and high on the hill flashbulbs shot off, intermittent and noiseless.

She stopped at the end of a long cement walk on their right that ran up to the center entrance of a house, a monstrous place that looked eighty years old, and over whose porch, for the present, as hung a vivid flag of crimson, gold and purple, illuminated by spotlights mounted on the lawn.

"This is it," she said.

They went up the walk and onto the porch. Both doors were opened back, but it was impossible to get through. People were jammed tightly in the vestibule, drinks and cigarettes held high into the yellow light made shimmering by the flowing layers of blue smoke. The staircase on the left was crowded all the way up with couples sitting two abreast as if at a stadium, and there was only a narrow aisle between them up and down which people struggled to pass. Charlie could see a few formal gowns and tuxedoes.

"Is there another way in?"

"A door to the kitchen," she said.

"Let's try it."

It was quieter in the back of the house, with the roar removed and muffled. The kitchen door was locked, but Charlie rapped on the glass. A thin, frail boy opened the door.

"Well, this is a novel way to make your entrance, or are you trying to go out backwards?" His blond wispish hair hung over his forehead, and his eyes were pink-lidded. He got up on his toes to look over Charlie's shoulder. "Elaine! The party is complete! Terrific!"

"Charlie, this is Bix, Cal's friend."

"Friend, roommate and political advisor," he corrected.

"How do you do?"

"Likewise. Enter. Some blast, huh?"

"When does it start?" Charlie asked.

Bix looked at him quizzically, vexed.

"Charlie lives in Greenwich Village. He knows all about parties."

"Terrific. Just the man we need."

"You've been drinking, Bix," Elaine said.

"Drinking? I'm stoned! I'm blasted right out of my mind! Oh, am I stoned! Come on, I'll show you where the bar is."

"Where's your date?"

"Upstairs. Drinking gives her diarrhea. I was in the kitchen just now looking for a cork."

"Terrific," Charlie said.

Bix led the way into the dining room. Charlie would have called it that—but not tonight. Tables were set up against two walls, and a bar, which was crowded three-deep, was against the third. All the tables were taken. The room opened out on a front parlor, which was done up like a night club with small round tables and a dance floor. Beyond the dance floor was a bandbox. Right now they were both empty.

"Here you are," Bix said. "I'm going to pull my girl off the seat, if you'll excuse me. If I see Cal, I'll tell him you're here. He said he'd invited you. Well. It's good seeing you again, Elaine." And he was off, staggering and pushing, like a man running a gauntlet.

"He seems keen on you," Charlie said.

"Aren't they all?"

"No, seriously."

"I know. He was always pleasant to me. This is the first time I've seen him drunk."

He shrugged. "What would you like to drink?"

"Do you think he told him?"

Charlie was confused. Then, "There's no point in hanging around to find out. We can leave right now."

"No, you wanted to come. Oh, I don't know," she said fretfully.

"It's up to you. You know them better than I do."

"You want to stay—and so do I, for the same reason. I want to *see*." She looked angry now.

"Scotch and soda?"

"Yes, please."

It took him a while to get the drinks. When he came back she was looking the other way, gazing. She saw him and came out of it. "I got depressed all of a sudden," she said.

"I was wondering."

"Anger runs out of me now as if I were a sieve. I used to be able to stay angry. Now, after a moment, I get depressed."

"As I said, we can leave."

"No." She sipped her drink.

He didn't feel like talking. He looked around at the party-faces, feeling like a cancer among them. The conversation was a roar. If there were enough like him, the party would run down and stop and the people would look at each other questioningly.

It was easy to imagine Torrenson telling about the good times. And tormenting a little fellow like his roommate in the process. The roommate had one of those crushes, obviously. Oh yes, Torrenson was a cutie. Charlie had not thought of it, but he was sure now that the roommate knew. Thus things were squared. If the little fellow could scratch through the liquor and the fog down to his fantasies, perhaps he might even come up with the location of her birthmarks, the effect of her tongue, and all the rest—Torrenson supplied. Perhaps he could work up a thesis on her, gleamed entirely from morbid conversations.

Charlie had to realize now that when it came to anger, this kind of anger, *he* was watertight. Given time enough, the rage would show on his face. But sure, tonight, his last night up here, was the night to work into a sweat about Torrenson. He wanted urgently to keep his pity up, think of Torrenson begging, but now all he could remember was this afternoon and his three friends in the luncheonette; what had they been talking about? What did they have to talk about? Along with the roommate. Terrific, just terrific.

Torrenson was coming, glad-handing and back-patting through the yakking crowd. "Steady," Charlie said aloud, and moved closer to her.

"What happened, did you have to come in the back way? I should have warned you. It happens all the time. How long have you been here?"

"Just arrived." Charlie raised his glass to show that it was still nearly full.

"Can I get you seconds? I have to get them for us. Wait for me a moment and we can go to the table. What do you think of our parties?"

"I don't see any marijuana, heroin, camphor balls or dirty pictures, but I guess you have your diversions."

"There's only so much you can do on a campus," Torrenson said with a straight face. "Wait for me."

When he was out of earshot, Elaine said, "Do you know that a year ago he seemed shy? By comparison. He was quiet in the classroom, and outside he was, well, self-effacing. He had an innocence about him."

"He's growing up. Now he has acne on his soul."

"You're going to make me spill my drink," she said.

"I haven't upset you with this stuff I've been throwing around about the parties in New York, have I?"

"Oh, no. I know why you're doing it."

In the lapse that followed he remembered the party last fall, after his first fight with Alice, when he had gone up to the Bronx in the Buick; he could picture going into the bedroom after his coat and that absurd moment, Hal and the girl in bed, himself trying to back out with some trace of—what? Savoir-faire? He remembered the girl's mother, and talking to her earlier. A creature from a nightmare, attacking him while her daughter was racing out of her clothes. "What *about* me?" the daughter had asked. Now, looking around at this, he almost wanted to think that the scene and been *driving* him toward that night and those people. A shudder went through him. Of Elaine, he asked, "Tell me, how do these things wind up?"

"Oh, they bunny-hop out to the street, and a lot of other silly stuff, and then they collapse onto the couches for fun and games. Those who are serious about it drive somewhere. Once in a while a drunk falls down into one of the gorges, and breaks his arm, leg or head, but that's rare—no, medium-rare."

"Terrific." He looked at her. "That idiot has planted that word in me and it's all I can think of to say."

"Try, bubby."

"All right. I'm a million miles away from here, anyway."

"Where?"

He shrugged, feeling the desperation of wanting to get a vague idea crystallized. "I don't know, I get the impression that I've fallen into something I left behind a long time ago. I had my fill of drunken parties, and maybe I even forgot about them, forgot they existed. But here they are, all of them, as though the same people had sped over back roads to get here before me, pulling the same antics, telling the same jokes, going through the same mannerisms and gestures."

"Little Swiss clock people."

"I don't follow you," he said.

"They're like the people in the Swiss clocks. They do the same things time and again, with the same blank expressions. But these people have a more profound vacancy in their eyes. Their glee wears through faster than that of the wooden figures. You get the idea that they all *want* to ship out tomorrow for combat—just to be doing something. They're crowding this in, as though there was nothing worth-while to do."

"Have you ever felt it?" he asked. Now he was thinking

of Korea. There had been a reason for tuning out over there. Fear slithered through a man like a snake in the night. You were close to part of the animal nature of things and you had a right to be afraid. In the beginning. This was all so far from everything, absolutely everything! Somewhere in the room was a sweet little girl crippled with cramps because she had to fart and she was afraid somebody would smell her, or worse, hear her. It was as if they were all trying to dip themselves in shellac.

Elaine said, "I felt it, when I was going out with him. Boy wonder. I let it go on for a couple of weeks, and then I had to run. That wasn't the only reason, of course."

"We shouldn't have come."

"As long as we're here, we might as well satisfy our curiosity. I've been wondering about the girl he's with, but I haven't said anything because I didn't want you to think I was being catty."

"You're about as catty as a lioness."

"I feel like a lioness around you. You give me pride, or you've been trying hard enough."

"Oh, a pride of lions. All right."

The band was getting up on the stand. There were six men, and Charlie was surprised. He tried to estimate the cost—hundred, hundred and fifty dollars. Perhaps even two hundred. It was really, though in a mild way, fantastic. Individual costs had to be tacked on, to get a good idea of what this amounted to, in plain human sweat. It had to be well over a thousand dollars, including, too, the cost of the gasoline the car burned to run Elaine and him up here from the motel. *I should have been an economist*, he thought. *Still, for this, a kid could pay his tuition here for a year*.

The band struck up a saxophoney arrangement of "Cherry Pink and Apple Blossom White." In a swarm, people got up from the tables and made for the dance floor. Somebody let out a shout of exuberance above the noise of the music. The people dancing folded into a solid wall and there was nothing more to see.

"All right," Torrenson said directly behind them, "we're ready to go."

Truer words were never spoken, Charlie thought wildly. He stepped aside to allow Torrenson to lead the way. His two drinks were on a very little tray, which was a bit of foolishness, considering the mob he had to get through. Charlie felt Elaine take his arm and hold him back several paces. She kissed his cheek and then whispered:

"You know what I'm thinking? Please don't break up. We could goose him now and send him, tray and all, across the room, and beat it the hell out of here."

"Be brave, will you?"

Torrenson wove a path around the side of the dance floor to one of the round tables quite near the band. Seated there was a blonde girl wearing a fluffy party dress of some indefinable dark color. But the color wasn't important, not at all, for the dress was cut low in the front, showing nearly everything of her small high breasts. She was wearing a push-up brassiere with her nipples tucked below, just below, the edge. She had lovely tan skin, marvelously even in texture.

"Oh, God," Elaine muttered.

"Now you're being catty."

"Do you know what I would look like in a bra like that? Do you?"

"You wear one and I'll paint the top of you green and use you for a golf course."

She giggled. "Please don't tell me what you would use for tees."

"Well, don't tease this innocent child we're about to meet."

"Now that is pathetic," she said.

Torrenson set the tray down and made the introductions. The girl's name was Betty. There were chairs around to spare and two extras were dragged up quickly. The table was not big enough for four, and they had to sit back from it and reach for the drinks. Still, it was clear that knees would be touching the rest of the evening. As Betty moved back she readjusted her skirt and crossed her legs. The petticoats caused the whole arrangement to float up and provide an ample view to the tops of her stockings.

"Well, here's to getting out," Torrenson said above the music.

"Getting what?" Elaine asked.

"Graduation," he said, not understanding. He was sitting opposite Charlie and out of line Betty's legs. Elaine, across from her, had seen most, apparently. As he raised his glass Charlie gave Elaine a nudge under the table. But for a moment it seemed as if she wanted trouble, this kind of cheap, pointless trouble, for she set her glass down and looked pleasantly across the table.

"Do you go to Cornell, too, Betty?"

"Oh, no. Cortland State."

"Charlie knows someone who went there, don't you, honey?"

Alice. "Well, she only went a year." People retained the oddest things. He had mentioned to Elaine only once that Alice had gone to that school. It was not one of the things that came to his mind when he thought of the girl, yet Elaine had remembered. He said, "She did her freshman year and then quit. That was last year."

"I'm a junior now," Betty said. "I doubt if I'd know her."

"I didn't think so."

"Charlie here is a teacher," Torrenson said.

"Are you? Where? What subject?"

The music blared up and Charlie had to wait a moment. He said, "In Brooklyn. I'm student-teaching History in a high school. I'm not sure how it's going to work out, but I'll probably get a substitute's license to stay on while I pick up my Master's at night."

Torrenson said, "You're not from the city, not with your speech patterns."

"No, I grew up right outside of town here. I live in the city now, though. I moved there after I got out of the Army, to go to college."

"Now there's something," Torrenson said. "Elaine's home is in Brooklyn and she goes to school up here."

"Is that right?" Betty asked. "It's positively uncanny."

"We know," Elaine said pleasantly. There seemed to be a thaw going on. Perhaps Betty had just one aberration:

what she thought she should wear. It might even be Torrenson's doing; if she was stuck on him she would wear
whatever he told her. At the same time Charlie noticed it,
Elaine put his new thought into words: "Congratulations
on your pin."

"Thank you," Betty said. "It's supposed to be over the
heart, but—"

"There's no point in being sadistic," Torrenson said.

"Or desecrating art," said Charlie, looking at him directly. He noticed that Elaine was not taken aback, and
he was glad. Maybe he had been less sure of her a
moment ago than he should have been; her one remark,
after Torrenson's toast, had been probably too delicious to
resist. His own thoughts at that point had been no more
benign. He had to think that he was still very much
off-balance. The idea that Torrenson—here he was across
the table laughing at what Charlie had just said—could
have spread it around among his idiot friends that he had
been sleeping with Elaine, still incited and enraged him.
And it was exactly that he, Charlie, had no proof that
anything of the sort had taken place, that had him reeling
inside. He was without a way to deal with Torrenson, just
as his thoughts of this Betty still swam around disunited:
her clothes had led him to expect one thing, but her
manner—and her treatment of Elaine, for that matter, for
all she could know, fraternity pin being the evidence of
what she could know—her manner made him think something else again, something else entirely.

The band finished the "Cherry Pink" number and
moved into something quieter, to give the saxophone players a rest.

Torrenson was lighting a cigarette. "You know, Cumberland, I've been thinking all evening about some of the
things you said this afternoon. I may have a rebuttal for
you."

"Oh, I thought we were pretty much finished with
that."

"Well, suppose we see if the girls object."

"I don't know how I could object," Betty said. "I've
been listening to it now for hours."

"What about you, Elaine?"

She was looking away from him toward Charlie. He nudged her again. "Charlie makes the decisions. If he says no, it's no."

In a deliberately dull voice, Charlie said, "If you really think you have something, go ahead. But let's not tie each other up the rest ofthe night." To Betty, he said, "This is the last time I'll be able to make this trip."

"Well, then."

He said to Torrenson, "Go ahead before you lose your train of thought."

Torrenson grinned. "I'm having trouble already.—Now it's all right." He drew on his cigarette. "Now, let me see if I have what you said straight in my mind. You object to the use of the depth interview because it opens the door to a possible abridgment of freedom. You say that since many men cannot or will not become aware of the things that can be used, let's say, against them, other men don't have the right to utilize them from the beginning."

"That's about it," Charlie said. "It's a question of freedom."

"Well, this is what I wanted to say: in going to the depth interview, the employer has as his object increased production, but it just so happens that he can only get that increase if the employee fits into his job and is happy with it. You have to concede that not all depth interviewing is confined to the search for the do-or-die type. There aren't that many in the world. The increase in production serves as a gain to others outside, consumers, users of the service, and so on. There's a gain in freedom for all in the sense that men have to work shorter hours because of increased production—" He looked up over Charlie's head. Charlie turned around. It was the thin fellow, Bix, with his date. She was a shy, plain girl.

"Well, I see you found each other," he said genially.

"That's right," Torrenson said without warmth. He just stared at Bix, who was waiting to be invited to sit down Charlie turned to his drink and gave Elaine a little sign to keep out of it. He wanted to see what Torrenson would do. As it was, he had already lost most of the answers he had formed while Torrenson had been talking. He labored to keep the one he could remember. Torrenson was still staring at Bix, silent. His control was a terrible and beautiful thing to watch. Of course he would win over the little fellow.

"Well," Bix said, "I thought I'd just introduce Susan to Elaine and, um, Charlie."

"Hello," said Elaine graciously.

Charlie said, "Hi," and Bix repeated the names and there were smiles and nods all around. Bix said he wanted to see some other people and he took Susan away.

"Where were we?" Torrenson asked in a bland voice.

"I remember," Charlie said. He took another swallow of his drink as he forced his mind back to the subject. A minute passed; it was almost impossible for him to escape the smooth cruelty of what he had just seen. "You said there would be an increase in production if the employee fitted into his job and was happy with it."

"That's right. There would be a gain all around."

"You have to examine what you mean by happy," Charlie said. It was the one point he had been able to retain. He was completely dissatisfied. He said, "The kind of happiness you were speaking of is the result of fitting into one's inner niche, so to speak, submitting to the handicaps of his personality."

"A man has to face his limitations," Torrenson said.

"Let's say, a man has to face his limitations if he wants to. That's all I'll buy of it. But that's not important here. What is important is the fact that the decision to face or not to face is being made for him in an employer-sponsored depth interview. Take it or leave it. Work at this bench or you don't work here at all."

"But he'd probably get the same advice from a guidance counselor with aptitude tests."

"Yes, but voluntarily. What a man does to himself is his own business. It's just that when he passes through that door to tamper with someone else's psyche that we all become concerned—"

"It isn't a door, though."

"Of course it isn't. To see where the one thing begins and the other ends requires thinking."

"It isn't much of a solution," Torrenson said.

"I didn't say it was a solution. It's the fact; if you're interested in your own freedom, you defy it as your peril. The question is: what is the right relationship between an employer and his workers?"

"But wait," Torrenson said. "We've gone right by one of the things I touched on before, and it's one of the most vital too. That's the increase that's made through this process—"

"That's the thing I wanted to say before," Charlie said. "We can't discuss this in quantitative terms—gain and loss. Freedom is a qualitative thing. The whole question of psychological probing is still a small one in our society, quantitatively speaking. There's not that much of it going on. It's things in terms of gain and loss in our society, you have to take into account the struggle built into the society. Who gets the gain is often the one with the most power."

"I thought we were assuming that," Torrenson said.

"I wasn't sure we were," Charlie said.

"Well, we just don't know each other well enough," Torrenson said pleasantly. "But I do want to discuss this quantitatively," he pressed. "We have to discuss this in terms of quantities and qualities both. We are dealing with the society as well as the individual, and the society no less than the individual has quantitative as well as qualitative needs. Excuse me."

One of the bartenders had come over. "Um, were running low on rye. It's going faster than we expected."

"Don't see me. See the chairman of the social committee."

"He's not around," the bartender said. He was about seventeen.

"So you want money? Here, here's twenty dollars. Do what you can with that."

The boy went away.

"They always run to me," Torrenson said. He looked at Charlie. "It must be a little like managing a class, eh?"

Charlie winced. "No, not quite."

"Well, let me go on. This thing works. The benefits are there to be measured. It has been done in practice. Call it human engineering to give it an historical base. Ford's Model T is the perfect example. Prices dropped five hundred dollars in ten years because of increased production and the increase came only through more efficient use of manpower. No one working for Ford enjoyed being reduced from a skilled laborer to an automaton doing one of many simple mechanical steps. Ford compensated his men by being the first in the industry to pay five dollars a day. That's my point: everybody gained."

"Ford gained most," Elaine said.

Charlie said to her, "That's back on the question of power, dear. We weren't going to discuss that, I think." He turned to Torrenson, who seemed suddenly pleased at something. His curiosity evoked, Charlie tried to go on, "You're right," he said. "Everybody gained. But again it's a question of which is more important, increased production and a more advantageous material position—being able to shoot golf every afternoon on your favorite course —" As he'd hoped, Elaine started to laugh. To her, he said, "Of course, it's still on my mind." To the others, "A family joke. Anyway, which is more important, being free to play games, or being free? It just happens that Ford was as guilty as anyone of the company paternalism Elaine mentioned this afternoon. No smoking by employees—ever. I'm sure that people would have been willing to pay an extra ten or fifteen dollars for a car—that's just a guess at what the paternalism saved—than force themselves or others to undue external influence on their private lives. If they had had a choice. A man has a private life even at his job, you know, and it's inviolable. Look at it this way: living well looks good, but I'd hate to pay the price of being continually forced into work that wasn't of my own choosing. Some men, anyway, see work as more than just the way to acquire leisure. Some see it as a way of making themselves grow beyond their limits."

"You're beginning to sound like *The New York Times*

Book Review. Man's immortal soul. Most men have to adjust—"

"I'll grant you that," Charlie said. "But the decision is being taken from them. Even you object to that. That you would bone up for the interview shows it. I'll always have you on that score."

"He will, too, sweetie," Betty said.

"All right," Torreson said sourly. "I'll revise it: some do and some don't. Have to adjust."

"He's been saying exactly that," Betty said.

There was a silence from the bandstand and then another slow number was started up.

Elaine said, "I think we'd all be right if we said, some do, some don't, and some do who think they don't. No, that's about the same thing. I'd better keep my mouth shut."

"No comment," Torrenson said, grinning.

Charlie knew what she had wanted to say: that the chance to decide had to stay open even though many people who thought they could move beyond themselves really could not, and had to stay with the rest. She was upset tonight, and had become tangled in the repetition of her own phrasing. Torrenson had thought it very amusing, for some reason.

He had taken Betty's hand. He looked away from Charlie toward Elaine. "I see what you're driving at. I've wondered why *I'm* so hell-bent to get into business—something. To wheel and deal. I don't think I'm going to find out, though, until I'm in it. It's probably a multiplicity of things. There's a word, multiplicity. Still, the idea holds a lure, a beckoning. It's important to me. Maybe I'm one of those who thinks he's more than he really is."

This was what Charlie had come here for, but he did not know how to pursue it. At the same time he noticed that Elaine was staring at the fellow and every once in a while dropping her eyes to the hand that held Betty's hand. Both of them had smooth, unblemished skin. Charlie was afraid Elaine was going to be too obvious, but then he saw that her gaze was not the one that went with a notebook and a pencil; there seemed to be a faint alarm in it, a projection of horror. It came to him that he wasn't seeing everything that was going on here. He had no perspective; of it all, this alone was what he knew. But she was seeing him now, having seen him for more than a year's time, and clearly she was seeing something.

Torrenson started again. "I don't know. I still don't buy what you say about freedom, Cumberland. As they're quick to say down at the Supreme Court, this doesn't constitute a clear and present danger. Not to my eyes, anyway." He paused, smiling affably. "I didn't mean to confuse you. I'm going back to something related to the original topic. In advertising as well as personnel they use depth interviewing techniques to find out what people like and are attracted to. Has Elaine told you anything about that? She used to work for B.B.D.&O."

"I know. She's told me a little."

"How do you feel about it? Advertising."

"Well, it stands to reason that if I don't like one for things that are inherent in both, I won't like the other, either."

"If A equals B, and C equals B, then C must equal A. Very good. But here is where I have you by the short hairs."

"Fine. I'm ready to learn."

Betty leaned over to Elaine. "Where does he get that stuff? Is he a Buddhist or something?"

Her pose showed everything but her nipples now, and all three of the others took notice of it. "Oh, no," Elaine said, "I'm a ventriloquist."

"Now, now," Torrenson said. "Anyway, Cumberland, this is what I was going to say—" But the first words were lost on Charlie, who was looking at him, trying to pay attention, but onto whose eyes was pasted the image of Torrenson's last gesture: a quick, totally revealing smile, a glance toward Elaine which possessed the assumption of all the things he fervently wished she could feel, so that he might rebuke her, chastise and reduce her with a superior, maddening, "Now, now," She had to be furious! But maybe this is what she had been seeing all the while. Betty had asked a silly question; Elaine could not have answered it better. There'd been nothing in her tone, and who could have missed seeing all that bosom—bared, possibly, at Torrenson's suggestion? Who wouldn't have taken a good look? Only Charlie himself, so as not to embarrass Elaine. Perhaps it was not Torrenson's only motive, but he had been wanting to catch Elaine, and he had. Sure, she must have been seeing Torrenson's hatred for her right along. Of course. He hated her. He *did* hate her. Where did they all stand now? Charlie's hands closed into fists as again his mind turned back to the chance—the excellent chance now—of Torrenson's flapping mouth. If Torrenson could do this in his hatred, he could surely do the other.

"But more deeply than that, the benefits, the increased standard of living, is the economic fact of our country: our economic health is dependent not on production, but on consumption, and not the consumption of necessities, either. Luxuries. The figures bear it out. You could say that nearly a third of the labor force is engaged in non-essential industries or services—movies, television, all these home appliances, cosmetics. You could go on and on. The point is, the country would be in chaos if the luxury industries collapsed or even suffered heavily. Just look at what people need and what they want. If they wanted just what they needed, half the country would be starving. I mean it. Advertising prevents that. It's the grease in the axle. It has to sell, just like any individual salesman, but through the mass media, because of the terrifically high pitch of production. And finding out what people want is part of the selling job. If a man likes his cars red, paint them red; if he likes them long, stretch them out a little—"

"For better or worse."

"Reason doesn't play a very big part in this, Cumberland. Most people aren't reasonable, and there's nothing that can be done about it."

"I like it even less now. It capitalizes on the immaturity of people and keeps them immature—"

"Come out of the clouds! This is the way it is!"

There was a shout from the bar, some laughter, and finally a cheer. A fellow came into view trying to shake liquor or soda from his head and shoulders. He was drenched.

"—Sure," Charlie mumbled, and sat back.

"You talk of freedom, but people can't stand freedom. They prove it every time."

"Dostoyevsky raises that question."

"Of course he does. The point is, what do people do with their freedom when they have it? They throw it away. They want to be controlled. At every turn they give up their freedom to whoever or whatever will protect them. In some cases—and you can't deny this, either— taking it away amounts to an act of kindness and compassion. Their minds, once opened, become instruments of self-torture and misery. They can't take reality; it makes them sick. Protecting them amounts to nothing more than being kind to animals—"

"Cal!" Elaine cried.

"Let him finish," Charlie said. "We all think it at one time or another."

"But only when we're upset or depressed—"

"That doesn't make it less valid," Charlie said. "What were we talking about before? Out at the bar. Some people choose to be animals, that's all. They bunny hop."

"Yes, I see. I'm sorry, Cal. You caught me off guard."

Torrenson smiled again. Smiled! Charlie could feel his rage charging up; in another moment he was fighting just to hold it. Torrenson said, "Now even when there's an abridgement of freedom, the abridgement goes, in most cases, unnoticed and seems even good. A life is filled. There's something to dream about. What else do people want? They can't take reality. I have the perfect example for you. I was in New York during intersession and I met a fellow, a member of the fraternity chapter down there. City College, is that where you go?"

Charlie nodded. "But it's a big place."

"I know, I won't bother you with his name. Anyway, this was the situation—I don't think anyone will be offended if I bring it up. He told me all about it. He was sleeping with his girl-friend, and he felt a terrible guilt over it. He was even physically sick with it. Possibly. He was an Episcopalian, and he'd gone to his minister, but the man had done no good at all. The kid really had a terrific situation inside: the moral conscience, but practically none of the faith of his religion. He was undecided, like most people." He stopped to wave to a couple across the room. "In any case, he wanted to be saved, told that everything was all right. He wanted to be protected—but from what? Simple: his own acts. He wasn't what he thought he was, so he wanted to be told the church was wrong and he was right. You know how I feel about religion, Elaine. I went through it with him point by point. He didn't want his freedom, though. He wanted only to be protected and assured. If it wasn't the loving arms of the church he wanted to fall into, it was the arms of his sweetie-pie. He didn't want to think, face himself. He wanted only to be titillated and satisfied."

"And you did all that?" Elaine asked. "You just went ahead and told him what was wrong with his religion and himself?"

"I tried," he said.

"My God, Cal, where are your brains? What have you learned in all the courses you've taken? You ought to know by now that you can't be sure of a thing, a cause, motivation, just because a person tells you it's so! It takes months and years of sitting and talking, gaining confidence and insights, having the subject himself examine what his life means and realize of his own volition what his problems are. Do you think that a college boy can adequately express his feelings? hey almost always go deeper than any language at his command. And even if his problem was what you thought, do you think he could have accepted it just because you told him of it? He has to go along his regrowth slowly. God, Cal, I thought you had more brains than that. I honestly did. For all you know, you might have pushed him down a flight of stairs."

"What have I been trying to say? That he wouldn't recognize the truth if he were hit over the head with it. And don't worry about what I did. I couldn't have done that much. I didn't attempt it. He asked me a question, a

series of questions, and I answered them. He was ready
for it. All right, in some parts he was a little reluctant,
and I had to help him along, but he was so close he could
have smelled it—" He stopped, as though he was remembering something, as if the truth was not quite what he
had just made it out to be. He had been caught unready
by this remembrance, and the reaction was etched on his
face. Charlie could see that Elaine had not missed it, that
she was wondering, too, what really happened on the
occasion of which Torrenson spoke, what happened to the
boy. And it was something they were not going to find
out, for already Torrenson was given over to lying. Lies
and distortions were already so intermixed with facts that
he could not sort them apart. The truth as gone, like the
last part of the wake of a ship at night, floating off
somewhere in the darkness of a foam-studded sea.

Charlie felt as if he had been slammed and slammed
again by an attacking animal, some huge stupid beast, and
that now he was giving up, waiting to be hit again. The
band came to the end of the number and there was just
the rumble of talk through the room.

Elaine said, "You meddled, Cal. There's a difference
between meddling and teaching."

Torrenson looked away from her disgustedly and
toward Charlie. "What do *you* think? You've been quiet
the last few minutes. Been preparing your rebuttal?"

"N-no."

"If you have a rebuttal, let's hear it."

"I think it's time we dropped the subject."

"Don't be silly. Speak up, there's nothing to be afraid
of."

Charlie felt Elaine's hand touch his, which had the effect
of reducing and dissolving his fury. How well she knew
him. This lunatic across the table was on the verge of
starting a riot, if he did not know it.

"I've been quiet, Torrenson, because some of the things
you said started my mind going. You said that the boy
didn't want to face reality, that reality made him sick, that
all he wanted was to be titillated and satisfied. Hasn't it
occurred to you yet that that's true of every human being

to his own degree? Hasn't it occurred to you that perhaps one of the reasons he can't face reality is that all he's ever encountered has been unreal and in that way, some way, gratifying? Not just the stale words of the church, but the whole putrescent corpus known as society?"

"Of course it's occurred to me." Smug. Very smug.

"That's my point, and I'm getting to it," Charlie said. The band started a Mambo; he raised his voice. "You asked for a rebuttal, and this is it coming up now. But let me touch on one other thing: you said he didn't want to be free, but what you didn't say—I didn't say it, either, earlier, though we've both been coming close—is that freedom isn't a pleasure or a right; it's a duty. Yes. Freedom is a duty. What you also almost said was that freedom and reality are interwoven, maybe even the same thing. Suppose I say it for you: a man *must* make himself free and stay that way so that he can find himself in relation to the world of which he's so intricately a part. Not just the near world, the universe."

"That's the old story. A man has to struggle for knowledge."

"That's right. That's right. Knowledge and freedom. I'm not done yet. I'll give you a hint of what I'm going to say: freedom from what?" Even as he spoke, however, something was filtering up; even as the words raced to his mouth to be spoken and thrown at Torrenson, something vague and dim was rising out of the night of his mind. The music seemed to be screaming behind him. "You know that man has to suffer for his knowledge and pay for it himself, but you're still willing to go down and join those whose job is merely to obscure life's first function— education, the pursuit of knowledge and the celebration of truth. Because of them and others like them—on one side, those Hollywood aberrationists that avariciously ply the more perverse aspects of our Puritan culture; on the other, but more forgivable—" What was he thinking of? It was coming up in his mind, but he could not hear it yet—"that old-time, new-time, any-time religion, say a word and save your soul—altogether surviving on the promulgation of the most vile idea of all: that man is from the start unworthy. It's not true. Man is worthy. On one hand, pockets are filled; on the other, coffers. In the latter case, let's hope, that isn't the prime issue. The point is, however, that when the coffins, not the coffers, are filled, all those who've gone the way other men have doomed them can have carved on their stones: 'We have not lived.'

"And you—you're going down to New York with what you know to disregard it, to suck up to those people who care for nothing but the putrid satisfaction of piling up more and more money; and at the same time, you're going to suck from people—who can do nothing to stop you because the way to them has already been made smooth—suck from them the very strength that might otherwise have powered them to the heights you know they can reach. You called them animals, Torrenson, but you're the animal. You know better, but you feed on your own kind. You're a disgrace, Torrenson, and you damned well know it."

Torrenson's eyes, wide and incredulous, were leveled at his own. He was too stunned to swing, or even to realize what had been said to him. But Charlie was not even thinking of him, and he knew he was leaving himself open. His strength had run out of him, and he was thinking of the night in the subway, the fight with the Puerto Ricans. Animals then. There were animals. The two swine who were going down to the station to file complaints—one of them the man who had cursed him and called him a Communist. And those who had pushed away from him as he came out of the subway car. It was strange that, when he thought of that sort of incident, he threw up his hands and maybe even tried to forget the children frozen on the roadside in Korea. It was that demoralizing. There was no really important point to the world. If anything, there was just one miniscule degree of improvement possible in each generation. No more, and so it would be when the dust blew up dry out of the bottom of the sea.

"Well," Betty said, "maybe we ought to dance." She stood up and tugged at Torrenson's coat-sleeve. "Come on, sweetie." She looked at Elaine. "Are you two coming?"

"We'll be along." When they were alone, Elaine said, "Would you like me to light you a cigarette?"

"Yes, thanks."

"We'll sit here and smoke, then get out. We don't have to say another word until you're ready."

"No, it's all right. I was right, but I did wrong. Isn't that odd? I've done it before. He's sick, I know it, and I judged him anyway."

"Don't think about it."

"That's another thing. I was almost thinking about it, that he's sick, as I was talking. Jesus."

She gave him the cigarette. "We'll be out of here soon."

The number ended, and there was scattered clapping from the floor. Torrenson and Betty came back. "Party poopers," she said. "You didn't even get up."

"Oh, yes," Charlie said. "We're very fast."

The band began a fox trot, slow and soft, and Betty grabbed his hand. "Come on, this will get you up. I won't take no for an answer."

Charlie looked quickly to Elaine. But she said, "Go ahead. I have to go up to the john. I do."

"We'll only be a minute, sweetie," Betty said to Torrenson. "He won't mind being alone," she said to Charlie.

"It's all right with me," Torrenson said disinterestedly. "I can get myself another drink."

Betty led Charlie out onto the dance floor and then turned to face him. "Loosen up," she said after a moment. "You're like a West Point Cadet."

"Elaine says Prussian Officer. I'm not a good dancer at all."

"You have to relax. That's better. You have to slouch a little when you dance. But hold me a little closer. We aren't playing London Bridge with the other kids running through underneath. There, isn't that much better?" There was a real note of insincerity in the last few words, and Charlie wanted to back away. But she was very close, and holding him firmly, and it would have been awkward. He could smell her perfume and make-up, thick and musky. As he turned her around he could see that the table was empty.

"You really poured it on him," she said in a low tone.

"I don't want to talk about it."

"What do you want to talk about?"

"Nothing, really."

"You're a strange one," she said.

"Not at all."

"What do you think of my dress?"

"What?"

"You heard me."

"All right, I think you're overdoing it."

"Why?" she asked.

"All women have tits."

It didn't shock her. "Not all."

"Most, then, and a tit is a tit is a tit."

"You ought to know," she said.

"What does that mean?"

"You've been around."

"I've had enough. Let's go back to the table."

"No."

"I'll go alone, then."

"No, you won't," she said. "You'll be in more trouble than you've ever had in your life. I can accuse you of something and make it stick. I can cry real tears whenever I want."

"I'll bet you can."

"Get closer," she said.

"Nothing doing."

"All right. But I can give you a good time, if you want."

"I don't want."

"How is Elaine?"

"What?"

"How is she in bed?"

"You're out of order now. I'll risk your real tears."

"Stay here. I know you're sleeping with her."

"How do you know that?"

"Cal laid her. He told me a long time ago."

"When?"

"A long time ago."

"And this is the first time you've seen her?"

"Yes."

"Why did he tell you?"

"I'd have to show you," she said, and smiled.

He pushed her away. "Now, listen, bitch: I want you to go up to the bathroom and stay there until we're out of here. I don't care what you do, but I want you to walk off this floor, and over to the staircase, without saying a word, giving a sign, anything. If you're not out of my sight in ten seconds I won't by worrying about your real tears, because they will be real. Your face will be split wide open."

She stepped back.

"Go on! I'm not kidding!" He watched her go and then he turned back to the table. He got there just as Torrenson was pulling up with his fresh drink. He sat down. Charlie stayed on his feet.

"Where's Betty?"

"She had to tend to nature," Charlie said.

"Is that the way she put it? She's a panic."

"Yeah, a pisser."

"That's very funny. I'll have to tell her that."

"That's right, don't stop now."

"What?"

"Nothing."

"You said something. What did you say?"

"I didn't say a thing."

Torrenson reared back in his chair and rubbed his arms. "Well, shit, it's cold in here. Maybe we'd better throw another Jew on the fire."

"What was that?"

"An expression."

"No, what did you mean by it? Come on, talking seems to be one of your strong points."

Torrenson smirked, as if at last satisfied. "Relax, boy. It's just something we say around here.

"It stinks."

"Come on, you needn't get indignant. I know Elaine is

Jewish, and you know I know. Maybe that's what has you
bugged: that I know everything about her."

"Don't be silly," Charlie said.

"What?"

"You heard me," Charlie said. "You haven't the men-
tality to know everything about her."

"Oh, now wait a minute. I took what you said before
only because—"

"Shut up, will you? You took it because you're a fool
and you have shit in your blood."

"You think you're pretty cute, don't you? How many
times do you think you can work me over? Maybe you
think the fact that I slept with your girl gives you the
right, I don't know—"

"You stupid slob, you just had to say that, didn't you? I
know all about that. I know the why of it." And, pausing,
he looked down into Torrenson's lap. "I know it down to
the smallest detail." It was the cruelest, wildest thing he
had ever done, but he'd had to do it. He'd had to match
madness with his own brand of madness, and for all his
thoughts, all his philosophical troublings, it had given him
exactly the satisfaction of squeezing a troublesome gnat
between his fingers.

"You bastard!" Torrenson breathed heavily. "You son
of a bitch!"

"There, you've had your say. As a matter of fact,
you've been having your say right along—"

But it was as if Torrenson hadn't heard him. He was up
now, his fists clenched, his breath coming hard. His head
was back so he could look down his nose, and suddenly he
had that begrimed look of a little boy fighting. He did
look faintly ridiculous, but Charlie could not help thinking, and remembering the night in the subway, and the
way the old man had returned with all the evils Charlie
had earlier sown, to lay them before the Puerto Ricans.
This is the result; this is always the result. For the first
time since he had told Elaine about it he recalled what he
had actually done to Murillo—almost strangled him. It
would have been better for Charlie if Murillo had taken
the recourse of the law. Charlie might have learned. This

would not have happened. He would not even know if he had achieved anything that night. Murillo could be in bed with Alice right now. "Don't be a fool, Torrenson. I'm not going to fight you."

"What's the matter, are you afraid?"

"Of course I'm not afraid. You aren't worth fighting. I have other plans for the evening. Now sit down and I'll go out to the hallway and wait for Elaine there, and that will be the end of it."

"You chicken-shit!"

"You have to fight, don't you? Well, I'm sorry. I'm sorry for everything I said, coming here—I'm sorry for you. I'm happy now, because I've gotten to that point at last. I'm sorry for you."

He turned around and pushed into the crowd of dancers toward the hallway. He was sure Torrenson would not follow. No one chased after this kind of a fight. And Torrenson could convince himself that it was Charlie who was dishonored. So be it.

He had to wait a few minutes before Elaine picked her way down through the cheering section on the stairs.

"Hi, I thought you'd be inside."

"I made our goodbyes," he said.

"Good, we're liberated. No, something's wrong. What happened? What happened back there?"

He hesitated. He did not want to tell her, but he did not think she would believe a lie. "Can we wait until we're in the car, anyway?"

"Yes."

She cried. He should have tried to lie at any cost, even with her. He drove them back to the motel. No one was around and he helped her the few steps to the door of their room. He did not turn on the light, but stood by while she undressed and slipped into bed. He was sure she did not want him in with her, and he was right, to a degree. She would not let him sit down in the chair by the window; she called him and asked him to stay by her, above the covers. He lay on his back and lit a cigarette.

He was very tired. The curtains were drawn and the room was black, but the windows were open and the cool

air moved over him like the passage of time. He kept his
eyes open to pay attention to the cigarette. Elaine was
quiet. She fell asleep. Out on the highway in front of the
motel a car passed, another car, tires whirring. Old, familiar sounds: his childhood had been filled with them. A
truck passed, a diesel, the motor hammering out. The
sound faded steadily and finally died. Charlie took another
drag of the cigarette, snuffed it out, and closed his eyes. He
thought of his childhood. He rolled over and took Elaine's
hand from under her pillow and held it. He thought of his
parents and how long now they were dead and how much
they had missed . . .

She awakened him near morning, kissing him, smiling.
The room was lit with a tender blue glow. She moved
back and put her hand on her pillow to watch him. The
damp of dawn was everywhere. She stayed silent. He sat
up, lit two cigarettes, and gave one to her. She moved her
head to his chest, twisting herself into a position that was
comfortable. The sheet was halfway up her thighs. She
had good, strong legs, classic and lovely.

She caressed his chest with her hand. "I realize I'm not
going to be a good wife in the beginning, if I become your
wife. I have so much to learn about you."

"No—no. I shouldn't have argued with him. I shouldn't
have let my feelings run away with me."

"I'm going to try, Charlie. I will try. Do you know what
I mean?"

"I know. Thank you for saying it."

"More than words. You'll see."

"All right, Shhh."

"I will try," she said again.

II

In the next three weeks Cal was more busy than he had
been in all the preceding three years and eight months of
his college career. He had papers to write, and letters to
New York. He had meetings to go to, and the election of
his successor to preside over. There were planned parties

and impromptu celebrations, addresses to take down and final, sentimental conversations too hold.

His last meeting as Chancellor was a triumph. The Treasurer's statement showed that the chapter was in better financial condition than it had been in years. The Alumni and Social Committees submitted favorable reports. In his own short valedictory Cal gave his views on the function of the fraternity. Its first role was to ease the way of the individual in his efforts to derive a satisfactory college experience. His opinion was that a genial atmosphere was more constructive than a hard, unremitting pressure to "make a good showing," or "keep the house average up." The fraternity was not a training camp, but it was not just a social club, either; it was a brotherhood that had been lost in recent years, the blame rested not just with the individuals in this house, but with the larger society as well. People came to college with their basic patterns already determined. A reasonable effort by the brothers could restore meaning, however, and for him, a reasonable effort consisted of no more than an honest attempt to accept the difference between individuals within a context of general good will. He believed in the fraternity, he said, and he had had a good time being Chancellor. He had tried to keep his policies easy, and he was sorry if he had hurt feelings in the process. He thanked them.

They cheered and afterward they came by individually and told him it was the finest thing they had ever heard on the subject, barring nothing. Even Ewing, whose thoughts had always run the other way, was impressed; and Bix, who had been waging a running, harping battle with Cal about "the way he was treating people," was awestruck. He had had an insibht, he said; Cal had given him the clue. He had wanted Cal to conform to *his* standards of behavior, when he should have accepted Cal's temperament as Cal had presented it.

Cal did not fail to notice the subtle needle even in that statement, and it just confirmed the plan for Bix he had made months ago: after graduation—nothing. No letters, no getting together. He had had enough of Bickerson and his pathetic, faggoty bitchiness. He had the feeling that

Bix knew this, and was simply trying to work back into Cal's good opinion. Too late, too late, for all that.

Cal saw Betty seven times. Seven times he enjoyed her rabbit habits. He was not going to see her after graduation, either, but he did not say goodbye. The ballet they had done over his fraternity pin prevented that. They had set a tone of deception, and though neither had ever fooled the other, they were not about to push their relationship to some new area of development, such as honesty. He had two regrets: one, that he could not take her to New York even on these terms, for what she was throwing was really that good; and two, that she might embarrass him later on, picking up with someone else in the fraternity, and then a third fellow, until the word got around. He had no intention of coming back here to visit, but he did not want to be humiliated. He considered heading her off by recommending her to someone of his own choosing—say, Pete Fuller. Fuller could appreciate her. But Cal was going to let it be; he liked Fuller, and it was foolish for anyone to know her too long—even a year was too long. Although Cal had not seen this side of her, he sensed she had a profound belief in trouble-making.

Right up to the last night, then, they were promising to write and visit and go on trips together. He could just see spending a weekend in her home. She lived in Johnson City, still a good distance from New York, she was the oldest of six children and she was just nineteen, and her mother worked in the Endicott-Johnson shoe factory. It was ridiculous.

He owed Betty and Bix one important debt, anyway; they had helped him get a fix on Elaine's boy-friend, Cumberland, and on Elaine as well. That night, Betty had come downstairs to tell her side of what had happened on the dance floor. She looked as if she had been crying all the time she had been gone, and she spoke before Cal had the chance to give her Cumberland's version and the opportunity to make something up. She was not that bright anyway. Cumberland had tried to rub her up, and she had been so surprised that she had said, in an easy, nervous way, to put him down, "What's the matter, aren't you getting enough from her?" She had forgotten herself, she knew, and had been absolutely wrong in revealing what Cal had told her in confidence. She had to go upstairs, both to get away from Cumberland's questions and attacks, and to be able to deal with her own sense of error, even though she knew Cal would be in for worse. She was sorry. She didn't want Cal to be angry. She wanted another chance.

She got it later, and she gave him something good to think about.

That same night Bix wanted to know what sort of person Cumberland was. It was almost dawn, and the evening had been a mixture of disaster and success for Bix, too. Susan had been sick in the beginning but then she had gotten better and Bix had done well. He was feeling fine. He wanted to know about Cumberland, he said, because the fellow had seemed the type he had expected Elaine never to go out with: a condescending, arrogant Greenwich Village Bohemian. He had made a crack about when the party was supposed to start. He knew all about parties, Elaine had said so proudly it had given Bix the shivers.

The two things tied it for Cal. Cumberland had never jibed: his ultra-liberal politics, some of his remarks. Cal had tried to like him, but like the fraud he was, Cumberland had had to impress Elaine with a whole series of aggressive remarks and vicious, sniveling attacks on Cal. He knew about Cal and her; he admitted it. It rankled him, and why not? Cal had been in her almost at the start. Maybe Cumberland had tried to rub Betty just to annoy Cal, but he was still a fraud. That he was so self-possessed to even consider it showed how much he cared for Elaine. He was too far gone to be capable of real feeling.

Not that she did not know it, deep, deep down. It worked both ways, and what Cumberland was, a Christian, was proof. She could not get involved with him, and his Christianity could justify in part what she was doing with him. He was only her stud, if he did not know it. Subconsciously, she had picked him on the basis of size, probably. She was a big woman and she knew it, because Cal had told her over a year ago. At least she was showing some sense; a fellow the size of Bix would get lost in her. Cal could see her lying back and gasping while Cumberland worked her over like a masseur. Sure. Jews like masseurs, anyway.

Cal wanted to see Cumberland's face when she told him she could not see him again. She could not overcome her parents' objections. She was sorry. Her voice would crack, or perhaps her speech would be clipped in her effort to be strong, but it would halt enough to let her anguish break through. Cal wanted to see Cumberland's face, because the fellow was feeling good and thinking he was riding high. The shock he was going to get would make up for what Cal had not done. Cal should have fought him. His kind were scum and fighting them was stupid, but Cal should have done it.

Cal knew what she would say and how she would say it, because he had heard it himself last year: her voice breaking when she told him of Marv, the patterns of words getting shortened and chopped when she told him of her parents and that actually, their objections had awakened her; she had been slow to see it but—here is where she stopped and took a breath and let the self-pity out—but she had really used him to forget about Marv. He had been caught in her reaction to Marv. This time she didn't have Marv and it would be more difficult, and she might even be crying, but it would be essentially the same. She had known from the beginning she would not be able to go all the way, but she had lied to herself, hoping. Maybe this was her way of getting back at her parents, she might say, getting close to the truth at last. It was a fitful rebellion, and she was sorry if he was hurt in the process, but it was all she was capable of. She was not strong enough to fight her parents. They had robbed her of her strength.

And him, the lover, the stud who had assured himself he was a lover, would feel it more intensely than anything Cal could have given him. Cal still regretted not hitting him. Cal could have kicked him once and sent him to the floor, clutching the penis he was so prideful of.

Cal wanted to see, too—and it was not as remote as it appeared at first—how she would look at forty-five or fifty: a Yiddish cow, her body a ruin, her breasts and backside sagging, the flesh hanging from her thighs like crepe. The full-blown ones went like that, and she was not going to be different. Really, her breasts were sagging already.

Not like Betty's.

Elaine Sellman was a shit and it had taken Cal a full year to realize it.

In the third week he began to receive answers from the companies in New York. There were employment application forms, printed material sketching the opportunities the companies offered, and several personal letters expressing pleasure in his record and background. A few noted that he was planning to move to New York anyway; he would be right if, on his arrival, he called for an appointment for an interview. One writer said he was "very interested" in seeing Cal.

There was one group of companies from which he received only those little printed acknowledgments saying that his letters were receiving attention. Almost daring himself, he had written to one of the oil companies with overseas operations. He understood that they needed people for training in administration and management outside the country. He was willing to travel, he had written, and able to honor any contracts he might be obliged to sign. He cast his letters in fine and earnest tones, in the attempt to indicate he had been thinking about such a career for years.

Of course he did not know that he was going to follow through. The idea had come to him in the middle of April, and it had been fascinating: two or three years overseas, coming back with eight or ten thousand dollars savings, to be able to deal with life much the same as his father had done in his way. He was aware that he would probably be assigned to some remote oil field and shuttled into a regimented life. He could function under those conditions, he was sure. There were so many advantages even in that part that he wondered why he had not considered all of it before.

He would learn something new. His life would be regular and orderly and he would get a chance to think. He would gain truly solid organizational and administrative experience, and the opportunity to prove and distinguish himself through his responsibilities far beyond what would be offered to him in New York. It was a frightening thing, to leave one's country for so long, but he had to consider it.

He had seen the crowds of New York. There were thousands of young men who would seem to someone over them all to be just like him, as clever and ambitious, more skillful in some things, and better educated. He could compete, but would he get the chance if he were digested to the bottom of some complex hierarchy? Thousands of clerks were clotted in single buildings in Manhattan; he had seen them on their lunch hours in the streets. He was afraid, and perhaps he was toying with this thing overseas because he was afraid, as if his emotions themselves were the final determinants of his fate. Where he would be in sixty days was as much a mystery to him as where he would be in sixty years.

In the final week, right up to the last evening, Cal was on the telephone with his parents, making arrangements, confirming them, changing them around again. His father did not want to stay overnight in Ithaca; the hotels both on campus and off would be too crowded. He and Cal's mother would arrive on Graduation Day in plenty of time for the ceremony, and then the three of them would leave that night after the party at the fraternity house was under way. They would spend the night in Sullivan County—reservations had been made at The Concord—and then go on to Groton Long Point, where Cal could rest three or four days or a week before going down to New York. Cal could not help thinking that at last he was going to spend a night at one of the Jewish resorts.

On the last evening Cal lay awake. The moon was up and enough light came through the branches outside the window to let him see the moon. The light flickered and played and blotted out as the branches bent and bobbed in the wind rolling up the hillside. The room was stripped bare. Suitcases were stacked by the door.

The next day was going to be a long one, busy and tiring, but he had given up hope of sleeping. His anxiety had his mind going with such speed and clarity that he might not wind down until dawn. That this was his last night in this room already had reminded him of the Tuesday last September when he had run through the big house in Darien. He could remember the stillness that had gripped his room that day, in the sunshine pouring through the unsettled light dust onto his old souvenirs and tattered books. Now again these things were receding into an even more distant past. He hated it. Childhood had been too short.

He should not worry. He had done well in college and had finished strong. There were good grades to look back on, and the highest office in his fraternity. He would do well from here on out. He would have a measure of success in his life.

His life. His short, short life. Cal remembered what that fellow Jerry Matthews had said about feeling the closeness of death, and he wondered if he were not beginning to feel it himself. At this juncture in his life, Cal seemed to see the perimeters of life. It trebled his unease. Matthews— more than once since Elaine's attack had Cal thought of that weekend; Cal could see Matthews again, thin and boyish and talking to him eagerly, and Cal was sorry he had met him at all. Matthews was indelibly associated with ugliness.

He tried to relax and turn his thoughts to being in New York itself. There would be a goodness about it, new and good and full of new faces. Maybe a chance with one of the oil companies would come up. Or maybe it would go as badly as possible, and he would have to bide his time with any kind of a job until his draft number came up. It would not be so terrible: a steady check, a place of his own, more free time and a lot less pressure. He seemed to keep forgetting; he could have it the way he wanted, and that could be just as difficult or pleasant as he pleased.

He thought of tomorrow again; his parents would be up

to watch him and he could see his father coming forward to shake his hand. It would be a good day.

A juncture in his life. What was it like? It was like coming out of a little woods and going into a forest. He could smell the dampness and feel the chill air. He was alone now. It would be the same, in a way—passing and meeting people all the time. Have a light lunch and pursue each other in the big trees. Strange, he could see the trees so well, tall and hard—the trees. In the distance were other people moving among them, over the debris of the forest floor. Maybe everyone was moving on a wheel, and he would see some of them again. He didn't know. Maybe it was done. Maybe it was really over. He imagined the cold air of the forest again and curled himself up small, holding the loose warmth of the sheet against him, his eyes open but his inner vision spreading icily and vividly before him in its secret fury. He thought again of his father coming forward, smiling, his hand reaching out. It was going to be good tomorrow. It was going to be very good.

The Friday after Elaine's graduation, Charlie drove directly from the school in Brooklyn up to City College. He had been going to wait until Monday to get his grades, there was a chance that not all would be posted today; but for this thing, at least, he was not going to hold himself back. It was a lovely day for a drive even through the city: mild, brilliantly clear, with a soft cool wind. He put the convertible top down and took Flatbush Avenue to the bridge and then went up Manhattan on the East River Drive. Dust blew in the shadows of the afternoon. On the benches at the riverside, old men and mothers and small children took in the sun. Tugs and barges pushed under the bridges up and down the brackish river.

His grades were posted and he came away pleased but not overjoyed. He started downstairs again at once. His tie was still on and his coat buttoned—he didn't know why, except that it was the kind of day that made him want to stay neat. He would celebrate—a hamburger in Prexy's and then a movie. He would be home early enough to pick up a book.

He had not heard from Elaine all week.

She had said to give her time. She wanted to do it her way, tell them herself forthrightly. She was not trying to spare him or keep him from the arguing of which she admitted she would be ashamed. There was going to be arguing, to be sure, and he would hear about it. She wanted to win for her own sake. If he stepped in her place and bore the worst she would keep in herself a core of weakness and ambiguity she could measure and weigh the rest of her life.

She just needed time. He had kept still when she told him her plans. That she wanted to try at all made him admire her more. As long as she saw it as a test she had no real choice, and though he wanted her and not an affidavit to her moral strength, he could not disagree with her. In her position, he would have to do the same thing.

But he had not heard in a week, he had not seen her in a month, and the time had come down like a periodic salve so that in his public moments as he tended to his business he could stop and almost be convinced that it could go either way and he would feel nothing—numbness. It was as upsetting as the trouble he was having within himself alone in the apartment, in the dark, listening to the empty roar of the city—those sessions, hours long now, which he declined to contemplate by day, because they showed him his weakness.

He drove the car slowly down Convent Avenue toward One hundred and twenty-fifth Street. The Avenue was full of shadow. There were colored children playing and shouting. "Fling that ball, man! Don't stand there with your mouth hangin' open! Fling it!"

Further south the land on the right went up on the deep hill of Morningside Park. The sun splashed down over the trees and shadow and pink light swam on the curving roadway below. The old town houses on the left facing the trees had the color of dark sunburn and above them the sky was turning a mild green.

He was afraid for her if she should fail. She would have her affidavit then, and to what would be just too clear. If she had to fail, so be it, but he wanted her to be happy some day. He did not want her remembering cowardice or lack of spirit, as he knew she would choose to call it instead of what it was, unnameable, horrible. She was fighting people she loved. It wasn't simple. He wanted the impossible: her, the person capable of so testing herself, without the test; and if she had to fail, he wanted her clean of her memory so that at least she could live again.

What she was fighting for was their civil acceptance of him from the start, instead of later, in some sleazy, half-withheld reconciliation. She wanted the conflict settled before it had a chance to begin. She wanted honesty among them—no secrecy, no surprises, no sudden terrible hurtings. She wanted honesty for Charlie and herself as lovers, the unquestioned, precisely imperfect honesty lovers needed and deserved.

In the nights he was thinking that he wanted to call her—she had asked him not to. Please let her do it alone. He spent the nights trying to remember to keep out of it for her sake. And a call would needlessly complicate matters. Suppose he got her mother, for example, what could he say to the woman? Oh, he had analyzed the entire situation down to its last atom.

Elaine would not keep him waiting long, she had promised. She had to have something real to tell him—did he understand? Yes, he did.

Don't worry, she had said Saturday night on the telephone.

It was not so easy. The time without her when he was alone had caused strange tricks to be played on him. He had told her none of it; he had wanted to keep the pressure off. Later, if there was going to be a later, he would tell her the things he had done and thought.

He had already moved her into his life. The weekends— he had kept her presence with him after them. Late one Wednesday night he rolled over for her and woke himself up. Another night, he heard her call him. Her voice, from the door. He had to turn on the light to be sure she was not there.

This past week he had seen a child with dark red hair and green eyes, with skin like Elaine's, and he was still thinking about her. He had wanted to get Elaine pregnant before this, but now he had seen her child, and it just intensified his desire. He had already plotted nine months' time from several possible starting dates. The irrational part of him wanted to get married at once. He did not know that he would be able to stand waiting six months or a year, for appearances.

All this, while he was thinking of and preparing for the other possibility, which he felt he had to do.

He drove steadily down the crowded avenues. The traffic streamed exhaust up between the buildings into the fading sky. The street noise was a vast hammering din.

In the mailbox when he got home was the following:

Darling:
I called at four o'clock, and came by at a quarter to five. I would have waited for you, but I had an errand to run. If you read this before seven, would you try to meet me at the luncheonette where we first had lunch together? If you can't make it, I'll call at eight. Don't worry.

All my love,
Elaine

It was done unevenly in pencil on the back of an envelope, as if she had used the wall for a backboard. He turned and went down to the car. It was six o'clock and he had plenty of time, but she did not say that she would not be there waiting.

What had happened? Whatever it was, it was now in the past tense, and it made his stomach roll and seize, as though he might be sick. His mind was a blank—a blank, and the realization that this thing was beyond his imagination infuriated him. He could feel his own sweat now; he had not noticed it before. When he got into the car and slid across the seat so that his clothes twisted about his body he thought he would go into a rage. He started the car and pulled it out of the parking space with such violence that the wheels screeched on the pavement for the first time in his memory.

He wondered how she had explained him. Who was he? His past stupidities ran after him—and the way he was driving now, he knew, was not very clever, either. His arrogance was suddenly stunning: no, the answer was no. He could see six months from now, him squirreled away in school, running up to college nights, her in an office somewhere, enduring the B.M.T. with the crowds in the evenings. It was going to be great in October and November, with the nights folding about them separately, steam on the windows. Tomorrow—tomorrow something inside them was going to look like a Christmas tree in an ash can.

Christmas—they had not even settled it. Perhaps it had settled them. Christmas tree, presents—what could she know about it? Could she believe in the love in it because he had told her to?

Sure he was afraid. Or it was a reaction, a preparation. He could be consoled on his garbage can of a Saturday by the thought that his Christmases might have been spoiled. This was the way of humanity, full of petty surprises. He wished he could be disgusted with himself, but he could not. There was no morality, no *real* morality. Things went whirling on, smashing into one another, the crippled and pathetic getting trampled, love being drowned, and in the stratosphere one could not hear so much as a squeak. His mind turned to them again, and the beautiful day this had been was now like something under glass, labeled and dry.

Freedom was a duty, yes, but it was about as attainable as tomorrow. We were hurt too easily. We were too weak—it was very nearly true. We capitulated, recoiled, attacked in return, until there was nothing left of our real selves. There was just the smallest chance for improvement, through the greatest effort. This winter at Seneca

Lake he had seen something for a moment—but too much of the time he was just not up to it. He had failed with Torrenson, he had failed with Murillo; and now, when perhaps he would have to do his best for someone who had given him so much goodness, he was failing again. His failures were getting the best of him. He had to try. This one time he had to try.

His hands were so wet with sweat they were sliding on the steering wheel.

The weekend traffic slowed him. Once over the bridge, he got into lane and let the car drone over the low undulations of the parkway. On the right Upper New York Bay spread out, the water pale and glittering in the very low sun. Freighters were pointed in and out, seemingly stilled by their own slow pace.

Her car was parked in front of the luncheonette, facing away. But she must have been watching for him in her mirror, for as he pulled up she got out and came back, crossing in front of him to the passenger side. She was smiling. Smiling! He leaned over and opened the door for her.

"Hi," she said. "Come on, give me a kiss."

"Wait. What happened?"

"I'm telling you. Give me a kiss."

"Oh. Oh, God." It was like being on a rocket. He kissed her.

"I'll remember this, the way you look, as long as I live."

"I love you," he said.

"I love you. Can we go somewhere? We have a while. I couldn't wait for you because I was picking up my father's paycheck. He's been home this week—oh, there's nothing the matter, but he told his boss my mother was sick. She's not, but that's part of what's been happening. Do you want to hear about it?"

"Of course I do."

"There's a little parking lot down by the highway."

"Fine."

"You're busy tonight—I hate to tell you this way. You

have to meet them. I'm sorry I couldn't ask you first. I was able to arrange it only this afternoon."

"That's all right."

They drove down to the parking lot, in which there was one other car, empty. The highway was behind them, cars going in both directions. At the water's edge a couple was sitting on a bench, and a child was tossing stones. Out on the water freighters were steaming for the ocean.

Her parents had gone up to Ithaca a week ago for the graduation. She was not going to tell them until they were all back in the city, and she didn't, though it was difficult. Her father kept looking at her, waiting for her to speak—to assure him that she wasn't seeing "that fellow." But he did not ask, and she kept still.

She drove them back Saturday, the car loaded with her clothes and four years' paraphernalia. It was when they were carrying her luggage up to the apartment that her father broached the subject. Her mother was upstairs preparing sandwiches.

"Listen, are you still seeing him? The fellow you told me about?"

"Yes. You'd better look at me, Pa. I'm going to be his wife."

He took a breath and held it. "Are you asking or telling?"

"I vote this year, but I still love you."

"Which means—hm." He stopped and reached for one of the suitcases. He started up the walk.

"I do love you, Pa."

He came back. "But you're going to do this?"

"Yes."

"Just like this?"

"Yes."

"You didn't tell me alone to get my help, did you? My help you won't get. I won't stop you but I won't help you."

"I told you because you asked if I was seeing him. I wasn't going to lie by not telling everything."

"Do you *know* what love is?"

"Not completely."

"You want this fellow to be the father of your babies? No hesitations? No reservations?"

"He's the only one I've ever wanted like that."

"And they're going to be Gentiles?"

"Not Gentiles, not Christians and not Jews. Not while they're children, anyway. What they do when they're older is their own affair. We'll train them as well as we can."

"What does this boy do?"

"Man, Pa."

"Man, then. What does he do?'"

"He's a teacher."

"Oh."

"He's a good one, Pa. He loves his work."

He nodded seriously, turned and went up the walk. Her meaning was not lost on him—her hope was that he would not take it for the cynicism it might have seemed. She *was* trying to impress him, but in the sense that she was trying to assure him, too. Her hope was that he would see that this was her stand—not a compromise, but not cruel. He did not tell her what he thought.

Her mother knew when Elaine got upstairs, and the woman was sick—with anger and frustration and what she thought was heartbreak.

"When will this happen?"

"When he says—now. The important thing was telling you first."

"But now he has the say? What do *you* want?"

"Oh, Ma, you know what I want. I wouldn't have said it that way if I didn't know what I wanted."

Her mother glared at her.

"This *can* be happy for all of us, Ma."

"You must be crazy to say such a thing."

"I mean it. I want you there. I want you to see it—"

"Never."

"There will only be this once, Ma."

Her mother walked away.

Sunday morning her mother started—shouting, yelling. Elaine kept her answers civil and brief. It put her mother on the defensive—and there was no defense against silence, Elaine knew. She stayed quiet. For a while Mrs. Sellman thought she had won a stalemate, until she tested Elaine and found it was not so. She became more desperate and petty. Until Wednesday, Elaine held fast. On that morning her mother resorted to name-calling, and Elaine started going for walks.

Her father took the week off and did nothing, as if he needed to consider it. Elaine saw the act as a good sign—he knew this was not a thing she was just saying. He watched television or went to the A. & P. for her mother or walked around in the neighborhood. He wasn't talking, and Elaine wanted to talk—and listen. He had things to tell her about marriage, counsel to give, and she wanted to hear it. He said nothing.

On Wednesday evening her mother realized she had nearly exhausted her resources. She tried to turn on Elaine's father. It was his fault. He could stop this. Elaine would listen to him.

He looked at his wife unhappily and got up and put on his coat and went out. He did not return until midnight. He had never stayed out so late before.

Early Thursday morning, before dawn, Elaine was awakened by something. Her eyes came open and she lay there, looking up. Moaning. She got up from the bed and walked lightly toward the living room, from which the sound had come. Her mother was sitting at the window, looking toward the street. The light on the corner was coming in the window and hitting her directly. She was wearing an old pink nightgown, loose from her shoulders, and it shuddered as she sobbed. The tears gleamed like oil on her cheeks, her eyes blinked continually. She did not see Elaine.

But Elaine could see her, a gnarled little woman, shapeless and old at fifty-two. Her mother—Elaine wanted to hold and comfort her. Now she could never know how much Elaine loved her.

"Ma," she whispered.

"Hm?"

"I'm sorry. It must be this way."

room.

"Please, Elaine, for my sake—"

"No, Ma, I can't. I could never be happy."

She waved Elaine away. She stopped and then did it a second time, averting her eyes. Elaine went back to her

There was no talk at all at breakfast, or afterward. Elaine went out and bought a *Times* and drove into Manhattan to look for work.

"I haven't found anything. The reason I didn't call you is that I had to be sure of what I felt. I felt it was settled; I wasn't sure. When my father asked me this afternoon to pick up his check I told him I wanted to bring you home tonight. As usual, he said I would have to ask my mother. It was settled. She told me to do what I wanted—she wouldn't look at me. I said you would come by after dinner for a little while. We have to see how this goes. It may be very difficult for you. If it is, I'll get you out in a hurry. We have to be reasonable in this part. It isn't perfect, but we have what we want, I think."

"Of course we do. You did beautifully, just beautifully."

"Tonight my father may want to talk to you, to satisfy himself."

"All right. I have to talk to him, anyway. I have to do that."

"Let him lead the conversation," she said.

"I know. I do it with my uncle."

"Are you really pleased?"

He smiled. "You know I am. I love you more than I have been able to tell you."

She kissed him. "I feel the same way." She stroked the side of his face. "When? When will you marry me?"

"The week after next. I have to give my family time. It's a long trip for them to make, if they're going to."

"Do you want to that soon? Do you really want to?"

He nodded, still watching her.

"Oh, I love you so much." She kissed him again and turned to look out at the water. She was very happy, he could see. Down below, the little boy was still tossing stones, shielding his eyes from the red sun. The air was growing cool. On the bay, another ship was streaming for the open sea.

"Come on," Charlie said. "They're waiting. We'd better get it done." He backed the car around and drove down the access road to the avenue that reached into the city.